Brenda Clarke was b
She is the author of s
Landscape, Under He *,* *,* *ers*
and Lovers, and *Beyond the World.*

BRENDA CLARKE

A DURABLE FIRE

CORGI BOOKS

A DURABLE FIRE
A CORGI BOOK : 0 552 13952 1

Originally published in Great Britain by Bantam Press,
a division of Transworld Publishers Ltd.

PRINTING HISTORY
Bantam Press edition published 1993
Corgi edition published 1993

Set in 10/11pt Linotype Century Schoolbook by
Chippendale Type Limited, Otley, West Yorkshire.

Corgi Books are published by Transworld Publishers Ltd,
61–63 Uxbridge Road, Ealing, London W5 5SA,
in Australia by Transworld Publishers (Australia) Pty Ltd,
15–25 Helles Avenue, Moorebank, NSW 2170,
and in New Zealand by Transworld Publishers (NZ) Ltd,
3 William Pickering Drive, Albany, Auckland.

Printed and bound in Great Britain by
Cox & Wyman Ltd, Reading, Berks.

But love is a durable fire
  In the mind ever burning;
Never sick, never old, never dead,
  From itself never turning.

SIR WALTER RALEIGH, 1552–1618

PART ONE
1971–5

CHAPTER ONE

'GRANDMA! Are you there? Can I come in?'

'Yes, of course, darling. I'm in here. You know you don't have to ask.'

Felicity Bryce was in her sitting-room, seated in front of her tapestry-frame. Behind her, the large picture-window of her top-floor flat looked out on to a panorama of Clifton roof-tops, silhouetted against the clear blue of an early-August sky. She paused in the act of selecting a strand of one of the brilliantly coloured wools draped across the arm of her chair, and glanced up smiling, as her younger granddaughter came into the room. She was fully aware that to have a favourite was wrong, and assiduously tried to conceal the fact that she preferred Anne to her older sister, Imogen. It was just, Felicity told herself defensively, that ten-year-old Anne was so much like her; they were compatible in every way, with shared interests in dressmaking, embroidery and fashion, and a mutual fondness for the same books and plays. Imogen, at fourteen, was more like her mother, Felicity's only daughter, Barbara. Her only child, in fact; she and Vincent, to their great sorrow, had never been able to have any more.

As always, whenever she thought of Vincent, Felicity's eyes turned automatically towards the silver-framed photograph which had pride of place on the shelf above the mantelpiece. She still missed him, even after all this time, and the happy life they had shared for thirty-five years. It was one of Felicity's chief regrets that Anne had never known her grandfather, not having been born until four months after Vincent's death.

'Are you all packed and ready, then?' Felicity asked, as Anne kissed her.

Anne perched on the free arm of her grandmother's chair and giggled. 'I am. I don't know about Mum and Im.'

Felicity frowned reprovingly. 'I do wish you wouldn't shorten names like that, my darling. It sounds so lazy.' She sighed. 'I can't imagine what takes those two so long. Neither of them has the slightest dress sense. If they just threw a few items in at random, it wouldn't make any difference. What time is the taxi coming?'

'I think it's ordered for one-thirty. We're going to have an early lunch first, then catch the quarter-past-two train from Temple Meads. Are you going to be all right on your own, Grandma, while we're away?'

Felicity laughed. 'My dear child, I'm not yet in my dotage. I'm only sixty-three, and perfectly capable of being in a house on my own. Besides, you always go to London to stay with the Haldanes every August. How do you think I've managed for the past six years? And before that, when I was still living by myself?'

Anne gave her grandmother a hug. 'I know. Silly of me. I worry about you, that's all.'

'I know you do.' Felicity's eyes were a little misty as she patted her granddaughter's arm. 'And don't think it isn't appreciated. It is. Very much indeed. But, in any case, your mother will be back in a fortnight's time. She isn't going on to Devon with you and the Haldanes.'

'She never does. She says two weeks is all she can possibly take off from the practice.'

Felicity heaved another sigh, but this time a mock one. 'Ah me! The rigours of the law!' Reverting to her normal voice, she added: 'Well, it was her choice to become a solicitor. It was what she always wanted.'

10

More than marriage, more than children; but Felicity was wise enough to keep these reflections to herself. Nevertheless, she couldn't help being of the opinion that Kenneth Seymour's early death, eight years ago, when Anne was barely three, had secretly been a relief for Barbara. Barbara had never been the marrying sort, and it had been a shock, therefore, when, at the age of twenty-eight, she had suddenly announced her engagement to a fellow-solicitor. She and Kenneth had been married in the March of 1954, and Imogen had been born two and a half years later. Felicity suspected that the marriage had been falling apart even then, but they had patched things up and soldiered on, because divorce was more uncommon, and more an admission of failure, than it was today. They had even had another child, and thank God they had! Felicity couldn't imagine life without Anne. But there was no doubt in her own mind that when Kenneth collapsed and died of a sudden brain haemorrhage, just before Christmas 1963, her daughter's mourning had been of a most perfunctory kind. Barbara had experienced no difficulty in picking up the threads of her single life again, even with the addition of two small children to support. A couple of years later, she had suggested that the top floor of the Victorian house at 4 College Close be converted into a self-contained flat and that Felicity move in with them.

'It makes sense economically,' she had said in her forthright no-nonsense fashion, 'and I'll be happier knowing that there's someone here for the girls when they get home from school in the evenings, especially when I have to work late.'

Felicity had been inclined to resent her daughter's single-mindedness, but she had moved in and not regretted her decision. She would never have got to know her beloved younger granddaughter nearly so well in other circumstances.

11

'Stand over there,' she commanded, 'and let me look at you.'

Anne obeyed, slipping off the arm of the chair and doing a pirouette in front of her grandmother. The straight, shining fair hair was drawn back into a pony-tail, and the soft grey eyes, the most striking feature of the little heart-shaped face, sparkled with health and a sense of fun beneath the darker gold wings of the eyebrows. The childishly thin body looked delicate, and the pale complexion gave an impression of uncertain health. Felicity, however, knew better. Anne was as strong as a young horse and, mentally as well as physically, was far better equipped to cope with anything life might throw at her than her elder sister. Imogen, her grandmother had long ago decided, was born to be one of life's victims, whereas nothing would ever get the better of Anne. She wouldn't let it. She had spirit.

Felicity surveyed her granddaughter critically. 'That's a very pretty dress,' she approved after a moment. 'That burned-orange shade gives your skin some colour, which makes me sure you must have had a hand in choosing it. Your poor dear mother could never have shown so much good taste.' She pursed her lips. 'It needs something, though, just to break up the solid mass of orange. I know. I shan't be a moment.'

Felicity disappeared into her bedroom and emerged a few moments later with a small linen handkerchief, sage-green. 'Tuck this into the breast pocket,' she instructed. 'There. That's it.' She also produced a length of ribbon, almost the same shade. 'And tie this round your hair, instead of that horrible elastic band with the plastic bobbles. Let me see. Right. Now you look extremely smart and fit company for one of the most distinguished of our theatrical knights.'

'Do you mean Uncle Cliff? It does sound funny when you talk of him like that. Anyway' – Anne returned

to her perch on the arm of her grandmother's chair –
'Mummy says Aunty Pen is just as famous an author
as Uncle Cliff is an actor. More famous even, because
millions of people read her books all over the world.
Not that many people go to the theatre. Although, I
suppose, they do see Uncle Cliff's films.'

Felicity looked down her nose. Ignoring the last
sentence, she said: 'More's the pity, especially when
you consider the sort of nonsense Penelope writes
nowadays.' She added repressively: 'I wouldn't have
one of her books in the house.'

Anne was intrigued. 'Why not? Mary James, at
school, said her mother said they're nothing but porn
. . . porno something, but Melissa Tate said her mother
always puts her name down for the latest one at the
library as soon as it comes out.'

'Mmm. Well, I can only say that Mrs James shows
more taste and discretion than Mrs Tate. However,
it's not for me to be the judge. I'm sure the next
book, which I understand is due to be published at
any moment, will head the bestseller-lists, as did
the last three.' A thought occurred to Felicity. 'Does
Barbara read them?'

Anne shook her head. 'Mum never reads novels, you
know that. She hates fiction. In fact, she and Aunty
Pen aren't much alike, are they? I've often wondered
how they came to be such great friends.'

Felicity turned her attention once more to her tap-
estry, choosing a length of crimson wool from the pile
at her side and threading it through her needle.

'You're not the only one, my darling,' she said, leaning forward and stabbing at the canvas. 'It's just one
of those inexplicable attractions. They met at school
and have been the best of friends ever since. Perhaps
it's because they complement each other; Penelope
is such an extrovert and your mother so reserved.'
Felicity stared consideringly at the stitch she had

made, glowing like a drop of blood against its sombre background. 'And they do have one or two things in common. They're both mad about cricket, which, as you'll find out when you go there yourself, is the school game, instead of tennis. And, although your mother may not read fiction now, she used to when she was younger, and they had the same sense of humour, which, incidentally, you've inherited from Barbara. She and Penelope used to spend hours shrieking with laughter over novels like *A Bullet in the Ballet*. And that, of course, is another shared interest: the ballet. So, you see, they're not as unalike as we might think.'

'No, I suppose not.' Anne swung one slim brown leg and sandalled foot. 'Anyway, I shall read Aunty Pen's books when I'm older. Mum says Aunty Pen says she only writes them for the money. Mum says Aunty Pen says she spent all those years writing high-class historical fiction and earned a pittance, so now it's fashionable to write this sort of thing she doesn't see why she shouldn't cash in. And Mum agrees.'

'Does she?' Felicity responded drily. 'I shouldn't have thought money was a consideration for the wife of Sir Clifford Haldane; but, then, I suppose one never knows other people's true circumstances. The theatrical profession is a notoriously uncertain one. Clifford Haldane has been exceptionally lucky. In his student days at the Bristol Old Vic, I don't think any of us would have prophesied his rise to fame and fortune.'

A voice was raised from the flat's little hallway. 'Mother! Is Anne up here?'

'In the sitting-room with me,' Felicity responded, and a few seconds later Barbara appeared, followed by Imogen.

At the sight of her daughter, Felicity winced. 'Darling, no!' she expostulated. 'Not a blue-and-white spotted blouse with a green-and-rust checked skirt, for pity's

14

sake. Whatever happened to that smart tan jacket and sleeveless green top I bought you?'

Barbara looked faintly irritated. 'I don't know. I've probably packed them. We're only travelling up to Paddington, for heaven's sake, not attending a royal garden-party. You set far too much store by appearances, Mother, and you're filling up Anne's head with the same sort of nonsense. Thank goodness Imogen's more like me.' She palliated her words by stooping to give Felicity an affectionate kiss, but continued in the same slightly peevish tone: 'Why on earth did I let myself be persuaded to call her that? Whose suggestion was it?'

'Not mine.' Felicity denied her guilt with an outflung hand. 'If I remember rightly, Clifford was appearing at the time in *Cymbeline*. You and Kenneth went to see it, while you were still pregnant, and liked the name.'

'I must have been mad,' Barbara said positively. 'It always reminds me of that awful book *What Katy Did*. She had a posh friend called Imogen, who came to tea.'

Imogen, who, having dutifully kissed her grandmother, had thrown herself down into the other armchair, now said unexpectedly: 'Well, *I* like it. It's different. It's better than plain old Anne.'

The two sisters were very alike, with the same straight fair hair, small-boned faces and thin coltish bodies. The one distinguishing feature was the colour of the eyes, Imogen's being blue like her mother's. She was also, being only a couple of months short of her fifteenth birthday, showing signs of maturity. The pale-blue cotton dress bulged gratifyingly over her burgeoning breasts. And, in spite of her recent outburst, she was really very fond of her younger sister. There was four years' difference between their ages, but they shared, by one of those coincidences that happen in families from time to time, the same birthday, 18 October. It had forged a stronger bond between them than might otherwise have been the case.

Anne demonstrated this now by refusing to take offence at Imogen's words, simply giving her an affectionate smile. Contrite, her sister got up and came over to hug her.

'Sorry. Didn't mean it,' she apologized with a sheepish grin. Seeing Felicity's critical eyes upon her, she said hurriedly: 'Don't start on me, Grandma. I can tell by your expression that you don't like this dress.'

'It's not the dress,' Felicity retorted, 'but the white patent shoes and handbag. White patent looks so common.'

Barbara intervened. 'Come along, girls. If we're going to have any sort of lunch before the taxi comes, we'd better hurry. Mother, if I don't have time to come up and see you again before we go, take care of yourself, and I'll see you in two weeks' time. If there are any problems, you have Penelope's new telephone number. I gave it to you the other day.'

'Ah, yes! A good job you reminded me or I might have forgotten. The new house in St John's Wood. That last film Clifford made must have been quite lucrative. You must tell me all about it when you return.'

Barbara stooped once again to kiss her mother goodbye. 'With the three boys, I suppose they felt they needed the extra room,' she murmured vaguely. 'Besides,' she added more briskly, 'it's very handy for Lord's.'

Felicity shook her head and smiled ruefully. 'If I live to be a hundred,' she said, 'I shall never understand this passion you and Penelope have for cricket. As far as I'm concerned, it's the world's most boring game.'

'This is a damn boring play,' Christopher Haldane said, looking up from the typescript he was reading, 'and it's going to be a monumental flop.'

16

His brother, Timothy, four years his junior, but just as big and blond and handsome, yawned in sympathy. 'Why do it, then? Wait for something else to come along.'

Chris, who had been lying stretched out on his mother's favourite sofa, swung his legs to the ground and made an abortive attempt to brush away the dirty mark left by his shoes.

'All very well for you to say that,' he retorted. 'You've got three halcyon years among the dreaming spires ahead of you. But I'm down, with only a modest degree in my pocket and my way to make in the world. If I want to be an actor – and that's all I've ever wanted to be – I have to do it without Dad's help. And parts don't grow on trees, not even parts like this. And I have a nasty suspicion I only landed this because of my name.'

'One of the penalties of having a famous father.' Tim yawned again. 'If it *is* a penalty, that is. I don't intend to let it inhibit me.'

His brother gave another ineffectual rub at the offending mark, then gave up the unequal struggle. He would just have to brave his mother's wrath. 'You still intend making acting your career, then?' he asked.

'Certainly.' Tim looked offended. 'If *you* can, why not me? Perhaps we shall be another theatrical dynasty, like the Redgraves or the Millses.'

Chris chuckled. 'Not Richard. He's made up his mind already to be a vet.'

'God! Don't remind me!' Timothy got up from his seat and strolled over to the open window, looking down into the quiet tree-lined road. The busy hum of traffic in St John's Wood High Street sounded faintly in the distance. 'That's one of the good things about this move. Rich is able to have the whole attic floor of this house to himself, where he can keep all those

17

stray birds and animals and revolting insects. I often wonder', he added idly, 'if Mother played Dad false over Richard. I mean, he's nothing like us, is he? Small, where we're big; dark, where we're fair. No theatrical leanings whatsoever.'

'Don't let Mother's books fool you,' Chris answered, laughing. 'She's really quite a prude.'

'Do you think I don't know that?' Tim turned back from the window. 'I was only joking. No, Rich is a throwback to some of Mother's maternal relatives. I've seen photos of them.' He flung himself down in his chair again. 'God! This is boring. Why do we have to stop in just to welcome Barbara and the girls? We've seen them two or three times a year for as long as I can remember. They're like a part of the family. Why do we have to stand on ceremony today? I had a date, too,' he added peevishly. 'I'm eighteen and you're twenty-one. Why do we let ourselves be imposed upon in this fashion?'

'Because', his brother pointed out shrewdly, 'we are both, at the moment, dependent on the parents' generosity, so it's only politic, as well as polite, to do as they ask now and then. As Barbara and the girls haven't been here before, Mother, for reasons best understood by herself, feels that it would be nice for us to be here when they all return from the station. Which reminds me, one of us had better go up and winkle Richard out from his attic. And, if your date was with who I think it was, perhaps it's all for the best. The parents most certainly wouldn't approve of your . . . er . . . *friendship* with Sylvia Gibson.'

Tim shrugged guiltily. 'She's a damn fine actress,' he said.

'What's that got to do with it?' Chris laughed. 'I don't imagine she's giving you tips on acting when you're alone together. What is to the point, though, is that she's twelve years older than you and, although

18

she's never married, she's lived with a number of different men. Mother might not disapprove of her as a family friend, but as a prospective daughter-in-law . . . ' He let the sentence hang.

'My life's my own,' his brother snapped defensively. 'I shall do what I like with it. And, anyway, what call has Ma got to be self-righteous, considering the kind of books she writes?'

Chris was suddenly weary of the debate. If the truth were told, he, too, was slightly resentful of being made to stay in on a fine summer's afternoon for no other purpose than to welcome visitors who were such a regular part of his life that he had long ago abandoned all formality towards them. Imogen and Anne were like the sisters he had never had, and it was many years since he had stopped according Barbara the courtesy title of 'Aunt'. He treated her nowadays with all the casual familiarity of an old friend. But he was less self-centred than Tim, more aware of other people's needs and feelings, and had realized that for his mother it was important to have the whole family present to welcome the Seymours to the new house. For Penelope, it was as much a symbol of her own new-found success as it was of her husband's rise to fame and fortune – a rise which had culminated, three years earlier, in his knighthood. It was Penelope's sudden need for a work-room of her own, instead of writing, as she had done previously, on the kitchen or dining-room table, which had finally precipitated the move from the house in Pimlico, where she and Clifford had lived for the greater part of their London lives, to this larger, far roomier one in a quiet backwater of St John's Wood.

It was three years since Penelope Fallon – she had always used her maiden name for business purposes – had taken the conscious decision to cash in on the legacy of the 1960s, with its lifting of most forms of censorship and restraints. If other writers could make money with the semi-pornographic novel, why shouldn't she? She was good at her craft and, once she overcame her natural inhibitions, had no doubt that she could make a similar success. She had not been disappointed, and with the active encouragement of her agent and friend, Irene Woodhouse, had, two years previously, published *Cravings*, a novel, according to the dust-cover blurb, of 'lust and passion' which had raced straight to the top of the bestseller-list. And the fact that she was Sir Clifford Haldane's wife had done her no harm at all, merely adding spice to the numerous interviews she had been requested to give, both in the popular press and on television. Nevertheless, as an interviewee, she had not been a spectacular success. In spite of her outgoing personality and her willingness to answer all questions openly and with candour, there had been nothing to discover about her private life except that she was a happily and decorously married woman who infinitely preferred talking about the achievements of her famous husband and three sons to discussing her book, which she frankly admitted writing for the money. It also became apparent that her heart was still with her original novels, and she displayed an unnerving – at least, from the interviewers' point of view – habit of digressing on such topics as the historical truth behind the characters of Macbeth and Richard III as opposed to the Shakespearian version, instead of revealing how she dreamed up the more salacious episodes in *Cravings*.

Two other books, *Moon in Capricorn* and *The Rococo Garden*, had followed in quick succession. A fourth, *Flung Roses*, a quotation from the poems of Ernest Dowson, was due to be published in September, and a pile of author's advance copies, which had arrived by parcel post during the morning, had been brought up to the first-floor drawing-room by the daily help, Mrs Clennan, and deposited on the coffee-table in the corner. Chris, noticing them for the first time, got up and slouched across to pick one up and examine its cover, remarking as he did so: 'We, of all people, shouldn't confuse Mother with Penelope Fallon, writer of purple prose. Between the pages of her books, you and Sylvia Gibson hopping in and out of bed with one another would be perfectly acceptable to her, but in real life she'll be down on you like a ton of bricks.'

'Do you think I don't know that?' Tim demanded peevishly. 'It's what makes it all so hypocritical. Anyway,' he added hurriedly, before his brother could take issue with him, 'Sylvia and I aren't hopping in and out of bed, more's the pity. She's as sensitive about the age-gap as Mother. Keeps talking about baby-snatching. It's so stupid in this day and age.'

'Not really. She's a colleague of Father's. They've acted together on a number of occasions. I don't know her personally, but she sounds like a sensible woman to me. You'll forget all about her when you go up to Oxford in a month or two's time.' Chris had been idly flicking through the pages of *Flung Roses* while he spoke and now began laughing uncontrollably. 'Oh my God! You ought to read this bit, on page forty-nine.' He staggered to a chair and sat down, wiping his eyes. 'It's physically impossible!' And he went off into another paroxysm of mirth.

Tim, curious, strolled across and twitched the book from his brother's limp hand. His eyes followed the closely printed lines until they suddenly stopped, widening in disbelief. 'You mean this bit featuring the custard tarts?' he asked uncertainly, before he, too, fell victim to uncontrollable mirth. 'Do you think', he gasped when he was eventually able to catch his breath, 'that Ma knows what she's talking about? I mean, do you think she and the old man

21

have ever . . . ?' Words failed him as the vision thus conjured up deprived both brothers of the powers of coherent speech.

And it was while they were reduced to near-hysteria, rolling helplessly around the room, that the drawing-room door opened and their parents came in, followed closely by Barbara Seymour, Imogen and Anne.

CHAPTER TWO

WHEN THE TRAIN had drawn into Paddington station, twenty minutes earlier, Barbara Seymour had been surprised, and secretly rather flattered, to see Clifford Haldane, as well as Penelope, waiting at the end of the platform to greet them. People, hurrying past, had turned their heads to look at him, conscious that they knew his face, without being able to put a name to it. A few found him instantly recognizable and gave a kind of half-smile, uncertain whether or not he would be offended if they hailed him. In the end, no-one spoke, but he did return one or two of the tentative salutations with a gracious inclination of his handsome head.

Barbara was never quite sure how she felt about her best friend's husband. In the days when he had been a student with the Bristol Old Vic theatre school, a year or so after its inception in 1946, and Penelope had first started going out with him, she had definitely disliked him. Or perhaps it would be fairer to say that she had been prejudiced against him because of his matinée-idol good looks and his air of arrogant self-confidence. He was not, in any case, the man to appeal to her, who, all her life, had never fancied the heroic type. Would she have married Kenneth Seymour if she had?

But as time went by, and she got to know Clifford Haldane better, she realized that beneath the arrogance was a vein of self-mockery which, together with the actor's ever-present sense of insecurity and constant self-doubt, made him a much more likeable person than she had at first imagined. She supposed, watching him as he advanced to greet her and the girls, that what she resented about him was his success; this feeling of being flattered by his attention. She recalled some years ago, when she had been in hospital for a minor operation, seeing one of the ward sisters, a bright, intelligent, highly competent woman and an excellent nurse, trying desperately hard not to be sycophantic and over-impressed when the surgeon had done his rounds. And failing, because the man himself had expected to be treated with the reverence and adulation that everyone else accorded him. Barbara always felt a little like that with Clifford.

She found herself saying, with a gush in her voice: 'Cliff! How good of you to come. You must be busy.'

'Resting at the moment, Babs. Delighted to be of service.' The deep distinctive tones, whose slightest whisper could be guaranteed to reach the back rows of the largest theatre, caused more heads to turn, and a couple of women who were passing nudged one another. Clifford turned his attention to Anne and Imogen. 'Hello, girls. Doesn't your poor old Uncle Cliff get a kiss these days?'

Imogen hung back shyly, eventually offering her lips for a chaste peck and quickly withdrawing, but Anne flung her arms about his neck, kissing him with unreserved affection. She knew he was famous, but the fact had never inhibited her. To her, he was simply Uncle Cliff, the husband of her mother's best friend, although nowadays he did have a more important role in her scheme of things as Christopher's father.

It was just before Christmas, when she and Barbara had been staying with the Haldanes for a few days' shopping, that she had suddenly become aware of Chris in a totally different way. Until then, he had just been another member of the family, ten years

24

her senior and therefore old enough to be classed as a boring adult. But during that brief holiday she had suddenly been conscious of him as a man, and had plunged headlong into her first real schoolgirl crush (that was if she discounted Marlon Brando and Sean Connery, which she now found it very easy to do). It was the prospect of seeing Christopher again which made her heart pound so fiercely as they crossed the station concourse and climbed into a waiting taxi.

Her mother and Penelope were already talking nineteen to the dozen; at least, Penelope was talking and Barbara was listening, getting in the odd remark now and then, with an all-consuming interest which excluded the others. Anne wondered why the great friendships of history and mythology – David and Jonathan, Damon and Pythias – were always male. Women were capable of great friendship, too.

'My dear, I do hope you like the new house,' Penelope was saying, as the taxi swept up the ramp and turned towards the afternoon bustle of the Edgware Road. 'Well, you'll see it for yourself in a minute. I knew it was absolutely right for us as soon as I clapped eyes on it. I think what swayed Cliff was the fact that it's called The Laurels. He couldn't resist it after that, and annoys all the other residents of Cameron Road by referring to the street as Brickfield Terrace. Half of them don't know what he's on about, and of course that pleases him no end. You know how he loves to be thought enigmatic.' She gave her husband's knee an affectionate squeeze, without turning her attention from Barbara. 'The basement is huge, and we've turned it into a rehearsal-room for Cliff and a writing-room for me – both, needless to say, soundproof. And darling Richard and his menagerie have been banished to the attics. And of course, my dear, Lord's is so handy.'

While Penelope rambled on, Anne watched her

25

quietly from one of the little fold-down seats opposite. Christopher and Timothy most decidedly resembled their father, tall and blond and handsome, whereas Penelope was almost plain. She had a round face, snub nose, bright blue eyes and a mop of naturally curly light-brown hair, which she rarely bothered to have styled. She dressed well, when the occasion demanded it, but her favourite clothes were tailored shirts and slacks and a long, loose, ancient caftan for writing in. 'I have to be comfortable,' she would apologize to unexpected guests, drifting into their midst in this voluminous garment, 'or I can't concentrate.'

Richard looked a little like his mother, Anne supposed, as the taxi turned into a tree-lined cul-de-sac and drew up in front of the tall Victorian house with the words *The Laurels* clearly painted on one of the two stone pillars which flanked the open gates. While Clifford settled with the driver, the rest of them followed Penelope up the path to the front door and waited while she found her key to let them in. The front garden consisted of a lawn set about with the shrubs which gave the house its name, and a central diamond-shaped flower-bed where a hydrangea was doing its best to push out a few dusty-looking blooms.

Clifford joined them as they stepped over the threshold into the hall, whose polished wood floor was patterned, in the afternoon sun, with lozenges of jewel-bright colour thrown by the two stained-glass windows, one on either side of the front door, and by a third on the half-landing of the stairs.

Penelope waved a comprehensive arm. 'Ground floor: dining-room, kitchen, laundry-room, study. But I'm not going to bother showing them to you now. You can have a guided tour when you've unpacked and rested. Come upstairs to the drawing-room, and I'll get Mrs Clennan to bring us up some tea. She's my daily help and an absolute treasure. One of a dying breed and nearly as extinct as the dodo. She used to "do" for the previous occupants of the house, and we inherited her when we bought it. That alone has made it the most inspired move we've ever made. As you know, I used to do everything when we lived in Pimlico.'

Still talking, Penelope led the way upstairs, where gusts of laughter could be heard emanating from the big front room. Anne recognized Christopher's voice, and her heart began to pound.

'What the devil are those two up to?' Clifford demanded as he reached past them and pushed wide the door. At the same moment, there was the thump of feet and Richard came charging downstairs from the second-floor landing, a small dog of indeterminate breed yapping excitedly at his heels.

'Hi, Anne,' he shouted, ignoring everyone else and flinging a proprietary arm around her shoulders. 'Come up and see my quarters. They're absolutely fab! I've got a whole floor to myself. Oh, this is my new dog, by the way. He's a stray. I've named him Sir Cloudesley Shovel.'

'I really don't see what's so funny about it. You and Tim have a depraved sense of humour.'

Penelope had snatched back the copy of her book from her eldest son, replacing it with its fellows on the coffee-table, and was now standing guard over the whole pile, like a tigress defending her young.

'If we're talking of depravity . . . ' gasped Tim, but dared say no more for fear of subsiding into laughter again. He contented himself, instead, by greeting Barbara and the two girls with a laconic: 'Hello, Babs. Imogen. Hi, Annie.'

He was the only person who ever called her Annie, and Anne hated it. She was not very fond of Timothy, which was strange, she thought, considering how

27

much he was like his older brother. But, at nearly eleven years of age, she was beginning to differentiate between looks and character; and although, like most young girls, and many older ones, she was vulnerable to a handsome face she had sense enough to realize that kindness was a great deal more important. Chris was kind, as well as good-looking, which was why she adored him, but there was an underlying dissatisfaction in Timothy's nature which made him, at times, both peevish and thoughtless, indifferent to the needs of others. When he was young, his pet phrase had been 'It's not fair'.

'What's all this about?' Clifford Haldane demanded, moving in his easy confident fashion centre-stage and immediately dominating the scene with his commanding presence.

'Ma's new book,' Chris said, grinning. 'Page forty-nine. The bit with the custard tarts.'

'That will do,' Penelope protested hotly. Her eyes swivelled in Richard and Anne's direction. '*Pas devant les enfants*, if you please.'

Her youngest son sighed wearily. He said to Anne: 'That means "not in front of the children". She thinks I don't know, but I do. I expect she's written something rude again, in her new book. It can be frightfully embarrassing when I get ribbed about it at school. But that's parents for you. No consideration.' He abandoned his slightly pompous manner and tugged at Anne's sleeve. 'Come on! Come upstairs. I'm dying to show you my new rooms. You don't want to stay down here for boring old tea.'

It was precisely what Anne wanted, to remain within sight and sound of Christopher in the hope that he might eventually single her out for special attention. But, in her heart of hearts, she knew that it wouldn't happen – he was already perched on the arm of his father's chair, deep in conversation – and what with Richard importuning her to 'Come upstairs now!' and Sir Cloudesley Shovel trying to nip her ankles she decided that the best thing to do was to comply. She didn't really want tea, because she had drunk lemonade from the buffet bar on the train, and she was tired of sitting down. So she followed Richard up another flight of carpeted stairs to the second floor, and then up a further flight, covered in a pale fawn drugget, to the attics.

These had originally been three small rooms, which had now been knocked into one. The walls had been painted white and the narrow windows fitted with blinds, which, when rolled up, allowed in the maximum light. The attics had also included a primitive bathroom, which had been refitted with washbasin, lavatory and shower, and its retention made the main space slightly L-shaped. That end of the room contained a single bed, wardrobe, chest of drawers, on which stood a black-and-white television set; and an armchair, covered in a coarse, hard-wearing, cream-coloured material, which looked as though it had never been sat in.

The remainder of the room was given over to shelves of books, a dog-basket, two cat-baskets and a long row of trestle-tables which supported several cages, one occupied by a large white rabbit, another by a couple of short-haired guinea-pigs, and a collection of cardboard boxes. On closer inspection, these proved to contain a starling with a broken wing, a hedgehog with an injured leg and a collection of snails gorging themselves on cabbage leaves.

'I'm studying snails at the moment,' Richard explained when Anne recoiled in horror. 'There's nothing to be scared of!' he added scornfully. 'They can't hurt you.'

'They're so slimy,' Anne protested. 'Like slugs in shells.' She went over to one of the windows, where

29

a black cat was sunning itself on the broad white-painted ledge. She stooped to stroke the short silky fur, and it purred softly without raising its head.

'That's Machiavelli,' Richard said, coming across and lifting the animal unceremoniously into his arms. Sir Cloudesley Shovel promptly expressed his jealous disapproval by jumping violently up and down, making pathetic little whining noises. 'Get down, Cloud! Down! That's right. No need to show off just because we have a guest. They're really quite good friends,' he assured Anne. 'Well? What do you think of it? Isn't it great?'

'It smells,' Anne complained, fastidiously wrinkling her nose.

'Of course it smells!' Richard was impatient. 'Animals do smell, including humans.' He replaced Machiavelli on the window-ledge, where he settled down once more to sleep. 'Come and be introduced to Alcibiades.'

'Who?'

'The rabbit. He's feeling a bit lonely. His mate died last week.'

'Why do you give all your pets such funny names?' Anne enquired, poking a tentative finger through the wire mesh of the cage and withdrawing it hurriedly as the rabbit made a grab at it with an excellent set of sharp pointed teeth.

'They're not funny! They're all names of real people. You don't suppose I'm going to call them Tiddles or Fluffy or Rover, do you?' His scorn was searing.

'I used to have a cat called Tiddles,' Anne said defensively.

Richard gave her a pitying look, but contented himself with asking: 'What happened to it?'

'She was run over, and we had to have her put to sleep. Mum said we weren't to have any more animals. She said they're an . . . an emotional and . . . and physical tie.'

'H'm! I'm glad she isn't *my* mother.' The guinea-pigs began squeaking. 'Come on! We'll go down to the garden and pick some grass for Bo and Berry. Boadicea and Berengaria,' he added grandly. 'We might find Alphonso, too. He's the tortoise.'

They went downstairs again. As they crossed the second-floor landing, there was a shout of merriment from the drawing-room, and Anne recognized Christopher's laugh. She hesitated a moment, tempted to go in, but Richard grabbed her arm and hustled her down the next flight, along the hall and out through the kitchen to the long, narrow, walled garden at the back of the house. This showed more signs of cultivation than the front one, with two neat lawns bisected by a crazy-paving path and the top half given over to a vegetable garden, at present crammed with all the abundance of midsummer. A flagstoned patio, nearest the house, displayed a variety of ornamental shrubs and miniature trees in green-painted tubs; and a peach tree provided some shade for the empty deck-chairs and sun-loungers, quilted in shiny floral polyester cotton.

Anne was impressed. 'Does Uncle Cliff do all this himself?' she asked.

Richard, leading the way along the path, looked astonished. 'Dad doesn't know the first thing about gardening. He has a man in twice a week to do it for him. His name's Mr Bone and he's great. See? He leaves this patch of grass by the wall uncut especially for the guinea-pigs. And the lettuces in that row are mine, for Alcibiades. Have a poke around under the cabbages over there. See if you can find Alphonso.'

Recalling, after a moment's thought, who this was, Anne began a half-hearted search for the tortoise. She liked animals provided they were soft and cuddly and furry, but had no great enthusiasm for the rest.

Spiders and reptiles she actively loathed, and so she was relieved when there seemed to be no sign of Alphonso. She was unable to share her childhood playmate's indiscriminate passion for the fauna of the world, and it always annoyed her when Richard assumed that she, too, wanted to be a vet when she grew up. She had no very clear idea of what she did want to do, but there were many years yet before she needed to make a decision. But at the back of her mind was the half-formed conviction that it must be something to do with the theatre so that she could be near Chris, or at least share an interest with him.

'Have you found him yet?' Richard asked, pushing the handfuls of grass into a plastic bag which he had taken from his pocket. Then, with a cry of delight, he swooped among the cabbage stalks, standing upright again, the tortoise clutched between his hands. Cloud, who had followed them into the garden, resumed his frenzied barking and brought Alphonso's wizened head poking out of his shell to see what was happening. Legs like crêpe rubber followed, and Richard held him out to Anne.

'Here you are. You can hold him if you want to.'

Anne hesitated, not wishing to give offence but feeling her flesh shrink. She was saved by the opening of a second-floor back window and the sound of Penelope's voice.

'Come along in, you two! Anne dear, your mother wants you to start your unpacking and have a bath before supper. Richard! It won't hurt you to have one, either. And you can change that filthy shirt.'

Richard was about to protest vehemently, but Penelope gave him no chance. She withdrew her head and closed the window.

'Parents!' he exclaimed disgustedly. 'Always wanting you to wash! What's the point, when I'm only going to get dirty again?' But he lowered Alphonso to his summer hiding-place among the cabbages and followed Anne indoors.

At supper, Anne, to her great confusion and delight, found herself sitting next to Christopher. Not that she could be said to gain much from it. After a friendly grin and a big-brotherly ruffling of her hair, he, like everyone else, gave most of his attention to his father, who was in an expansive anecdotal mood – his natural reaction to any fresh audience. By the time Anne had regained her composure and taken her first few mouthfuls of macaroni cheese, Clifford was in full flood with a story about some actor, whose name she had failed to catch.

'This woman pursued him everywhere. But everywhere! Whatever theatre he was appearing in, there she was, in the box nearest the stage, wearing one of these terribly *décolleté* gowns of hers, tits flopping over the edge of the box like a couple of over-ripe melons. And the upshot was that no-one ever watched the performance when she was present. The audience was too busy looking at her, hoping the dress was going to fall off completely. God! Didn't the poor sod curse! But of course there was nothing he could do about it. She was perfectly at liberty to come and see the play.'

'What happened in the end?' Barbara asked, joining in the general laughter but keeping an uneasy eye on her daughters. Really, Cliff was not at all careful with his language in front of children. It always surprised her that the boys had all turned out so well.

'She found a new object for her affections and made his life a misery instead. Fans, God bless 'em! Our livelihoods depend on them, but they can be a terrible menace at times.'

'Ah, well! I shan't have that problem for some considerable time,' Chris said, ignoring Tim's *sotto voce*

'If at all'. He addressed himself to his mother at the other end of the dining-room table. 'I'm starting rehearsals on Monday, so get me up when you get yourself up, would you?' He added for his father's benefit: 'Some ghastly, fly-blown, disused church hall in Camden Town. Do you know it?'

Before her husband had time to reply, Penelope demanded peevishly: 'Does that mean you won't be able to come to Irene's wedding? You know she was anxious for you to be there.'

Christopher looked irritated. 'For heaven's sake, Ma, I never had any intention of going. She's *your* agent, not mine. I hardly know the woman, and I've never even met the fellow she's marrying. I don't suppose she'll care if I'm there or not. You'll have Dad with you, and I'm sure you could wangle an invitation for Aunt Babs.'

'Your father isn't coming,' Penelope said, adding waspishly: 'He has to see a man about a revival of *Volpone*. At least, that's his story and he's sticking to it.' Chris shot his father a glance of deep respect. Penelope went on: 'And to say you don't know Irene Woodhouse is ridiculous. She's been to dinner with us on lots of occasions.'

'But I've been up at Oxford for the past three years,' her eldest son pointed out gently. 'So why on earth she should be keen to have me at her wedding I can't begin to imagine. You've probably got me mixed up with Tim. He's been making up to Irene behind your back. He likes older women.'

Tim sent him a furious warning look across the table, which no-one seemed to notice but Chris himself and Anne. But she was too young to speculate on what it might mean, and was more interested in the arrival of one of Mrs Clennan's delicious summer puddings, flanked by a huge bowlful of cream.

'You *have* met Irene more than once, Chris,' his

34

mother insisted, 'and I know she sent you an invitation to her and Jeremy's wedding next week because she likes you. But if you can't come, I suppose you can't. I'll take Barbara in your place.'

If Chris was surprised at being let off the hook so easily, he declined to push his luck by enquiring the reason. His mother could be persistent when it came to getting her own way, and he was just grateful that, this time, she had given up without a struggle.

But it had occurred to Penelope, while she was talking, that Irene's interest in Chris might not be as ingenuous as she made it sound. Her eldest son was a very handsome man, and Irene was susceptible to good looks. Penelope also suspected that Irene's marriage to Jeremy Grantham was far from being a love-match – on her side anyway. In the few years they had known one another, Penelope had come to realize that Irene had a roving eye.

CHAPTER THREE

IRENE WOODHOUSE had graduated from Cambridge in the summer of 1967 and, in the autumn of the same year, had joined the publishing house of Herrald & Simpson as an assistant editor of romantic fiction. Six months later, as the result of a desire to be her own boss, and with a substantial legacy willed to her by a favourite aunt, she had left to set up her own literary agency, operating from an office near Covent Garden. The rent was exorbitant, but she was aware of the necessity of a good address while still unknown and struggling to make an impression. Her short time with Herrald & Simpson had not been wasted, and, as an easy-going popular member of staff, she had left behind her a fund of goodwill, not least on the part of her editor, Jeremy Grantham. He had fallen heavily for the long-legged redhead with eyes which were definitely green, however much jealous detractors might insist that they were blue. Irene had only to put on a green dress to prove them wrong.

By dint of working her laborious way through piles of publishers' catalogues and looking up the authors mentioned in the *Writers' and Authors' Who's Who*, she compiled a list of names whose owners appeared to have no agent. She wrote to each of them a letter pointing out the advantages of having someone else to do the unpleasant job of haggling and bargaining, and who had time to study the various markets. One of the first to reply, accepting her offer, was Penelope Fallon.

The name meant nothing to Irene, but a visit to her

local branch library soon acquainted her with the fact that Penelope was the author of a number of historical novels, popularly known as 'faction'. They were undoubtedly good, and had even been described by one provincial newspaper critic as brilliant, but they had never earned very much money. Aimed at a specialist market, they were issued only in hardback and were mainly borrowed from libraries. Irene rang Penelope – and was amazed when the phone was answered by the unmistakable tones of Clifford Haldane.

'But why on earth don't you make it known that you're married to him?' she demanded, when Penelope had paid her first visit to the Covent Garden office. 'It would be invaluable publicity for you.'

'I've never thought about it,' Penelope admitted. 'Publicity has never been very high on my publisher's agenda.'

Irene nodded. She knew Harper Bennett's mode of operation: lots of authors, small advances, short books – sixty thousand words the maximum. Never reprinted. To do the firm justice, they had given a start to a great many writers who might otherwise have remained unpublished, but she felt that someone like Penelope should have spread her wings and moved on by now.

'You need an agent,' she told her firmly. 'And you need to write something different. Try your hand at romantic fiction. Not the Mills & Boon type. This decade has liberated women's reading habits. Explicit sex scenes are in. That's what's making the big money nowadays. I don't say it will last. Nothing lasts for ever. But just at present it's definitely in. Do you think you could do it? Not everybody can, especially older women. But you're – what? – early forties? That's still young.'

Coming from someone of twenty-three, this was flattering, and Penelope had promised to see what she could do. In the event, she had found it easier than she had expected, and the runaway success of *Cravings* – the one-word title was extremely popular just then – had cemented the basis of a relationship which quickly ripened into friendship. Irene became a frequent dinner guest at the Pimlico house, often escorted by Jeremy Grantham, but they had never seemed to Penelope to be more than just good friends. It had therefore come as something of a shock to her when, a month or so earlier, Irene had announced that she and Jeremy were getting married.

At the time, Penelope had been involved in all the turmoil of the move from Pimlico and, with Clifford working on a film at Shepperton, most of the work had devolved on her. Apart from proffering her somewhat startled congratulations, she had given the matter very little thought until now, sitting propped up against the pillows beside Clifford, the rest of the house quiet, everyone in bed.

'You know,' she remarked, after a protracted silence, 'I started to wonder this evening exactly why Irene *is* marrying Jeremy Grantham.'

Clifford, who, in the light of his bedside lamp, was studying a much-thumbed copy of *Volpone*, grunted. 'Perhaps it's that old thing love ... You know, if Carl can swing it with the backers and a decent theatre becomes available, we might get this on by Christmas. There's room for a good classic revival in the West End just now. Casting might be a bit of a problem. It would need the right Mosca. I wonder if Alan Dobie's available. Saw him do it at the Oxford Playhouse ... oh, fifteen years ago.'

Penelope, recognizing the mood of self-absorption, gave up trying to interest her husband in Irene's affairs and resumed her silent contemplation of the opposite wall with its paper of trellised roses. She didn't really like it, but it would do until such time as she could arrange to have the room redecorated. A thought occurred to her. Was Irene pregnant?

The more she considered it, the more she was convinced that she had hit on the truth. Irene had looked pale and thin when she had last seen her, two days ago. She had lost her usual bloom of health, that glowing patina to her skin. At the time, Penelope had put it down to pre-marriage nerves, but now she saw it in a different light. She recalled how she herself had looked in the early weeks of pregnancy; and she suddenly felt uncomfortable, as though she had opened someone's private correspondence by mistake. Furthermore, for no discernible reason, she felt glad that Chris would not, after all, be able to accompany her to the wedding. It would be a great deal more comfortable, in the circumstances, to have Barbara with her. She must telephone Irene in the morning to make sure that it would be all right. Now that she came to consider the matter carefully, she couldn't really see, either, why Irene had invited Chris.

Irene Woodhouse, soon to be Grantham, stood at her bedroom window, looking out at the dim grey distances of Hampstead Heath. Behind her, in the bed, Jeremy was snoring, having insisted on champagne at dinner to celebrate her news.

'Pregnant? My God, that's wonderful!' he had exclaimed, his thin narrow features lighting up with pleasure. It didn't seem to occur to him that maybe her pregnancy was the reason she had finally accepted his oft-repeated offer of marriage. His conceit was too securely armoured for that. He had always known that, in the end, he would prove irresistible.

'It's this damn silly career of yours, isn't it?' he would say. 'Forget it. A woman needs a home and children.'

And now, through her own carelessness, she had

39

played straight into his hands. She had been on the Pill, but forgotten to take it. Only the once, but it had been enough. So here she was, expecting a baby.

That didn't explain, however, why she felt impelled to get married. There were plenty of single parents about these days. She knew a few herself; but she also knew that they found it very difficult to bring up a child, give it all the love and attention it needed, and pursue a career as well. So she had gone for the easy option: marriage, a husband and a settled home. But she had misgivings. She wasn't in love with Jeremy and never had been. She was no more attracted to him than she was to any of her other admirers; and there had always been plenty of those since her teens. In fact she had thought herself incapable of love until she met Chris Haldane.

Irene stirred restlessly, watching a late-Saturday-night reveller hurrying past, below her, along the empty street. She despised herself for the way she had succumbed to Chris's obvious charms: the superb body, the handsome face, the aura of glamour that hung about him because he was Clifford Haldane's son. He was five years younger than she was, too, although these days such a small age-gap really didn't matter. It wasn't as though she had met him that often, either; just a few dinner-parties in the Haldanes' old home in Pimlico. He wasn't even aware of her existence as a woman, only as his mother's agent. So why did she think of him so constantly? Why did his presence disturb her dreams? Because she was a stupid romantic fool; the sort of woman she had always affected to despise. She was crying for the moon, instead of being willing to settle for what she had. Jeremy was a decent man, in love with her in his way; older than she was; a widower, with a house on the other side of the Heath from her poky little flat, with a decent-sized garden where a growing child could play. Of course, she had no intention of abandoning her career after the baby was born, but Jeremy didn't know that. She would cross that bridge when she came to it.

Anne woke with a start, unable for the moment to place her surroundings. She was not in her bedroom at home, nor was she in the familiar Pimlico house where she had spent so many happy hours. Then she remembered. This was Aunt Pen's new house in St John's Wood. She wondered what had disturbed her, before recollecting that she was sharing with Imogen. She had never found it easy to sleep in the same room as her sister.

She glanced over at the other bed to discover it empty. 'Im,' she whispered. 'Where are you?'

'Over here,' came the muffled reply. 'Sorry, did I wake you? I couldn't get off, so I thought I might find something to read.'

Anne, her eyes growing accustomed to the darkness, made out Imogen's crouching form beside a bookcase which stood in an alcove near the window. She glanced at the clock on her bedside table, the illuminated dial informing her that it was just gone two.

'You can't read now!' she protested. 'It's the middle of the night. I wish you weren't such a light sleeper. Come back to bed, for goodness' sake.'

Imogen rose and came reluctantly, her white cotton pyjamas gleaming palely in the light from a street-lamp, making her look like a small lost ghost. She climbed into the other single bed, drawing the sheet up to her waist but rejecting the blanket. It was a sultry night.

'Can't you sleep?' Anne enquired after a moment's silence. Then, when her sister did not answer, went on: 'It is very warm. And the house is a bit strange, too. Very quiet compared to the one in Pimlico. It's quiet at home, but I don't notice it there. I suppose

41

Grandma's all right. I don't like to think of her being alone.'

'Of course she's all right,' Imogen replied irritably. She lowered herself against the pillows and stared up at the shadowy ceiling. After another silence, she asked suddenly: 'Do you think Tim even knows that I'm alive?'

'Tim?' Anne was startled. She mulled the question over for a few seconds, before saying incredulously: 'Don't tell me you're keen on Tim!'

'Why not?' Imogen's tone was aggressive as she turned her head to look at her sister. 'What's wrong with him? He's every bit as good-looking as Chris.'

'He's not as nice, though.' The words were out before Anne had time to gauge her sister's possible reaction. Imogen flounced into a sitting position and snapped: 'You're like all the others! Everyone seems to think that Chris is superior to Tim. Just that bit handsomer, cleverer, bound to make a better actor. It's nonsense, of course, but for some reason or other Chris is universal favourite. Tim's always in second place.'

Anne raised herself on one elbow and regarded her sister with wide eyes.

'Sorry,' she breathed. 'I didn't know you liked him that much. How long have you felt this way?'

Imogen sighed and lay down again. 'Oh, ages,' she said. 'I knew for certain last summer, when we were staying at the cottage with them and we went for that picnic on Dartmoor. You know, near the Burrator reservoir. It was such a lovely day, and he was so kind, taking trouble to talk to me when everyone else ignored me.'

Anne, young as she was, was yet old enough to realize, a little guiltily at times, that Imogen did tend to get overlooked. Not because people intended deliberately to be unkind, but because Imogen was so self-effacing. She was painfully shy, and always had been, in spite of her grandmother's efforts to imbue her with confidence.

'If she only had half your spirit!' Felicity had once lamented to Anne. 'Or if only your mother would encourage her to think more highly of herself! But there! Barbara never does see what's going on under her nose. She's too self-centred.'

Anne had the impression that her grandmother had later repented being so outspoken, because she had warned her not to repeat her words to her mother. Anne never had. She was essentially trustworthy. She had also been a little shocked at this overt criticism of Barbara, still being at the age when respect for adults effectually blinkered her to their faults. But now, recalling Felicity's words, she began to have an inkling of the truth behind them.

'People don't mean to ignore you, Im,' she said. 'It's just that sometimes you're so quiet they forget you're there.'

'Well, Tim didn't ignore me or forget that I was there.' Imogen's momentary elation faded. 'At least', she sighed, 'not that day. But since then he's been like all the rest. He's hardly spoken a word to me today. Nor last Christmas. Anne, what do you think I should do?'

Surprised at being so appealed to, Anne could only shake her head. She was, after all, the last person to give advice. Wasn't she in a similar position as regards Chris? Then the common sense which would always make her so clear-sighted told her that the two cases were hardly the same. There was a ten-year age-gap between herself and Chris, and even though she was convinced that her adoration of him would last for ever she could hardly expect him to wait for her until she grew up. She also recognized that there was an element of fantasy in the situation, even if she were too young to put it in just those words. But Tim was only three years older than Imogen; and, although he might now regard her as still a child, in a couple of years the age-difference between them would be unremarkable. Many people, indeed, would see it as just right.

'You think I'm being stupid,' Imogen said defiantly, misinterpreting her sister's silence.

Anne shook her head. 'I think it's romantic,' she answered. 'If you and Tim ever did get married – I mean some time in the future, after he's finished at Oxford – Mum and Aunt Pen would be delighted. They've always been such very close friends.'

'Oh heavens!' Imogen petulantly flung back the sheet in order to cool down. 'I don't suppose anything like that will ever happen! And, for goodness' sake, don't repeat what I've told you to anyone. If you do, I'll never speak to you again.'

'I shan't say anything,' Anne assured her sister, hurt. She hunched her thin shoulders and turned on her side, presenting her back to Imogen. She felt suddenly burdened down by confidences, things she wasn't supposed to mention. Her grandmother and sister had no business telling her their secrets. Secrets were only fun if they could be shared with somebody else. It would be nice to talk to Richard; to ask him if her mother were really self-centred, if Tim liked Imogen. They had always been the greatest of friends ever since they were small, and had always discussed everything together. But she hadn't told him how she felt about Chris: she had been afraid that he would laugh at her. She accepted, sadly, that she and her childhood playmate were growing away from one another. The age of innocence was coming to an end.

'I had no idea you'd be at the wedding,' Tim said, delighted. 'I didn't realize you were a friend of Irene Woodhouse.'

Sylvia Gibson smiled. 'I'm here as a guest of the groom. Jeremy and I lived next door to one another when we were children, in Birmingham. And, if it comes to that, I didn't expect to meet you here, either, although I naturally guessed your mother would be present.'

'The whole family was invited, but Chris and Dad chickened out. Ma's none too pleased about it, although she'd have been madder if Babs and the girls hadn't been staying with us. She wangled invitations for them at the last minute. They're all over there, by the buffet.'

Sylvia Gibson nodded. She had acted with, and been a friend of, Clifford Haldane long enough to know all about what he called 'my other family', and she had met Barbara Seymour and her two daughters on more than one occasion in the past, during their frequent visits to London. She glanced across at the little group, caught Penelope's eye and waved. Penelope waved back and mimed her inability, for the present, to fight her way through the crush of people separating them. Sylvia grimaced understandingly.

At the age of thirty, she was a striking-looking woman, who would have stood out in a crowd even if she hadn't been a familiar face to thousands from her stage, film and television appearances. Her tall elegant figure was always impeccably dressed, the very dark, almost black hair swept back into a classic chignon at the nape of her neck. The high cheekbones, sallow skin and slanting eyes of a deep liquid brown ensured that, more often than not, she was cast as an exotic foreigner – a fact which irritated her immensely, although she was growing more reconciled to it as she got older. Envious theatrical friends told her that she was lucky to be so constantly in demand; but one of the reasons she liked working with Clifford Haldane was that he so often

45

asked for her in roles which cast her against type.

But there was no doubt that her looks had been her fortune in more ways than one, gaining her a steady stream of male admirers since she was twelve years old, when she first began taking a serious interest in the opposite sex. And, although she had never felt intensely enough about any one of them to want to get married, she nevertheless had enjoyed a number of good relationships, some of which had ripened into lasting friendships. Recently, however, she had found herself wondering if, by refusing always to take the ultimate step, she had missed out on something – some sacred mystery, ordained by God in the joining of hands and exchanging of vows. In her heart of hearts, with so many of her friends divorced or separated, she couldn't quite believe it, although, because of her unmarried state, she had denied herself the luxury of children. But sitting today in St Clement Dane's, listening to the beauty of the marriage service, she had once again been seized by the same vague longing for a more permanent involvement. But with whom?

Her latest liaison, with Timothy Haldane, could hardly be classed as a serious affair. Not on her part, at least, although she sometimes suspected that Tim felt differently. Of course, he was far too young for her, and she was not even sure how their friendship had started, except that she had known him for years and was flattered that someone so handsome, and twelve years her junior, should find her exciting. They had been to bed together once or twice; but he was a boy, who had only just left school, with three years at Oxford before him. So no thought of marriage had so much as crossed her mind until, astonishingly, this afternoon, when she glimpsed him among the guests on the opposite side of the church. And even then, for a brief moment, she had mistaken him for his elder brother. He had remained unaware of her presence until they reached the Savoy, where the reception was being held, but the look of delight on his face when he eventually spotted her, and the alacrity with which he had pushed his way through the crush to her side, had suddenly made her feel that here, after all, might be the great love of her life. Ridiculous, of course. She would be accused, with some justification, of cradle-snatching. Besides, she would probably feel quite differently tomorrow. She was being over-sentimental, influenced by the day, the transparent happiness of her old friend Jeremy Grantham, and the general whiff of orange blossom which pervaded the air.

Not, of course, that Irene Woodhouse – Sylvia corrected herself: Irene Grantham – was wearing orange blossom. (Did anyone wear it any more? she wondered.) The cream lace two-piece with its short revealing skirt, was far removed from the conventional idea of a bridal gown. And there was no veil, either, just a tiny wisp of a hat perched over one eye – a mistake, perhaps, since something less revealing might have preserved the illusion of an equal happiness on the part of the bride. Sylvia grimaced secretly. 'There you are,' she told herself. 'Disillusionment is setting in already.' Yet, even so, she could not shake off the longing for something more permanent than just another affair.

She became aware that Tim had been speaking to her, asking her a question, and was now waiting for her answer. 'Sorry, darling,' she apologized. 'I didn't quite catch what you said. I was admiring Irene's dress.'

'I asked if you had anything lined up for the immediate future? If not, would you like to come down to Devon with us in ten days' time? Originally, it was going to be the five of us and the two Seymour girls, but Chris has had to pull out because he's landed a part in this play I was telling you about the other day. So you could have his room, if you'd care to come. I know Dad wouldn't mind. He's planning this new production of *Volpone*. He might even be thinking of offering you a part.'

'Well . . . ' Sylvia had to admit that the prospect was tempting. Her agent had mentioned the possibility of a small film role in the autumn, but she had heard nothing more from him for over two weeks now. And, anyway, August was still the summer. She wouldn't be needed yet. 'What about Penelope?' she asked. 'Has she been consulted?'

But just at that moment, right on cue, Penelope appeared, having managed, at last, to make her way through the press of fellow-guests. In her wake came Richard, the two young Seymour girls and their mother, who was wearing a strange shapeless navy-blue dress, with gloves, shoes and handbag in a vivid eye-catching shade of cerise. Sylvia tried hard not to stare.

Before Penelope could do more than open her mouth in greeting, Tim was appealing to her to endorse his invitation. 'I told Sylvia Dad wouldn't mind. What do you think?'

'I should think he'd probably welcome her with open arms,' his mother agreed. 'Yes, do come, my dear, if you feel you can. You'll be someone for Cliff to talk to about things the rest of us can't possibly understand. At least, that's his theory, and I dare say he's right. Even after all these years, there are aspects of acting and actors that still confuse me.'

Sylvia laughed. 'Very circumspectly put. You should have been a diplomat, Pen, as well as a writer. By the way, I hear you have a new novel coming out next month. Congratulations.' She saw the embarrassed expression on Penelope's face, recollected that she hated talking about her books, and hurried on: 'Of course I'd love to come down to Devon with you, if you're sure that's all right. Dartmoor's a part of the country I'm particularly fond of.'

'Good. That's settled, then,' Penelope said, glancing around her. 'Can anyone spot a waiter? The speeches are due, and I've nothing to drink.'

CHAPTER FOUR

'THAT'S TORMENTIL,' Richard said, pointing to a patch of bright yellow flowers, waving gently on slender stems. 'In the Middle Ages, people used to boil the roots in milk and eat them to cure stomach ache. Ssh!' He flung out a peremptory arm, stopping Anne in her tracks. 'Look,' he whispered, 'there's a wheatear, grubbing for insects. It hasn't seen us. If we keep perfectly still . . .'

The afternoon silence was shattered by Cloud's excited barking, as he launched himself after a ball thrown by Imogen. The wheatear rose up with a furious flapping of wings, its white rump gleaming against a cloudless sky. Richard sighed in exasperation and said 'Bugger!' very loudly, eliciting an immediate reprimand from his mother.

'You are not to use words like that, Rich! You know that very well. Don't let me hear you swearing again.' Penelope hesitated, realizing that her last injunction was slightly ambiguous, but it was too hot to think properly and she left it there. She reflected that everyone's temper seemed a little frayed today. No-one appeared to be in the best of spirits.

Perhaps that was not surprising. They had been at Fourmile Cottage for over a week now, and today was the first really fine day that they had had. There had been the inevitable excursions into Tavistock and Plymouth, and a visit to Sir Francis Drake's old home, Buckland Abbey, but they did these trips every summer, and nothing compensated for the lack of good weather. It was particularly trying for the children, who liked to run free on the moors; although Penelope doubted if that sort of amusement appealed any more to Imogen. She had grown up a lot since last year, and without her mother's sheltering presence seemed even shyer and more withdrawn. She had never been a communicative child and was obviously finding the trauma of adolescence hard to handle. There was an aura of unhappiness about her, and none of Penelope's efforts to cheer her made any difference. It never occurred to Penelope to associate Imogen's silent misery with Sylvia's inclusion in the party, although she was conscious that the invitation might have been a mistake. Far from keeping Clifford company, Sylvia seemed to have spent all her spare time with Tim during the past ten days.

Penelope leaned back against an outcrop of rock and glanced around her: at the debris of their picnic lunch; at Clifford, lying flat on his back, fast asleep and snoring, his much-annotated copy of *Volpone* slipping from his fingers on to the short tough moorland grass; at Imogen, the same dispirited look on her face that she had worn all week, desultorily throwing the ball for Cloud; at Richard and Anne, chatting amicably together as they disappeared over the horizon; at Tim and Sylvia . . . But, as usual, they were nowhere to be seen. Penelope stirred uneasily. What was this sudden fascination for one another's company? What did they find to say when they were alone together? She recollected Sylvia's reputation, her numerous love-affairs, facts which had previously seemed of no importance, but which suddenly assumed great significance when considered in relation to Tim. Tim was twelve years younger than Sylvia and had his whole life in front of him. Surely he couldn't be such a fool as to get embroiled with an older woman . . .

Penelope pulled herself up short. She, the writer of

modern sexy novels, the epitome – to her readers – of the new-found freedom of the sixties, was thinking like a Victorian mother, with the same rampant morality and desire to protect her young. Deliberately, she closed her eyes and tried to sleep, feeling the warmth of the sun-soaked granite through the thin cotton of her dress. But sleep refused to come, and she found herself continuing to speculate on the whereabouts of Tim and Sylvia. In desperation, she switched on the small portable radio at her side, turned down the volume and listened to the latest cricket scores.

'Now, what bird is that?' Richard demanded. 'Over there, on that gorse bush. Anne! You're not looking. Red breast, white marking above the eye, makes a noise – there, listen to it! – as though it's tapping stones.'

'Robin?' Anne hazarded vaguely, and immediately opened the vials of her companion's wrath upon her head.

'Robin!' His scorn was withering. 'It's a *whinchat*! I don't know what's got into you this holiday, Anne. You used to know all the moorland birds as well as I do. You'll have to do better than that, you know, if you're going to marry a vet.'

'Who says I'm going to marry a vet?' Anne asked indignantly. 'I've never said I was going to marry a vet.'

Richard turned his head to look at her, mildly surprised. 'We always said we'd get married when we were older. You know we did. We agreed it ages ago.'

Anne shrugged. 'I've changed my mind.'

'Oh.' Richard was momentarily nonplussed, but took this setback to his future plans with stoicism. 'Oh, well, if you have, you have. That's your pre . . .

prerog ... prerog-something. It means you can do what you fucking well like.'

Anne regarded him thoughtfully. 'I think "fucking" is another of those words you ought not to say. I don't know what it means, but I think it's something really awful. I used it once, because I'd heard one of the girls at school say it, and it was the only time Mum has ever slapped me.'

'Really?' Richard evinced interest. A serious, some said precocious, child for his age, he nevertheless had a deep-seated vein of mischief, which at present manifested itself in a desire to shock his elders out of the wary condescension they displayed towards him.

He and Anne were sprawled at the very edge of the ridge of high ground which sheltered Fourmile Cottage. Just beyond where they lay, the grass-covered slope shelved steeply to the valley floor, studded with rocks and boulders. The cottage itself, seen from the back and surrounded by its garden, seemed deceptively close in the still sunlit air. Every detail was clearly defined, and its origins as two cottages knocked into one, with a small modern extension, uncompromisingly revealed. As a permanent dwelling-place, it had its limitations, but as a holiday home it offered the prospect of peace and tranquillity. Clifford had bought it four years earlier with the money from a particularly lucrative television series, and he and his family had been coming to Devon each August ever since. Now, however, Chris's absence was the first indication that there was bound to be a gradual diminution in their numbers, as school holidays and university vacations became things of the past.

'Well, if you aren't going to marry me, who are you going to marry?' Richard asked after a protracted silence.

'*I* don't know,' Anne said, a shade too defensively. 'I just know it's not going to be you.'

As she spoke, her heart gave a painful lurch and the blood rushed into her cheeks as she saw the back door of the cottage open and Chris come out ... Then, almost at once, she realized that distance had deceived her. The shining cap of fair hair belonged to Tim, and he had one arm around Sylvia Gibson's shoulders. They walked a little way down the garden path, then stopped to kiss, the two bodies so closely intertwined that they looked like a single person. Anne nudged Richard and directed his gaze in their direction with an embarrassed giggle.

Richard sat up, hugging his knees and screwing up his eyes against the sun. 'Why do you think they've been indoors', he demanded disapprovingly, 'on a lovely afternoon like this?'

'Perhaps they were thirsty and wanted a drink.' Anne could come up with no better reason. As the kiss continued, her eyes met Richard's, and the next moment they were both rolling on the ground, convulsed by stifled laughter.

'What a couple of wallies,' Richard gasped, when at last he could speak. He scrambled to his feet. 'Come on, let's go and tell the others.'

But Anne shook her head. 'No, I don't think we ought to,' she said. 'Kissing's ... well, *private*, isn't it? That sort of kissing that grown-ups do. I mean ... well, it's just between them. Tim wouldn't like it if we told anyone.'

Richard considered this, then nodded. 'All right,' he agreed. 'It'll be our secret. But I bet Tim'll tell everybody, sooner or later. That sort of kissing', he added knowledgeably, from his vast store of wisdom, 'nearly always leads to marriage.'

'Anne! Wake up! There's an awful row going on downstairs.'

Anne opened her sleep-drugged eyes to see Imogen

bending over her, shaking her violently by the shoulder. For a second or two, she stared vacantly, not sure what was happening; then the sound of raised voices floated up the staircase from the ground floor of the cottage. A moment later, Richard appeared in the open doorway of their bedroom, wearing green-striped pyjamas.

'There's a fucking great row going on downstairs,' he hissed, in a more colourful echo of Imogen's words. 'I think Tim wants to marry that Sylvia Gibson. I told you that's what would happen,' he added to Anne, with an air of self-congratulation. He jerked his head towards the landing. 'Come out here and we can hear what's going on. Mum sounds really angry.'

Penelope *was* angry, although she would have been hard put to it to explain why she felt such white-hot rage. After all, she had nothing against Sylvia except her age; in fact, until now, she had always liked the woman. She hadn't exactly approved of Sylvia's string of affairs, but she certainly would never dream of sitting in judgement. As far as Penelope was concerned, people were free to do what they wanted with their lives provided that they didn't impinge on hers. And there, of course, was the rub. Tim had, presumably, already been to bed with Sylvia and was now, incredibly, proposing to marry her; Tim, who was only just eighteen to Sylvia's nearly thirty; Tim, who, in Penelope's eyes, was still not much more than a schoolboy.

Until that moment after dinner, when the three younger members of the household had been packed off to bed, when Tim had dropped his bombshell, Penelope had had no idea how strong a maternal instinct she harboured.

'I'm afraid I'm not a very good mother,' she had always disclaimed with a deprecatory laugh. 'Too busy writing. I wonder sometimes if either Cliff or I is really cut out to be a parent.'

But the moment Tim had said defiantly, 'Sylvia and I are going to get married,' she had known the truth: her self-derogation was a pose. She had always been an excellent mother and cared deeply what happened to her children. Looking back, she realized that she had never willingly missed a school concert, sports day, prizegiving; had supervised homework and made sure that uniform and all necessary equipment was bought on time and ready to hand. It was Cliff who, more often than not, had been missing, away filming or busy with rehearsals.

She blamed herself for not seeing this coming, for misreading the signs. She had assumed that Tim was simply being polite to Sylvia; entertaining a guest, his father's fellow-actor and friend. Instead of which, he had fallen, as half a dozen others before him had fallen, for those strikingly exotic looks. That in itself was not surprising. He was going to make a fool of himself over a pretty face, lose his head over an attractive older woman, at some time or another. No; the amazing thing was that Sylvia had actually accepted him. Sylvia, who had adamantly remained single throughout her thirty years, who had dropped far more suitable and eligible men friends without, apparently, a second's regret, was willing to marry Tim.

'Why?' Penelope demanded furiously, viciously jabbing her needle into the tablecloth she was somewhat inexpertly embroidering. 'Why, Sylvia? Why do you want to ruin Timothy's life? What harm have we ever done you?'

Clifford Haldane got up and came to sit beside his wife, perching on the arm of her chair and slipping an arm about her shoulders.

'Now, hang on, Pen,' he said quietly. 'Before we sink under a mass of clichés, don't you think we ought to let Sylvia speak? Sylvia my dear, this has come as a shock. I don't think either of us realized that you and Tim knew each other all that well, and most certainly had no idea that you were lovers. I . . . er . . . I assume that you are?'

'Yes, we are,' Tim struck in defiantly, without giving Sylvia a chance to reply. 'I suppose I might have guessed you'd both react like this. Neither of you has ever given a thought to what *I* want, or what's good for *me*. If it were Chris, now, that would be different. You've always considered *his* wishes, consulted him about what *he* wants to do, just because he's the eldest. It's so damnably unfair!'

'That's not true!' Penelope gasped, appalled at the unjustness of the accusation. 'All your father and I have ever wanted is what's best for both of you. And Chris has never proposed marrying a woman so much older than himself. How do you think you're going to manage while you're up at Oxford?'

Sylvia, having at last got control of her voice, raised it for the first time since entering the little low-beamed parlour. Tim, lingering with her in the dining-room after the evening meal, had warned her that telling his parents might not be easy. She had agreed with him fervently, anticipating many more objections than he seemed to do.

'As far as money goes, I'm quite able to support Tim. I'm never out of work for long. Luckily for me, my face has been, if not my fortune, at least a constant supplier of bread and butter.'

Penelope snapped at her son: 'Is that what you want out of life – to be a kept man?'

Clifford squeezed her shoulders again. 'Pen! Pen! Remember what I said just now about the danger of too many clichés.'

She rounded on him, glad of the excuse to avoid Tim's accusing stare. 'Don't you *care* what happens to your son?'

'Yes, of course I do.' Her husband slid off the arm of her chair and drew himself up to his full height, lifting his chin in a gesture his many fans would have recognized immediately: Angelo in *Measure for Measure*; Becket in *Murder in the Cathedral*; King Lear; the grand heroic pose which he could, in a moment, slough off for the vulnerability of Marlowe's Edward II or the cringing pathos of Shylock. 'Sylvia, my dear girl, you do realize the pitfalls of marrying a man so much younger than yourself? Tim's had no experience of life as yet. Whereas you . . . ' He paused, floundering a little, on the brink of indiscretion.

Sylvia laughed. 'Oh, I know what you're trying to say, Cliff, and of course I've thought about it; considered the implications of the age-gap in ten or fifteen years' time. But . . . ' She broke off, shrugging.

But what? she asked herself. That there was a 'but' she was perfectly well aware. She had astonished herself this afternoon, when, after they had finished making love in his room upstairs, he had asked her to marry him and she had said 'yes'. Now she couldn't believe that she really had said it and wondered what had come over her. But she could hardly back out now, even if she wanted to. And she was not at all certain that she did. There was something about Tim that attracted her enormously; yet, at the same time, something else that repelled. One moment he was a sophisticated man of the world, the next a petulant schoolboy. Her feelings for him were ambivalent. Had she allowed them to be seduced by the calm and peace of the Devon countryside? By the strange sensation of timelessness induced by the wild open spaces of the moor? She had no idea; nor, at that moment, did she particularly care. She was possessed by a kind of recklessness. She had been cautious, where men were concerned, for far too long.

'Well, I think it's obscene!' Penelope declared, too

angry to think what she was saying, and snatching words out of the air. 'She's nearly old enough to be your mother!'

Tim began to shout. 'Oh, knock it off, Ma! How many pregnant twelve-year-olds do you know? You can give Sylvia fourteen years. You just hate to think that I've grown up. You don't want to give up possession.'

Penelope, her mouth open to reply, was halted in her tracks. She stared at her son, horrified. Was that how he saw her, a possessive mother, afraid to let go? Worse, was that how other people saw her, undeceived by her protestations of maternal deficiency? And, even worse than that again, was it true?

Tim went on: 'And I really don't think you have any right to use a word like "obscene". Not after some of the stuff you put in your books.'

'Now, stop it, both of you!' Cliff ordered, in the voice he used to reach the back of the stalls. 'All this wrangling is getting us nowhere. Tim's proposed and Sylvia has accepted him, so there's nothing we can do to alter that fact. But I do feel', he added, looking directly at his son, 'that your mother and I have some wishes and conditions that should be respected. Therefore, I ask you both to wait until Tim has graduated before rushing into marriage. If you love one another, three years isn't going to make all that difference.'

'More clichés,' Tim sneered, but was interrupted by Sylvia, who reached across and held his hand.

'I think we should do as your parents wish, darling,' she said quietly. 'Cliff is right. We ought to wait a little while, just to make sure of our feelings for one another. And if I can afford to wait three years' – her smile was ironic – 'I'm sure that you can.'

'I'm sure of my feelings now,' he protested. 'I shan't feel any differently in three years' time.'

'For me. To please me,' she coaxed, and experienced

a treacherous little surge of relief that Cliff's suggestion had bought her a breathing-space in which to discover what it was that she really wanted.

Tim's expression grew surly, but it was three against one, and he knew he stood no chance now that Sylvia had joined the opposition. He addressed his parents. 'Oh . . . all right, if it's what Sylvia wants. But I shan't change my mind, if that's what you're hoping. It's not fair. You've always thought that Chris is the one who's more mature for his age. I'm just good old Tim, his shadow. Well, you'll see. You'll be proved wrong, both of you. I know what I want and I'm going, for once, to get it, in spite of everybody.'

Clifford glanced at Penelope, daring her to say any more on the subject. She hesitated, then nodded her acquiescence.

'Right,' he said. 'That's settled, then. I think we could all do with a drink.'

'Phew!' Richard exclaimed, joining Anne and Imogen in their bedroom as the three of them stealthily removed themselves from the landing, where they had been hanging over the banister rails. 'What a carry-on. Fancy Timmo wanting to marry Sylvia Gibson. She must be ninety if she's a day!'

'You're talking rubbish,' Anne said, preventing him settling on her bed and pushing him towards the door. One look at Imogen's white unhappy face told her that Richard's pleasantries would not be welcome. 'It's time we were in bed. Your mother will be up in a minute to see if we're asleep. You'd better go now. Go on, Rich! Get back to your own room.'

'I'm going. I'm going,' he assured her, offended. But he was still inclined to linger. Fortunately, at that moment, a sleepy Cloud, woken by the sound of Richard's voice, left his basket beside his master's bed and came snuffling and whining across the landing in search of him. 'Hell's teeth!' Richard bent and scooped the dog into his arms. 'This won't do, Sir Cloudesley. If Mum hears you up and about, she'll be upstairs like a shot. 'Night, Anne. 'Night, Im. See you both in the morning.' He paused in the doorway, glancing back over his shoulder. 'Who'd ever have thought it, though? Timmo and old Sylvia!'

He was gone, finally, and Anne was free to give her attention to Imogen, who had climbed back into bed, drawing the sheet and one thin blanket up to her chin. Her young body was rigid beneath the bedclothes.

'Are you all right?' Anne whispered, getting into her own bed, but not attempting to lie down. 'Do you want me to fetch you anything?'

Imogen shook her head, staring mutely in front of her. The curtains, with their pattern of daisies and forget-me-nots still visible in the waning light of the late-summer evening, were drawn back to reveal the sweep of the moor beyond. The bedroom which the girls were sharing was at the back of the house, in the small extension which gave an L-shape to the original structure. A few stars were pricking the deep blue of the sky. An owl hooted in the distance, and the outline of a tree was etched against the window.

'A glass of water?' Anne suggested, feeling useless in the face of such concentrated misery.

Imogen snapped: 'Leave me alone, can't you? Go to sleep.' But a moment later she broke out fiercely: 'I hate this place! I want to go home! I don't think I can bear it for another four days.'

'You'll have to,' Anne said. 'Aunt Pen and Uncle Cliff have arranged to drop us off in Bristol before going on to London. Besides, how would you explain it to everyone if you suddenly asked to leave? Four days will soon go. It won't be so bad.'

'It'll be purgatory!' Imogen turned on to her side,

facing her sister. 'Whatever does he see in that horrid old woman?'

Anne, while sympathizing, felt constrained to take Sylvia's part. 'She's not that old. She's a lot younger than Mum or Aunt Pen. And she's quite nice when you get to know her. She talked to me a lot, that afternoon we went to Buckland Abbey, telling me stories about her life in the theatre. She made me laugh.'

'She's horrible,' Imogen answered with conviction. 'I *hate* her and I hate Tim and I hate this cottage. I'll never come here any more, ever. And don't you say anything nice about her again, or I'll hate *you*, too. I wish I were dead.'

There seemed to Anne to be no suitable answer, and she watched silently while her sister rolled on to her stomach and turned her head in the other direction. Anne stared at the shadowy patterns on the ceiling as the last of the daylight drained away and full darkness set in. If this was what love did to you, she decided, she hoped it would never happen to her. She thought of Chris, but was wise enough to know that the little ache in her heart which any memory of him conjured up had nothing to do with the emotion that Imogen was feeling. Her sister had been miserable ever since they arrived at the cottage; ever since she had heard of Sylvia Gibson's inclusion in the party. She had resented being treated like a child, being made to go to bed at the same time as herself and Richard. Not that they had been going to bed that early, Anne reflected, but Imogen had wanted to be classed with the grown-ups, not with the children. It diminished her in Tim's eyes. Imogen had been resentful.

All was quiet downstairs now; only the faint murmur of voices. Everyone was being stiffly formal and very polite to each other, Anne guessed, in the way adults had when they had quarrelled; avoiding one another's eyes and making stilted conversation. No; the holiday this year had not been as happy as the last three. She herself had found Richard more irritating than she used to do. At one time, she had liked nothing more than to accompany him on his rambles across the moor, while he instructed her in the different species of plants, animals and butterflies. But now she found his all-absorbing interest in nature rather boring. She preferred the trips to Plymouth, window-shopping in Royal Parade and New George Street, looking at the fashions, eating at Humphrey's on the Hoe. She no longer enjoyed getting dirty, grubbing around for insects. Richard seemed to her, in some ways, to be still a baby.

The owl hooted again, this time right over the cottage. It must be late; she could hear the others coming upstairs to bed. She heard the murmured 'good-nights' on the landing. Only another four days and she would be home in her own room, in her own bed. Anne suddenly realized that she was looking forward to it.

CHAPTER FIVE

'HAPPY BIRTHDAY, darlings.'

Felicity Bryce came into the kitchen just as Anne and Imogen were finishing their breakfast. Barbara was already at the sink, starting the washing-up, neatly dressed in the navy blue suit and white blouse which she wore for work – the only outfit in her wardrobe which had her mother's unqualified approval. Felicity kissed her granddaughters and handed each a carefully and prettily wrapped parcel. 'Happy birthday,' she repeated.

She reflected that the last fifteen months had matured Anne beyond recognition. Today was only her twelfth birthday, and she still had the same slender under-developed figure that she had always had, so it must be her manner, her general air, that gave the impression of someone older. That and her protective attitude to her sister.

Felicity's gaze switched to Imogen. The girl was altogether too quiet and introverted. At sixteen, she should be enjoying life, out with boys, not moping around the house every weekend, watching so much television. It wasn't even as though she studied hard; her O level results had been far from good, and Felicity doubted that her A levels, in two years' time, would be any better. Yet Barbara persisted in her delusion that both the girls would go on to university.

Something had gone wrong, that summer holiday of last year, during the trip to Devon. This year, despite much persuasion, they had declined to go, returning home with their mother after the usual two weeks

64

in London. Barbara had been cross at their refusal, calling them rude and ungrateful, but Felicity had told her sharply to leave them alone; the girls were growing up, and had minds and lives of their own.

'Take them abroad,' she had advised. 'Broaden their horizons. Show them some new countries.'

'You know I don't like going abroad,' Barbara had answered. 'And, if I don't go to London, when else do Pen and I get a chance to see one another? We're both too busy most of the time.'

'You're selfish,' her mother told her roundly. 'Always have been, always will be.'

But no strictures of Felicity's influenced Barbara, who had gone her own way all her life, forcing other people to fit in around her. Felicity knew when she was beaten and had abandoned the subject.

'Oh, Grandma, it's lovely!' Anne was exclaiming, holding up a pale pink nightdress of fine cotton lawn. Discarded wrapping-paper was strewn across the table. 'Look, Mum! Isn't it pretty?'

Barbara turned her head. 'Very.' She glanced at her mother. 'A little old, perhaps, for a twelve-year-old? And I thought pink wasn't one of your favourite colours.'

'Not if it's an insipid acrylic jumper worn with a coffee-and-cream suit,' Felicity responded tartly. 'But it has its place in lingerie and nightwear. As for being too old, Anne is at the age when she needs to feel grown-up. Imogen darling, I hope yours is all right.'

'It's lovely, Grandma. Thank you.' Imogen smiled, holding up one thin wrist around which was clasped a narrow silver bracelet. 'It's really beautiful.' There was more warmth in her tone and smile than Felicity had heard and seen for a long time.

'That's fine, then. Now, show me all your other cards and parcels.'

'They'll be late for school,' Barbara scolded, coming over to the kitchen table to gather up the rest of the dirty crockery and carry it back to the sink. 'Come to that, I shall be late myself, if we don't all get a move on.'

'We'll show you this evening, Gran,' Anne promised, getting up and beginning to search for her things. 'What have I done with my satchel? You haven't seen it, have you, Im?'

'By the door,' Barbara said impatiently. 'Imogen, you could show Grandma what the Haldanes sent you.' She returned to the table, rummaging amongst the litter of cardboard and brown paper until she found a flat red leather box, which she snapped open. 'Look at that!' She displayed a delicate gold chain, supporting a heart-shaped locket set with a single pearl. 'Isn't that beautiful?'

'And very expensive,' Felicity commented drily. 'But I imagine it's from all of them.'

'Oh, yes, it's from all of them,' Imogen answered tonelessly. 'At least, that's what it says on the card. But I expect the truth is that Aunt Pen chose it and packed it up. Uncle Cliff and the three boys just signed their names. I don't suppose Tim even did that, because he's up at Oxford at the moment. Anyway' – she kissed Felicity's cheek – 'I'd rather have your bracelet, Gran.'

'Oh, really!' Barbara exclaimed in vexation as she began peeling off her rubber gloves. 'I don't know what's got into you two girls lately, where the Haldanes are concerned. Talk about ingratitude! Well, let me tell you here and now that we have all, including you, Mother, been invited to Cameron Close for Christmas, and I have every intention of accepting. It's no good looking like that, Imogen. If you want to stay here on your own, you can, but I'm going. The rest of you can do as you wish.'

Felicity, noting the sullen look on Imogen's face and Anne's obvious agitation, said smoothly: 'That will be very nice. I haven't seen the house in St John's Wood yet, so it will be a treat for me. I'm sure we shall have a lovely time. Now, get along, all of you. I'll finish clearing up here before I go upstairs and have my breakfast. Babs, you won't need that heavy coat. It's a beautiful autumn day. The sun's shining. Hurry up, Imogen, Anne. I'll cook you both your favourite supper this evening. And afterwards, when you've done your homework, we'll watch television.'

'And at the weekend there's the party. Great!' Anne picked up her satchel. 'And don't let me forget to watch that new series that's starting on TV tomorrow night. "Colditz." David McCallum's in it. He's fab. I've been mad about him ever since "The Man from UNCLE". Come on, Im, or we'll miss the bus. 'Bye, Gran. 'Bye, Mum. See you tonight.'

Barbara sighed as the kitchen door closed behind her daughters. 'It's nice to see one of them happy. I just wish Imogen would buck herself up. She's been so miserable lately.'

'Adolescence,' Felicity reassured her. 'It's a difficult time, especially for girls. You were a pain in the arse.'

'Really, Mother!' Barbara protested, at her most austere. Then she relented, grinning momentarily as she powdered her nose. 'I dare say you're right. But I wish she'd hurry up and grow out of it.'

Her mother started to clear what was left on the table. 'Don't worry. It's a phase and it'll pass.' But, even as she spoke, Felicity wondered how many people had used that comforting phrase, only to find that it simply wasn't true.

'Sylvia! Sylvia!' A hand descended on her shoulder and a familiar voice said: 'I thought it was you.'

She turned. 'Chris.' Her face lit up with pleasure. 'What are you doing here?'

He grimaced. 'Chasing up my agent to see if there was an offer of work he'd forgotten to tell me about. And you?'

She jerked her head towards the New Theatre behind them. 'There was an extra rehearsal called for this morning. Did you know I'd managed to land a part in the current production? One of the leads has had to quit for personal reasons. I was just going to get some lunch at the Salisbury. Come with me. My treat.' Chris hesitated, while the traffic roared along St Martin's Lane, polluting the soft October sunshine with a cloud of exhaust fumes. 'Now, don't be silly. When you're in work, you can return the compliment.'

'Oh, all right.' He stopped frowning, and his face broke into a big friendly grin, which made Sylvia reflect – not for the first time – that, although he and Tim were so alike to look at, by nature they were totally different.

The Salisbury, with its opulent interior of red plush seating, superbly etched windows and abundance of highly polished wood, was crowded, as it always was at lunchtime, with more than a sprinkling of familiar theatrical faces amongst the rest. But Chris and Sylvia managed to find a corner where the noise was not too deafening, and were eventually served with generous portions of ham, fried eggs, salad and chips.

'I'll never eat it all,' Sylvia protested. 'It's far too much.'

'In other words,' Chris said, 'you had no intention of coming in here until you met me. And you've spent far more money than you intended.'

'Oh, for heaven's sake! It's hardly going to put me in debt. And, if I can't take my future brother-in-law to lunch when he's resting, who can I take? I was sorry your last play folded.'

Chris shrugged. 'It was inevitable. I was amazed that it ran as long as it did. It was an absolute stinker.'

'Yes, I know. I saw it.'

'Did you? Why? You must have heard that it wasn't up to much. Are you into masochism?'

She laughed. 'I came to see *you*, as a matter of fact. And I was glad I did. You were good. You made up for all the rest.'

He paused, laying down his knife and fork, and looked round at her. 'Do you mean that? Or are you just being kind?'

'You know I'm not. The critics said much the same thing. One day you'll be an actor to measure up to your father. I mean it, Chris. Maybe you'll be even better.'

He regarded her thoughtfully for a moment, before resuming his meal. 'Don't let the old man hear you say that,' he advised her. 'You might forfeit his friendship for good.'

'Oh, I think I've done that already.' Sylvia tried to sound indifferent, but did not quite succeed. 'I haven't been in favour with either Cliff or Penelope since I got engaged to Tim.'

'Why did you? Get engaged to Tim. I shouldn't have thought he was really your type. Too immature for someone like you.'

'You mean I'm almost old enough to be his mother.'

'Hell, no!' Chris dismissed the idea with scorn. 'This age business, which seems to obsess Ma and Pa's generation, doesn't mean a damn thing nowadays. No, I meant exactly what I said. Tim's only three years younger than I am, but sometimes I feel like his grandfather. Mind you, to be fair, my parents often make me feel that way, too.'

Sylvia laughed, and Chris suddenly wondered why he'd never noticed before how extremely attractive she was. Those slightly foreign, cat-like features, with the high slanting cheekbones and dark liquid-brown eyes, were very exciting. No wonder Tim had fallen for her. And Chris felt a spurt of annoyance that his younger brother should have been so much more percipient than he had been. He had always prided himself on being wide awake to the charms of the opposite sex, yet somehow or other he had overlooked Sylvia Gibson. Maybe it was because he had always thought of her as his parents' generation. But of course she wasn't; and it was irksome that Tim had got in ahead of him; had, moreover, wooed and won the lady. His pride took a nosedive.

Sylvia, who had eaten very little except the salad, and was now pushing the rest of the food around her plate, said so softly that Chris had to strain to hear her: 'I know what you mean about Tim. He is a bit young for his age. At first, that was what appealed to me. I'd got very fed up with worldly-wise smart-arse men and wanted something different. But now . . .'

'But now?' Chris prompted her after a moment's silence.

'Now . . . perhaps I'm not so sure.' She glanced at the bare third finger of her left hand; bare because Tim had been unable to afford a ring and his parents, naturally enough in the circumstances, had refused to help him. 'It's not as though we're officially engaged as yet.'

'That's true.' Chris moved a little closer to her, allowing their thighs to touch. 'Would . . . would Tim be very upset, do you think, if you ended the engagement?'

'Maybe at first . . . But he's young. He'd get over it. People always do.'

She returned the pressure of Chris's leg, her heart beginning to hammer against her ribs. What a fool she'd been! What a stupid bloody fool! She wasn't remotely in love with Tim: it had always been Chris. She recalled Jeremy Grantham's wedding the previous year, just before she had accepted Penelope's invitation to go down to Devon. She remembered looking across the church and mistaking Tim for his brother, and the sense of longing which had engulfed her. And she had been sufficiently unaware of her true feelings at that time to believe that what she felt was for Tim. How on earth could she have been so blind?

Chris asked abruptly: 'Are you busy this afternoon?'

'What?' She jumped, and her breath caught in her throat. 'No. No, the rehearsal was just this morning. My time's my own now until six-thirty, when I have to be at the theatre. My first time on, tonight. Always nerve-wracking, but especially when you're joining an established cast.' She gave a small dry laugh. 'Why do you ask?'

Chris finished his last chip and placed his knife and fork together on the empty plate, aligning them with painstaking precision and carefully avoiding her eyes. 'I thought we might spend the time together,' he said after a moment. 'That is, if you'd like to. The cinema, maybe. Or a matinée.'

She hesitated, but only for a second. 'Or you could come back to my flat,' she suggested.

His eyes swivelled to meet hers. 'That would be nice. Thank you.'

'So this is the house I've heard so much about.' Felicity's approving glance took in the Christmas tree standing in one corner of the hall; the pile of discarded raincoats and wellington boots which had been dropped in a heap on the floor, instead of being put

71

tidily away in a cupboard; the dog lead festooned over the back of a chair and the saucer containing cat food under the telephone-table. 'This is how a house should look. Lived in. I congratulate you, my dear Penelope.'

'If that's a dig at me, Mother, I'm ignoring it,' Barbara cut in drily. 'I'm not going to quarrel with anyone this Christmas, not even you. I've come to enjoy myself.'

'Quite right,' Penelope said, laughing. 'Just leave all the luggage where it is for the moment while you all have some tea. I'll get the boys to hump it upstairs later.'

'Felicity!' Clifford descended the stairs, hands outstretched. 'Welcome to Brickfield Terrace.'

'To where?' Felicity was confused as her host embraced her, kissing her on both cheeks.

There was no time for explanations, however, as Richard appeared, hanging over the banisters on the first-floor landing and shouting: 'Anne! I'm up here.' As if to confirm this fact, Machiavelli sprang gracefully on to the newel post, demonstrating the art of the impossible by clinging on to the shiny spherical surface with the claws of just three feet while cleaning the fourth paw with a bored insouciance. At the same moment, Sir Cloudesley Shovel rushed downstairs, hurling defiance at the intruders. 'Shut up, Cloud! Shut up!' Richard adjured him.

Clifford shrugged and raised his eyes heavenwards. 'You see nothing has changed, Felicity, since our move from Pimlico. It's still the same old madhouse.'

'True.' Penelope led the way up to the drawing-room, where strings of Christmas cards and shiny decorations were haphazardly suspended from walls and ceiling. A real log fire was burning in the grate, adding to the already considerable warmth of the central heating. Tim was lounging in one of the deep armchairs, his handsome face wearing a petulant expression.

'I've phoned Sylvia's flat four times this afternoon, and there's still no answer. She's being damned elusive this vacation. Oh, hello, Babs. Hi, Imogen. Hello, Annie.'

Anne reflected that it was typical of Tim to air his grievances before bothering to greet them. She thought he looked sallow and unwell, as though he were suffering under some kind of tension.

'Anne!' Richard flung an arm about her neck, almost choking the breath from her body. 'Why didn't you come down to the cottage this summer? Come up to my room. I've tons of new things to show you.'

Anne thrust away his arm and smoothed her hair. 'I'll have my tea first, thank you.'

'That's right, Anne dear,' Penelope encouraged her. 'Don't let him bully you. Now, sit down, all of you. Mrs Clennan left everything ready before she went. Oh, this is nice,' she went on, seating herself behind a small table on which the tea things were set out, flanked by two plates of sandwiches, a large chocolate cake and a dish of recently baked mince pies. 'It's lovely to see you all again. We did miss you in the summer.'

With great restraint, Barbara refrained from looking at her daughters, merely remarking: 'We did spend a fortnight with you here, in London. And the girls did have some rather sticky holiday projects to finish for the school.'

Clifford seated himself on the sofa, next to Anne, putting an avuncular arm around her shoulders. 'How's my favourite girl?' He glanced guiltily at Imogen and added hurriedly: 'I count Imogen as grown up, now that she's turned sixteen. And why didn't any of you come up to town to see me in *Volpone*? It ran for over six months.'

Anne giggled and helped herself to a sandwich. 'We meant to, didn't we, Mum? But somehow we never quite managed it.' She put her head on one side, looking up into Clifford's face. 'I was wondering the other day, how did you first meet Aunt Pen?'

He laughed. 'It was during my first year in Bristol. A few of us had been sent backstage to watch the mechanics of a performance and all that it entailed. Afterwards, your Aunt Pen was waiting outside the stage door, hoping to get Paul Rogers' autograph. She got me instead.'

'A very poor substitute,' his wife said, handing round cups of tea, but the look she sent him told a different story. 'Of course, a lot of the first-year students were older in those days than they are today, because they'd been in the forces. Cliff had had a distinguished career in the Royal Pay Corps by the time I met him, and risen to the dizzy heights of lance-corporal.'

They all laughed. 'Didn't he convince you he'd been in the D-Day landings?' Barbara asked. 'I seem to recollect something of the sort.' She took a piece of chocolate cake.

'Oh, he told me all kinds of lies when we first met,' Penelope agreed. 'I nearly believed them, too. He was so convincing. He's always been a good actor. I'm not sure, even now, when he's being himself or when he's playing a part. Don't ever marry a member of the acting profession, girls. It complicates life enormously.'

'I don't intend being an actor,' Richard announced grandly, sharing his fourth sandwich with Sir Cloudesley Shovel, who was sitting beside his chair, watching him intently with bright intelligent eyes. 'They're quite safe with me. I don't know what you're all grinning at. Being a vet's a proper job, not like acting. Look at Chris. He's only been on stage once in the last twelve months. He's been working as a barman for ages.'

'You know,' Clifford said, eyeing his youngest son with ironic affection, 'you can be quite disgustingly sententious when you put your mind to it, Rich. All the same, you're right about Chris. But that's partly his own fault. He came down from Oxford, where, admittedly, he'd done some acting with the OUDS, thinking he was going straight into an acting career on the strength of his name. Unfortunately, the idea was reinforced by my agent wangling him a part almost immediately in that dreadful play. Since when, he's hung around London, hoping, like Mr Micawber, for something else to turn up, when what he should have done was to get himself taken on by some reputable provincial repertory company and learn his craft from the bottom up. I thought, back in the autumn, that I'd persuaded him to see sense; but then, quite suddenly, nothing I could say would induce him to leave London. I feel in my bones that he's up to something, but I don't know what.'

'Probably involved with some woman,' Tim said laconically. He was still lounging in his chair, apparently very much at ease, but he had eaten nothing, and Anne noticed a nervous tic at one corner of his mouth. His hand, too, when he drank, was clamped rigidly round the handle of his cup, the knuckles white with tension. Suddenly, he propelled himself to his feet. 'If you'll excuse me, I'll go and phone Sylvia again. She must be home by now.'

'Problems?' Barbara enquired as he left the room, and Penelope sighed.

'Hopefully. I know that sounds mean, but I really don't want Tim to marry Sylvia. I thought one or the other of them would have cooled off by now. Anyway, let's talk about something else. I've managed to get a box for Boxing Day evening at the

Palladium, and I might tell you I had to pull a few strings.'

Richard, bored by the grown-ups' talk, and having decided that two mince pies were all that he and Cloud could manage just at present, again leaned over and tugged at Anne's sleeve. 'Come on upstairs.'

'I'm still eating,' she hissed indignantly and, to prove her point, took another slice of chocolate cake, which she did not really want. But she could hardly say that she was hanging on in the hope that Chris might put in an appearance. Richard would laugh at her, and the grown-ups would exchange small, secretive, indulgent smiles. So she munched slowly, making the cake last, and pretended to an interest in the conversation.

Her mother was asking about Irene Grantham's baby daughter, born the previous April.

'I'd like to be able to say that Debbie's a dear little thing,' Penelope answered, pouring Felicity a second cup of tea, 'but I'm afraid it wouldn't be true. She's one of those babies who cry a lot unless they get perpetual attention. And, with Irene and Jeremy both working, they were finding it difficult to cope, so they've engaged a full-time nanny. Not a very satisfactory situation, but I don't know what else they could have done. I was fortunate. All my three were perfectly content provided they were fed – and still are,' she added, reaching out to slap Richard's hand, which was straying in the direction of the last mince pie.

Tim wandered back into the room, his face set in lines of angry discontent. 'She still isn't there,' he grumbled. 'Where the hell is she?'

'Have you tried the stage door?' his father asked mildly. 'She might have decided to go to the theatre early for some reason.'

'I thought of that. But she isn't there.' Tim threw himself into his chair again and stared balefully at his younger brother. Richard put out his tongue.

Before either of his parents could issue a reprimand, there was a diversion. The drawing-room door opened yet again and Chris came in, closely followed by Sylvia Gibson. Tim was on his feet immediately, his face transformed, alive and glowing.

'Darling! I've been trying to phone you for hours. Where on earth have you been?'

He would have thrown his arms around Sylvia, but Chris moved to intercept him. He was looking extremely pale, Anne noticed.

'Wait, Tim.' Chris met his brother's bewildered stare squarely, but his hands were trembling and he thrust them into the pockets of his overcoat. Sylvia came and stood beside him, taking his arm. Chris went on: 'Mother. Dad. There's something I have to tell you. Sylvia and I were married by special licence at two o'clock this afternoon.'

CHAPTER SIX

THE CHAMBERS of Bryce & Seymour, Solicitors and Commissioners for Oaths, were to be found in a narrow passage connecting Small Street and Broad Street, in the oldest part of Bristol. The alleyway, although undoubtedly marking some medieval site, was Victorian, or more specifically Dickensian, in appearance; and Irene Grantham, making her way there from the nearby Grand Hotel, would not have been surprised to see Mr Tulkinghorn emerge majestically from one of the doorways. But her only encounter was with a marmalade-and-white cat, stretched out contentedly in the warm May sunshine.

Having wandered up and down for a few moments, she eventually located Bryce & Seymour near the entrance to Small Street. The highly polished brass plate indicated that the solicitors' office occupied the building's upper storey, the ground floor being apparently given over to the importation of bananas. Irene pushed open the street-door and mounted the dark twisting staircase almost immediately inside it, a musty smell of dust and old papers, which she felt to be entirely appropriate to her surroundings, assailing her nostrils. At the top of the linoleum-covered stairs was another door, this time of glass, bearing the name of the firm in gold lettering. She opened it and went inside.

The room, obviously the outer office, was, to Irene's surprise, light and airy, the sun pouring in through a large skylight, partially shielded by a fawn roller blind. The office fittings were functional and modern, a battery of green filing-cabinets taking up the whole of one wall, plain fawn drugetting on the floor and a desk made of some pale-coloured wood on which reposed an electric typewriter. Behind this sat a plump middle-aged woman, sensibly dressed in a fawn woollen suit which caused her to melt into the background. As soon as she saw Irene, she stopped typing, smoothed a wisp of greying hair into place and asked: 'Can I help you?'

'I . . . er . . . I wondered if Mrs Seymour was free. I'm a friend of a friend of hers. I'm afraid this is purely a social call,' Irene added, feeling suddenly guilty under the other woman's stern unblinking gaze.

'You mean Miss Bryce. Mrs Seymour goes by her maiden name during working hours.' The cool impersonal tones managed to convey that this arrangement had the speaker's unqualified approval. 'There has been, of course, no Seymour in the partnership since Mr Kenneth's death. If you'll tell me your name, I'll ask if Miss Bryce can see you.'

This given, the woman disappeared through another door into the inner office, and Irene was left alone, beginning to wish she hadn't come. She felt uncomfortable, over-dressed in her high-heeled shoes and vivid emerald-green dress, like a peacock who had strayed into a kitchen garden. But a moment later Barbara herself appeared, one hand outstretched in greeting, saying: 'Irene! How lovely to see you. What are you doing in Bristol? Come in. Muriel, do you think you could rustle us up two cups of tea?'

The plump woman looked none too pleased, but murmured something about seeing what she could do. As the door to the inner sanctum closed behind them, Irene asked with a nervous laugh: 'Who's the dragon?'

Barbara smiled, waving her guest to the chair normally occupied by clients, and resumed her own seat behind the big walnut desk which faced the window.

This looked down into the alleyway at the front of the building, making the room seem much darker than the other. A pine-green carpet and matching curtains, together with tiers of oak shelving which supported an impressive array of law-books, added to the general sense of solemnity. All in all, it was not a place for frivolity, Irene decided.

'That's Muriel Bates,' Barbara said, answering her question. 'She's been with me for years and is very efficient. In fact I don't know what I'd do without her. She seems a bit forbidding, I know, on first acquaintance, but she's really a dear. Now, tell me what you're doing here.'

'I had to come down to see one of my authors, Madeleine Deane. You may have read some of her books. Writes those rather up-market crime-stories. She loathes London and won't set foot in it, so, if the mountain won't come to Muhammad, etc ... I like to keep in touch with all my flock, if I can, at least once a year on a personal basis. The telephone's all right, but now and then you need to meet people face-to-face. We had lunch at the Grand, in Broad Street, but she had to rush off immediately after. I had an hour or so to kill before catching my train, and I suddenly remembered Pen telling me that your chambers weren't far from the hotel. So here I am. I do hope you don't mind.'

'Not a bit.' Barbara sounded genuinely pleased to see her. 'As a matter of fact, it's a slack afternoon. I've a client at four o'clock; but, apart from that, nothing. Now, tomorrow's absolutely hectic. Ah! Tea. Thank you, Muriel.'

Miss Bates, who had entered so silently that Irene had not heard her, placed the tray she was carrying carefully on top of the walnut desk and withdrew just as quietly, but managing to leave an aura of grave disapproval behind.

Barbara poured the tea into two delicate china cups and handed one to Irene. 'Do you *have* to go back to town tonight?' she asked. 'Couldn't you stay over? I can offer you a bed, and I'll ring Mother to tell her there'll be an extra mouth for supper.' As Irene hesitated, she smiled conspiratorially. 'If you're worried you'll be imposing, there's no need to be. My invitation isn't exactly disinterested. I'm dying to find out all about Chris's marriage to Sylvia Gibson and Tim's reaction to it. For once in her life, Pen won't discuss it with me, and that hurts. We've always told one another everything. Besides,' she added, sipping her tea, 'Chris will be coming in later on. He's appearing in Bath this week in a touring version of an Agatha Christie play, and I thought the least I could do was to put him up. So a little information about the current state of play, before he arrives, wouldn't come amiss. You'd be doing me a favour.'

Irene was silent for a moment, her thoughts racing. When Barbara had first issued her invitation, she had meant to decline it. For one thing, she doubted very much if she knew any more about the Haldanes' affairs than Barbara herself: Penelope had been unusually reticent about the whole messy business, she and Clifford closing ranks against outsiders' gossip. And, for another, she was inundated with work, having at least three unread manuscripts on her desk and a meeting tomorrow afternoon with her least favourite editor, from her least favourite publisher. But at the mention of Chris's name, with the realization that he would be there, under the same roof, her resolution faltered. The mere thought of him still had the power to turn her bones to water, and the prospect of a chance to see him, to talk to him, was one she was unable to resist. She knew it was foolish. She was a married woman, he a married man. Moreover, she had a thirteen-month-old daughter. Jeremy was a kind, attentive, considerate husband who desperately wanted her to love him, and she had done her best. God alone knew how hard she had tried! She had even attempted to persuade herself that she loved him, and sometimes she had almost succeeded. But she had only to hear Chris Haldane's name for the illusion to be shattered into a thousand pieces.

'Well . . . ' She made a show of reluctance, telling herself that she was staying for Barbara's sake and not for her own. 'I mean, I've no nightdress or anything with me. And I'd have to catch an early train in the morning.'

'No problem.' Barbara was obviously pleased. 'I can lend you some pyjamas and a spare toothbrush, and the girls and I are always up and dressed by seven. You can have your breakfast with us. Mother will attend to Chris. That's settled then, as long as you don't mind waiting around for an hour until after I've seen Mrs Gosling.'

Irene shook her head. 'No, that's fine. Can I use the phone in the outer office to ring Jeremy and Nanny Gray? Oh, and I'd better warn Phyllis that I shall be in late in the morning.' She wondered if there was any insanity in her family. She was putting herself to all this inconvenience, and for what? A possible brief glimpse of Chris before they all went to bed. And tomorrow she would be on her way back to London before he was up. She was almost twenty-eight years of age, and here she was behaving like a love-sick schoolgirl. She felt guilty and ashamed, but at the same time knew that nothing was going to shake her resolution to stop in Bristol overnight.

Chris shouted his good-nights, nodded to the stage-doorkeeper and went in search of his car, a battered old Renault, which he had parked in one of the streets behind the theatre. It was a lovely night, warm without being sultry, stars glittering overhead, the perfect end to a fine spring day. The performance had gone well this evening, with none of the upsets and fluffed lines which the cast had experienced this time last week, on the opening night in Manchester, or a fortnight ago, in Bournemouth, when the leading lady had fallen over and wrenched her knee. Perhaps it was because this was the final week of the tour, and they were all looking forward to getting home and sleeping in their own beds again at night. (It was, of course, a euphoria which wouldn't last, once the realization of being out of work, and with nothing else lined up, sank in.)

In the circumstances, Chris should have been feeling on top of the world; instead, he was bad-tempered and irritable. What on earth had made him agree to stay with the Seymours for the week? He must have been out of his mind. Three months ago, however, at the beginning of the tour, when Barbara had issued her invitation, he had jumped at the offer. After thirteen weeks of lodgings and theatrical digs, the prospect of a soft bed and decent food for seven whole nights had seemed irresistible, even if it meant travelling home to London on the Sunday between engagements to pick up his car.

But the reality was somewhat different. For a start, he had forgotten that he would have to drive a distance of some twelve or thirteen miles each evening after the end of every performance, and back again the following day. Second, the cast had got on well together, with no sign of the petty feuding and quarrels which marred some tours; probably because there was no big name in the production. Over the weeks, they had become good friends; and now, instead of going out with them for a meal and to a club, or back to one of the members' digs for a chat and a laugh over the day's events, Chris was committed to a lonely journey into Bristol. Cursing silently to himself, he got behind the wheel of the Renault and let in the clutch. He blamed his mother. Barbara Seymour would most likely never have thought of inviting him to stay without some prompting by Penelope.

Twenty minutes later, having, more by luck than by good judgement, finally mastered Bath's labyrinthine traffic system, and in a worse temper than ever, he found himself heading towards Bristol. The lighted houses gave way, temporarily, to open country, and he was able to let his concentration relax a little. Immediately, his uneasy thoughts, never far from the surface of his mind, came crowding in. This time next week, he would once again be out of work, living in Sylvia's flat on Sylvia's money; and he had the cold comfort of knowing that the only reason he wasn't referred to as Sylvia Gibson's husband was because he was even better known as Sir Clifford Haldane's son. He had made a mess of his life, and he had no-one but himself to blame.

He passed the Globe Inn, a lighted galleon in a sea of darkness, just as the home-going crowds were spilling out on to the pavement at closing time. Noisy, convivial, they were heading for the carpark or crossing the road to wait for a bus. Chris braked sharply, mouthing furiously behind the windscreen, as a young couple, arms entwined, eyes only for each other, stepped out almost in front of the Renault. He pushed on, following the signs to Saltford and Keynsham. Why had he married Sylvia? He had never been in love with her, not for a single instant. Was it because she had been Tim's fiancée? Was that why he had wanted her? He hated to think that that might be the reason; but there had always been a rivalry between himself and his younger brother. Their friendship had always been an uncertain one; and whereas there was

84

no doubt about their fondness for Richard, the baby of the family, the relationship which existed between Chris and Tim had not bred in either a similar mutual affection. As a child, Tim had been jealous of his elder brother, clamouring for his attention, but suspicious of Chris's motives when it was given. On Chris's part, he had found Tim a bit of a bore, fun enough to be with for a while, but whose whining and perpetual sense of ill-usage made his company quickly pall. And there had been occasions when Chris had taken a spiteful pleasure in deliberately doing his brother out of something he had particularly wanted.

But they were grown up now, and Sylvia was not some toy or treat which could be handed back or restored, with a careless smile, at a later date. So surely, *surely* that couldn't have been his reason for marrying her! At the back of Chris's mind, a doubt still niggled, but he couldn't admit it, even to himself. His marriage had caused a terrible rift between himself and Tim which showed no signs of healing, caused his parents deep distress and had been the source of a great deal of theatrical gossip. And for what? For a relationship which had been not only one-sided from the start, but also doomed to failure by the sense of guilt which weighed heavily on both himself and Sylvia. Had he felt for her what she so obviously felt for him, they might eventually have been able to work something out; but as it was, even after only five months, he knew that as far as he was concerned the marriage was over. They would struggle on for perhaps another year, maybe two, for appearances' sake, but the end would still be the same whenever it happened.

Chris realized with a start that he was already in the Bristol suburbs, and concentrated once more on his driving, looking for the signposts which would direct him towards Clifton. He felt dog-tired, and the anger at his own stupidity increased. He liked the

Seymours – indeed, in an elder-brother way he was extremely fond of Imogen and Anne – but not enough to justify driving all this way after each performance. As he negotiated the city centre, he decided to make his excuses to Barbara and to look for digs in Bath tomorrow. Feeling slightly better, he drove up Park Street and, fifteen minutes later, having twice taken the wrong turning, arrived outside 4 College Close. As the engine died, the front door opened and Barbara came down the path to greet him.

'Chris, you found us, then. When it got so late, I was afraid you might have lost your way.' Her cool detached tone expressed neither concern nor pleasure, but he received the impression that she was glad to see him. In similar circumstances, his mother would have been extravagantly welcoming, fussing around and wanting to know every detail of the journey. He thought, as he had thought all his life, that they were unlikely friends.

'Sorry,' he said, locking the Renault and pocketing the keys. 'Have I kept you up? The play overran a bit tonight, and I did lose my way, twice, but not until I was nearly here.'

'Clifton can be a bit confusing,' Barbara said easily, 'but you'll know the route tomorrow. Come inside. We've saved some supper for you. I hope you like bacon-and-liver hotpot. It's one of Mother's *pièces de résistance*. And we've another guest, just for tonight. Irene Grantham. She was in Bristol today on business, called on me at my chambers, and I persuaded her to come home with me and stop over.' She led the way indoors. 'And the girls have waited up to see you as well.'

Chris followed her, cursing silently. The last thing he wanted was to be met by a deputation of women to whom he had to be polite; to answer the inevitable barrage of questions as to how the performance had gone, who was in the company, and what was he going to do when the tour finished at the end of the week. It would have been bad enough just coping with Barbara and her mother; but it was piling Pelion upon Ossa to have to be courteous to Irene Grantham as well. He hardly knew the woman except as a social acquaintance, and on the infrequent occasions when they had met they had exchanged very few words. And then there were the girls. He quite liked them; Imogen, at least, was a quiet child with not much to say for herself, but Anne unnerved him. She had a way of looking directly at him with those clear grey eyes of hers which he found oddly intimidating, as though she were trying to peer into his very soul. And he wasn't sure that he wanted anyone to know that much about him. He guessed that she had an uncomfortable habit of always saying what she thought, like young Richard. He was another one who let you have it straight from the shoulder. They were well matched, that pair. They should get together when they were older. And, finally, he hated liver; any kind of offal made him feel sick.

Barbara ushered him into the drawing-room: a big pleasant room on the ground floor, furnished with old-fashioned, heavy mahogany furniture, and lit with the subdued glow of various table-lamps, rather than the glare of one central overhead light. A small fire burned on the hearth against the sudden chill of the spring evening, and the velvet curtains, which were drawn across the windows, were of a rich deep chocolate brown. A huge white vase filled with red and yellow tulips brightened up one corner.

For the first few seconds, the room did indeed seem distressingly full of women; and Chris, his tired senses reeling, had to stop himself turning tail and heading back to the car. But then, suddenly, he was aware of nothing and no-one but Irene Grantham, as she rose from her chair to greet him. His tiredness dropped away, and he stood there, in a daze, conscious that she was speaking but not hearing a word that she said. She was wearing an emerald-green woollen dress which clung to her figure, displaying its every magnificent contour to advantage. Her auburn hair was dusted with gold in the flickering light of the fire, and her eyes were as green as her dress. He wondered why he had never before realized how attractive she was, and then recalled, guiltily, having once thought the very same thing about Sylvia. But this was different. Irene was not merely attractive, she was beautiful; although there was a lot more to it than that. What he felt, standing there, holding her hand in his, staring at her as if he had just been granted a glimpse of the Promised Land, was not simply physical arousal, even though, heaven knew, he would have taken her to bed there and then, if he could. No; it was more as if he had met the one person in the whole world to whom he truly belonged; the one woman without whom his life would be incomplete; his soulmate, to use a hackneyed phrase. He knew that his mother wrote about such things in her novels, but had never believed them until now; yet the only sense of astonishment he felt was that recognition of the fact should have come so late. He should have known years ago, the moment he first set eyes on Irene Grantham, or Woodhouse as she had been in those days. But Fate had played a dirty trick on him, blinding him to the truth until after they were both married to other people.

He became aware of the silence all around him, and realized that it was his turn to speak. What on earth had Irene been saying to him? He found he had no idea.

'Irene, it's lovely to see you. You must forgive me if I'm a bit stupid. I'm dog-tired, and driving over to Clifton on top of a performance has fuddled my senses. Just let me get my bearings. Mrs Bryce!' He turned and shook hands with Felicity. 'Hello, girls.' He acknowledged Anne and Imogen's presence with a wave of his hand.

Barbara handed him the whisky she had poured him. 'Your supper won't be a moment. I only have to get it out of the oven, and you can have it in here on a tray. Sit down and talk to Mother and Irene while I see to it. Girls! Bed. It's gone eleven, and you know you were only allowed to stay up on condition that you went to bed as soon as Chris arrived.'

Imogen looked as though she would like to protest that she was, after all, sixteen, but she said nothing except to wish everyone a quiet good-night. Anne did the same and followed her sister upstairs. She had hardly washed and undressed, however, when Imogen came through from her own room, wanting to talk. Anne, whose one desire was to be left alone with her thoughts of Chris, sighed and moved her legs so that her sister could sit on the edge of the bed. At least Imogen was a pleasanter person to be with, these days. Since Chris's marriage to Sylvia, she had been much happier, even though it was obvious to Anne that Tim was still in love with his ex-fiancée.

'What is it?' she asked. 'I'm tired.'

Imogen swung her legs on to the bed and wriggled her feet under the eiderdown. 'Do you think Mum will kick up a fuss in two years' time if I don't go on to university after I leave school? The fact is, I don't think I'm university material, but you know what Mum's like. She made up her mind when we were small that we were both going to have brilliant academic careers.'

'Well, I'm not,' Anne said decidedly. 'I know what I want to do. Stage design. I'll be good at it, too, like those three women who call themselves Motley.

I'll be even better known, and directors will be falling over themselves to engage me.' She spoke with the confidence of a twelve year old, no doubts as yet clouding her horizon. She had it all planned out in her mind. Chris, by then, would be as big a star as his father, and would absolutely insist on her designing the costumes and sets for all his plays. And gradually he would come to realize that he loved her, and they would get married after Sylvia had died of old age. It was a splendid scenario, and one which she often played over to herself after she was tucked up in bed.

'You always have everything mapped out,' Imogen said admiringly. 'My trouble is that I've never known what I wanted to do, except marry Tim. Mum's certain to insist that I try for a place at university.'

'She can't if your A-level grades aren't good enough. And they probably won't be,' added the practical Anne. 'The most she can be is Disappointed, with a capital D, and anyone can cope with that. She doesn't sound off, after all. She just goes quiet.'

Imogen laughed. 'With a capital Q. Yes, I know, but it makes me feel awful. I'd rather she raved and shouted in a way.'

'Look!' Anne snuggled down in bed, pulling the sheet and blankets up to her chin. 'You've another fifteen months before you need worry about it, and then you've got me and Gran to back you up. We can deal with Mum, even if you can't. Why don't you take a decent secretarial course with a couple of languages? You've always been good at French and Latin, which is more than you can say for me. I got thrown out of the Latin class because I'm such a duffer at it, and now I have to do extra French with horrible old Mademoiselle Carrier. You could learn Italian or Spanish, I dare say, and find them quite easy.'

It struck neither of them, either then or before or after, that their relationship was topsy-turvy, with

Anne behaving like the older sister and Imogen coming to her for direction and advice. It was the way things had always been for most of their lives, and they both took it for granted.

Imogen slid off the bed and kissed her sister goodnight. 'Thanks,' she said, before disappearing into her own room again.

Anne closed her eyes, and immediately the present slid away, giving place to those rosy visions of the future in which, in their different spheres, she and Chris took the London theatre world by storm. Fantasy and dreams began to merge, and Chris had just insisted on bringing her on stage to be greeted by a rapturous first-night audience – 'Marvellous, marvellous sets and costumes, you'll all agree . . . My wife . . . So proud . . . ' – when she was suddenly wide awake. Unsure what had disturbed her, Anne rolled over and switched on her bedside lamp. It was two o'clock, and the house was silent. Everyone must have long since gone to bed. She sat up, straining her ears, but could hear nothing. Then, just as she was lying down again, she heard the gentle opening and shutting of a bedroom door. Reassured, she settled once more on her right side and closed her eyes. Nothing to worry about; just someone returning from a nocturnal trip to the bathroom.

CHAPTER SEVEN

'SO I'M VERY DISAPPOINTED, as you can imagine.' Barbara's voice, at the other end of the line, sounded weary and depressed, but also a little indignant, as though Nature had deliberately dealt her a badly flawed hand by presenting her with a daughter who was not academically bright. It alienated Penelope's sympathies; and, besides, she had worries of her own. Barbara went on: 'You know how I'd set my heart on both the girls following me into the law.'

'It serves you right. It's wrong to make plans for one's children.' The words were more sententious than Penelope had intended. 'All right, we're all guilty of doing it, I agree, but we ought to know better, that's what I'm saying. So what does Imogen intend to do, now that she's left school?'

'Secretarial college, extending her knowledge of French and learning Spanish. Apparently it was Anne's idea. It would be.' Barbara's tone was slightly bitter. 'Imogen has always listened more to her sister than to me. Mind you, Imogen's A-level grades weren't good, so there was no question of university unless she sat them again, and she's flatly refused to do that.'

'Probably because she knows her own limitations,' Penelope said coolly. 'And Anne's proposal seems to be eminently sensible, if you ask me. She's always had her head screwed on the right way. Whatever she decides to do in four years' time, I should back her to the hilt if I were you.'

'You sound like Mother.' Barbara's voice was momentarily acerbic. Then she laughed. 'Of course, I know you're right. It's just that ... well, I've had my dreams.'

'Haven't we all?' Penelope pushed the hair back from her forehead. The August day had been warm, and the evening seemed to be still hotter. 'Look, Babs, I must cut you off. I'm in the middle of a dinner-party.'

Barbara was horrified. 'Why on earth didn't you say? I could have phoned tomorrow. And I've been rabbiting on for hours.'

'Only fifteen minutes,' Penelope answered with a wry grin. 'And I could tell you were upset and needed to talk. What are old friends for? Come up to Town one day soon and we'll unburden our souls to one another.'

When Penelope returned to the dining-room, she found her guests halfway through the first course of avocado and watercress salad, provided by the invaluable Mrs Clennan. They had evidently finished discussing last month's bomb outrages at Westminster Hall and the Tower and the impending resignation of President Nixon, and were now safely launched on their own favourite topics: the world of theatre and publishing. Clifford was giving his eldest son the benefit of his advice.

'The thing to do with any stage in any theatre is to find the spot before the rest of the cast discover it.' He added for the non-theatrical in their midst: 'There's always a spot on every stage from which an actor can be heard all over the auditorium without having to raise his voice. Once you know where it is, you're quids in.'

Chris shrugged. 'All very well,' he said, 'if you can work your moves to include it. But directors have their own ideas. We're not all stars who can override them.'

His tone was regrettably snide, Penelope thought,

as she once more took her seat at the end of the table opposite her husband. 'Sorry about that interruption,' she murmured. 'It was Barbara needing a sympathetic ear.'

'How is she?' Irene Grantham asked, more from politeness than from any genuine interest. Her thoughts were completely dominated by the fact that Chris was sitting immediately across from her. It needed all the restraint at her command not to reach out with her foot and touch his under the table. Surely everyone in the room must know that they were lovers; had been lovers for over a year now. She couldn't believe that their guilty secret wasn't writ large on both their faces. She was trying not to look at Sylvia, just as Chris was avoiding the eyes of both Jeremy and Tim.

'Oh, she's fine. Fine,' Penelope replied a trifle vaguely, wondering what on earth had possessed her to invite such an uncomfortable collection of dinner-party guests. It had seemed a good idea, last week, to get Tim and Chris together for a meal.

'Now that Tim's graduated, he and Chris are bound to see more of one another,' she had said to Clifford. 'We have to do something to heal the breach between them. Perhaps if Tim gets used to seeing Chris and Sylvia together, sees that they're happy, then perhaps he'll be more reconciled to the fact of their marriage.'

But the trouble was, Chris and Sylvia didn't appear to be that happy. It had struck Penelope forcibly this evening, when they had first arrived, that there was tension between them. In spite of her careful make-up, there were dark smudges beneath Sylvia's eyes which suggested she had been crying; and it became increasingly obvious, as the night wore on, that all was not well between them. Chris was placatory and over-anxious to please, Sylvia withdrawn and unresponsive. Penelope wondered how long this state of affairs had existed, and blamed herself for not having sensed that the marriage was in trouble sooner. But she had been immersed in a new book for the past six months and, as usual, oblivious to what was happening around her. To make matters worse, Tim had spotted at once that there were difficulties, and was regarding his elder brother with smouldering resentment. He had always blamed Chris and not Sylvia for her betrayal, blindly persisting in his belief that she was the innocent victim of duplicity and cunning.

Penelope had been relying on Irene and Jeremy Grantham to lighten the atmosphere, but they, too, seemed listless and out of sorts with one another. Irene had snapped at her husband on two or three occasions, to everyone's embarrassment except her own, and was now ignoring him completely, even though, for the past minute, he had been trying to attract her attention. Instead, she was listening with exaggerated interest to something Chris was saying.

The onus of keeping the conversation flowing was therefore falling on Clifford and the young actress he had invited to partner Tim and make up the numbers. A nice enough little thing, Penelope thought, but not all that bright: Amanda something; she hadn't quite caught her other name. But the girl was plainly flattered at having been singled out for an invitation to the home of Sir Clifford Haldane, and burst into her high-pitched whinnying laugh at his slightest pleasantry. It was beginning to get on everyone's nerves, even Clifford's. Serve him right, Penelope decided.

Somehow or other they got through two more courses, and then Penelope suggested taking coffee and liqueurs out on to the patio where it was cooler. Chairs had been set up earlier among the tubs of ornamental shrubs and trees, and an outside light illuminated the flagstones like a stage, shining softly through the flickering leaves of the peach tree, turning everything it touched to gold.

Mrs Clennan had already placed the tray of coffee things on the round, white-painted metal table, and through the open kitchen window she could be heard clattering the plates and cutlery as she washed up.

Sylvia, sitting down in the chair next to Penelope, said enviously: 'That woman is marvellous. She must be one in a million. You wouldn't catch my daily agreeing to work at night.'

Chris, who had drunk a little too much at dinner, and who was growing tired of his friendly overtures being rejected by his wife, said sharply: 'Don't you mean "our" daily? Now that I'm working again, I don't think my contributions to the household budget should be overlooked.'

Even in the subdued light, it was easy to see Sylvia's hurt expression. 'I'm sorry, darling,' she answered quietly. 'I didn't mean it the way it sounded. I wasn't thinking.'

Chris, who was already feeling ashamed of his outburst, was ready to apologize, but found himself under attack from his brother. Tim, who had refused to take a seat and was drinking his coffee standing up, leaning against the wall of the house, sneered: 'The great actor! A minor role in a Pinter revival! And you probably only got that because of your name. Sylvia must earn five or six times what you do in a year. She's been supporting you ever since you got married. She was wonderful in that Dickens serial she did recently for the BBC, and now she has this part in the new Bond film lined up. You've been living off her for the past two years. You've no right to criticize her.'

The apology died on Chris's lips, and he heaved himself up out of his chair.

'I'm damned if I'm going to sit here and listen

tamely while my younger brother takes me to task. Just mind your own bloody business, Tim.'

He slammed down his coffee-cup, to its imminent peril, and went indoors. Unnoticed by the others, who were all looking at Sylvia, Irene followed him. She found him in the little room known as the study on the ground floor. Quietly, she closed the door behind her and went across to him.

'Darling, don't let Tim upset you.' She wound her arms about his neck. 'It's natural he should still be bitter.'

Chris turned to her at once, enfolding her in his embrace, feeling as he always did when near her: comforted and safe. He could smell her familiar perfume, feel the softness of that wonderful auburn hair against his cheek.

'This is ridiculous,' he murmured. 'We can't go on meeting in corners for the rest of our lives. We have to do something about it. Make a clean break. I love you. I love you so much.'

'And I love you. But I have a two-year-old daughter to consider. I can't disrupt her life without a great deal of thought. If I leave Jeremy, I might not get custody of Deborah.'

'I think you're worrying about nothing. Children, particularly girls, are usually handed over to their mother, whoever's at fault. And Jeremy would surely agree to it.'

Irene's arms tightened their hold. 'I can't bring myself to tell him, that's the·trouble. He still loves me.'

Chris sighed. 'I know,' he said. 'I'm just as much a coward where Sylvia's concerned. What the hell are we going to do?'

'Wait a bit longer,' she counselled him, stroking his hair. 'Wait and pray for a miracle to happen.'

The study door was opened with a wrench of the

knob which almost tore it off its spindle. Tim stood in the doorway, flushed with wine and anger.

'You thought no-one saw you slope off after my lecherous brother, didn't you?' he asked Irene. 'Well, I saw you. I had a feeling something was going on between you two, the way you've been eyeing each other up all evening. The rest must be blind to have missed it. You've both been reeking of the farmyard at copulation time. Talk about on heat!' He leered offensively, before turning on his brother. 'You randy bastard! You took Sylvia away from me, and now you don't want her any more. You're quite prepared to toss her on one side while you fuck a married woman. You want to watch out, Irene. You'll be for the scrapheap, too, once he finds another, younger model. Don't forget you're five years older than he is. He's working his way slowly down the age-scale. What about our nubile little Amanda? Couldn't you fancy her, Chris? Or is she still a bit too young?'

It was at that point that Chris hit him, a strong upper-cut to the jaw, sending Tim sprawling. Chris had meant to keep his temper, but in the face of his brother's taunts it proved too Herculean a task. He regretted the blow instantly. He had recently begun to feel a deep sense of guilt about Tim, now that he himself knew what it was to be in love. He imagined someone taking Irene away from him and knew at last what Tim must have suffered; because there was no doubt that Tim still loved Sylvia. His three years at Oxford hadn't changed him or diminished his affection for her.

Chris reached down a hand to help his brother up, but Tim was already scrambling to his feet, a murderous gleam in his eyes. He launched himself at Chris, knocking him backwards across the desk which stood in the middle of the room. Irene screamed, 'Stop it, Tim! Stop it!' and pinioned his arms just long enough for a shaken Chris to heave himself away from the desk and recover his balance. The next moment, Tim was free of her restraining hands and had his brother by the throat. Chris kneed Tim in the groin. Queensberry rules had gone out of the window.

An authoritative voice exclaimed: 'That'll do, you two. Just stow it!' And Richard forced himself between his brothers.

He was fourteen now, and had been out for the evening to a friend's house. He was wearing flared blue jeans and a tie-dyed T-shirt in shades of orange and red. A blue nylon bomber jacket, with welts and cuffs striped in a deeper blue, hung over one arm, but slipped to the carpet as he used all his strength to separate Tim and Chris. And to everyone's surprise, except his own, he managed it.

'My God, you're a wiry little devil,' Chris panted, glaring at him. 'How did you become so strong?'

'I grew up,' Richard answered coolly. 'In case it's escaped your notice, my voice has broken.'

The sarcasm was lost on Chris, who continued to stare at his youngest brother as though he had just arrived from Mars. It was true; Richard had grown up, almost without anyone noticing. He was still short, especially amongst his own generation or compared with the other males of his family; about five foot three or four by Chris's reckoning, but still with time to grow taller. The real change, however, was in his general physique; the way he had filled out. The thin coltish child had gone, to be replaced by a tough young man, full of latent strength and very much in command of himself. And, it would appear, of other people. Looking now into those wrathful brown eyes, Chris felt every inch the delinquent schoolboy. He gave a reluctant grin.

'Yes, you have grown up, haven't you? I admit I hadn't registered the fact.' He glanced at Tim's bloody nose and could feel his own left eye swelling. He must have knocked it against the desk when he fell. 'God! We must look an unedifying sight. Ma will kill us for ruining her dinner-party.'

'I don't know that I'll go that far,' Penelope said from the doorway. 'But I'm damned annoyed.' She surveyed her two elder sons grimly, her eyes taking note of Irene's presence, and drew her own conclusions. 'I think', she added quietly, 'you'd better come outside again and finish your coffee. You both look as though you need it. And I shouldn't bother cooking up any explanations. Nobody will believe them. Just trust to people's good manners, and the British dislike of scenes, to ask no awkward questions. At least, not in public.' She waited until Chris, Tim and Irene had left the room, then kissed Richard's cheek. 'Thanks, darling,' she said.

Her youngest son stooped to pick up his jacket. 'No sweat,' he answered. 'But you can't really be surprised that I prefer animals to humans, can you?' He hesitated, then his eyes twinkled. 'Well, sometimes anyway. And you're always an exception.' He returned the kiss. He went on shyly and a little awkwardly: 'I love you more than anyone. More than Sir Cloudesley Shovel or Machiavelli, or even my tropical fish.'

Penelope fought to keep a straight face and just succeeded, her spirits insensibly lifting. 'Thank you, sweetheart,' she said. 'I'm very flattered.'

'So there you are.' Penelope swivelled round on the dressing-table stool to look at her husband, who was already in bed. 'Rich loves me more than his tropical fish, and I can't tell you how *proud* and . . . oh, how full of *joy* that simple declaration made me.' She swivelled back again to stare at her face, caked with cleansing cream, in the mirror. 'It made the whole sordid unpleasant evening worthwhile.'

'As bad as that, eh?' Clifford laid aside the book he had brought up to bed with him. 'You really think there's something going on between Chris and Irene?'

Penelope started to wipe off the cream with handfuls of cotton wool, which she disposed of in the wastepaper-basket by her feet. 'I know there is,' she answered simply.

'Woman's intuition?'

'Mother's intuition. And don't scoff at it. It's something that works.'

'I wouldn't dream of scoffing,' her husband said blandly. He caught her eye in the mirror and smiled, but a moment later was serious again. 'I wonder who Chris gets it from.' He had no need to specify 'it'. 'Certainly not from us.'

'No.' Penelope dropped the last piece of cotton wool in the basket and began, slowly, to brush her hair. 'Although I've often wondered why not. Why you haven't been unfaithful to me,' she added, by way of explanation. She saw his startled face and laughed. 'Well, I mean, you're so handsome. And you're famous, which, as everyone knows, is a powerful aphrodisiac. And I'm plain and dull. I always have been. I could never understand what you saw in me.'

There was silence, and Penelope had the distinct impression that her husband was trying not to laugh. But when he finally spoke his tone was more exasperated than amused.

'For God's sake, get into bed, woman. For someone who's convinced she's plain, you spend one hell of a time on your appearance. And there's absolutely no need if it's for my sake. You've never been less than beautiful to me.'

Penelope climbed in beside him and they put their arms around one another. 'But I still don't see', she objected, after a moment, 'what it is about me you like.'

'Well, if you'd just stop talking, I could show you. No, no,' he added, catching her look of mild reproach, 'it isn't only sex, I promise you, although you're everything a man could desire in that department.' He wanted to make love, but he could tell that the evening's events had upset her more than she liked to admit, and that she was in need of comfort and reassurance. 'There's never been anyone else for me, not since I saw you standing outside the stage door, all those years ago, with your autograph-book in your hot little hand, and that look of desperate disappointment on your face when you realized I wasn't Paul Rogers. There was just something about you that told me you were the right one for me. It's no good asking me to define it. I'm just an actor. I repeat other people's words. I don't make them up. Look, you're a writer, and I, as I have just said, am an actor, both candidates for all the neuroses and insecurities going. But are we neurotic? Are we, hell! Instead, we're a boringly well-balanced couple, the despair of the gossipmongers. And that's because of our rock-steady marriage. And why is it rock-steady? Because we're as much in love today as we were twenty-seven years ago, when we met. There's that certain something between us – chemistry, or whatever. Something that Chris and Irene obviously haven't found with their current partners. Perhaps they've found it in each other.'

Penelope was unhappy. 'But that would mean divorce.'

'Divorce is a fact of life, Pen.' He squeezed her gently. 'Like infidelity. And who should understand that better than the author of such sagas as *Moon in Capricorn*, *Flung Roses* and whatever the new book's called?'

She twisted her head to look him in the eye. 'Does the sort of novel I write nowadays shock you?'

Clifford burst out laughing. 'Good God, no! You

can't shock actors. But, then, you know that. And stop worrying about the boys. They've had a stable loving background all their lives. They're fundamentally sound, all three of them. I've no fears at all for their future. They'll make mistakes – children do – but they won't be our mistakes. They're their own men, particularly young Richard.'

Penelope nodded. 'Yes. He's different from the other two. He knows exactly what he wants from life, and he'll get it. Like Anne Seymour.'

'Ah, yes.' Clifford disposed himself more comfortably, settling his wife against his shoulder, within the circle of his arm. 'What did Barbara have to say that was so urgent?' He listened while Penelope told him, then said: 'Good for little Anne. She'll make sure Imogen does what she wants. It needs someone to stick up to Babs. I still don't understand why you and she are such friends.'

'Yes, you do. You know very well she's not as stuffy as she seems. And we like the same things.' Penelope smiled reminiscently. 'We used to read P. G. Wodehouse novels under the desk during Latin. We both made up our minds we were going to be picked for the school's first cricket eleven, and we were. We both adore the theatre and the ballet and detest opera. We love Jane Austen and Mrs Gaskell. We'd do anything for one another and one another's children. We might have a disagreement now and then, but we never quarrel.' She sat forward suddenly, glancing back at Clifford, her eyes glowing. 'Do you know what would really make me happy? If Anne and Richard were to get married some day. I've just realized that they're absolutely made for one another. I don't know why I haven't seen it before.'

Her husband pulled her gently back against his shoulder. 'Don't get carried away with the idea, my love. You know what we've just been saying. Children have a knack of doing the unexpected. Besides, at the moment, unless I'm very much mistaken, Anne fancies herself in love with Chris.'

'Impossible! She's still a child.'

'A schoolgirl crush, nothing more. Did you never have one?'

Penelope considered the matter. 'I remember once writing a fan letter to Basil Rathbone. I don't think I ever got a reply.' She slid a hand inside Clifford's pyjama jacket and began stroking his chest. She could feel the soft blond hair beneath her fingers.

He responded at once, his arousal immediate and complete. What he had told her was nothing but the truth: she satisfied him in every way; he never had had, never would have, need of another woman. An actor's life was full of opportunities, temptations even, but he felt not the slightest desire to succumb. He remembered her as he had first seen her, on that chill autumn evening in 1947, waiting in the light of the open stage door, a plainish girl in a well-worn blue coat – clothes were still rationed in those days – not nearly as good-looking as Barbara, who stood beside her. But there had been something about her, a twinkle in the blue eyes, an upward tilt to the generous mouth, that had drawn him like a magnet. They had been married the following February and set up their first home in a grotty little furnished flat in Redland. Clifford recalled that his parents-in-law, now both dead, had not at all cared for the idea of their only child marrying an actor.

'Such a precarious profession,' Mr Fallon had said.

And when Chris had been born two years later he and his wife had been sunk even deeper in gloom, because Penelope had had to give up her job in George's bookshop. But things had worked out far better than anyone, least of all Clifford himself, could possibly have imagined. He had been lucky, and in any actor's life luck was nearly as important as talent; in some cases, more so.

And later, when they had finished making love, lying quietly side-by-side, listening to Penelope's peaceful breathing, Clifford knew that he had been profoundly lucky in other ways, as well as in his chosen career. He was, he told himself, the original Man Who Had Everything, so he could hardly complain if, now and then, his sons gave him cause for anxiety.

Penelope's thoughts were running on much the same lines. She knew herself to be a most fortunate woman. But she couldn't help wondering uneasily what was going on between Irene and Jeremy Grantham, or Chris and Sylvia. If Jeremy and her daughter-in-law had suspected nothing before, they could hardly remain in ignorance after tonight. Some explanation had to be offered for Chris and Tim's fight, and for the fact that Irene had been there with them. If Penelope had been able to draw her own conclusions, then so could the others.

With a sigh, she rolled on her side and snuggled into Clifford's back. She was too tired to think about the problem any more now. It would have to keep until morning.

CHAPTER EIGHT

'WHAT WAS THE FIGHT between Tim and Chris about? I'd like an answer, Irene.'

She had seen the question coming all the way home in the car, and had been dreading it. As soon as they were inside the front door, she said: 'I'm very tired. I'm going up to bed. I have a meeting with your crime editor, Jessie Lang, first thing tomorrow morning.'

But Jeremy had seized her arm, roughly for him, and guided her into the dining-room, flicking on the lights with his free hand. In the pink-shaded glow, his face looked greyish, as though all the blood had been drained from the skin. Irene felt a surge of tenderness for him – tenderness, but not love – and she thought desperately: I have to tell him the truth. It's not fair on him or me. She wondered what Chris was saying to Sylvia: they had had no opportunity to confer before leaving The Laurels.

Upstairs, she heard Deborah start to cry. Their arrival home had disturbed her. But, a few moments later, there was silence: the efficient Nanny Gray had evidently been close at hand. Irene glanced round the room, and it struck her, as if for the first time, how little her personality was stamped on any of the furniture or fittings. Indeed, the whole house, now she came to think of it, was hardly altered from the time of Jeremy's first marriage. After the wedding, he had given her *carte blanche* to do just as she liked; to throw out or change anything that did not please her. But she had done nothing. It was almost as if she had known, deep down, that she was only a bird of passage; that before very long she would leave him.

'Well?' Jeremy asked. 'I'm waiting.'

Irene went over to the sideboard and poured herself a gin with very little tonic. Dutch courage, a voice jeered inside her head; but, then, maybe the Dutch knew a thing or two when it came to sticky situations. She kicked off her high-heeled evening sandals and sat down at the table, the pale oval of her face and the shimmer of her silver-beaded dress reflected in its polished surface. She gulped at her drink before raising her head to look at Jeremy.

'They were fighting because Tim accused Chris of being unfaithful to Sylvia.' She added, after a protracted pause, during which she swallowed half the glass of gin: 'With me.'

'I see.' Jeremy drew a rasping breath. 'And is there any substance in the allegation?'

Irene gave a small hysterical giggle. 'You sound just like the prosecuting counsel in a courtroom. If you mean, is it true, then, yes, it is.' She ventured another glance at his face and said angrily: 'Don't look at me like that! God knows, I didn't want it to happen!'

But she knew it was a lie. She had wanted Chris Haldane since before she was married; and if she could hear the insincerity in her voice, then so could her husband.

'In that case, why did you let it?' His tone was abrasive, and he sat down opposite her rather suddenly as if his legs had unexpectedly given way. He made no attempt to fetch himself a drink. He found solace in music and books, not in alcohol.

'How do I know?' Irene was aware that she sounded peevish. She wished he would make it easier for her by ranting and shouting and calling her names, instead of this painful earnestness and desire to understand. 'No-one wills these things to happen. They just do. There's no rhyme or reason to them.'

'No. Quite.' Again, there was silence. 'So what do you intend doing about it?' he asked after a few moments. 'And what about Deborah? Don't you think you should consider her?'

'Of course I'm considering her!' Irene's voice cracked, and she got up to fix herself another gin and tonic. She was drinking too much. The two gins, in addition to what she had drunk during the evening, were beginning to make her head swim. She just wished that they would blot out her sense of pain and guilt. 'Of course I want her to have a good, settled, loving home. But I can't help my feelings, and surely it won't be good for her to grow up in the company of two people who don't love each other.'

'I love you,' Jeremy said simply.

Dear God, there was no answer to that! Then she realized that he wasn't going to fight her, oppose her, tell her that she had forfeited all right to their daughter: he only wanted what was best for her. He loved her, but he would give her her freedom. She acquitted him of deliberately choosing the one course of action calculated to make her stay: Jeremy wasn't devious enough for that. But, unwittingly, he had spiked her guns, taken the wind out of her sails or whatever other metaphor there was for making certain that she would have to give their marriage another go. Her mind was filled with a silent scream of protest; every fibre of her being rebelled at the thought. But what else could she do, if she were to live at peace with herself for the rest of her life?

All at once, her body felt leaden, her mind refused to function. She got up, returning her empty glass to the tray on the sideboard, and went round the table to her husband, putting a hand on his shoulder.

'Come on, let's go to bed now. We'll discuss this again tomorrow.'

108

He asked: 'Do you want me to move into the spare bedroom?'

Irene bit her lip, suppressing the overwhelming desire to yell at him: 'Oh, for God's sake, tell me what a lying bitch I am! Hit me! Swear at me! Anything! Just don't be so bloody humble!' Instead, she answered wearily: 'Of course I don't. Come on. I'll be able to see things more clearly in the morning.'

It was a lie. She could see things clearly now. And she had no idea what she was going to do about them.

'You bastard!' Sylvia rounded on Chris almost before the front door of the flat had closed behind them. 'You fucking bastard! You and Irene Grantham have been having an affair, haven't you? And don't bother to deny it. I'm not still wet behind the ears!'

'There wouldn't be much point in denying it,' Chris answered calmly. 'Tonight's unfortunate little episode spoke for itself. And the whole of Chelsea must be aware of the fact by now. Can't you keep your voice down? Or is this one of those theatrical exercises to see how far you can make it carry?'

'Oh, that's right!' She slammed down her evening bag, bright with metallic sequins, on the hall table. 'Be sarcastic! After all, sarcasm is the cheapest form of wit.'

'And that is a very over-used quotation.' Chris took a deep breath and tried again. 'Let's discuss this like two adults, shall we, instead of two angry squabbling children?' He opened their bedroom door and went inside, drawing the floor-length velvet curtains across the window. As he switched on the various lights, the room sprang into focus.

It was a very feminine room, furnished in shades of beige and a deep crushed-strawberry pink. Roses rioted over the bedspread and up the walls, only stopping short at the carpet and curtains. The built-in wardrobe, occupying most of one wall, had mirrored doors, giving the room back its reflection. There was no overhead light; everything was softly illuminated by wall- and table-lamps, suffusing the room in a soft pink glow. Like Irene, a few miles away, Chris suddenly felt his surroundings to be alien. There was nothing here that he had helped to choose or been invited to alter. When they married, he had been expected to take Sylvia lock, stock and barrel.

And honesty forced Chris to admit that, until recently, he had been content to do just that; which perhaps said something about his state of mind at the time of the wedding. He should have known that such indifference could not possibly augur well for the future. But it was only since the realization that he was in love with Irene Grantham that he had felt the need to start afresh; to create his own home in his own way and not inherit everything secondhand from another person. All the same, he had no idea what he was going to do about it. He owed Sylvia some loyalty. He wondered what was happening between Jeremy and Irene.

Sylvia followed him into the bedroom, slamming the door shut behind her.

'Oh, it's all very well for you to strike a reasonable attitude! You're the one at fault! What hypocrisy!' And suddenly, to her own consternation as much as to Chris's, she slumped on to the bed and began silently to cry, tears and mascara coursing down her face together.

Chris stood irresolute, fighting against the sensation of being trapped by another's grief and pain. It wasn't fair that he should be made to feel so guilty. But the phrase immediately reminded him of Tim, and a fresh wave of guilt swept over him. He felt as though he were drowning. He moved round the bed to

110

sit beside Sylvia, putting an arm across her shoulders.

'Look, I'm sorry. I have been having an affair with Irene Grantham.' He noted his dishevelled appearance, reflected in the wardrobe mirrors, and his swollen, unsightly left eye. Bill Brewer, his director, would be furious. He would have to disguise it as best he could with heavy make-up. 'But . . . ' But what? He felt Sylvia's body shake, as she was racked by another spasm of misery. 'But it's over.'

He told himself in later years that he had meant it when he said it. At that moment, he saw no alternative in the face of such concentrated misery. He had been responsible for breaking up Sylvia and Tim, and he owed both of them the expectation that he would at least try to make a go of the marriage. His and Sylvia's second wedding anniversary was not until December: he owed it to his own peace of mind to stick it out as long as possible.

'I'm sorry,' he whispered, kissing Sylvia's cheek. 'If you'll forgive me, we'll start again. If you want me, that is?'

She sniffed and gave a wintry smile, attempting to wipe away her tears with her fingers. If she had heard a note of hope in that last question of his, she chose to ignore it.

'Of course I want you. I'm in love with you. I always have been. I'm sorry I made such a fuss. I might have guessed that, sooner or later, you were bound to have an affair with a younger woman.'

Chris was tempted to point out that Irene was still five years his senior, which rather destroyed her theory, but he refrained. The theory was Sylvia's protection against any acknowledgement that the affair might be serious. He owed her that, but his heart felt as though it were being torn out of his body. He loved Irene. For the moment, however, there was nothing he could do about it.

111

*   *   *

She thought: He's not a child any more. He has grown up. And so have I.

The discovery took Anne by surprise. Until this moment, it had not occurred to her that adulthood was so close at hand. She was not yet fifteen, and neither was Richard, but they would both have birthdays during the course of the approaching summer and autumn. When she had accepted Penelope's invitation to come to Devon for part of the Easter holidays, she had done so more in a spirit of resignation, and to please her mother, than because it was what she had wanted. Now, on this Good Friday morning, climbing with Richard to the top of the ridge overlooking the cottage, she was glad that she had agreed to come.

It was a small party, just Penelope, Richard, Chris and herself. Clifford was busy, filming in France; Tim was with some obscure repertory company, in some equally obscure corner of the country, learning his chosen trade as an actor; Sylvia was appearing in a current National Theatre production. Imogen, busy at secretarial college, had refused to give up even part of her holiday to go to Devon.

'Tim won't be there, so what's the point?' she had asked succinctly.

'Oh, you and Tim!' Anne had exclaimed disgustedly; but honesty forced her to admit that her own decision had been more than a little influenced by the knowledge that Chris would be present, the run of the Pinter play having finished at Christmas and no new work being as yet on offer.

'Try to cheer Chris up, you two,' Penelope had instructed Anne and Richard. 'He's always depressed when he's not working.'

She deliberately closed her mind to the fact that there might be another cause for her eldest son's unhappiness. No-one had been more astonished or delighted than Penelope when, following the unfortunate dinner-party, last August, Chris and Irene Grantham seemed to have ended their affair. She had said nothing to either of them, keeping her relationship with Irene on a strictly business footing; but she regretted, all the same, that her friendship with her agent should have become a casualty of such an unpleasant situation.

Richard, always good-natured and very fond of his eldest brother, was willing to comply with his mother's wishes. Anne was only too pleased to do so. But Chris had other ideas. He spent his days going for long lonely walks across the moors, refusing all offers of company. And in the evenings, as soon as supper was finished, he shut himself in his bedroom with his portable radio, spurning television or his brother's suggestion of a card game.

'Leave him alone, then,' Penelope had advised them. 'Let him be miserable by himself. It's his loss, not ours.'

But she herself was busy, having brought the proofs of her latest novel with her. The job was one she hated, time-consuming and requiring concentration. Every morning, she shut herself away in the dining-room, typescript and proof sheets spread out across the table, and dared anyone to disturb her until lunchtime. Then she would emerge, a little irritably, to forage in the refrigerator for cold meat and salad. Her youngest son complained that they would all soon look like rabbits, to which his mother responded tartly that surely that would suit him, as he preferred animals to human beings anyway. Chris, on the other hand, paid no attention to what he ate, even if he put in an appearance.

So Richard and Anne found themselves thrown almost exclusively into one another's company, tramping across the moors or taking bus trips into Tavistock or Plymouth. And Anne made her momentous discovery that Richard had changed; that he was no longer an exuberant, slightly rowdy child, full of wild enthusiasms which he expected other people to share, but a quiet and dignified young man, still as dedicated to the idea of becoming a vet as he always had been, but interested, too, in the desires and ambitions of others. He listened while she told him of her wish to study stage design, laughed at himself for having once thought that she, too, wanted to be a vet and reminded her, jokingly, that, at the ripe old age of twelve, he had proposed marriage. They both laughed at that, looking back to those children they had been only a year or two ago as if they were inhabitants of another planet. The friendship between them ripened and deepened, maturing into a quiet contentment in one another's company, the ability to be silent without embarrassment, a shared sense of humour. They found that they liked one another, and that they could be together without any conscious awareness of their difference in sex. In later years, Anne looked back on that Easter as being an interim period in their relationship; a time of complete happiness and understanding.

As they reached the top of the ridge and began walking across the high plateau of moorland, she slipped a hand into one of his with the easy natural camaraderie of youth. They both wore jeans and denim bomber jackets over warm jumpers, causing a friendly farmer, on his way into Tavistock, to remark: 'Can't tell which are maids and which are lads these days. 'Tweren't like it when I were a boy.' They grinned shyly, city-bred children unused to exchanging words with total strangers. After a while, they sat down in the lee of some rocks and Richard produced a bar of thick milk chocolate from his pocket. Carefully, he broke it in half and they munched in companionable silence, looking at the panorama of tufted moorland grass and granite outcrops spread before them.

A curlew rose suddenly from its nest, flapping skywards with its call of 'curlwee, curlwee' echoing sadly in the still morning air. They could see the long curved bill and make out the barred and patterned brownish plumage. A little distance from where they sat was a patch of gorse, golden flowers embattled behind sharp black spikes. Pale lanterns of bilberry glowed against dark green leaves; cushions of emerald moss clung to the rocks behind them. The cloud-smudged heights promised a warm day later on, and Anne stretched her arms and legs in great contentment.

'I *am* glad I agreed to come,' she said. 'I nearly didn't. Jackie Kent asked me to go to Switzerland with her and her parents.'

'I'm glad you came as well.' Richard turned and smiled at her. 'It's odd, you know, and I wouldn't admit it to the guys at school, but you're my best friend.'

'And you're mine.' She wiped her chocolate-stained fingers in the grass and felt once again for his hand. 'I suppose it's because we've known one another since we were children.'

Satisfied with this explanation, by mutual consent, they scrambled to their feet and continued walking, occasionally breaking into snatches of the current number-one pop tune, 'Bye Bye Baby,' a smash hit for the Bay City Rollers. Sir Cloudesley Shovel circled them, barking loudly, giving an excellent imitation of a dog who is forced to keep an eye on his simple-minded owners, while at the same time carrying on his own important business. Now and then, he deigned to chase the ball which Richard threw for him, but made it clear that it was only done as a favour. There were too many exciting scents demanding his urgent attention.

'That dog's getting too big for his boots,' Richard complained affectionately, as Cloud, ignoring the offer of tug-of-war with a stick, began exploring a rabbit burrow.

Anne glanced at her watch and saw that it was nearly twelve-thirty. 'Lunchtime,' she said. 'We ought to be getting back. I'm hungry.'

'Well, don't expect anything but salad again,' Richard warned her. 'I don't know why Mum has to work on holiday. I suppose', he added, quoting Penelope, 'because the publishers want the proofs back the day before yesterday.'

They retraced their steps across the moor and descended the ridge, holding hands and laughing breathlessly. Cloud, tearing ahead of them, waited patiently, and a little contemptuously, at the bottom until they finally slithered to a halt. Then he led the way indoors.

The telephone was ringing as they entered. Penelope erupted from the dining-room and snatched up the receiver, at the same time placing a hand over the mouthpiece.

'Rich darling, be an angel and make something on toast for yourself and Anne. Another hour and I'll have got this damned proof finished, then I can pack it up and post it in Tavistock tomorrow. I think there's a tin of baked beans in the cupboard next to the pantry.' She removed her hand. 'Hello. Who is that? I'm sorry, but I haven't heard a word you've said up to now.'

Richard grimaced at Anne as she followed him along the stone-flagged passage and into the kitchen. 'What did I tell you? Never mind, baked beans at least make a change from salad.'

As it happened, there was also a tin of spaghetti, and faced with such an embarrassment of riches they sat on the floor, haggling amicably over which to have, while Sir Cloudesley Shovel whined pathetically and nosed his empty plate. From the other side of the half-closed door, Penelope's voice rose sharply, taut with horror.

'Oh my God! Jeremy, this is dreadful!' Richard glanced at Anne, raising his eyebrows, both their faces suddenly serious. He got up and opened the kitchen door to its fullest extent, making no pretence of not listening. 'What?' Penelope was supporting herself against the newel post at the bottom of the staircase; her free hand gripped the edge of the narrow hall table. 'No . . . No, he's not here at the moment. He said he was going into Plymouth this morning and would probably get lunch at a pub . . . Yes . . . Yes, of course. But, Jeremy, do you think that's a good idea? . . . Well, I mean, what about Sylvia? . . . All right, I'll tell him . . . Yes, I promise. But what he does then is entirely up to Chris . . . Give Irene my love when you see her . . . Goodbye, Jeremy . . . Goodbye. Take care.'

She replaced the receiver slowly, lost in thought, and stared at Anne and Richard without really seeing them. Richard hissed at Anne, 'Put the kettle on,' and went forward to slip an arm around his mother. 'Come and sit down,' he urged. 'Is it bad news? Something to do with Irene Grantham?'

Penelope allowed herself to be led into the kitchen, where her son installed her in the rocking-chair in front of the old-fashioned range. The uneven stone floor was dotted with multi-coloured rag rugs, bought from a secondhand-stall in Tavistock market some years before, and lovingly restored to their pristine brightness. Richard pushed one of them under his mother's feet and began gently chafing her cold hands. Anne busied herself with making tea and rummaging in the pantry for sugar and biscuits.

Richard repeated: 'Is it bad news? Tell us.'

Penelope nodded. 'Irene was knocked down by a car yesterday evening. Of course, she wasn't on a pedestrian crossing; she never is. I've been warning her for years about that habit she has of jay-walking.'

'Is she badly hurt?'

'A broken leg and a couple of fractured ribs which caused some internal bleeding. A dislocated shoulder.' Anne handed her a cup of hot sweet tea, and Penelope took it gratefully. 'She was in pretty poor shape when Jeremy saw her at the hospital last night, but she's slightly more comfortable this morning. But she's pretty low and tearful, as you can imagine, and she keeps asking for Chris. She begged Jeremy to ring us.'

'Will you tell him? Chris, I mean,' Richard wanted to know.

'I promised, because Jeremy was so insistent, but do you think I should? The only person Jeremy's thinking about is Irene. That man's so idiotically altruistic that sometimes I could murder him! The only person I can think about is Sylvia. She and Chris seem to have been making a go of it lately. And now this! It's bound to affect things.'

Richard got up from crouching beside her chair and kissed his mother on the forehead. 'That'll depend on Chris, won't it?'

'Do I hear my name?' Chris, unnoticed by any of them, had appeared in the kitchen doorway. 'I decided to come home for lunch after all.' His eyes fell on the tins of baked beans and spaghetti standing on the table. 'What delicacies do we have here? A change from salad, I suppose,' he added, echoing Richard. Then, becoming aware of the silence, he asked: 'What's the matter?'

There was a pause, while three pairs of eyes stared at him with differing degrees of speculation. Penelope, sipping her tea, raised her brows at Richard. He shrugged, as much as to say: 'What else can you do but tell him?'

'It's Irene,' Penelope blurted out. 'She's had an accident.' The details stumbled unwillingly off her tongue, but Chris barely stopped to hear them.

'I must go and pack,' he said. 'I suppose I can't take the car? No, I thought not. Rich, telephone for a taxi to get me into Plymouth, then ring North Road station and find out the time of the next London train.'

He was gone, his face white and set, running upstairs two at a time. Penelope finished her tea and leaned back in the chair, rocking herself gently. She looked tired and resigned. Richard left the kitchen to do his brother's bidding.

'What will happen now, do you think?' Anne asked.

Penelope hunched her shoulders. 'God knows! Probably divorce. Remarriage.' She added after a moment: 'One good thing might come of it, I suppose, if that does happen. Tim could eventually get Sylvia back. He's still in love with her.'

PART TWO
1976–80

CHAPTER NINE

'MY GOD, it's hot,' Barbara complained. 'I can't ever remember a summer as hot as this one. There'll be water restrictions soon, I shouldn't wonder.'

'There already are in some parts of the country. Let's sit down for a moment.' And Penelope led the way to a nearby seat overlooking the long blue vistas of Nightingale Valley.

It was Sunday afternoon, and the Downs were crowded, the bright cotton dresses of the women making vivid patches of colour on the grass. The sun beat down relentlessly from an almost cloudless sky. There had been no rain for months, following a very dry winter. Penelope and Clifford were spending a long weekend with the Seymours and, the previous evening, had taken them to see the Royal Shakespeare Company's production of *Henry V*, which was playing in Bristol for this last week in July, and in which Tim had a very small part. It had been, in a hectic summer, their only opportunity to see him. A visit to Stratford had been out of the question.

After a heavy Sunday lunch, lovingly prepared by Felicity, Clifford was stretched out in a deck-chair in the garden, the two girls were off somewhere about their own business, and Felicity herself was sound asleep on her bed. Barbara and Penelope, however, had decided, in spite of the heat, on a walk.

'I loved coming up here as a child,' Penelope recalled. 'I loved running up and down the sides of what I used to call "the hollows". You know, what's left of the old quarry workings.'

Barbara nodded, but she hadn't brought her friend out to reminisce. There were other subjects she wanted to talk about, which she didn't quite like to discuss in front of Clifford. He still, after all these years, had the power to make her feel uncomfortable when he turned those slightly mocking, bright-blue eyes upon her. She had always been a little in awe of him, and since his knighthood more so; a fact which she resented. She frequently forgot that her friend was Lady Haldane, introducing her as 'Mrs' – lapses which never worried Penelope, who often forgot herself. But Barbara suspected that Clifford would be less tolerant.

'So what's happening about the divorce?' she asked, lowering her voice a little.

'Divorces, you mean,' Penelope answered gloomily. 'Sylvia and Chris's became absolute in June; I thought I'd told you. Jeremy and Irene will have to wait a little longer. I believe I heard October mentioned.'

'And then?' Barbara raised her eyebrows.

'And then, presumably, Chris and Irene will marry. I say "presumably" because they don't keep us informed any more. They both know how strongly we disapprove of the whole shoddy business.'

'It must be difficult for you, Irene being your agent.'

'It is, rather, but we keep our relationship now strictly business. I thought of going to someone else, but decided it wouldn't be fair to either of us. She's damn good at her job, and I'd be lost without her. And I'm her top-selling author.'

'Was there much opposition from Jeremy and Sylvia?'

Penelope grimaced. 'From Jeremy, no. He's too much the perfect gentleman for his own good, that one. And he's perfectly willing to let Irene have custody of Deborah, provided he has reasonable access. But Sylvia was a different matter. She fought long and hard to keep Chris, and the divorce was fairly acrimonious. But she gave way in the end, when she realized that he was serious about Irene.' Penelope sighed. 'To be fair, they really are in love with one another, and I think this marriage, when it happens, will last. At least, I hope so. As a family, we don't want any more scandal. The trouble is that Sylvia still loves Christopher, too. That boy has always been Nature's spoilt darling.' She watched as some children ran by, oblivious of the scorching heat, screaming and laughing, while their parents tagged wearily behind them, sweating and crumpled. 'Kids!' she added despairingly. 'Who'd have 'em?'

Barbara nodded in agreement. 'Were we as unsatisfactory? I can't believe it. I seem to recollect that we were models of good behaviour and filial duty.'

Penelope chuckled, sloughing off her sombre mood. 'Oh, I don't know. You remember how strait-laced Mother and Dad were. They thought the end of the world had come when I married an actor. And I'm sure Felicity would have preferred a much more dashing daughter. I always got the impression she thought you a bit of a bore.'

Barbara laughed, albeit a trifle grimly. 'She still does. You and I should have swapped parents. Everyone would have been happier. However, Mother's got the granddaughters she wanted, especially in Anne. They're as alike as two peas in a pod.'

They sat in silence for a moment or two while all around them the heat hung in a shimmering haze. A dog, a streak of brown and white, lay panting beneath a tree. People moved slowly, in a kind of torpor, and the whole scene took on a dream-like quality. Then Penelope asked abruptly: 'What's Imogen going to do, now she's left secretarial college?'

'Look for a job, of course.' Barbara wished she'd followed her mother's advice and worn a paler-coloured dress instead of this black-and-orange cotton. She

125

swung a red-sandalled foot slowly back and forwards.

'I was wondering . . . ' Penelope hesitated momentarily before going on: 'I was wondering if she would come and work for me?'

'But you already have a full-time secretary,' Barbara objected.

'She's leaving to get married in a month or two, and I thought it would be cosy to have someone that I knew around me.'

Barbara eyed her friend suspiciously. 'This is very fortuitous, isn't it? What are you up to?'

'Nothing,' Penelope protested. 'Susie French really is leaving in September to get married. She'll be going to live up north with her husband, so there's no question of her being able to carry on working for me. And, if Imogen is willing, it'll save me having to scout round the various agencies. Interviewing people is time-consuming, and a lot of secretaries are so independent. I can train Imogen from the ground up, so to speak, to do things my way. Do you think she might agree?'

'She'll jump at the chance,' Barbara answered drily. 'She'd be a fool not to. Added to which, of course, there's a chance that she'll be able to see more of Tim. I think she thinks that I don't know how keen she is on him. Girls always imagine their mothers are less observant than they really are. And I guess, too, that you've known it for quite some time. Penelope' – she slithered round on the seat so that she could study her friend's profile – 'there isn't any ulterior motive in this offer, is there?'

'I've told you, no!' Penelope returned Barbara's questioning gaze with a wide-eyed stare.

All the same, she was not as innocent as she looked. Barbara was right; she had been aware for a long time that Imogen was fond of Tim, to put it no higher, and she harboured a vague hope that, one day, he would return that affection. What worried Penelope was her second son's continuing infatuation for Sylvia Gibson – or Sylvia Haldane as she supposed she had been for the past four years. Now that Sylvia was a free woman again, Penelope feared that Tim would try to renew the relationship. With Imogen a permanent resident at The Laurels, she hoped to offer him an alternative.

At twenty, Imogen had grown into a very pretty girl, more than fulfilling her early promise. She had developed a good figure to go with the long slender legs which had always been one of her most eye-catching features. The blonde hair, which used to hang loose and straight, had been permed, giving her rather thin face a necessary fullness. And the blue eyes were enhanced by the current fashion for heavy eye-liner and mascara. All in all, Penelope thought, when Tim was at home he could hardly fail to notice her. Could he? But children were so perverse; they rarely did exactly what you wanted. She sighed for the second time that afternoon, reflecting on the trials of motherhood.

'Leave them alone and don't interfere,' would be Clifford's advice, and in her heart she knew it was sound. But sometimes it was too difficult to do nothing.

'Shall we go back?' she asked. 'I really don't think I can take much more of this heat. It's so oppressive.'

Barbara agreed with alacrity. She had discovered all she wanted to know, and was more than willing to return to the house, whose thick Victorian walls offered at least some relief from the sun. She got up, and the two women walked slowly back towards the top of Pembroke Road, each busy with her own thoughts and plans.

'Sylvia!' Tim's voice, at the other end of the phone, was low and urgent. 'I'm coming home this weekend. I have to see you.'

127

Sylvia lit another cigarette, her fifth in the past hour, the telephone receiver jammed beneath her chin. She blew out a cloud of thin blue smoke, before speaking into the mouthpiece.

'I've told you, Tim, a dozen times already, that there really is no point. We have nothing to say to one another.'

'We do. You know we do,' he pleaded. 'You were in love with me once. Why can't you be again?'

He was, she thought, like a small importunate child demanding the bag of sweets which had been taken away from him by his elder brother. Now his brother no longer wanted the sweets, he saw no reason why they shouldn't be returned to him.

She said quietly: 'Tim dear, I'm trying to tell you as gently as I can, without doing too much damage to your feelings. Our engagement was a mistake. It was always Chris I wanted. And I still love him. I'm not going to change my mind. So, please, don't bother coming all the way from Stratford this weekend. It won't do any good.'

'I'm coming anyway, whatever you say,' he repeated obstinately. 'I don't have a performance on Saturday evening. I'll drive down. One of the other guys in the company has offered to lend me his car.'

He rang off abruptly before she made another attempt to dissuade him. Sylvia replaced her receiver.

'Oh, hell!' she said to the darkened room. It was late, and outside a thin September rain was falling. She could hear the swish of car tyres on the wet roads. Her current engagement was at the Albery, the renamed New Theatre, outside which she had met Chris that day, four years ago. It brought back memories, and it needed all her powers of concentration not to let them interfere with her work. By the time she returned to the empty flat at night, she was exhausted, ready for the oblivion of sleep. It was the only thing which brought her peace of mind, and her doctor had prescribed her sleeping tablets.

In moments of bitterness, she had toyed with the idea of taking an overdose; not enough to kill herself, but just sufficient to look as though she had meant to do so, thus arousing Chris's concern. But would she? He was not in love with her as he was with Irene. Oh, he might well feel concern, guilt, misery, but would those emotions bring him back to her? And would she want him, if they did? She had forced him once before to stay with her, but what had she achieved? Two unsatisfactory years during which she had known all the time that he was hankering after another woman.

She sat down, lit yet another cigarette and stared at the blank television screen. By the time she returned from the theatre at night, most of the programmes she wanted to see were over, and she was alone in the all-embracing silence. In the days before her marriage, she had not noticed it, always having been used to her own company. Now she was alone once more and would have to re-accustom herself to the quiet. She had broken her golden rule about never getting married; first, when she had foolishly got engaged to Tim, and then when she had married Chris. But it wouldn't happen again. She would never put herself through such heartache a second time.

The hot tears stung her eyelids. She wanted to shout out 'Chris!' at the top of her voice, like an animal in pain; a howl which would reach out across the London streets and bring him hurrying to her side. But of course she couldn't. And it wouldn't have the desired effect in any case. There was no doubt that he did love Irene Grantham, and that they would be married as soon as possible after her divorce from Jeremy became final next month. Sylvia herself was already a free woman; free to take up her life, to start afresh, to go out with whomsoever she chose. The trouble was, there was no-one she wanted – certainly not Tim.

She stubbed out her cigarette half-smoked and went into the kitchen to warm some milk on the stove, sending up a small prayer as she did so. Dear God, don't let him keep his threat of coming home this weekend! But she had very little hope of her plea being answered. And as she didn't really believe in God she supposed she had no right to expect it anyway.

Imogen, as Barbara had predicted, had jumped at the chance of becoming Penelope's secretary. The job had seemed like the answer to her dreams. It had a cachet, a glamour about it which made her the envy of her friends. In reality, it was more mundane and harder work than she had imagined, Penelope insisting on office hours while she was working on a book, and making Imogen responsible for all her and Clifford's social correspondence. Nevertheless, Imogen knew herself to be especially fortunate, and living on the premises did not worry her. Always shy and retiring, she had never prized independence very highly, preferring, even at twenty, the comforting reassurance of the presence of older people. Moreover, there was always the promise of a visit from Tim to brighten her days, and the even happier prospect that, after his stint in Stratford, he might be based in London for a while. So far, she had seen nothing of him, but she had only been at The Laurels for just over a month, and surely he must return to see his parents soon.

Weekends were her own, when Penelope encouraged her to do as she pleased. But, as yet, Imogen had made no friends and was inclined to be intimidated by the capital's volume of traffic and an Underground system she had not, in the past, ever had to tackle on her own. In consequence, she hung around the house or went down to the basement to work – a fact which deeply worried Penelope.

'Serves you right,' Clifford said unsympathetically, as they sat up in bed that mid-September Saturday morning, drinking tea. 'I warned you that mixing business and friendship never works. In fact it's always a stupid idea. And having Imogen to live with us was even sillier. Now you have a secretary for whose welfare you feel responsible twenty-four hours a day, seven days a week. You'd have done far better to get a stranger from one of the agencies.'

'Don't rub it in,' his wife answered irritably. 'I know I'm to blame. I just didn't think it through. I hadn't realized just how diffident Imogen is. If it had been Anne, now ... However, it's no good crying over spilt milk, and she's a very competent secretary. My work has never been so up to date.' She swallowed the last of her tea. 'I wonder if Rich is doing anything this morning?'

'Oh, no, you don't, Pen my love!' Clifford eased himself out of bed, displaying the full glory of crimson pyjamas. 'You're not saddling Rich with your responsibilities. You know that's one of our golden rules: we never pass the buck to the children. And don't look at me, either. I intend to relax this morning before the matinée. God knows, it's nerve-racking enough playing two performances of the Scottish play in one day, without arranging entertainment for Imogen as well.'

Penelope nodded gloomily. 'Everything going all right?' she enquired, but not much attending to the answer. She knew from experience that nothing ever went perfectly during a run of *Macbeth*. Having once written a historical novel about the much-maligned king, she had her own theories as to the reason.

'So I'm going to run my bath now,' her husband concluded at the end of a recital about what had gone wrong so far. 'If you don't want yours first, that is.'

Before Penelope could reply, there was a peremptory knock on their bedroom door, and, without waiting for permission to enter, Tim walked in. His mother gave a little crow of excitement and held out her arms.

'Darling! What a lovely surprise! What are you doing here?'

Tim approached the bed and kissed her briefly, managing to dodge her embrace. His mother grinned in acknowledgement of this dexterity.

Clifford frowned. 'Don't you have a performance this evening?'

'Sorry to disappoint you, Dad, but no. So', Tim added defiantly, 'I've come down to see Sylvia. I'll stop overnight and go back tomorrow.'

'What do you mean, you've come down to see Sylvia?' It was Penelope who spoke, but both parents turned disapproving eyes in his direction.

'Oh, for heaven's sake!' Tim exclaimed irritably. 'There's no need to look like that. You can't pretend that you don't know how I still feel about her.'

'Tim.' Penelope swung her legs over the edge of the bed and grabbed her dressing-gown, while her husband, telling himself that she was quite capable of dealing with the situation, slunk cravenly off to the bathroom. 'Please don't do it. Neither your father nor I wants to see you get hurt again. Sylvia doesn't want you. She's in love with Chris, and probably always will be. She's the sort of woman who has a once-in-a-lifetime passion. Forget about her. You can't mend matters. You can only make them worse. She's thirty-five now. God knows, she ought to know what she wants, and it isn't you. Please, for everyone's sake, leave her alone.'

Tim's handsome face set in the mulish lines Penelope knew so well from his childhood. He wanted something and he had made up his mind to have it. And, as had happened so often in the past, he was going to be hurt and disappointed when thwarted.

'I don't see how you know what she wants,' he answered belligerently. 'Anyway, as soon as I've eaten, I'm going over to see her. I told her the other evening, on the phone, that I was coming.'

He didn't add that he had specified no particular time of day, and hoped, by leaving Stratford at five that morning and arriving in time for breakfast, to make certain of finding Sylvia at home.

Penelope sighed and gave up the struggle. She wasn't going to dissuade him, she could see that. Indeed, if she persisted in trying to do so, she might even make things worse, hardening his determination.

'Very well,' she said. 'You must do as you please. Go on down and have breakfast. I expect Mrs Clennan has it ready by now. You'll probably find Imogen already in the dining-room. She's an inveterately early riser.'

'Of course. I'd forgotten she'd be here.' Tim's face brightened a little. At least, with Imogen present, his mother would be more reluctant to continue their conversation during the meal. 'How's she getting on?'

'Very well. She's an admirable secretary. In fact she's a charming girl altogether.' But Penelope's recommendation went unheeded. Tim was uninterested in anyone but Sylvia.

He was, none the less, pleased to see Imogen when he entered the dining-room a few minutes later; flattered, too, by the way her face lit up at the sight of him.

'Tim! How . . . how marvellous! Are you home for long?'

He shook his head, taking a seat at the table beside her. 'Only for one night. There's some . . . some business I have to attend to. One of the other blokes in the company lent me his car, and I drove down very early this morning.'

She smiled, and he thought suddenly how pretty she had grown. Not to be compared with Sylvia's exotic beauty, of course, but attractive all the same. A girl he would not be ashamed to be seen with. And she was staring at him with such a look of adoration! Here was a woman who would never compare him unfavourably with his elder brother, and he found that thought extremely comforting in a world where all the women seemed, unaccountably, to prefer Chris.

'You must get Ma to give you some time off soon,' he said, 'and come up to Stratford to see me. I only have a couple of small parts as yet, but it's all experience. One day, I intend to be as good an actor as the Old Man. If not better.'

Imogen saw nothing outrageous in a statement which was usually greeted with smiles of derision, and her eyes told him so. 'I saw you in *Henry V*', she said, 'at the Hippodrome in July. We came backstage afterwards to see you, if you remember.' Tim realized, guiltily, that he had been quite unaware of her presence. 'I thought you were wonderful.'

Tim, always receptive to praise, positively glowed. 'That's sweet of you, Imogen.'

Richard's imminent arrival at the breakfast-table was heralded by the excited entrance of Sir Cloudesley Shovel, whose advancing years, and a touch of arthritis in one of his back legs, could never persuade that he was not still a puppy. Barking fiendishly he advanced on Tim and tried to nip his left ankle. Machiavelli, who followed in a more decorous manner, ignored Tim altogether, but sprang up on the empty chair beside him. Richard, appearing in their wake, grinned at his brother and said 'Good morning', but evinced no interest in how he had got there or why.

'Pass the toast, Imogen,' was all he said, 'there's a dear.'

Although the last thing Tim wanted was any further discussion of his affairs, Richard's detachment nevertheless still managed to annoy him. He sometimes felt that he was the odd one out in the family, whose talents and charm had never been properly appreciated. It was all the more pleasant, therefore, to be able to turn to Imogen and be assured of an admiring audience. He wondered why he had not realized before how very sympathetic she was. He found himself wishing that he had more time to spend with her on this brief visit. He felt that he could pour out his troubles to her and that she would understand. She, too, was the unappreciated one, or so he told himself, in a household of much bossier, stronger-minded women. Unfortunately, his time was limited and what there was of it belonged entirely to Sylvia. He had to make her see reason; to convince her that he was the one she had always really loved; that Chris had been a mere aberration. He was confident of the fact in his own mind; it was simply a matter of making Sylvia admit it. At the moment, her pride had taken a battering, but he was sure that it would soon recover.

He smiled to himself and started to eat his breakfast.

CHAPTER TEN

'NO!' Sylvia exclaimed furiously. 'I've told you, there's no chance of us getting back together again. I thought I'd made that plain when you phoned me the other evening.'

She was in her dressing-gown, Tim's ring at the doorbell having caught her still in bed. Had she known who it was, she would not have answered, but Saturday was the milkman's morning for collecting his money. So, half-asleep, she had hunted round for her purse, extracted a couple of pound notes, made her way to the front door of the flat and opened it, only to discover Tim standing in the corridor. Her reaction had hardly been welcoming.

'What the hell do you want?'

Slightly daunted, Tim had replied, 'I want to come in,' and, like a fool, she had let him.

But, once inside, she gave it to him straight from the shoulder, ruthlessly interrupting his first few stumbling words with an explosion of anger.

'I didn't think you meant it,' he protested, looking hurt, like a small boy who genuinely could not understand why he was being punished. 'You loved me enough, once, to get engaged to me. What's happened?'

She sighed in exasperation, leading the way through to the kitchen. She craved a cup of coffee and her first cigarette of the day, and could no longer postpone them. She filled the electric kettle and plugged it in, setting two mugs on the table.

'Chris happened,' she answered shortly. 'Do you take milk and sugar? I've forgotten.'

'What? Oh ... milk, no sugar. But, Sylvie, Chris doesn't want you.'

'Do you think I don't know that? And please don't call me Sylvie! You know how I hate it.' She took a cigarette from a wooden box on the dresser and lit it, inhaling deeply and blowing out a cloud of blue smoke.

'Well, then?' Tim looked hopeful.

She spooned instant coffee into the mugs and filled them up with hot water, pushing one towards him and indicating the blue-and-white milk-jug. 'Help yourself ... Well, then, what? The fact that Chris doesn't want me doesn't automatically mean that I want you.'

Tim ignored the coffee. 'But you loved me once. You must have done, to accept my proposal of marriage.'

Sylvia pulled out a stool from under the table and sat down, wrapping her white towelling robe more firmly around her. With one of her feet, she pushed another stool towards Tim and told him to be seated.

'Tim,' she said quietly, 'I know this may be difficult for you to understand, and I don't know of any easy way to put it. I'm not sure I understand it myself, not altogether. I think what happened was that, somehow or other, I'd got you muddled in my mind with Chris. You're very alike to look at, and once, at Irene and Jeremy's wedding, I actually mistook you for him.' She stubbed out her cigarette in the big glass ashtray which stood in the middle of the kitchen table and lit another. 'What I'm trying, not very successfully, to say is that my mind played a trick on me. It made me believe that I was in love with you, when all the time I was really in love with Chris. Does that make any sort of sense?'

'No, it bloody doesn't!' His face was crumpled and petulant, a parody of his elder brother's, who, in similar circumstances, would have been blazingly angry. Sylvia was afraid he was about to burst into

137

tears. 'You're just making excuses, trying to put me off, hoping that Chris will come back to you. Well, he won't! So you might as well make do with me.'

'Oh, for God's sake, is that what you want? That we should "make do" with one another?' Sylvia was losing patience, and her tone was scathing. 'Can't you get it through your silly thick head that I don't want you? What woman in her right mind wants the shadow, when she's known what it is to have the substance?'

Something snapped inside Tim; but his rage, when at last it came, was hysterical rather than threatening. He swept his mug of untouched coffee off the table, sending it spinning to the floor, where the hot liquid ran in a pale brown stream across the plastic tiles, with the shattered china making small jagged islands.

'You don't love Chris!' he shouted. 'You can't! I won't let you! You've got to love me! I'll make you.'

He got up and lunged round the table towards her, but slipped in the pool of coffee and fell heavily, banging his head against one of the legs. It was a débâcle somehow so typical of Tim that Sylvia's anger evaporated, and she burst into uncontrollable laughter. She slid off her stool, desperately trying to control her mirth, and bent over him.

'Tim love, are you OK?'

He pushed her away and struggled to his feet, his lower lip trembling. 'Oh, very funny!' he exclaimed. 'Very funny indeed! I suppose if something like that had happened to Chris you'd be all consideration.'

'No. I think I should have laughed just the same. And Chris would have laughed with me.' The smile died out of her eyes, and her voice caught in her throat. 'I'll get a damp cloth to sponge down your jeans,' she said. 'They're stained with coffee.'

Tim, who by now had picked himself up off the floor, made a grab for her, forcing her back against one of the kitchen units and trying to kiss her. Furiously angry, she averted her face and brought up her hands to fend him off, hammering with her clenched fists against his chest.

'Stop it, Tim! Let me go! If you don't, you'll be sorry!'

It was doubtful, she realized later, if he even heard her, so intent was he on proving that he could still arouse her ardour; but when he persisted she kneed him smartly in the groin. He gasped and released her, staggering backwards and finally lowering himself into her vacated chair.

'That hurt,' he protested, staring at her in bewilderment.

'And would have hurt a damn sight more, if my aim had been better.' Sylvia went over to the sink and rinsed a cloth beneath the cold-water tap. 'For heaven's sake, Tim, grow up and start behaving like an adult. I'm thirty-five, and I can do without this sort of juvenile hassle.' She returned and began dabbing at the rapidly drying coffee-stains on his pullover and jeans.

Tim pushed her hand away and stood up, a little unsteadily. With a visible effort, he drew himself to his full height, gathering the rags of his dignity about him.

'I'm going,' he said. 'As I'm so unwelcome here, I shan't trouble you any further with my immature attentions.' The last words were spoken with such bitterness that Sylvia was filled with remorse and guilt, emotions which quickly evaporated as Tim added spitefully: 'You won't get Chris back, you know, whatever you might think. He only wanted you in the beginning because I had you.'

Sylvia flinched, as though Tim had struck her; but, at the same time, one part of her mind registered surprise that he should prove to be so percipient. She had underrated Tim's powers of understanding.

'Do you think I don't know that?' she asked him quietly.

Tim hunched his shoulders. 'Oh, well, Chris has made fools of us both, then, hasn't he? I'm sorry I made a mess of your floor. Do you want me to clean it up?'

She made a noise which could have been either a laugh or a sob and shook her head. 'No, I'll do it. It won't take long.' She followed him through the sitting-room and out into the flat's narrow hallway. As he went to open the door, she detained him, with a hand on his arm. 'Tim, I really am very sorry. And . . . and, whatever Chris may have done to us both, I honestly don't believe he did it deliberately. Not with malice aforethought. I feel sure he truly does love Irene. Don't think too badly of him. He is your brother, and for your parents' sake you must try to forgive him. I appreciate – who better? – that it isn't easy; but you, at least, ought to make an effort.'

He neither looked at her nor answered, merely shaking off her hand. A moment later, the front door of the flat shut with a snap behind him.

Tim stared at his reflection in the brightly lit mirror of the dressing-room he shared with several other of the Royal Shakespeare Company's less exalted players. His face, still wearing the heavy theatrical make-up, was scarcely recognizable as his own. Slowly, almost reluctantly, he smothered it in cream and began to wipe it clean with a handful of cotton wool. Gradually, his own features began to appear, and, with their re-emergence, his worries, which he had managed to forget for the past few hours in the world of Shakespeare's medieval England.

Since that last encounter with Sylvia, when he felt he had made a humiliating spectacle of himself, he had tried very hard to forget her. Not only his pride was at stake, but also, he felt, his reason. He would go mad if he thought about her too much or too long. Years ago, he remembered, his mother had taken himself and Chris to see some play in which their father was appearing. He had long forgotten the name of the piece, but one line had stuck in his memory. 'The only antidote for a broken heart', one character had proclaimed cynically, 'is another affair.' Which was why Imogen was waiting for him, right this minute, at the stage door, having dutifully sat through the evening performance.

Dropping further handfuls of stained cotton wool into the wastepaper-basket, and oblivious to the general buzz of conversation all round him, Tim continued to mull over the events of the past few weeks. It had been his suggestion that Imogen should visit him in Stratford. True, she had jumped at that suggestion with a flattering eagerness, but it was at his own instigation that she was here. He liked Imogen; he liked her very much. He always had, he told himself fiercely. Why, then, did he have this sinking feeling in the pit of his stomach?

He finished cleaning his face and got up from the stool, shedding his dressing-gown and pulling on his street-clothes. Then he hung his last-act costume on the rail at the end of the room and called his good-nights. In reply to enquiries as to his movements, he said he had someone waiting and went out into the corridor. Imogen was chatting to the stage-doorman and gave Tim a small shy smile as he approached.

'How did you enjoy the play?' he asked, stooping to kiss her.

She flushed with delighted surprise at this mark of affection, firmly suppressing the knowledge that amongst actors kissing was a normal mode of greeting.

'I thought you were absolutely marvellous,' she told him warmly.

141

He laughed. 'If you'd blinked more than once, you'd have missed me.' But he looked pleased, nevertheless, the rather hard lines about his mouth disappearing. He was aware that the two small roles he doubled in offered insufficient opportunities to warrant such unstinted praise, but it bolstered his self-confidence and confirmed his own assessment of his acting abilities. And Imogen's open adoration underlined the stark contrast of Sylvia's almost contemptuous dismissal. Maybe Imogen was, after all, the right person for him.

He put an arm around her shoulders, and they walked slowly along the banks of the Avon. Overhead, it was a clear starlit night, and somewhere in the distance an owl gave its long ululating cry. Tim was washed by a sudden wave of peace and contentment. He did not stop to think that this could be a reaction to his earlier mental turmoil. He had never been much given to self-analysis. All he knew was that he was unexpectedly happy and needed to make love, and he could tell by Imogen's response, when he stopped to kiss her again, that she felt the same way.

They walked on until they were free of the town, and found a place to lie down amongst a belt of trees. It was a chilly night, but neither of them was in a mood to notice. Tim took off his jacket and laid it on the ground.

It came as something of a shock to him to discover that Imogen was still a virgin. In the enlightened and female-emancipated seventies he had not expected it, and it rather spoilt his pleasure. However, her whispered assurance that she had never wanted to make love with anyone but him was an added sop to his vanity. He reflected that Sylvia, so much older and experienced than himself, had often made him feel gauche and inept. Imogen made him feel like a man of the world. When he kissed her good-night at the entrance to her hotel, he said: 'You must come and visit me again. Often.' And as he set off back to his digs, whistling softly to himself in the dark, he found that he meant it.

Anne was bored, not by Stratford-upon-Avon, which she had visited some years previously with Felicity, but by the organized school trip and the regimented visits to places of interest. Moreover, she objected to giving up a Saturday to the project and had argued unavailingly with her mother.

'A trip to Stratford will do you more good than loafing about the house all day watching television.' Barbara had been adamant. 'And don't try roping in your grandmother to back you up, because I shan't listen to her, either. Besides, if you're still set on doing stage design – although I shall do my best to dissuade you – I should think it's right up your street.'

'It might be if we were going to the theatre, but Miss Warboys organized the visit at the very last minute, and the Saturday performances were sold out.' Anne had been suitably indignant. 'Going to Stratford and not seeing one of Shakespeare's plays is like going to the Savoy Grill and not eating.'

But her mother had been unimpressed by this brilliant piece of reasoning, and insisted on paying for the trip. So Anne and her friend Jacqueline Kent had been on the specially chartered coach leaving the school gates at eight o'clock on that warm early-October Saturday morning, and by midday were eating a packed lunch on the banks of the Avon. After which, the coach transported them to Shottery, to look at Anne Hathaway's cottage, then back to the town centre for visits to Shakespeare's birthplace, the church of the Holy Trinity, the Guild Chapel and Harvard House. Miss Warboys then decided it was time for a break and ushered her twenty

143

or so charges into a Sheep Street café for tea.

'Thank heaven,' Jackie groaned, as she and Anne managed to find two seats near the window, as far as possible from their form mistress's eagle eye. She giggled. 'The proprietor doesn't look too pleased.'

'Can you blame him?' Anne glanced round her. 'He'd rather have a load of tourists, all scoffing expensive cream teas, than a lot of schoolgirls on a diet of sticky buns.' She peered out of the window, hoping to see a member of the theatre company. Her wish was granted, but instead of leading man Alan Howard, or the handsome Charles Dance, who had so taken her fancy back in the summer in *Henry V*, she saw Tim Haldane walking along on the other side of the road, one arm linked through Imogen's.

'There's my sister! What's she doing here? And with Tim!' She gripped Jackie's wrist. 'I must speak to her. Cover for me.'

'How am I going to do that?' wailed Jackie as Anne rose to her feet and began surreptitiously edging towards the café door.

'Just try to look like two people,' Anne hissed in reply and, before her friend could raise any further objections, was through the entrance and across the street, chasing after Imogen and Tim. Once out of earshot of the café, she yelled: 'Tim! Imogen! Wait!'

At the sound of her name, Imogen slowed and glanced over her shoulder, her face registering both surprise and pleasure when she saw her sister.

'Anne! What brings *you* here?'

'School trip.' Anne came to a halt beside them, holding her side. 'Can't stop a minute or Warboys will be on the warpath.' It was an old school joke, and Imogen smiled in recognition. 'What's more to the point, what are *you* doing here?' Anne countered.

'I often come up to see Tim. As often as Aunt Pen doesn't need me. As a matter of fact ... ' Imogen glanced questioningly at Tim. 'Is it all right to tell her?'

'Tell me what?' Anne asked curiously. Now she came to study her sister and Tim more carefully, there was something definitely furtive-looking about the pair of them.

Tim hesitated, then shrugged with a kind of resignation. 'Why not? She'll have to know sooner or later.'

'Tim and I are engaged. He's asked me to marry him.' Imogen smiled triumphantly.

Anne only just prevented herself from asking: 'Are you sure?' Her last information was that Tim was still trying to win back Sylvia. Instead, she murmured: 'That's wonderful. But when did it happen?'

'Yesterday evening, as soon as I arrived. You're the first to know. We're going to phone Mum and Aunt Pen this evening.' Imogen held out her left hand to display a thin band of gold and a very small solitaire diamond.

'Gosh!' Anne was stumped for words. She still found it difficult to believe and glanced at Tim for confirmation.

He smiled, hoping that his future sister-in-law would not notice the effort it caused him. He thought of the letter he had received yesterday morning from Sylvia, now reposing in his landlady's dustbin. A few days previously, in one last desperate appeal, he had written to her with all the eloquence at his command: an outpouring of his love which he persuaded himself must move her at least to pity, if not to a resurgence of the feeling that he was sure had once existed between them. And when he had come down to breakfast yesterday, to see an envelope bearing her writing beside his plate, his heart had lifted. If it contained what he hoped, then tonight, very gently but firmly, he would tell Imogen that it was over between them.

The shower of torn paper fragments which had cascaded on to the tablecloth had momentarily bewildered him until he suddenly realized what they were: his own letter ripped to pieces. Fortunately, he was the first down and no-one else had been witness to his distress. He had scooped the bits back into the envelope, which he had then savagely crumpled and taken outside to throw in the dustbin. And that same evening, after the performance, he had asked Imogen to marry him in a gesture of defiance which common sense whispered that he might later regret – a warning he had resolutely ignored.

Looking now at Anne's doubtful face, it came home to him exactly what he had done. But there was no going back. He said with forced jocularity: 'The parents will be pleased, don't you think? I know it's what Mum wants and has for a long time.'

Anne had an uneasy feeling that there was something not quite right with this answer, but she was too delighted with the news to examine her doubts too closely. She flung her arms around first one and then the other, proffering excited congratulations.

'I must go,' she said at last with some reluctance. 'I'll be in trouble if Warboys discovers I'm missing.' She regarded them both with misty eyes. 'Oh, I am pleased. Try to ring Mum before I get home.' She began retracing her steps before remembering something. Turning her head, she shouted at their retreating backs: 'I hope I'm going to be chief bridesmaid!' But they were already out of earshot.

In the café her absence had gone unnoticed. A gleeful Jackie told her: 'Sheila Weston threw up in the ladies'. Warboys managed to head her in the right direction just in time.' She noticed her friend's face and asked: 'What's up with you? You look like a pregnant chicken.'

Anne gave her Cheshire-cat grin. 'Shut up and

146

listen. I've got the most wonderful news.'

And so it was. It was odd, therefore, that during the drive home, while her form mates slept and the darkened countryside flew by outside the coach windows, Anne found herself beginning to worry. The more she thought about that scene in Sheep Street, the more she felt that Tim had been a little too subdued. He had received Anne's congratulations with a restraint which seemed strange in a newly engaged man. Everyone knew, of course, that he had been in love with Sylvia for years, but surely that must now be over. He would never have asked Imogen to marry him otherwise.

Her mother had driven to the school to pick her up and was waiting with the car when Anne alighted from the coach, close on midnight. She could see from Barbara's expression that Imogen had already telephoned her. As she slid into the front passenger-seat, she said: 'You've heard, then. I expect Im told you that I saw her and Tim in Stratford. Well? What do you think?'

Barbara replied cautiously: 'Penelope's over the moon. She's been on the phone to me half the evening.'

'But what do *you* think?' Anne enquired as her mother carefully negotiated the main road which ran across the Downs. 'Are you pleased or not?'

'If it's what Imogen wants, then, yes, naturally I'm pleased. I think she's rather young to get married and I would have preferred her to carve out a career for herself first. And Tim's track record hardly inspires confidence. All that unfortunate business with Sylvia Gibson. Let's hope he's got over her, for everyone's sake, especially Imogen's.'

Her mother's somewhat pessimistic attitude inevitably forced Anne back to the side of optimism.

'Tim's probably seen sense at last and realizes that Imogen will make him the perfect wife. And she will,

147

you know. She's been in love with him since she was about fourteen.'

Barbara snorted derisively. 'No girl knows her own mind at that age. She's far too immature.'

Anne felt too tired to argue any further. All she wanted was her bed. She would think about things tomorrow; but for now, relaxing against the seat and lulled by the car's smooth onward-rushing motion, she gave herself up to romantic dreams of bridesmaids' dresses and wedding bouquets. And before she knew it she was home.

Barbara's doubts were shared, had she known it, by Clifford. He had returned late that evening from the theatre to be greeted by Penelope's ecstatic report of the engagement, and kept awake late into the night by wedding plans. But it was all too sudden and too unexpected for his liking, given the volatile nature of his second son. Clifford discerned his wife's hands, pulling the strings behind the scenes, but he had no wish to spoil Penelope's whole-hearted pleasure in the event, so he kept his misgivings to himself. He could not feel, however, that Imogen's uncritical adulation would do Tim any good either as a man or as an actor. Tim needed encouragement, it was true: he had always lacked Chris's self-confidence. But he needed constructive encouragement. Had it been Anne, now, instead of Imogen whom Tim was marrying, that would have been a very different kettle of fish . . .

But Clifford was too tired and too drained by the evening's performance to stay awake longer, wrestling with his children's problems. Tim would have to learn to fend for himself. Penelope had at last stopped talking. Clifford turned on his side and slept.

CHAPTER ELEVEN

'WHAT ELSE could I have done', Penelope asked Barbara, raising her voice to make herself heard above the din, 'but have the reception here? Chris is my son, after all, and Irene is still my agent.'

Her friend nodded. 'And now she's your daughter-in-law, too.' Barbara also had to shout to make herself intelligible, so great was the babel of conversation all about them.

Chris's register-office wedding to Irene, the previous day, had been very quiet, with only the participants and a couple of witnesses present; but the wedding breakfast was a different matter, and The Laurels was packed to suffocation with the Haldanes' relatives and friends. There were, however, three notable exceptions. Neither Tim, Sylvia nor Jeremy Grantham was anywhere to be seen. The latter two, naturally enough, had not been expected, but Penelope had done her best to ensure Tim's presence. Having appealed unavailingly to his better nature, she had attacked on a different front.

'Imogen will be on her own. You're engaged to her, for heaven's sake! She'll be upset if you don't put in an appearance.'

'No, she won't,' Tim had retorted. 'She understands. A very understanding girl, is Imogen!'

He had, nevertheless, detected an undercurrent of resentment when he had made it plain that he had no intention of attending the wedding reception. Imogen had not gone so far as to reproach him, but she had looked hurt. Obviously, she had assumed that his engagement to her would have cancelled out his feelings for Sylvia. Tim tried to reassure her, explaining, a little too vehemently, that his absence was to mark his disapproval of his brother, and had nothing whatsoever to do with his affection for his former fiancée. Imogen had continued to look unconvinced.

Anne, who had been searching for her sister for at least half an hour, finally ran Imogen to earth in the basement, sitting at her desk, an untouched plateful of food from the buffet in front of her. Sir Cloudesley Shovel, with the unerring instinct of a dog who knows exactly where the greatest source of sustenance is to be found, was lying at her feet, gazing up adoringly, waiting for the next sliver of cold chicken to fall into his slavering mouth.

'It's all cupboard love, you know,' Anne reproved him, perching on the edge of the desk. 'Im! What on earth are you doing down here on your own? Why aren't you upstairs with the rest of the guests?'

'Oh!' Imogen shrugged and tentatively offered Cloud a ham-and-mushroom vol-au-vent, which disappeared as if by magic. 'I don't like crowds, you know that.'

Anne looked sceptical. 'You mean Tim isn't here, and there's no-one else you want to be bothered to talk to. I think it's mean of him,' she added bluntly.

Imogen fired up immediately. 'It's not! I don't blame him. He feels strongly about the way Chris treated Sylvia.'

'That's Sylvia's business, I should have thought. Not Tim's any longer.' Anne fed a pâté-covered biscuit to Sir Cloudesley Shovel. 'You'll be sick, and serve you right,' she informed him. Cloud curled his lip in disdain and wolfed down the biscuit. Anne went on: 'Im . . . Look, I know it's none of my business, but you are certain you're doing the right thing, aren't you?'

It was cold for November, and a flurry of sleet spattered against the basement windows. Outside,

Cameron Road lay embalmed in a Sabbath quiet, except for the noise emanating from The Laurels. One or two disapproving faces had appeared at windows during the course of the afternoon, but it was generally accepted by most of those residents who had not themselves been invited to the party that 'theatricals' were different; Sunday was the one day when everyone was sure to be free.

'What do you mean?' Imogen enquired fiercely. 'Of course I'm doing the right thing! Tim and I love one another!'

Anne made no answer. She was fully aware that her sister loved Tim, but did he truly love Imogen? It was a question which had been worrying her for the past six weeks, ever since she had first been told of the engagement. It seemed, from all the information she had managed to glean on the subject, that Tim was very probably still in love with Sylvia Gibson; and his behaviour today, indicating a refusal to forgive and forget, only confirmed her misgivings.

She slid off the desk and urged: 'Do come upstairs. Mum and Gran have been asking where you are. We shall be going back this evening, and you know they like to see as much of you as they can. Nowadays they don't get the chance very often.'

Imogen shrugged, as though indifferent to anyone's feelings for her except Tim's. Anne resisted the urge to shake her; to tell her not to be so selfish.

'Oh . . . all right,' Imogen at last agreed reluctantly. 'I'll be up presently. Be a dear, and take my plate back for me.'

'You've eaten nothing,' Anne protested. 'Besides,' she added, 'you'll lose an admirer if I do.' She nodded towards Sir Cloudesley Shovel. 'That hell-hound is a very fairweather friend, I do assure you.'

Imogen was betrayed into a laugh. 'OK. Leave him and the plate here. But he'll get most of it.'

Anne bent down and lightly kissed her sister's cheek. 'I'm sure he will. But do try to eat something yourself. As for you' – she addressed Cloud, who turned hopeful eyes in her direction – 'you'll be an obese old dog who won't be able to run after the bitches.' But, as even this dire threat failed to deflect him from his interest in food, Anne laughed and went upstairs again.

The entrance hall, like the rest of the house, seemed full of people. After she had fought her way through the dining-room to the buffet-table, she refilled her plate with a variety of what was on offer, before continuing upstairs to the first-floor drawing-room, where Chris and Irene were chatting to some of their guests. A quick glance round showed her her mother, in an over-fussy pale mauve suit and nondescript white blouse, talking to Penelope at the far end of the room; her grandmother, elegant as always in a softly draped dove-grey dress and matching shoes, being entertained by a suave elderly gentleman with silver hair, whose face Anne immediately recognized from his several television appearances; Cliff, who had been buttonholed by a very earnest lady with a massive bosom, trying to take an intelligent interest in what his companion was saying and only succeeding in looking miserably bored; and Richard, listening with his usual courtesy to a middle-aged man who was thumping the upholstered arm of the sofa in his anxiety to emphasize the point he was making. There were also a number of other people, all equally unknown to her, as well as a sprinkling of famous and familiar faces.

'Hi!' a man's voice said behind her. 'I don't think I know you, do I?'

Anne turned to see a young man with bright hazel eyes and a mop of curly brown hair standing at her elbow. He was, she judged, about her own age, and would have been called plump had he been just a little bit shorter. But his height distracted attention from his girth, although his features were distinctly cherubic.

'No, I don't think you do,' she answered coolly. 'But, then, I don't know you, either, so that makes us quits.'

He grinned, not at all deflated by her distant manner. 'Oh, I'm Ivo Kingsley,' he said. 'My mother's a second cousin of Cliff Haldane. She was invited to this shindig, but couldn't make it, so she sent me instead. We live in Grange-over-Sands. It's a long way to come, and she's not well at present. So here I am.' He gave a brilliant smile, as though expecting Anne to be as delighted with the fact as he was. 'I'm staying here for the weekend,' he went on. 'Managed to get a couple of days off school. Well, what the hell! I'm leaving, anyway, next summer. Do you live in London?'

Anne, who thought him conceited, but harmless enough in his own way, debated whether to give him a set-down or to play along. 'No, Bristol,' she said after a moment. 'We came up by train early this morning, and we're going back tonight. That's my mother, my grandmother and myself. My sister lives here. She's Aunt Pen's secretary and she's engaged to Timothy Haldane.'

'Ah! You're the other Seymour girl. I've heard about you. Of course, I've met Imogen, and your mother is Penelope's best friend.' He seized her elbow and guided her to two empty chairs placed against one wall. 'That's better,' he went on, helping himself to a slice of cold meat from her plate. 'Now we can talk.'

Anne found, however, that this was something of an exaggeration. Ivo Kingsley talked; she listened. Within minutes, she was in possession of most of his life's history, from birth to the present day. He was a year older than herself and Richard; a posthumous child, born two weeks after the death of his father. His widowed mother had gone back to teaching, and had hoped that Ivo would follow her into education, after first obtaining a university degree. But Ivo had other plans, and was determined to try his luck on the stage.

'It's in the family, after all,' he said, nodding towards Clifford. 'I'm hoping to get into RADA. I've already made an application, and I'll be eighteen by the time I leave school. Actually, I think I'll make a very good actor. I've been in several school plays, and our drama coach assures me I definitely have talent.' He glanced once again at his cousin. 'Oh, God! Look out, I think they're going to start making the speeches. I hate all that crap. It's so boring. Besides, I've finished my drink. I'll just make my way downstairs to the buffet.' He stood up, reaching down a hand. 'It's been very nice talking to you. We'll meet again, perhaps, some time.'

Not if I know anything about it, Anne thought to herself. She looked up and smiled as she saw Richard coming across the room towards her.

'I see you got nobbled by cousin Ivo,' he commiserated. 'I'd hoped to rescue you earlier, but I couldn't get away myself from old Charlie Dearman. Nice chap. One of Herrald & Simpson's chief crime writers. Does all those detective novels about Inspector Whatmough. What did the ineffable Ivo have to say for himself?'

'He regaled me with a potted autobiography,' Anne replied tartly. 'I didn't realize you had any North Country relations.'

'I've only met him once or twice myself. But he's all right, is Ivo, when you really get to know him.'

Anne looked doubtful. 'I'll take your word for it. He says he's going to be an actor, too. You must really be odd man out in your family. How did you get on, by the way, with your O levels?'

But before they could compare notes on the past summer's triumphs and disasters Clifford rapped on the mantelpiece and loudly called for silence. People began crowding into the drawing-room and gathering round the open doorway, as word was passed that the speeches were about to begin. There was a kind of uneasy excitement at the prospect of what Clifford would find to say on such a sensitive occasion.

Clifford himself had agonized over the matter and decided to keep it short and simple. 'Ladies and gentlemen,' he said, raising his glass, 'I'm sure you'd all like to join me in wishing the bride and groom every happiness in their new life together. So I ask you to drink a toast to Irene and Christopher.'

There was a general murmur of 'Irene and Chris' as the guests downed the rest of their champagne. Four-year-old Deborah, red-haired like her mother, but with bright blue eyes instead of green, solemnly drank from her glass of lemonade. Anne, observing her, couldn't help feeling that she was too precocious for a child of her age. There was something a little knowing in the way she constantly glanced around for adult applause. And she was so perfectly groomed, not a smear of dirt nor a hair out of place, that to Anne she looked like a doll.

As if to confirm her thoughts, Richard hissed in her ear, 'A right little madam, I should say, wouldn't you?' – nodding towards his newly acquired step-niece. 'Bet she's a tyrant when she's older.'

Chris had risen to reply to his father's toast. He, too, had realized the wisdom of keeping his speech to the minimum.

'On behalf of my wife and myself, I should like to thank you all for your good wishes and for being here today. Irene and I appreciate it very much. I just want to add that I consider myself a very lucky man.'

'Well, you don't bloody deserve to be!' The crowd

around the doorway was falling back to let Tim through. He must, Anne thought despairingly, have spent the last few hours in a pub, drinking steadily. 'You don't deserve anything after the way you've treated Sylvia.' His enunciation was slow, but precise, without any slurring, even though he was lurching from side to side. 'You're a bastard!' he shouted. 'And you've married a whore.'

Clifford muttered, 'Oh, my God!' and tried to get hold of Tim's arm, only to be landed a blow which sent him sprawling. Somebody screamed, and Chris was rocking on the balls of his feet, a red glint in his eyes. The next moment, he had knocked his brother flat on the carpet and was sitting astride him, his hands locked around Tim's throat.

'I'll kill you!' he shouted. 'I'll kill you for saying that about Irene!'

Several of the male guests tried to pull him away, but Chris's anger gave him abnormal strength and he simply shook off their restraining hands. Penelope moaned, 'For pity's sake, someone *do* something!' and kneeled beside her husband, trying to revive him.

Suddenly, in a voice of deadly calm, Richard said: 'That'll do, Chris. Let Tim alone or you'll have me to reckon with.'

There was a surprised silence, during which Chris's hold on Tim's throat slackened and he glanced up angrily at his younger brother. The thin young face was set in hard unemotional lines, and Richard returned the look without flinching. Tim was spluttering and coughing, shocked into sobriety. After a moment or two, the anger faded from Chris's face, to be replaced by a reluctant grin.

'I believe you would take me on, too,' he said softly.

'You're damn right,' his brother answered. 'The pair of you want thumping for upsetting Mother in this way.'

Chris nodded slowly and got to his feet. 'Sorry, Ma', he said contritely, 'for spoiling your day. Is Dad OK?'

'I think it would be more appropriate if you apologized to your guests,' Penelope replied tartly. 'Yes, your father's recovering.'

Clifford was sitting up, rubbing his chin and moaning about its probable disfigurement. 'A good job I'm playing Macbeth in a beard,' he muttered.

Imogen came bursting into the room, throwing herself down beside Tim and putting her arms around him. 'What have you done?' she demanded fiercely of Chris.

By this time, many of the guests were making excuses to leave, some out of sheer embarrassment, others anxious to circulate the story amongst their friends. Within half an hour, the house was cleared of almost every guest except for a few diehards, determined to stick out any party until the bitter end; Anne, Barbara and Felicity, who still had a couple of hours before their train left Paddington; and Ivo Kingsley, who seemed unhappy at having missed all the excitement.

'Why on earth didn't you come and get me?' he reproached Anne. 'You knew I was only downstairs.'

'I had other things on my mind,' she retorted acidly. 'And it wasn't some sort of raree-show. It's a pity a lot of the others weren't down in the buffet with you.'

He was unabashed. 'Still, it's not often you get a punch-up at a wedding, and I'm sorry I wasn't here to see it. It would have made my visit really worthwhile.'

Bereft of speech, Anne moved away to join her mother, who was seated on one of the sofas, offering what comfort she could to a devastated Penelope. Clifford had retired to his room to nurse his swollen jaw. Tim and Imogen had also vanished, while Chris

157

and Irene were preparing to take their departure.

'Sorry, Ma,' Chris said, sitting down on the other side of Penelope and taking one of her hands in both of his. 'I shouldn't have lost my temper.'

Penelope smiled, but failed to offer the reassurance he was so obviously seeking. It would have been easy to say, 'It wasn't your fault,' but would it have been true? Always scrupulously fair, she couldn't help feeling that Chris was really responsible for the quarrel. That wasn't to excuse Tim's behaviour, of course, and she would let him know what she thought of him in no uncertain fashion. All the same, there was something to be said in his defence; but, for now, she was too exhausted to say it.

Irene came to stand behind the sofa, pressing her hands on Penelope's shoulders. 'Why don't you lie down for an hour or two?' she asked. 'Leave all this mess until tomorrow morning, when Mrs Clennan's here to help you. I'll take the morning off as well and give you a hand.'

'No honeymoon, Irene?' Felicity enquired, beginning to stack the dirty crockery from the various tables.

Irene shook her head. 'No, we decided against it. For one thing, there's Deborah.' She indicated her daughter who, worn out at last by the day's excitements, was curled up in an armchair, fast asleep. 'For another, we felt it wasn't really appropriate. And, lastly, Chris may have the offer of a part in a film next month. We can't risk being out of London.' She raised her eyebrows at her husband. 'Darling, I think we really should be going.'

Chris got up, first giving his mother's hand a final squeeze. 'I'll call you in the morning. And give the old man my apologies, will you?'

Ten minutes later, they had gone, to the Hampstead house which, until recently, Irene had shared with

Jeremy. It was an arrangement which Penelope did not care to think about too closely, but it was felt to be in Deborah's best interests. She smiled wanly at Barbara.

'I think I will go and lie down for a bit, if you don't object. You're too old a friend to stand on ceremony with. Oh dear, what a dreadful sentence. Never mind. I'm not writing my deathless prose now. And stop your mother tidying up. Mrs Clennan will see to it in the morning. And in case I'm asleep when your taxi arrives I'll say goodbye. Not', she added dramatically, 'that I'll ever sleep again, but just in case ... ' She managed a wry grin, blew them a kiss and left the room. Barbara and Felicity immediately went into a huddle.

Leaving her mother and grandmother to discuss the events of the day, Anne went in search of Richard, guessing correctly that he would be in the attic. He had discarded his jacket and tie, rolled up his shirt sleeves and was bending over a cardboard box on one of the long trestle-tables. Machiavelli was curled up on the end of the bench, pretending to doze, but in reality keeping a close eye on the proceedings. When she got near enough, Anne could see why: the box contained an injured bird.

'Mac thinks that's his supper,' she said, laughing.

Richard glanced round and smiled a welcome. 'Don't worry.' He pointed to some fine wire mesh. 'That's going over the top to foil him. Poor old chap,' he added fondly. 'His evil little plans are always being thwarted. I take it you've very wisely absconded. What exactly is going on downstairs?'

Anne told him. 'And I think you were wonderful,' she continued, feeling unexpectedly shy and embarrassed, two emotions she had never experienced before in Richard's company. 'The way you spoke up to Chris was splendid.'

Richard looked equally uncomfortable. 'He's my brother,' he replied awkwardly. 'I'm not afraid of him. No reason why I should be, is there?'

'No.' She smiled uncertainly. 'I suppose there isn't.'

The uneasy silence lengthened, neither being able to think of anything else to say. It was suddenly as though they were strangers. Machiavelli, taking advantage of the fact that his master's attention was temporarily distracted, uncoiled himself with sinuous grace, and began picking his way along the table-top, his eyes fixed hungrily on his prey.

Anne smiled nervously. 'I ought to be going. Our taxi will be here very soon. I ... I expect we'll see each other over Christmas. We usually do, if our mothers know anything about it.'

Richard nodded. Then, without warning, he lunged forward, seized her shoulders and kissed her full on the lips. As kisses went, it was fumbling and inexpert; and Anne, who, by now, had been the recipient of a number of amorous embraces from various boy-friends, judged that he had not had much experience in such matters. It might have surprised her, if she had stopped to think about it; her generation, as Barbara never tired of pointing out, enjoyed far more sexual latitude than any previous one. But Anne was too preoccupied with the strange emotions which the kiss had aroused to give Richard's rough-and-ready approach much thought. She felt exactly the way she had always imagined she would feel if Chris kissed her; a little faint, her heart beating much too fast. It was ridiculous, she told herself. Impossible. This was only Richard, her childhood playmate, who was already looking as if he, too, found something ludicrous in the situation.

'Sorry,' he murmured. 'Don't know what came over me. It's been one of those days. Mac! Don't you dare, you monster!' Alerted by the bird's frantic cheeping,

Richard turned with relief to the cat, who was just about to insinuate a lethal paw into the cardboard box. Anne half reached out to touch him, then thought better of it and dropped her hand back to her side. She heard the door at the bottom of the attic stairs open, and her mother's voice calling her name.

'I have to go,' she said. 'Well . . . ' She edged reluctantly towards the door. 'Goodbye, then.'

' 'Bye.' Richard didn't look round. He had picked up the frightened bird and was cradling it between his hands. Machiavelli, balked of his prey, had jumped down and was sulking under the table.

'Anne!' Barbara's shouts were growing insistent. 'It's time to get ready! I know you're up there.'

'I must go,' Anne said desperately. 'See you.'

'See you,' he answered.

She was almost at the door of the room, and still he was refusing to look her way. On an impulse, she went back and kissed his cheek. 'You really were wonderful this afternoon,' she told him. He gave her a quick sidelong glance but made no answer.

Anne went downstairs. Her mother and grandmother were already in their outdoor clothes, waiting for her in the hall. Imogen had appeared to see them off, her eyes red and puffy as though she had been crying. The sisters hugged one another, but said nothing. There really didn't seem to be much to say. Indeed, Anne found herself unable to concentrate on anything or anyone but Richard and the scene in the attic; and in the taxi which took them to the station, and afterwards in the train, she paid only scant attention to Barbara and Felicity, who were discussing the stirring events of the day.

'You're very quiet,' her mother observed as the train pulled out of Swindon. 'Aren't you feeling well? Some of that food was exceedingly rich.'

'I'm fine. Just tired,' Anne said, and lapsed once more into silence.

It was pitch dark by now, and she could see nothing of the countryside beyond the carriage windows, only her own reflection in the glass. She realized with a shock that, for the first time in years, she had left the Haldanes' without giving Chris a second thought. She no longer cared what happened to him, where he went or what he did, and she could see her schoolgirl crush for what it really was. The only person she could think about was Richard, who had so suddenly and unexpectedly replaced his elder brother in her affections.

Perhaps this, too, was just a crush; an ephemeral fleeting emotion she would grow out of. But, somehow, she didn't think so. Looking back, she knew that Richard had always had a corner of her heart. Now it would seem that he had all of it.

CHAPTER TWELVE

PENELOPE STOPPED SPEAKING, switched off the dictating machine, and sat for a few moments, lost in thought, staring in front of her. Then she got up and went through to the outer office, where Imogen was industriously typing. The old caftan, which she had bought years ago in Carnaby Street, billowed around her ankles. With each wash, it grew more faded and more decrepit, but she refused to abandon it. By now, she had a superstitious belief that she couldn't write successfully unless she was wearing it. Above her, the house was quiet. Richard was at school, in the throes of sitting his A levels; Cliff was away on location for yet another film; Tim was touring as Biff in a production of *Death of a Salesman*; Mrs Clennan had failed to put in an appearance because her husband was ill.

Imogen glanced up, lifted her fingers from the keys and switched off her dictaphone. As the chatter of the typewriter and Penelope's recorded voice was momentarily stilled, she could hear birdsong through the open basement windows. Someone, somewhere, was mowing a lawn, and there was the faint sickly-sweet smell of honeysuckle. She said: 'I've nearly finished chapter five, if you want to revise it. I shan't be a few minutes.'

Penelope shook her head and pulled up a chair. 'I want to talk to you. I think it's time we had a chat, don't you?'

Imogen looked genuinely surprised. 'What about?' she queried.

Penelope arranged her caftan more comfortably over her knees. 'About you and Tim,' she answered.

Imogen was immediately defensive, twisting the diamond engagement ring round and round on her finger. 'What's there to discuss?' she demanded.

'Don't take that aggressive tone with me,' Penelope reproved her gently. 'You and Tim have been engaged now for almost two years. Don't you think it's time you got married?'

The blood stained Imogen's cheeks. 'We're not in any hurry.'

Penelope raised her eyebrows. 'You mean Tim isn't in any hurry, don't you?' She hesitated before her next question. 'Are you sleeping together?'

The blush deepened. 'I don't think that's anyone's business but our own.'

'You're quite right.' There was another pause, then Penelope went on: 'There's no reason at all that I can see why you shouldn't get married. Indeed, why you shouldn't have married long ago. What are you waiting for?'

Imogen shrugged, her mouth set in a thin resentful line, her eyes fixed on the sheet of paper in her typewriter. 'We'll get married when we're ready.'

'When Tim's ready, you mean.' Penelope decided the time had come to be ruthless. 'When he's made up his mind it really is you he wants to marry, and stops chasing after Sylvia Gibson.'

'He's not chasing after her!' Tears welled up in Imogen's eyes, but she blinked them away. 'It's me Tim loves. He's told me so, lots of times. He just wants to wait until he's a bit more established as an actor. He doesn't even see Sylvia nowadays if he can help it.'

'She's in *Death of a Salesman* with him,' Penelope answered drily. 'Playing his mother. Did he tell you that?'

'Yes, of course! He tells me everything!' Imogen protested fiercely; but it was obvious to Penelope that she had had no idea. Her fingers had stopped hovering over the typewriter keys and were knotted tightly together in her lap, the knuckles gleaming whitely. She looked, too, as though she might be about to be sick.

'I'm sorry.' Penelope got up and bent over her, putting an arm around Imogen's shoulders. 'Darling, I didn't mean to be cruel, but something has to be done soon about Tim, or you'll lose him. He's my son, and I can't bear the thought of him wasting his life running after a woman who doesn't care two straws for him. I want to see him happily married, with children. I know it's selfish, but I want to be a real grandmother, not just a pretend one to Debbie Grantham. I want *you* for my daughter-in-law.'

Imogen's carefully controlled composure suddenly gave way, and she burst into violent sobbing. 'What can I do?' she asked through her tears. 'I can't force him to love me.'

Penelope did her best to offer comfort, silently reproaching herself for having been so heavy-handed. She had hoped to spur Imogen into some sort of action, to have provoked her into fighting for Tim, but she realized now that she should have known better. Imogen was not the battling type: she folded under outrageous fortune's slings and arrows.

'We'll think of something,' she murmured reassuringly.

But what? she wondered, when, half an hour later, she had coaxed Imogen upstairs to lie down on her bed and, having abandoned work for the day, seated herself, with a long cool drink of iced lemonade, in the quiet drawing-room. She switched on the television, hoping for some cricket to calm her jangled nerves, but it was June and Wimbledon was in progress. Never having played tennis, the game irritated her because she could not understand the rules, so she switched the set off again and began prowling restlessly about the room. If the rest of her day was

165

ruined, she had only herself to blame. She should have been patient and minded her own business; instead, she had stirred things up – a bad habit for which Cliff frequently took her to task.

'Leave the boys alone,' he would beg in exasperation. 'God knows, they're old enough to run their own lives, without you poking your nose in.' But even as he said it they both knew it was like asking King Cnut to turn back the waves.

The rift between her two elder sons worried Penelope and kept her awake at nights. Chris, she had to admit, seemed completely happy, and would have made up the quarrel long ago if Tim had been willing. Not only was his marriage to Irene proving a complete success, but his career, in the past two years, had also taken an upswing. The film he had made, just after his marriage, had set his foot on the first rung of the ladder to ultimate stardom. Made on a small budget, the story about an autistic child was thought, at the time, to have limited appeal but, against all the odds, had proved to be a commercial as well as an artistic success. Chris, playing the part of the boy's drunken father, had given a performance which earned him unanimous critical acclaim and got him nominated for a Hollywood Oscar. As a result, he had been much in demand ever since and his career was thriving.

Tim, on the other hand, continued to struggle for even the slightest recognition, and was not helped by gratuitous press comparisons, on those rare occasions when his work was noticed, with his brother. He had long become inured to his acting being unfavourably compared with Cliff's, and could live with that. There was, after all, only one Sir Clifford Haldane. But being told that his interpretation of Flamineo, in *The White Devil*, was as much like his brother's as a 'candle flame is to the sun' upset him deeply and made him ever more resentful. If he was present when

166

Chris and Irene visited The Laurels, he immediately left the house without speaking to either of them – a state of affairs Penelope felt she could no longer put up with. Richard, if his A levels went well and he got the university of his choice, would be going away to Edinburgh in the autumn, and she would miss his stabilizing presence. She needed to have her other two sons at least outwardly friendly.

She had persuaded herself that Tim's marriage to Imogen was the answer. In moments of honesty, she was forced to admit that she had no sound basis for this conviction; but, for the most part, she was able to ignore the still small voice of reason. And she could think of no-one she would rather Tim married than the daughter of her best and oldest friend. She had been delighted with the news of the engagement, but dismayed by the subsequent delay. The plans she had made for an immediate wedding had come to nothing as, with one excuse after another, Tim and Imogen had put off getting married. So, in this June of 1978, Penelope had decided it was time to take a hand. Her ploy to goad Imogen into action having failed, it was obvious that she would have to use other measures. But the question still remained: What exactly could she do?

Her glance, roaming the room in search of inspiration, fell once again on the television set and reminded her of the tennis. Some words of Tim, before he left on tour, stirred her memory. 'We shall be in Bath for the second week of Wimbledon.' She ran upstairs to her bedroom for the leather-bound diary, which she kept on the lower shelf of her bedside table. In the back was a list showing Tim's tour itinerary, and 'Bath' was scribbled in for one of the last two weeks in June. Triumphantly, she sat on the edge of the bed and dialled the telephone number of Barbara's chambers.

* * *

Anne was sitting in a deck-chair in the garden, surrounded by textbooks and notes, trying to revise for her examination on the history of art, which she was sitting the day after tomorrow. She had sat the practical part of the art exam the previous day, and thought that she had done quite well, so it was essential that she do equally well in the theory. But the warmth of the day was against her, and she had to keep jerking herself back from the borderline of sleep. Perhaps it would have been more sensible to remain at school, like Jackie, who was revising in the cool and calm of the library, instead of opting to come home to do it. However, she had made her choice and must get on with it. She refocused her eyes on the textbook open on her lap.

The telephone rang, its strident tones disturbing the afternoon quiet. Pleased at the distraction, Anne got up and went indoors. It was Penelope.

'Anne? I've just phoned Barbara at work, and that Miss Bates tells me she's off sick. What's the matter with her?'

'The doctor says it's a touch of summer flu. Nothing serious, but she has a slight temperature. Doctor Wright says she must stay in bed for a few days. Did you want to speak to her? I rather think she's asleep. She was when I looked in a little while ago, but I could wake her up if necessary.'

'No, don't do that.' Penelope sounded resigned, almost dispirited. 'Give her my love and say I hope she'll soon be better. It's so unusual for her to be ill,' she added plaintively.

'Was there something you wanted, Aunt Pen? Something I could do for you?' And then, before Penelope could reply, Anne continued: 'How . . . how's Richard?'

'What? Oh, Rich. Yes, he's fine. In the midst of A levels. Which reminds me: you must be, too. How are they going?'

'All right, I think. You can never be sure. But I feel they're going OK. I've applied to Wimbledon, in case you didn't know, to take the course in stage design.'

'Then you must live with us,' Penelope said promptly. 'If Rich goes to Edinburgh, as he hopes, you can have his room during term time. I was only thinking today how empty the house was going to be without him. You'll be a wonderful substitute.'

Anne felt her heart miss a beat. 'Rich wants Edinburgh?' she asked hollowly. 'But why? It's so far away.'

'That's what I said,' Penelope sighed. 'But he's got this bee in his bonnet that for veterinary training it's the best. Been reading too many of those James Herriot books, I shouldn't wonder.' She hesitated, then went on: 'Look, Anne love, the reason I phoned your mother was that Tim's appearing in Bath all this week. I was going to ask her to go over and see him and act the heavy mother. Ask Tim what the hell he's playing at, and when he and Imogen are going to get married. The delay's all his doing, I'm sure of it. And when Cliff gets back from Italy I'll make him have a word as well. If we all lean on Tim, he won't have any option but to set a date. I'm pretty certain Imogen won't raise any objections.'

It flitted through Anne's mind that pressuring Tim – or anyone, for that matter – into making a decision against his will was an unwise thing to do. She suppressed the thought, however. Apart from wanting her sister's happiness, and being young enough to desire a wedding for its own sake, she had her private reasons for wishing to see the two families united by marriage. It brought her that much closer to Richard.

'I could go over and see him,' she offered, 'if you tell me where to find him. I don't have another exam until the day after tomorrow, and our time's our own

169

in between. I don't suppose I'll be as heavyweight as Mum, but I'll do my best.'

Once again, Penelope hesitated. At the back of her mind, she had the feeling that, had she been able to speak to Barbara, her friend might have refused the challenge: Barbara had never been one for interfering or trying to influence people against their natural inclinations. Even the girls, once she had realized that they were serious in their choice of careers, she had allowed to go their own way. So ought she to encourage Anne to do something of which her mother might disapprove? But it was not in Penelope's nature to stand idly by and do nothing.

'Well . . . I suppose you could go, if you're free. But shouldn't you be doing revision tomorrow?'

'Officially, yes. But, honestly, Aunt Pen, I don't think I could cram another fact into my head if I tried. Last-minute revision is never much good anyway. I can go over by bus and look round the shops afterwards. It would make a nice day out. Gran's looking after Mum.'

'Perhaps you really ought to consult Barbara first,' Penelope suggested uneasily.

'Well . . . I don't think I'll say anything about meeting Tim. I mean, I don't want to worry her as she's ill. Whereabouts is Tim staying in Bath?'

Penelope gave her an address in Widcombe, her voice sinking to a conspiratorial whisper, although there was no-one around to overhear. Anne wrote it down on the pad beside the phone, then tore off the top sheet and slipped it in her pocket.

'I'll try to ring you tomorrow night,' she promised, 'and let you know what happens.'

After she had replaced the receiver, Anne stood for a few moments, staring sightlessly at the picture on the wall, a reproduction of 'Ladies Reading' by John Singer Sargent. Richard was going to Edinburgh

University, if he could get in; hundreds of miles away. She shivered, suddenly cold in spite of the warmth of the day. Then she shook herself mentally. It wasn't the end of the world. He would be home in the vacations: they would see each other, especially if she were living in the same house. Aunt Pen had said that she could use his room; up in the attic with Cloud and Mac. They would be missing Rich, too. They could comfort one another. And in the meantime she could bring herself and Richard closer together by ensuring that Tim married Imogen. She had no clear idea of what she was going to say to Tim in order to bring this about; all she knew was that it was a consummation devoutly to be wished. Which reminded her that she ought to be revising *Hamlet* for her first English exam next week. Some of her misgivings returned, but she resolutely shrugged them off. She would go over to Bath tomorrow and try to talk some sense into Tim.

Sylvia pushed Tim away, sat up in bed and reached for her packet of cigarettes. Her hands shook slightly as she lit one.

'How the hell did I get myself into this situation?' she demanded of the room at large. 'I must be the world's number-one prize idiot.'

The morning sunlight sifted through curtains of a particularly virulent purple rep, violently at odds with an orange-and-brown patterned carpet and a peacock-blue bedspread, quilted and ruched in some repulsive shiny material. The furniture, consisting of bed, wardrobe, two bedside cabinets and a chair, was cheap and equally shiny. The washbasin in one corner had a dripping tap, and the basin itself was streaked with green. As theatrical digs went, Sylvia had seen worse, a lot worse, but the Victorian boarding-house in Widcombe was nevertheless depressing; although

171

her own room, across the landing, did overlook the back garden.

Tim's arms slipped around her waist as he cuddled into her back. He kissed her bare shoulder. 'You're here because you love me,' he said confidently.

Sylvia dragged on her cigarette and blew a cloud of blue smoke down both nostrils. Once again, she freed herself from Tim's clutches and swung her legs out of bed.

'I don't love you, Tim,' she replied with suppressed violence. 'For heaven's sake, do yourself a favour and stop pretending. I slept with you last night because you'd worn me down with your importuning. You haven't let up since the start of the tour – nagging, nagging, nagging. You've worn me to a frazzle, and it's played hell with my performance. I only agreed because I thought it might get it out of your system and you'd leave me alone for the next two weeks.' She did not add that she had been feeling desperately lonely, or that he had reminded her poignantly of Chris. 'I knew it was a mistake agreeing to take this part with you in the cast, but I persuaded myself that you'd be sensible, especially as you're engaged to Imogen Seymour. You ought to have contacted your future in-laws, I suppose you know that. I don't believe you've even let them know that you're here.'

'I don't want to see them,' Tim answered sulkily. 'They're bound to want to know when Imogen and I are going to get married.'

'And when are you?' Sylvia demanded.

'Never,' he told her eagerly, rolling once more towards her, dragging the loosened bedclothes with him. 'Not if you'll have me. I'll break off the engagement tomorrow. Today. Just say the word. Please, Sylvia. Darling!'

She stood up swiftly, as if his touch might burn her, stubbing out her cigarette in a blue pottery ashtray and grabbing her discarded pyjamas and dressing-gown from the chair. A pair of feathered mules lay abandoned on the floor. Sylvia wriggled her feet into them, then turned to face Tim.

'I've told you,' she said fiercely. 'I don't love you. I don't want you. Last night was a terrible mistake. Sweet Christ, can't you understand that? All the time we were making love, I was pretending you were Chris!' She glanced at Tim's travelling clock on the bedside table and groaned. 'Dear heaven, it's nearly ten-thirty! Mrs Bigwell, or Bidwell, or whatever she's called, will be up to do the bedrooms in a minute. I don't want her finding me here like this, even if she is used to "loose-living theatricals". She's been clattering around downstairs for ages, now I come to think about it. And there's the front doorbell. It could be Fred. He said he might call round this morning, and I don't want the rest of the company getting any wrong impressions about our relationship.'

Tim got out of bed and came towards her. 'Sylvia, don't go. You loved me once. Why can't you love me again?'

He tried to take her in his arms, but she wrenched herself free. 'We've been through all this, Tim!' she shouted at him, losing control and not caring who heard her. 'Get bloody lost!'

The bedroom door opened. 'Tim!' Anne's voice preceded her. 'Your landlady said to come on up. I told her I was your fiancée's sister.' She was inside the room now, and her arrested gaze took in the scene before her. Her cheeks turned scarlet. 'I'm ... I'm sorry. . . ' She realized suddenly who the woman was and she gave a strangled gasp. Her impulse was to turn and run headlong down the stairs and never see Tim again, but somehow or other she forced herself to stand her ground.

Sylvia swore and shrugged on her dressing-gown. Tim snatched the quilt from the bed and wrapped it round him.

'Annie!' He sounded dazed. 'What are *you* doing here? And how did you know I was in Bath?'

'Aunt Pen told me and gave me the address. I came', she added furiously, 'to talk about you and Im and when you're going to get married. But I can see I've had a wasted journey.'

'No, you haven't.' Sylvia pushed past Anne to the door. 'This was a one-night stand, and the biggest, stupidest mistake of my life. I've just told Tim that, in case you don't believe me. If you can knock some sense into his silly head, I'll be forever grateful. 'Bye for now, Tim. See you tonight at the theatre, but just keep out of my way until then.'

She went, closing the bedroom door behind her. Anne was left alone with Tim. He slumped on to the bed. 'I can't believe she really means it,' he said.

Against all the odds, Anne found herself feeling sorry for him. He looked so pathetic, so abjectly forlorn, that her heart went out to him. There was a fleeting look of Richard about him, which she had never noticed before; an expression of the eyes which tugged at her heart-strings. She stopped being angry and went to sit beside him on the bed.

'Tim.' She shyly squeezed his arm. 'It's silly to go on chasing after someone who so obviously doesn't want you, when there's someone else who loves you very much. You're engaged to Imogen, for heaven's sake!' A little of her anger returned, and the squeeze became a shake. 'You had no right asking her to marry you, if you didn't mean it. Everyone would be so pleased if you set the date. You've been engaged for nearly two years, and I don't think you're being very fair to Im, keeping her hanging about like this.'

Tim avoided her accusing eyes, but he looked uncomfortable and shamefaced. 'I know,' he muttered. 'It's just that . . . I wanted to be sure.'

'You can be sure of one thing.' Anne surprised herself with the way in which she was handling the situation. 'Sylvia doesn't love you, and never has. She wouldn't have married Chris otherwise, would she? And, even though he's treated her so badly, she still wants him. My guess is that she'd have him back tomorrow, if he decided it was her he loved, after all, and not Irene. So why don't you just admit it to yourself, get dressed and call Imogen? There's a phone downstairs in the hall. I noticed it as I came in. It's the only sensible thing to do, and you know it.'

He turned his head slowly and looked at her. His eyes were blank with misery, and she was afraid that her arguments had fallen on deaf ears. But, after a moment, his hand crept out to grasp one of hers. 'I know,' he answered in a suffocating voice. 'And I am very fond of Imogen. Truly.'

'Well, then!' Anne's voice was full of artificial brightness, and she made herself ignore the misgivings of her heart. 'That's all right! You and Im will get on together famously, and once you're married you'll forget all about Sylvia Gibson.'

His hand tightened on hers, like a frightened child seeking reassurance. 'Promise you'll be around if I need you.'

'How . . . how do you mean?' She was suddenly wary.

There was a momentary silence. Then Tim shrugged. 'Just promise that you'll be around. I like you, Annie. You're like Rich. You're comforting to be with.'

He seemed to have difficulty in explaining any further, so Anne did not press him. 'I'll certainly always be your friend,' she said, 'if that's what you mean.'

He nodded, released her hand and stood up. 'I'll get

175

dressed now. Wait for me down in the hall, and we'll phone Imogen together. I shan't be long.'

He was as good as his word, and joined her in the dark hallway, with its depressing brown wallpaper, within ten minutes. He had not bothered to shave, but with muttered apologies said that he would do so later. He slotted in his money and dialled the London number. It was obviously Penelope who answered.

'Hi, Ma! Let me speak to Imogen, would you?' There was a moment's hiatus before he went on: 'Im! Darling. I've got Annie here with me. She wants to know when we're going to set a wedding date, so I thought I'd call you and we can do it right away . . . Yes, this minute . . . I don't know. Just pick one out of the air . . .OK. The first of September. I'll leave it to you to make all the arrangements.'

Standing beside him, Anne was suddenly frightened, wondering what exactly she had done; what burden she had taken upon her shoulders.

CHAPTER THIRTEEN

'ANNE! ANNE!' Ivo Kingsley had to run, dodging in and out of the Saturday-afternoon crowds thronging Oxford Street, to catch up with his quarry. Drawing abreast of her, he grabbed Anne's arm, laughing and panting. 'Hey! Slow down. Where are you going in such a hurry?'

Anne swore under her breath. She was aware that Ivo had been trying to attract her attention for some moments past, so she had feigned deafness. He was becoming something of a problem.

Anne had won a coveted place on the stage design course at the Wimbledon School of Art the previous autumn, and had come to London to live with Penelope and Clifford. Ivo Kingsley was at RADA, in his second year; and the acting bug, which ran so fiercely in the Haldane blood, had resulted in his being already marked down as one of the more promising male students. Moreover, his natural arrogance gave him the necessary panache for the heroic classical roles. In the two and a half years since Chris and Irene's wedding, his face had lost some of its plumpness; and, although he would never be traditionally good-looking, he would find no difficulty in obtaining romantic leads.

Anne said: 'I can't stop, Ivo. I'm sorry.'

He made a moue of disappointment, which might or might not have been genuine. There was no shortage of girls interested in Ivo – a fact of which he was well aware – but Anne's very indifference to him was a challenge. He pursued her relentlessly and, although he shared a small flat just off Tottenham Court Road with two other students from the Royal Academy, he consistently managed to get himself asked to The Laurels for meals. Anne had hinted to Penelope that she found this something of a strain, but as it was not her house, and Ivo was Clifford's cousin, her hints had been too subtle to be effective.

'I think it's nice for you to have someone of your own age around,' Penelope had said on the occasion of Ivo's last visit. 'This house is like a morgue, now that the boys have all left home. And now that Tim and Imogen are married you don't even have her for company.'

Anne had refrained from pointing out that she had plenty of friends of her own choosing, because she was conscious that she brought very few of them home. Her fellow-students fell mostly into two categories: those who were too shy and overwhelmed to accept an invitation to meet Sir Clifford Haldane, and those who would have shamelessly made use of him, trading on his good nature and fondness for herself. So she confined her social life to pubs, cinemas, coffee-bars and other people's flats. It had crossed her mind on more than one occasion that she would be better off in a place of her own, and she had been offered a share in more than one friend's bed-sitter, but two considerations militated against her acceptance. First, she knew it would upset Penelope, who liked having her around; and, second, she would miss Richard's occasional flying visits home, plus those times when their paths crossed at the beginning of vacations. She therefore had little option but to remain in St John's Wood and endure Ivo's frequent visits.

Ivo said: 'Let's go and have a coffee. No. A better idea. Why don't you come and have dinner with me at the flat? The others will be out tonight. They're going to the Lyttleton to see that new Simon Gray thing – *Close of Play*, I think it's called – so we'll have the flat to ourselves. What do you say? Go on! Say "Yes, please".'

'I'm sorry, Ivo.' Anne freed her arm. 'I've promised to spend the evening with Imogen and Tim. I really ought to go. I'm late already.'

Although it was the final week of May, there was still a nip in the air, after a winter which had seen what the popular press had termed the Great Freeze. Anne, who had rashly chosen to wear a thinner blouse and jacket, deceived by some early-afternoon sunshine, now found herself shivering in a sharp breeze which whipped along the pavement, sending sweet- and chocolate-wrappers bowling along the gutters. Ivo was immediately all concern.

'You're not dressed warmly enough,' he protested. 'Look, come round to the flat and I'll lend you one of my sweaters.'

Anne hesitated. She wasn't really late. Imogen had invited her to supper, and it was only just after four o'clock. However, they would eat early because, at the moment, Tim had a small part in one of the productions at the National. It was his first role for some time, and for most of the nine months since their marriage it had been Imogen's salary that they had relied on. Imogen still retained her job as Penelope's secretary, and worked, weekdays, from nine until four-thirty at The Laurels. Little wonder, therefore, Anne reflected, that there was no talk of children. She had no idea how much help Tim received from Clifford and Penelope, either directly or, far more likely, indirectly, but suspected that it was considerable. She knew that her mother and grandmother did what they could in the way of extra-special presents whenever possible.

'Well?' Ivo asked. 'Are you coming?'

The strengthening wind caught them a buffet, and Anne nodded. As they turned into Tottenham Court Road, Ivo put an arm around her shoulders. Anne tensed, wishing she had never decided to go shopping but had gone straight to Earls Court. If Ivo felt this resistance, he gave no sign, but continued to press her closer, at the same time pursuing a totally impersonal line of conversation. What would the country's first-ever woman prime minister and the new Tory government mean for the arts? A topic which lasted them until they reached Ivo's flat.

This was over a greengrocer's shop on the corner of a side-street. Anne had been there on three previous occasions, to parties, but this was the first time she had seen it in daylight. The street-door, which Ivo unlocked, was coated with peeling and faded paint, while the narrow flight of stairs inside twisted upwards into darkness. A strong smell of rotten vegetables pervaded everything. Ivo flicked down a switch, and the stairs were flooded with a harsh white light from a bulb hanging over the stairwell. He led the way up, his feet clattering on the uncarpeted treads.

The living accommodation comprised a kitchen-dining-room and two small bedrooms, all of which, seen through the open doors, were as untidy as each other. Clothes were strewn across floors and unmade beds, a stack of unwashed crockery filled the sink and yesterday's papers still littered the three arm-chairs.

'Squalid, isn't it?' Ivo laughed. 'Hold on, while I find you that sweater.' He disappeared into one of the two bedrooms, emerging after a couple of minutes with a pale-lemon V-necked woollen pullover in his hands. 'Here,' he said, holding it out. 'I thought it would go with that grey blouse you're wearing.'

Surprised, and a little touched, by such foresight, Anne slipped off her denim jacket to reveal fully the short-sleeved dove-grey cotton blouse beneath. She wore, as well, a pair of much-worn and slightly scruffy jeans, which clung lovingly to the contours of her legs and hips, while her slim waistline was emphasized by a wide, glossy, chestnut-coloured leather belt. The straight fair hair was swept back into a pony-tail, tied with a scarlet ribbon, showing off to advantage the fine bone structure of the delicate heart-shaped face. She looked as though a puff of wind might blow her over, but was, as she so often laughingly said of herself, as 'strong as a horse'.

She slipped the sweater over her head and was busy wriggling her arms into the sleeves when she was seized in a bear-like hug and Ivo's lips descended roughly on hers. Caught off-guard and thrown off-balance, she toppled over into one of the threadbare armchairs, Ivo sprawled on top of her. For a moment, she found herself almost enjoying the sensation, before anger took over. Exerting all her strength, she pushed against his shoulders, at the same moment managing to bite his lower lip. With a sharp cry of pain, he rolled off her on to the floor, where he sat trying to staunch the blood flowing from his rapidly swelling mouth.

'You bitch!' he protested as well as he could.

'You shouldn't have tried it on, Ivo.' Anne stood up, pulling the sweater down around her hips. 'This isn't the Dark Ages, you know. Next time, just ask if I mind before you kiss me.'

'Who says there'll be a next time?' he demanded, but the words came out oddly, hampered by his bloated bottom lip. 'You do realize, I suppose,' he went on in the same garbled sound, 'that I'm playing Trinculo in a scene from *The Tempest* in class on Monday? How the hell am I going to do it now?'

Guiltily, Anne surveyed the damage she had wrought. It was his own fault; but her reaction, she felt, had been a shade too drastic. She went over to the sink, rinsed out a cup and filled it with cold water. 'Do you have any TCP and cotton wool?' she asked him.

This, however, was expecting too much, it seemed, so she had to make do with a clean handkerchief, which she found in her shoulder-bag, turning it into a cold compress with some ice cubes from the fridge. When the swelling had gone down a little, she was relieved to see that the actual damage to Ivo's lip was negligible: a very slight wound, but one which had torn the soft inner flesh – a fact which accounted for the copious bleeding.

'The least you can do is make me a cup of coffee,' he mumbled after a few minutes.

Anne surveyed the kitchen area with deep misgivings. 'You mean you'd rather die of food poisoning than blood poisoning. Oh, well, I'll see what I can do. Wait there.'

She managed to find a jar of instant coffee, a half-full bag of sugar and a waxed-cardboard carton of milk, whose sell-by date was already two days old. She retrieved two mugs from the sink and washed them carefully, relieved to discover that the flat at least possessed a good supply of hot water. A minute or so later, she resumed her seat on the floor beside Ivo and handed him one of the mugs, filled with steaming coffee. He took it gratefully, but gave a yelp of pain as the hot liquid scalded his torn lip.

'You're bloody determined to get me one way or the other, aren't you?' he demanded fretfully.

Anne suppressed a strong desire to laugh and slid an arm around his neck, at the same time giving his cheek a friendly peck. He really wasn't too bad when one got to know him. There was a sense of the ridiculous lurking beneath all that arrogance and carefully cultivated charm. He glanced sideways at her, then put down his mug and turned his head to return the kiss – a gentle salutation on her slightly parted mouth. Then he drew away and regarded her speculatively.

'Friends?' he asked.

'Friends,' she agreed. He was certainly very attractive and, had it not been that she loved Richard, she felt she might have enjoyed a brief fling with Ivo. Even as it was, she was perfectly willing to accept this new phase in their relationship.

'And you'll stop all this nonsense of avoiding me and pretending you don't hear when I'm chasing after you, shouting your name and waving my arms about like a demented windmill? And don't bother to deny it. I'm not quite such an idiot as you take me for.' He kissed her again, but in a brotherly spirit, without passion.

Anne coloured guiltily. 'Was it so obvious?'

'Obvious? People three or four yards in front of you were turning their heads to see what lunatic was disturbing the peace.'

'I'm sorry,' she said penitently. 'I promise it won't happen again. You're not such a bad sort really.'

'Thanks. Remind me to come to you when I need a character reference.' He sipped his coffee, which was cooling rapidly. He seemed about to add something further, but there was the sudden clatter of feet on the uncarpeted stairs and, a moment later, the living-room door burst open as the other two students, with whom he shared the flat, came in. They were laughing, chatting over the day's events, and did not immediately notice Anne. When they did, they both grinned knowingly.

'Oops!' Melanie Hibbert, a tall girl with strong, rather masculine features, which marked her down as a potential character actress, subsided into one of the armchairs. 'Have we interrupted something?'

183

'Not at all.' Anne scrambled to her feet. 'I was just going, as it happens. I should have been at Earls Court a quarter of an hour ago.'

Ron Townsend, a small vital man, with darkly piercing eyes and the lilting tones of the Welsh valleys, said: 'Thought you lived in St John's Wood. You're Sir Clifford Haldane's niece, aren't you?' He nodded towards Ivo. 'Everyone in the bleedin' place seems to be related to him.'

'A gross exaggeration,' Anne replied, slipping her jacket on over Ivo's yellow sweater. 'And I'm not Sir Clifford's niece nor any relation to him. It just happens that my mother and Lady Haldane are very old friends. I've known the family all my life.'

Melanie was regarding Ivo with interest. 'What have you done to your lip?' she asked. 'It's all swollen. Looks like a dirty great love-bite to me.'

Ivo got to his feet, grinning, while Ron Townsend said disapprovingly: 'You don't make personal remarks like that, girl. Not when you're sharing a flat.' He held out his hand to Anne. 'Nice to have met you properly. I've seen you around.'

'Yes.' Melanie Hibbert also held out a hand, although she made no attempt to get out of her chair. 'Sorry if I spoke out of turn just now.'

'Why didn't you say something?' Anne demanded furiously as Ivo accompanied her downstairs to the street-door. The smell of vegetables was again over-whelmingly potent.

Ivo grinned lazily. 'I thought you deserved a little punishment. And, after all, Mel wasn't completely wrong.'

'Oh, you're impossible!' Anne exclaimed indignantly. 'We're friends. Nothing more. Remember!'

'Yes, ma'am.' The hazel eyes, in the cherubic face, met hers with a deadpan seriousness which forced her into a reluctant grin.

'No stepping out of line,' she warned him.

But when he had closed the door behind her he stood for a minute or two, resting his back against the wall, staring at nothing in particular, his expression suddenly serious. His tongue probed the cut inside his lower lip, but he felt nothing. He had liked Anne from the first moment they had met, at Chris and Irene's wedding. He found it difficult to analyse exactly what it was about her that attracted him so strongly. She had made it plain, even then, that she thought him brash and pushy – facts of which he was himself well aware, but which, he felt, were necessary attributes for a budding actor, and one, moreover, who intended to be successful. But her transparent disapproval had in no way undermined his liking for her; nor had that liking diminished in the intervening nine months before he returned once more to London, to take up an acting scholarship at RADA. During the year which followed, he had seen her briefly, on odd occasions when she visited the Haldanes and he managed to wangle himself an invitation for Sunday lunch or dinner. Her indifference to him was both a spur and a challenge to one who normally had no difficulty in attracting whatever girl he fancied; but it was also more than that. The genuine liking for her was as strong as ever.

Her arrival, the previous September, as a permanent term-time guest of the Haldanes, while she studied stage design, engendered in him a state of near-euphoria. He began to haunt The Laurels. But nothing he did or said seemed to make any impression on Anne, who continued to treat him as a nuisance, to be avoided at all costs. Until this evening. Now, quite suddenly and for no apparent reason, she had mellowed towards him.

When she had kissed his cheek, his first impulse had been to seize her and smother her in an ardent embrace.

Fortunately, the mug of coffee he was holding had acted as a natural deterrent. By the time he had put it down, he had had time to reflect on the unwisdom of any such action. A cunning entirely foreign to his nature prompted him to take a casual approach. Win her trust and friendship first, said a voice inside him. The rest can come later. That there would be more, he had no doubt whatsoever. Already, he was beginning to think of her as his girlfriend. Suddenly galvanized into life, he went bounding up the stairs, two at a time. Under his breath, he was whistling.

'Sorry I'm late. I got held up by Ivo Kingsley.' Breathlessly, Anne dropped her jacket and shoulder-bag on a convenient chair and crossed the room to hug her sister. She noticed how thin and fragile Imogen was looking. 'You're working too hard,' she reproached her.

Tim and Imogen's two-bedroomed flat was on the third floor of a faceless block erected in the late nineteen forties, in a flurry of postwar activity, when homes were urgently needed to replace the thousands that had been destroyed in the Blitz. *Functional* had been the watchword in those days, with the result that architectural embellishment had been kept to a bare minimum, and Anne always found the outside of the building grim and forbidding. The corridors, lifts and staircases gave her much the same feeling, but once safely inside the flat she was more in harmony with her surroundings.

Imogen had proved herself to be a natural home-maker, doing wonders with limited resources. Some of the furniture Anne recognized as having come from either The Laurels or from College Close; other pieces were obviously secondhand. But all of them were lovingly restored and polished, and vases of flowers brightened all the rooms. Anne reflected that this ability was something Imogen had inherited from their grandmother. Barbara had never been gifted at turning a house into a home. Anne trusted that when she married Richard – as she had no doubt, one day, she would – she would be able to make him equally comfortable. She only hoped that Tim appreciated her sister's loving efforts.

'Everything OK?' she enquired. 'Where's Tim?'

Imogen shrugged. 'I found a note when I got back half an hour ago. He says he's gone over to Julia Berry's place, so they can run through one of their scenes together. Apparently the producer thinks it could be improved. He'll be home soon. The performance starts at seven-thirty, and he's on stage at rise of curtain. He needs to be at the theatre at least by half-past six to fix his make-up.'

Anne found herself wondering where Tim really was, then dismissed the thought as unworthy. Whatever affection he still retained for Sylvia Gibson, she certainly felt nothing for him. Anne remembered the angry way she had spoken to him, that day nearly a year ago now, in Bath. However compromising the situation had been, Anne had no real doubt that Sylvia regretted her part in it, and that it would not happen again. Indeed, rumour had it that Sylvia had recently thrown away the torch she had been carrying all this time for Chris, and had acquired a new man-friend, who had moved into her flat; her accountant, Anne had been informed by one of her fellow-students, who always had her ear close to the theatrical grapevine. Anne wondered if Tim knew yet.

Imogen called from the kitchen: 'Steak and salad all right? Or are you going through one of your vegetarian periods?'

Anne wandered over to the kitchen door and propped herself against the jamb. 'That's fine. You ought to know that no-one can be a vegetarian if they're living

187

with Penelope. Mrs Clennan gets highly offended if you don't eat every morsel, and she's a great believer in the dietary benefits of meat.'

'Yes, I remember.' Imogen laughed, but to Anne it sounded forced.

'You're sure everything's all right?' she asked again.

'Why shouldn't it be?' Imogen switched on the grill, unwrapped the steaks and began pounding them with her rolling-pin. 'You could wash the lettuce for me, if you like. While these are cooking, I'll mix the ingredients for the dressing.'

Anne picked up the lettuce, which her sister had left on the draining-board, and started to wash it under the tap. There was something amiss, she felt certain. Imogen's manner was strained, and once again Anne was haunted by the fear that forcing Tim into marriage had been the wrong thing to do. But whenever she tried to share her misgivings with Penelope the older woman summarily dismissed them.

'Nonsense! Anne love, some people need a helping hand to point them in the right direction. Tim's like that. What we did, we did for his own good. He and Imogen are very happy.'

And Anne had to admit that, for a while, they had indeed appeared to be. It was only in recent months that she had begun to worry; to have renewed fears about the part she had played in arranging the marriage. It was nothing she could put her finger on; just a feeling, when she saw Tim and Imogen together, that all was not well.

'You're not pregnant, are you?' she asked bluntly.

There was silence. Then her sister said quietly: 'As a matter of fact, I am.'

'Im! That's marvellous!' Anne dropped the lettuce in the sink and turned to embrace her. 'How excited everyone will be! Have you told Mum and Penelope?' A thought struck her. 'Does Tim know?'

Imogen extricated herself from the bear-like hug and returned her attention to the grill, where the steaks were hissing and spitting. 'No, not yet. No-one does, except you.'

'But, for heaven's sake, why not?' Anne was incredulous. 'I should have thought you'd want to trumpet it from the roof-tops. I know I should, if it were me.'

'Well, you're not me.' Imogen's tone was curt. 'I'll let them know in my own good time. I only found out, myself, two days ago. I . . . I just wanted some time to get used to the idea, before everyone else started fussing.'

'Of course. How silly of me.' Anne kissed her sister's cheek. 'I didn't mean to be critical. Look, I've finished doing the lettuce. I'll go and lay the table.'

'Anne!' Imogen held out her hand. 'I'm sorry. I shouldn't have been so short with you. And I'm glad you're the first to know. Honestly.'

Anne nodded, reassured. Pregnancy did odd things to women, or so her mother and grandmother had always told her. It explained her sister's funny moods of late. She began to hum softly under her breath. In nine months' time, she would be an aunt. She wondered happily if she would have a nephew or a niece as she laid the dining-room table with three places. Everything was going to be all right after all. She could stop feeling guilty.

Imogen came through from the kitchen with two plates. 'The steak's ready,' she said. 'We might as well go on. I've put Tim's to keep hot in the oven. Serves him right if it's overdone. I told him what time we'd be eating.'

Again, there was that abrasive note in Imogen's voice. Anne's contentment was jarred a little. Then she told herself not to be stupid: all wives got annoyed when their husbands were late for meals. She helped

189

herself to salad and attacked her steak. It was too rare for her liking, but she forced herself to eat it. She was, in fact, bravely swallowing the final mouthful, when she heard Tim's key in the lock. The front door opened and shut, and he crossed the small lobby. Imogen did not look up.

He stood in the open doorway, swaying slightly and beaming at them. 'Hi, Annie! Forgot you were coming. Sorry I'm sho late.' He made his way to the table and sat down. Imogen rose without a word to fetch his dinner.

Anne stared at him, her heart sinking. She could smell the whisky on his breath, and she wondered how often nowadays he came home drunk.

CHAPTER FOURTEEN

RICHARD DUMPED HIS CASES on the hall floor and shouted: 'I'm home! Anyone around?'

There was an immediate surge of activity. The hitherto silent rooms disgorged their various occupants, like characters in a fairy-tale, webbed in an enchanted sleep until such time as he returned to wake them. Penelope came rushing upstairs from the basement, to fling her arms about his neck and plant a resounding kiss on one thin cheek; Anne appeared on the first-floor landing, leaning over the banisters, her little, heart-shaped face split wide in a delighted grin; Mrs Clennan bustled through from the kitchen, an oven-glove in one hand, a tea-towel in the other, determined not to be left out of the family welcome; while Clifford emerged from the small cluttered back room, known euphemistically as the study, pausing for dramatic effect while he pressed a slightly blood-stained handkerchief to his mouth.

'Dear boy.' He embraced his youngest son. 'You behold me, bloody but unbowed, from the hands of the dentist.'

'Take no notice of him,' Penelope advised disgustedly. 'He's only had a minor extraction and a filling. The way he carries on, you'd think it was major surgery.'

Richard laughed. 'And Daniel Hartley's one of the best dentists in the world, Dad. You've always said so.'

Clifford regarded his wife and son reproachfully. 'Dan Hartley is. But Dan, unfortunately, is sick. I had

191

to suffer at the less competent hands of his assistant. I think he must have an O level in metalwork. Anne my dear, come and bear witness to the torment I have been in.'

Anne, who had by now reached the bottom of the stairs, shook her head at him. 'You were in the kitchen half an hour ago, scoffing chocolate biscuits.' She smiled shyly. 'Hello, Rich. Welcome home. I've moved out of your attic, by the way. I'm in one of the guest rooms until *I* go home at the end of next week.'

He regarded her equally shyly. 'Aren't you coming down to Devon with us this year?'

'I've asked her until I'm blue in the face,' Penelope told him. 'But she reckons she has too much studying to do in the holidays. Perhaps you can persuade her to change her mind.'

'I'll try,' Richard offered. 'Now, what about some food? I seem to have been on that train for ever.'

'Heavens, yes! You must be starving.' Penelope turned with a swirl of her caftan. 'Mrs Clennan stayed on specially to cook a late lunch for us. It's all ready, so we can eat at once. Leave your cases; you can unpack later. At whatever ungodly hour did you leave Edinburgh this morning?' And, without waiting for Richard's reply, she led the way into the dining-room.

After the first pangs of hunger had been assuaged, and Mrs Clennan complimented on her steak-and-kidney pie, always his favourite, Richard asked: 'How's Imogen? I was thrilled with the news that I'm going to be an uncle. What was Tim's reaction?'

There was a fractional pause before Anne and Penelope spoke together.

'Delighted, naturally.' That was his mother.

'Over the moon,' Anne assured him.

Richard glanced instinctively towards his father, but Clifford appeared to be totally absorbed in the necessity of eating on only one side of his mouth. 'I don't think that fellow even has an O level,' he said fretfully.

Richard looked thoughtful, but made no further comment until Mrs Clennan had removed the empty dinner-plates and replaced them with dishes of fruit salad and clotted cream, listening to his mother and Anne's bright inconsequential chatter about the possible choice of babies' names.

'Poor Imogen's suffering from morning sickness at the moment,' Penelope added. 'But she insists on coming to work. She was even willing to come in today, Saturday. I ask you! I had to put my foot down.'

The dining-room door closed softly behind Mrs Clennan. Richard stopped chasing an elusive piece of apple around his dish and laid down his spoon. 'Is Tim all right?' he asked his mother. 'There was a piece in one of the national dailies, a few weeks ago, about his understudy having to go on for him because he was indisposed. Reading between the lines, there was an implication that illness was not the real reason.'

Penelope was immediately on the defensive. 'What a load of nonsense! I read the piece myself, and I know what you mean. It makes me furious. If Tim weren't our son, no-one would be interested in his doings. It's most unfair! Of course he wasn't well. What other reason could there be for him to miss a performance? Anyway, the run of the play has ended now, so perhaps the gossip columnists will leave him alone.'

Clifford said quietly: 'Tim *is* drinking. And it's no good you springing to his defence, Pen. He's drinking quite heavily, and you know it. He was too drunk to go on that time, which is why they had to employ the understudy. Some "friend" tipped off the press, but the reporter was too cautious to use the information without proof. Hence the subtle hints and underlying tone of vilification. Unless Tim pulls himself together pretty soon, he'll find no management will touch him. Once you get a name for unreliability in our business, no-one wants to know you.'

'But lots of actors drink,' Anne protested, alarmed for Imogen's sake by this gloomy picture. 'And some of them drink quite heavily.'

Clifford shrugged. 'If you're a big name, a money-spinner, you can afford to take a few chances; but, even so, you have to watch it. Let too many people down too many times and it doesn't matter how big a star you are. Money's the name of the game in both the commercial and the subsidized theatre. And other actors don't want to work with someone they can't rely on.'

Richard frowned. 'Is Tim's problem as bad as you're saying?'

'No, of course not! Your father's exaggerating as usual.' Penelope resolutely changed the subject. 'So what's your news? You've told us hardly anything about yourself and what you've been up to. So get started.'

And Richard, recognizing the voice of authority, obeyed.

During her stay in St John's Wood, Regent's Park had become one of Anne's favourite haunts, particularly Queen Mary's Garden, with its lake, cascading rockeries and magical rose plantation. Sir William Reid Dick's delicately carved statue, 'Boy with the Frog', had become like a personal friend, to whom she went for comfort and solace whenever she felt depressed. But this afternoon, strolling along the paths with Richard, happy in the expectation that, at any moment, he would reach out and take her hand, she felt on top of the world. Nothing, not even her ever-present worry about Imogen, had the power to spoil the warm late-June sunshine or her pleasure in the rainbow-hued banks of flowers. When Richard had suggested a walk, to counteract the effects of Mrs Clennan's calorie-packed cooking, she had agreed at once, only stopping to change her much lived in jeans and sweatshirt for her prettiest summer dress. This was a dove-grey cotton, whose colour exactly matched that of her eyes, patterned with a tiny print of pale-pink geometrical figures. Its full swirling skirt emphasized her slender waist, while the fitted bodice showed up the contours of her breasts. These were an increasing source of pride to her, because, when younger, she had feared she was going to be flat-chested. But suddenly, around the age of sixteen, she had begun to fill out, and now, three years later, she was quietly pleased with the result.

She nodded towards the lake. 'That's filled by the Tyburn, did you know? I always think it's a shame that something so beautiful should be part of such an infamous river.'

Richard smiled. 'It's only man who's made it infamous, by using its banks for such a shameful purpose.' Then as if to reassure her that his words were not intended as a reproof, he put an arm around her shoulders. 'Anne. There's . . . there's something I wanted to say to you.'

She turned her head expectantly towards him, her heart suddenly beating faster. She could feel the colour rising in her cheeks. 'Yes?' she queried.

His grip tightened. 'It's just that . . . well . . . just that . . . ' He hesitated.

It was a fatal pause. Before he could continue, a voice was heard shouting: 'Anne!' And coming along one of the paths was Ivo Kingsley. As he caught up with them, Richard withdrew his arm. To Anne's fury, Ivo's replaced it. 'I've been looking for you,' he told her accusingly. 'Had you forgotten I was calling round this afternoon? You were going to hear my

195

lines for the end-of-term performance. Hi, Rich!' He suddenly became aware of his cousin's presence. 'You home for the long vac already?'

Richard, Anne noticed with a sinking feeling, was looking wary, trying to assess the relationship between herself and Ivo. And Ivo was giving a good imitation of a man with proprietorial rights. She hunched her shoulders, shrugging off his all-embracing arm. Nevertheless, she had agreed to meet him at The Laurels. He had a genuine grievance.

'I'm sorry, Ivo,' she apologized guiltily. 'I'm afraid I forgot. Rich asked me to go for a walk. Perhaps some other time.'

Surely anyone who did not have a skin like a rhinoceros would be able to interpret the message, but she had reckoned without Ivo's rhino-like qualities. 'I'll join you,' he said affably. 'I could do with the exercise. And Penelope's asked me to stay to supper, so you can hear me when we get back.' He grinned across her head at Richard. 'She's a great girl, you know. I'm the envy of all my friends.'

Anne tried to catch Richard's eye, but he resolutely avoided looking at her. She must make the situation clear to him as soon as possible. Ivo's arm was round her shoulders again, and he began talking about their mutual friends and acquaintances, interlaced with various snippets of gossip, some of which made her laugh, no matter how hard she tried not to be amused. Nor was she able to disguise totally her interest in what he was saying. The theatre was becoming their world; a shared interest from which Richard was more or less excluded.

It was the same at supper. Chris and Irene had also been invited, and the theatre vied with publishing as the chief topic of conversation. Veterinary science was barely mentioned. Richard sat quietly eating, contributing very little to the general talk, but with

196

plenty of opportunity to study the others. His chief objects of interest were Ivo and Anne, whom Penelope had seated together, on the opposite side of the table. Their attitude towards one another puzzled him. It was plain that Ivo considered Anne to be his girl, and that, to a certain extent, the rest of the company did also. They were spoken of as a couple, their names constantly linked. Yet Anne herself seemed to treat Ivo with an amused tolerance which suggested that she was far from serious about him. But there was affection in her manner, too, although Richard doubted if she were conscious of it.

He had returned home after his first year at university unprepared for any changes; expecting to find the same Anne whom he had known nearly all his life. But a year of standing on her own two feet in London had inevitably wrought subtle differences in her. She was more self-assured than he remembered; more able to hold her own in any conversation; more assertive in her opinions. She occasionally called people 'darling', with no more meaning to the word than if she were using their Christian names; perhaps slightly less. If he had to sum up the new Anne, Richard thought, he would say that there was a gloss to her which he found a little forbidding. She had grown extremely attractive; and that, too, alienated him somewhat. She was no longer 'his' Anne; there were other people – other men particularly – who considered that they had a claim on her time and company. Even Chris, who in the past had barely noticed her existence, now appeared to find her amusing and listened to what she had to say.

They were laughing together now over some recent incident in a West End play, with Ivo joining in, one of his hands gripping Anne's wrist, shaking it to emphasize the point that he was making. And then Irene, who had been deep in earnest discussion with Penelope over an alternative title for her latest novel, turned her head to invite Anne and Ivo to a party that she and Chris were giving the following week.

'And you must come, too, Rich,' she added as an afterthought, 'if you want to.'

He smiled and shook his head. 'Thanks all the same, but I shan't know anyone. I don't think I'll bother.'

Anne said: 'Oh, but you must come, Rich. You'll enjoy it. Chris and Irene give marvellous parties. You can come with us, can't he, Ivo?'

She had not intended to refer the question to Ivo, as though asking his permission; it had just slipped out. She cursed silently. She wanted to lean towards Richard and reassure him that she and his cousin were not a pair. But Richard merely smiled thinly and said: 'No, thanks. Three's a crowd.'

Anne wondered despairingly how she had allowed herself to get into this situation with Ivo. It was becoming ridiculous. People were taking far too much for granted. So, after the meal was over, and while Ivo had vanished upstairs to the bathroom, she suggested to Richard that they went for a walk round the garden.

'Cloud needs a romp,' she urged. 'Since you went away, he's growing fat and sluggish. I do my best with him, but we're all out so much, or your mother's busy writing, and he doesn't get sufficient exercise.'

Richard hesitated a moment, then nodded. 'Right. You'd better get a jacket. It's quite a chilly evening. I'll rout out Cloud from whatever corner he's lurking in.'

Of all Richard's animals, only Sir Cloudesley Shovel, Machiavelli and Alphonso now remained. Alcibiades, the rabbit, and the two guinea-pigs Boadicea and

Berengaria, were long since dead, and Penelope had insisted that their successors were given away before Richard departed for Edinburgh.

'Five years is a long time; and, if you think I'm going to look after your menagerie while you're at university, think again. And Mrs Clennan has far too much to do without playing nursemaid to a lot of animals.'

She had done her best to persuade him to part with the tortoise as well, but on that score had found him intractable. Alphonso still roamed the garden in summer and was put to hibernate in the shed during the winter months. Richard, Cloud ambling grumpily at his heels, insisted now on searching for him beneath the cabbages and lettuces in the top half of the garden, still lovingly tended by his old friend John Bone. Anne, wrapped in an ancient jacket of Cliff's, taken from a downstairs cupboard, sat on the garden seat and watched him. Love for him welled up inside her. It astonished her that she could ever have imagined that she felt the same way about Chris. This was real; the other shadow. A mature emotion as opposed to a schoolgirl crush. She had to find some means of reassuring him about Ivo; convince Richard that, whatever appearances might lead him to think, she and his cousin were, in that most hackneyed of terms, just good friends.

'Here he is,' Richard called, and she glanced across to see him smiling, holding the tortoise between his hands. Then he stooped and tenderly replaced Alphonso beneath the cabbages where he had found him. 'Come on, Cloud!' he added, throwing a stick. 'Fetch, boy! Fetch!'

Cloud, who was lying at Anne's feet, opened a leery eye and blinked once or twice before closing it again. Snuffling slightly, he buried his nose between his front paws, pretending not to have heard. Richard paused to fondle the dog's ears before sitting down beside Anne.

'He's getting fat and out of condition. What he needs is a good run every day in the park. I don't suppose you could . . . ?'

'No,' Anne said firmly, but with a laugh in her voice. 'And don't think I haven't tried. But Cloud's idea of exercise nowadays is what you've seen tonight. A quick foray round the garden, followed by a good long sleep. I simply haven't the time to waste in trying to make him go for a walk. You could always make the effort, during the holidays. I'm only sorry I shall be home in Bristol and miss the fun. But in a battle of wills, yours and his, I put my money on Cloud.'

Richard grinned. 'You might lose,' he told her. 'I can be very determined when I want.' He hesitated before asking: 'I suppose you really do have to go home at the end of next week?'

She grimaced ruefully. 'Yes, I'm afraid I do. I don't see much of Mum and Grandma since I came to live in London. At least, not as much as they'd like. And Grandma was a bit cut up because I didn't apply to the Bristol Old Vic school for my stage design course. So I feel I owe it to her to be at home for a part of the holidays. And afterwards Mum and I are going for a fortnight to Greece.'

'Why *did* you apply to Wimbledon?' Richard asked. His tone was interested, showing a genuine concern, in direct contrast to Ivo who asked her questions but never listened to the answers.

Anne shrugged. 'I think because I wanted to get away from home. I'm very fond of both Mum and Gran, but there comes a time when you have to spread your wings. Why did you choose Edinburgh, if it comes to that?'

Richard's arm crept round her shoulders. 'For the same sort of reason. I, too, am very fond of my family, but sometimes', he added vigorously, 'they can get right up my nose. I hate this quarrel between Chris and Tim. I looked up to both of them when I was young, and I can't stand to see them squabbling like a couple of kids. I know Chris is to blame, but he's done his best to make amends. It's Tim who won't play ball. Anyway, why are we wasting time talking about them? Let's talk about us instead.'

'What about us?' Anne asked in a voice which was not quite steady. Her pulse was racing.

Richard paused, marshalling his thoughts. What he wanted to ask was if there were indeed a 'them' to talk about. What was Ivo to her, or she to Ivo? But it was a difficult question to put. It smacked of impertinence, and he was afraid of a snub. Richard had no means of knowing if he meant anything to Anne at all. She certainly seemed to have become very popular during the past year, while he had been away in Edinburgh. Ivo was obviously keen.

'Well . . .' he began, but out of the corner of his eye he was already aware that they no longer had the garden to themselves. Chris had come out on to the patio and was now running up the shallow flight of steps leading to the lawn.

'Anne!' His tone was urgent. 'Ma said will you come at once? Tim's on the phone and asking for you. Apparently, he won't speak to anyone else. I don't know what's wrong, but it sounds like trouble.'

Anne stared at him uncomprehendingly. 'But why does he want me?' she demanded. 'Why doesn't he tell your mother?'

Chris spread agitated hands. 'Look, I don't know. Please just come! That's the message.'

The urgency in his voice finally got through to Anne, and she got up from the seat in such haste that she almost stumbled. Richard caught and steadied her, but she was unaware of his touch, which, a moment ago, had sent a thrill of anticipation down her spine. Now all she could think about was Imogen and what might have happened. She pulled herself free and ran indoors.

Penelope was standing by the phone in the hall, still holding the receiver and trying to talk to Tim. Clifford was hovering anxiously in the study doorway, where he had been reading a new film script, sent to him that morning by his agent. Irene and Ivo were hanging over the upstairs banisters, unashamedly eavesdropping. There was a general air of unease.

'For goodness' sake, Tim, tell me what's happened,' Penelope was saying as Anne arrived, breathless, at her side. 'I'm your mother. Why can't you tell me? If there's trouble, I think I have a right to know. Here!' she added, pushing the receiver into Anne's hand. 'See if you can get any sense out of him.' And she turned with a shrug to Richard, who had followed Anne into the house.

'Tim? What's wrong?' Anne could hear him breathing heavily at the other end of the line. 'Why do you want to talk to me? Why can't you tell your mother?'

'Because she and Dad would only kick up a hell of a fuss. But you promised to stand by me when I let you persuade me to marry Imogen. I want a divorce, Annie, but Im says no. No way will she give me one.'

'I'll come round,' Anne said. 'I'll be there as soon as I can. Stay there and wait for me.'

She hung up and faced the others. 'I'm sorry, but I'll have to go,' she told them. She forced a reassuring smile. 'Just a row, that's all. I think they just want someone there to referee.'

'I'll drive you,' Clifford said, coming forward.

'And I'll come with you,' Penelope added.

'No!' Anne realized from their startled faces that she had been too emphatic. 'No, please. It's just a

202

disagreement. They don't want it to turn into a family inquest. I'll go by Tube and get a taxi back. I'll just run upstairs and fetch a coat.'

When she came down again, it was obvious that they had all been discussing the affair. 'We've decided that I'll go with you,' Richard said quietly. 'If Imogen's your sister, Tim's my brother. We have a right to know what's going on.'

'There isn't any need,' Anne retorted sharply. 'I can handle things better on my own. Tim will only resent it if you poke your nose in. It's something between him and me. He might just listen if I go by myself.'

She did not wait to argue, but ran out of the house, slamming the front door behind her, and sped along the road. Her shoulder-bag, which she had remembered to grab along with her coat, bumped against her side.

After her departure, the others stared at one another in angry frustration. 'Really,' Irene remarked, giving voice to all their feelings, 'I do think Anne's taking an awful lot on herself. Still, as we can't be of any use, Chris, I think we'd better go home. We can let the baby-sitter off early.'

Richard said drily: 'I didn't realize that Anne and Tim were so close.'

Ivo answered cheerfully, plainly unruffled by the episode: 'Oh, Anne's a great girl for sorting things out. People rely on her judgement. I've noticed it at the school. I don't let it worry me, though. I know, when all's said and done, that she's my girl, and they know it, too. But it's a good job I'm not the jealous type. You and her, for instance, roaming around the garden this evening. Any other fellow might resent it, but I know that you're just friends who've known one another for ever. So I take no notice.'

Penelope had gone upstairs to the drawing-room with Chris and Irene, Clifford had disappeared once more into his study, leaving Richard and Ivo alone in the hall; so there was no-one to dispute, or even question, Ivo's statement.

'I'm sorry,' Richard said stiffly. 'I had no idea how things stood between you.'

'That's OK,' Ivo assured him. 'I told you, I understand. She's a great girl, is Anne. I think we probably deserve each other.'

'I'm sure you do.' If there was any acerbity in Richard's tone, Ivo failed to hear it. He grinned, with the sort of smug self-satisfaction which always riled his Haldane cousins. Richard went on: 'I'll say good night. If Mum asks where I am, I'm in my bedroom. I've a lot of work to get through this vacation.'

'Right. Sounds like a pretty dull life to me. I'm going home at the end of next week. Until then, see you around.'

Richard went upstairs without making any answer.

CHAPTER FIFTEEN

ANNE COULD HEAR THEM arguing as she rang the bell of the flat; Tim shouting; Imogen's voice, also raised, filling the spaces in between. The interior walls were not thick, and several of the neighbours were already poking interested heads out of their respective front doors. One harassed young woman, with a pale pinched face, said: 'Try to shut them up, will you? They've been at it for hours and they keep waking the baby.'

Anne smiled thinly and promised to do her best. She pressed the bell again, and this time they heard it. There was a sudden lull before Tim opened the door and let her in. 'For heaven's sake, stop making such a racket!' she pleaded. 'You're disturbing the entire landing.'

Tim's face immediately set in the sulky lines she knew only too well, and her heart sank. 'Im's being unreasonable,' he muttered.

'Unreasonable!' Anne rounded on him furiously. 'What else do you expect her to be? She's pregnant for God's sake! And you tell her you want a divorce!'

She went into the living-room, where Imogen, with swollen tear-stained eyes, was curled up at one end of the sofa. She gave a little sob when she saw her sister, and Anne sat down beside her, taking her in her arms. Tim followed sullenly and flopped into the armchair with a show of bravado. Anne's anger increased. She reminded herself, however, that the play at the National had ended its run the previous week and Tim was not in the current production. Nor

205

in the two after that, with the result that he had time on his hands in which to get tired and irritable. Time to think of Sylvia Gibson. It was the perfect recipe for disaster.

'Right,' she said more calmly. 'Now, what's this all about? And why have I been dragged into your quarrel?'

'You promised,' Tim accused her. 'You promised that, if I needed you, you'd be there.'

'All right, so I'm here. But you seem to have made up your mind already. If you really want a divorce, I can't dissuade you.'

She could guess, by Tim's face, that it was something he had flung at Imogen in the heat of the moment; something he would no doubt have retracted if her immediate intransigence in the matter had not put his back up. Before she could say anything further, however, Imogen said in a high-strung angry voice: 'I won't divorce you, Tim. Not ever! I'll never set you free to marry that woman!'

'There you are!' Tim shouted. 'That's just like her! Never gives an inch!'

'What do you expect me to do? Say "Yes, of course, dear, you can have a divorce, even though I'm expecting your baby"? What kind of a wimp do you think I am? You must be simple!'

'Imogen, be quiet!' Anne's grip tightened about her sister's shoulders. 'You'll make yourself ill, and that isn't good for the child. You're less than six weeks pregnant.' She turned her attention to her brother-in-law. 'Why don't you admit that it was just something you said because you were angry? That you don't really want a divorce. That it was a rotten thing to say and you're sorry. What was the original row about anyway?'

Tim looked sulkier than ever. Imogen said bitterly: 'He'd promised to take me out to dinner tonight. I

206

wasn't feeling very well this morning, so he said he'd make the necessary arrangements. Instead he went out drinking with his friends and forgot all about it. He didn't come back until half-past six, and I'd been waiting for him for hours.' Her voice broke, as she indicated the pale-cream silk frock she was wearing. 'I was all dressed up, too.'

'Seems to me you're the one with grounds for a divorce.' Anne tried to keep her tone light. She recalled the overpowering smell of drink as Tim let her in. He'd probably been at it for hours, going from one all-day club to another with his friends.

'That's right! Side with her!' Tim was beginning to sound ashamed. 'But you should have heard the things she said to me before I was even inside the door. Said I was a lazy drunken sot who couldn't even provide for her and the baby.'

'And you retaliated by saying the most hurtful thing you could think of. Look, why on earth don't you both kiss and make up? Admit that neither of you meant what you said and you're sorry.'

But had they really not meant it? Didn't people when they were angry, as when they were drunk, often speak the truth? Wasn't it then that their secret thoughts came out into the open? Accepted convention always refuted this argument, so truth got swept under the carpet. And perhaps, Anne told herself, it was just as well or marriage would become an even more frequent casualty than it was already. She looked pleadingly at Tim.

'Well ... ' he was beginning reluctantly, but got no further. Imogen suddenly doubled up with a cry of pain.

'What is it?' Anne asked sharply.

'I ... I'm not sure.' Imogen gave another gasp of terror. 'Call Doctor Michaels, quick! I think I'm losing the baby.'

*   *   *

207

The next few hours remained in Anne's memory only as a series of disconnected pictures, like a camera lens clicking open and shut: Tim's white face as he made for the telephone; Imogen's stifled screams of pain; the doctor and ambulance arriving almost together; Clifford and Penelope racing along the hospital corridor; the endless cups of tepid coffee; the equally endless attempts at explanation; her mother coming straight from Paddington, having caught the first available train; above all, her own irrational sense of guilt, as though she were somehow to blame.

I talked Tim into marrying Imogen, she kept thinking. I shouldn't have interfered. I should have let matters take their course. I feel responsible for their marriage. So why doesn't Penelope feel the same way? It never seems to cross her mind. But I'm never going to poke my nose into anyone's affairs ever again. I've learned my lesson. And Tim looks like death. Probably feels like it, too. That's all I've done for him. Saddled him with a sense of guilt even greater than mine. And I can't even pretend that Imogen's happy. God, what a mess!

Imogen was out of hospital by the end of the week, and Barbara insisted that she return with her and Anne to Bristol for a few days' rest and recuperation. A silent Imogen allowed herself to be persuaded without any demur, and Tim promised to come down to fetch her whenever she was ready to return home. And in all the confusion of the week Anne had no time to think about Richard. It was only after she was back in College Close that she had the leisure to recall how polite and distant he had been; the punctilious way he had enquired after Imogen without ever expressing any concern for herself, or once enquiring as to why Tim had sent for her in the first place and not his mother. In fact, when she came to think of it, he had been quiet and withdrawn almost to the point of indifference. She worried and fretted over it at night, when the silence was broken only by the distant nocturnal roarings of the animals in the zoo. Perhaps she had been wrong about what he felt for her; maybe she had misread the signs. She wanted nothing so much as to catch the next train back to London and have it out with him, but she couldn't. Imogen clung to her, monopolizing her presence as the one person who really knew what had happened to make her lose the baby. She needed to discuss it over and over again, and Anne was the only one she could talk to without betraying Tim. Barbara and Felicity knew that there had been a row, but not exactly what had been said, and Imogen was wise enough to keep that a secret from them.

Anne also found herself the recipient of her mother's and grandmother's confidences. It was true, what she had told Richard: Felicity missed her during term-time. She and Barbara had never had a great deal in common. Then there was her mother, making plans for their holiday in Greece at the end of the month. She seemed really to be looking forward to her younger daughter's company, even going so far as to ask her advice about what to wear, and permitting Anne to accompany her when she went shopping.

'Miracles will never cease,' Felicity said. 'Make the most of it, and for God's sake don't let her take that awful orange-and-black dress or those red sandals she insists on wearing with it.'

Anne felt trapped by her own indispensability. She tried telephoning Cameron Road, but it was always Penelope or Clifford who answered. Richard, it seemed, was out a lot. She left messages asking him to ring her, but he never did. In the end, she gave up and let it ride. Ivo, on the other hand, never failed to phone her at least twice a week, ignoring his mother's agonizing over the cost of calls between

Grange-over-Sands and Bristol. 'Why doesn't *she* ever phone *you*?' Mrs Kingsley would demand plaintively, but her son ignored that as well.

Tim arrived to take Imogen home. He was very quiet and subdued, barely opening his mouth. It was obvious that he felt bad about what had happened and expected to be blamed. Anne managed to trap him on his own, in the garden, the second morning of his visit. Barbara was upstairs with Imogen, helping her to pack, and Felicity was in the kitchen preparing lunch.

'Tim,' she said, sitting beside him on the garden bench, which circled a medlar tree in the middle of the lawn, 'do you know what's happened to Richard? He never answers any of my calls.'

'Richard?' Tim looked vague. 'He's around. Busy, I suppose. Studying. Looking up old friends. Annie! I never meant this to happen, you know. I didn't want Im to lose the baby.'

'No. Well, perhaps you should have thought a bit more before you threatened her with divorce. Did you really mean it?'

'No ... yes ... I don't know. I may have meant it when I said it.' He raised his hand and began tugging at one of the tree's lower branches, absentmindedly stripping off the leaves.

'And now?' Gently, Anne released the mangled branch from his clutches.

'Of course not.' He spoke a little too vehemently, she thought, as though trying to convince himself more than her. He turned his head to look at her. 'I'm very fond of Imogen, you know.'

'I know,' Anne sighed. 'But you don't love her.'

'No. I suppose I don't. It's always been Sylvia.' He took a deep breath, as though glad, at last, to have the truth out in the open. 'I can't explain why. She's years older than I am, and she doesn't care for me at all. For her, it's always been Chris.' He added

210

viciously: 'He's the cause of all the rotten mess, but he's the one who's come out of it smelling of roses. Happily married to Irene! And the stupid bitch dotes on him. Everyone takes his side, that's what gets me. Everyone says forgive and forget, even young Rich. A fat lot he knows about it!'

'Tim, about Rich . . . ' Anne began hopefully, but he did not even hear her.

Instead he went on: 'If ever I can do either of them a bad turn, I'll do it.'

'You know you don't mean that,' Anne said quickly. 'Tim dear, when you get home this evening, would you phone Richard and ask him to call me?'

Tim hesitated. 'I will if I remember,' he agreed, but so reluctantly that Anne guessed he would manage to forget it. 'He's off to Devon at the end of the week with Mum and Dad. He and Mum will probably stay there most of the summer.'

'You and Imogen ought to go with them. It would do Im good. Help her to recover.'

Tim shrugged. 'Imogen can go if she wants to, but I daren't be away from London for very long at the moment. I've a promise of a part in the next NT production at the Cottesloe.' Felicity appeared at the kitchen door, waving her arms to indicate that lunch was ready. Tim laid a hand on Anne's arm. 'I truly am fond of Imogen. I promise I'll try to make things up to her. I know I've been drinking a lot lately. That's going to stop. I mean it.'

Anne put one of her hands over his. She wasn't sure that she really believed him, but she wanted to, desperately. For the sake of Imogen's future happiness, she must.

'I know you'll do your best,' she said, standing up. 'Come on. Gran hates her meals to be kept waiting. And, Tim, you won't forget to ask Rich to call me, will you?'

Richard did not telephone, either that evening or the following day. Nor the day after that, nor at any time before the end of the week, by which time he was in Devon with his parents. Anne debated whether or not to ring the cottage, but decided against it. She had her pride after all. And in mid-July she and Barbara went to Greece for three weeks.

Anne sent Richard a highly coloured picture postcard of the Parthenon, and another to Ivo of the monastery at Daphni. At a distance, she found she could think of Ivo more kindly; almost, to her surprise, with something like affection. And on those occasions when Barbara spoke to Felicity by phone there was always a message for Anne: Ivo had called to know how she was getting on; Ivo sent his regards and, sometimes, his love; Ivo was looking forward to seeing her again at the beginning of next term. But there was no word from Richard.

'Is there something going on between you and Ivo Kingsley that I should know about?' Barbara asked one evening, as they were dressing for dinner. She went across to close the bedroom window against the incessant volume of noise in Omonia Square. It was somehow typical of her mother, Anne reflected, that a holiday in Greece meant a large fashionable hotel in the noisiest part of Athens.

'We're just friends,' she said, wondering how to suggest tactfully that royal blue sandals and evening stole were a little garish when worn with a cyclamen-pink dress.

Barbara raised her eyebrows. 'I should have thought that frequent telephone calls from Grange-over-Sands to Bristol, when there is no chance of even speaking to you, but simply to enquire how you are getting on in Greece, is well beyond the limits defined by friendship. On Ivo's part, at least.'

'Well, I can't prevent him, can I?' Anne demanded pettishly. 'I can't stop him doing silly things.'

'You could offer him a little more definite discouragement than you seem to be doing at present,' her mother commented drily. 'I can't believe he'd carry on this way if he thought you indifferent to him. Or are you not really as indifferent as you sound?'

Anne wrinkled her nose. 'I'm fond of him.' Where had she heard that recently? 'But I'm certainly not in love with him.' A picture of Tim flashed through her mind. 'OK. Next term, I will try to be less friendly, but it's very difficult. We meet all the time, and he has a skin like a rhinoceros when it comes to putting him down.'

Barbara gave a short laugh. 'You make him sound like a dog that's outlived his usefulness. All right. I'll mind my own business. But I've met a lot of Ivo's kind. They never know when they're beaten. Watch out that you don't find yourself trapped against your will. And don't make the mistake of thinking it couldn't possibly happen to you. That you're too smart.' She surveyed her daughter, frowning slightly. 'That dress could do with some brightening up. Why don't you borrow my diamanté necklace and drop-earrings?'

Although this was his second winter in Edinburgh, Richard could still not accustom himself to how much colder it was than in London. He invariably, as now, went out too lightly clad, with the result that, within half an hour, he was chilled to the marrow. This morning, however, he was glad of the icy February wind which swept across Calton Hill and cleared his head of all the lingering alcohol fumes left over from the night before. Yesterday had been Gordon Fraser's nineteenth birthday, celebrated in suitably liquid fashion by a bring-a-bottle party, held in the tiny flat which he shared with Richard and two other students from the university. And the four of them, waking to a cold grey Saturday dawn, nursing mammoth hangovers and faced with the debris of a highly successful evening, agreed without hesitation that the clearing-up could wait. Gordon, Sandy Mason and Pete Jenkins had immediately gone back to sleep; but Richard, having once forced himself awake, found it impossible to stay in bed, so had dressed and gone out for a walk.

He made his way, almost automatically, to Calton Hill, which had, over the past eighteen months, become his favourite place in a city he was coming to know and love as though it were his own. He stood by the Dugald Stewart monument and stared out over the panoramic view of the old and new towns which made up modern Edinburgh; a view which, someone had once told him, had been the favourite of Robert Louis Stevenson. In the distance, the castle lowered at him, safe on its impregnable rock. The crowned head of St Giles and the delicately rearing pinnacle of the Scott monument also peered at him through the chill morning mist.

Richard shivered suddenly, aware that his duffel coat was insufficient protection without a sweater underneath. Jeans and a long-sleeved T-shirt were all very well inside the flat, which, with the body heat of four people, was inclined to be stuffy; but here, on the top of Calton Hill, they were not enough to prevent the icy blast from penetrating right to the skin. He had also forgotten his scarf and the pair of good leather gloves that Anne had given him for Christmas. But at the thought of Anne his mind sheered away in a hurry. He wasn't sure what he felt about her any more. Last summer, when he had gone home for the long vacation, everything had seemed settled in his mind. He had kept a framed photograph of her on his bedside table in the flat, and spoken of her to the others as his girlfriend, with the underlying implication that he and she might one day get married. It hadn't stopped him going out with other girls, but he had felt himself in some way committed, and had therefore treated these affairs lightly. Word soon got around among the female students that anyone looking for a serious relationship should give Richard Haldane a wide berth.

But last summer had put paid to all that. He had arrived home to find Anne elusive, her time monopolized by Ivo and Tim; one of the central figures in a domestic drama which no longer seemed to have any bearing on his own life. He hadn't realized until then how much he had grown away from his family and his London life during the past year in Edinburgh. Ivo's revelation that he regarded Anne as his girl might have come as a bit of a shock, but not, Richard admitted to himself with some surprise, as a numbing disappointment. It was something he found that he could live with. He told himself, too, that she had changed; become more sophisticated as she was inevitably sucked into that world of the theatre, of which he himself had never wished to be a part. From infancy, he had soaked up its hothouse atmosphere of uncertainties and mild hysteria, its rivalries and jealousies, from which even someone like his father was not immune. His brothers had been infected by the acting bug at a very early age, and Richard now found it difficult to recall when he had taken the conscious decision to reject it; to do something entirely different; to become his own man. And for a long time, when they were small, he had believed that Anne shared his dedication to the idea of becoming a vet . . .

'You look blue with cold,' said an amused female voice behind him; and Richard turned to see a freckle-faced snub-nosed girl of about his own age, warmly wrapped up against the cold, holding a small yapping cairn terrier on the end of a bright red lead.

There was something in the warmth of her smile

that made him grin in return. 'I am,' he answered. 'It comes of being a poor stupid Sassenach who hasn't yet got the hang of your northern climate.' He added, holding out his hand: 'My name's Richard Haldane. I'm from London.'

She encased his hand in a green woollen mitten and shook it with a firm no-nonsense grip. 'I'm Georgina Frere. And this' – she indicated with a nod of her head the terrier, who was eyeing Richard's ankles with evil intent – 'is Barkis, so-called because, where bitches are concerned, he's always willing.' She creased her brow with a quizzical look. 'Haldane. That's a famous name. I don't suppose there's any possible connection?'

It was on the tip of Richard's tongue to deny the relationship, but a faint small voice at the back of his mind warned him that this random meeting was destined to be of importance to him, so he might as well begin by telling the truth. 'Sir Clifford Haldane's my father,' he admitted.

To his delight, the information did not overwhelm her, as it did so many other women. 'My, my!' she mocked gently, pulling down the corners of her wide mobile mouth. 'We are in exalted company, Barkis.'

Barkis, deciding that he had shown self-restraint for long enough, made a dash at Richard and nipped him smartly on the ankle. With a cry of apology, his mistress bent and scooped him into her arms, giving him a tap on the nose as she did so.

'You're a naughty, naughty dog! What are you?' Barkis gave her the puzzled innocent stare of an animal who has only been doing his duty. Georgina's effort at a reprimand collapsed; she gurgled with laughter and kissed his nose. 'I – I'm sorry,' she said, turning to Richard. 'Has he . . . has he drawn blood?'

Richard, who had crouched down in order to examine the damage, glanced up to meet bright hazel eyes brimming with barely concealed amusement. He made an attempt at severity. 'Luckily, no. But he has ruined a perfectly good pair of Marks and Spencer's socks, only put on for the second time this morning.'

'Oh dear. Look, let me take you home and my mother will make you some coffee. And I'm sure Daddy will stump up for a new pair of socks.'

Richard hastened to reassure her. 'It doesn't matter about the socks, honestly. And your mother isn't going to take kindly to your bringing some strange man home for coffee.'

'Oh, she won't mind,' this friendly girl told him cheerfully. 'And when she finds out you're Sir Clifford Haldane's son she'll probably invite you to dinner. She's an enormous fan of his. I think she has a signed photograph somewhere, which he sent her years ago, after she sent him a letter.' They began descending the hill by one of the paths. 'Are you at the university?'

He nodded. 'I'm going to be a vet, if I ever manage to pass the exams.'

'Are you really?' She swept off her dark-green knitted bobble hat and shook out a shock of carrot-coloured hair – an amazing brilliant orange which flamed on the wind. 'Daddy's a vet. How's that for coincidence?' She fell silent for a moment, then added, almost accusingly: 'I've been thinking . . . If you're Clifford Haldane's son, doesn't that mean Penelope Fallon's your mother?'

'Yes. Do you disapprove?'

'Of her books?' Again there came that delicious gurgle of laughter. 'I love them. So do all my friends. They're so . . . well, you know . . . *explicit*. But my mother's a wee bit strait-laced.'

'Oddly enough,' Richard replied drily, 'so is mine, though I don't expect you to believe that. It's true, all the same. I've come to the conclusion that writers are really two people. There's the Dr Jekyll personality, when they're being themselves, and the Mr Hyde, who escapes whenever they sit in front of a blank piece of paper or a typewriter . . . Look, are you sure your mother isn't going to mind your bringing me home like this?'

Georgina once again reassured him; and indeed, when Richard was introduced to Margaret Frere, he discovered her to be every bit as friendly and hospitable as her daughter. The family home was in Ramsay Lane, an exclusive part of the Old Town, with windows overlooking Princes Street Gardens. There seemed to be no other children apart from Georgina, which explained the love and affection lavished on her by both her parents. Callum Frere, who was getting ready for his Saturday-morning surgery, welcomed Richard as though he had been a long-lost friend; and when Richard revealed that he was reading veterinary science at the university his reception was, if possible, even more effusive.

The morning was well advanced before Richard finally managed to tear himself away, resisting all Mrs Frere's pressing invitations to stay for lunch.

'Much as I'd love to,' he told Georgina, 'I really ought to get back and help the others clear up.'

'Will I see you again?' she asked, as she stood with him at the front door. Her gaze was frankly inviting. 'I can't help feeling that our meeting this morning was more than chance.' She added candidly: 'I like you, Richard Haldane. More than any other boy I've ever met.'

As he walked away, it occurred to Richard that he, too, liked Georgina Frere and wanted to see more of her. She was the sort of uncomplicated, forthright, open-hearted girl he found it easy to understand.

PART THREE
1981–5

CHAPTER SIXTEEN

THE FIRST TIME Anne set eyes on Georgina Frere was when Richard brought her home to Cameron Road during the Easter vacation. Georgina had come to London with him on two previous occasions, once in September and again at Christmas, but neither time had Anne been present. Now, however, there was no avoiding the meeting. Clifford had decided to celebrate his fifty-fifth birthday with a family party; and, as he said, the Seymours were as much a part of that family as his own children. Not only that, but they were united by marriage. Barbara and Felicity, as well as Anne, received invitations and Clifford would brook no refusal.

'Of course I'm expected to drop everything and arrange it all,' Penelope grumbled to Barbara, during one of their lengthy bi-weekly telephone conversations. 'Cliff's always thought that my novels write themselves and that I'm really a lady of leisure.' But her tone was without rancour, and Barbara suspected that, secretly, her friend enjoyed the pressure. 'So make a note in your diary, and tell your Miss Bates that she'll have to manage on her own for a couple of days. Anne says that she'll stay on here until the party. Then she'll travel back with you for the holidays. Oh, and Rich is bringing that girl of his from Scotland. I have a feeling that they may be about to make an Announcement.' Penelope lowered her voice conspiratorially, speaking in capital letters.

'An engagement, do you mean?'

'I shouldn't be at all surprised. Rich is very *épris* in

221

that direction. At least, I thought so the last time he brought her home. And we've had a pressing invitation to visit her parents.'

'Will you go?'

'Well, my dear, if Rich and Georgina do get engaged, we'll have to, won't we?' Penelope chuckled. 'I gather Mummy doesn't approve of my books, although Georgy, intelligent child, loves them. But Margaret Frere is a great fan of Cliff's, so he'll be in his element. Look, I must go. Cliff'll be apoplectic when he sees the size of his next phone bill.'

Barbara snorted. 'Tell him you pay your fair share. Besides, after two Hollywood films in a row, he can easily afford it. Nevertheless, I must go, too. Mother's watching "The Borgias" on TV, and if I'm not there to unravel the plot she gets terribly confused. History was never her strong subject.'

'Tell her to switch to "Brideshead". Much easier to follow.' They murmured their goodbyes, and Penelope replaced the receiver. Turning her head, she saw Anne standing at the open study doorway behind her. 'Hello, darling. I didn't know you were there. You could have had a word with your mother. I was just speaking to her.'

'Yes, so I gathered.' Anne twisted her hands together. 'Is it true, what you were saying? That Rich and Georgina are going to get engaged?'

'Well, I don't know for certain but, yes, I think it probable. Mothers get an instinct about these things. Now, supper will be in ten minutes – if you're not going out, that is.' Anne shook her head, and Penelope went on briskly: 'You mustn't mope around just because Ivo's away. If you're going to marry an actor, you'll have to get used to these separations. They have to go where the work is when they first start out, you know.'

Anne was in her last year at Wimbledon and, after

the holiday, would be starting her final term. Ivo had left RADA the previous summer, to join the hundreds of other aspiring young actors in the country's dole queues. For three months, he had worked as a waiter in a wine bar near Victoria station, but then the luck had run his way. He had been offered the post of assistant stage manager at the Nottingham Playhouse, with a promise of one or two minor character parts in future productions. Not the sort of prestigious beginning to his stage career that he had once seen himself making; but he had long ago given up on the idea that being Sir Clifford Haldane's cousin would afford him an instant passport to fame and fortune. Therefore, when a chance presented itself to join the famous Playhouse, he did not hesitate. Even leaving Anne behind in London became of secondary importance.

He was, in any case, extremely unsure at present how he stood with her. Twice during the past year he had asked her to marry him – the first time, confident of her acceptance – and twice she had turned him down. She had offered no reasons for her refusal, apart from the conventional ones that they were both too young, had no money nor any immediate prospect of making any. But he had gained the impression that there was more to it than that. Not normally a very perceptive young man, he had, on both occasions, been conscious of a certain reserve in her manner, as though she were harbouring a secret, and for the first time he had begun to question her affection for him. Being Ivo, it was not a doubt which lasted for more than a few days, and he had set out for Nottingham with a little more reluctance than he would otherwise have done, but with no intention of allowing anything or anyone to stand in his way.

He nevertheless wrote and telephoned Anne, wherever she happened to be, with a regularity she found difficult to match. She felt profoundly guilty about

Ivo, and about the cowardice which prevented her from telling him the truth: that she was in love with Richard. But somehow she could never quite bring herself to deflate the self-confidence so important to an actor. So she permitted, without actively encouraging, his attentions, buoying herself up with the hope that everything would be sorted out once she and Richard had got over their ridiculous estrangement. But then, suddenly, Penelope and Clifford were talking about Georgina Frere, Richard's Scots girlfriend, making preparations for first one visit and then another, during the summer and Christmas vacations. And now here was Penelope talking about an engagement, and assuming, which was just as bad, that Anne was pining for Ivo.

'I'll be in to supper,' she told Penelope rather curtly, adding: 'Then Trish Ransome and I are going to the pictures.'

Patricia Ransome was a fellow-student in Anne's year, also doing stage design. A tall gangling girl with straight black hair cut in a heavy fringe, and with what appeared at first glance to be equally jet-black eyes, she had a laconic laid-back approach to her chosen career which masked an extraordinary talent. Anne recognized Trish's superiority in almost everything they did, but never felt in the least bit jealous – a fact which was entirely due to Trish's quickness to praise others while gently deriding her own capabilities. It was this generosity of spirit which had first attracted Anne to her, and resulted in the two becoming fast friends. Trish, who hailed from Newcastle and had a Geordie accent which could be cut with a knife, had soon become a firm favourite at The Laurels. She had won Cliff's heart by revealing herself to be a lifelong fan of *The Diary of a Nobody* and tuning in at once to his inevitable reference to Brickfield Terrace.

'Bring her home as often as you like,' Cliff had begged. 'It's nice to meet someone with intelligence.'

Penelope, overhearing this remark, had wondered if it were a dig at Georgina Frere. For some obscure reason – known, possibly, only to himself – Clifford had not joined in the general family admiration of the young Scots girl.

'Oh, nice enough. Nice enough,' he had grudgingly admitted to Penelope in the privacy of their bedroom. 'But a little too ... too chocolate-boxy. I like my women with a bit more brain.'

Penelope had flown to Georgina's defence. 'Rubbish! She's a charming girl, and you know it! You're just harbouring some unfair prejudice against her. A vet's daughter! She'll make Rich a splendid wife, if it ever comes to that. And he dotes on her.'

Clifford, sitting on the edge of the bed, arrayed in a dark-blue silk dressing-gown, had sighed dramatically. He was appearing in a Noël Coward revival at the time, and totally unable to leave the part behind him at the theatre.

'I'm afraid that's true. He *is* giving an impression of someone completely besotted.' Another sigh. His cynical wife expected him, at any moment, to produce a cigarette in a long cigarette-holder or burst into a chorus of 'One Day I'll Find You'. 'I had rather hoped', he added, with just the correct touch of pathos, 'that Anne would have been our other daughter-in-law.'

'There's never been any suggestion of that,' Penelope had answered briskly. 'I've always imagined that she'll marry Ivo.'

Clifford grimaced, but had said no more, to his wife's great relief. She wanted to like Georgina, and had so far managed to do so without any difficulty – a state of affairs she hoped would continue. The last thing she needed was Cliff planting doubts in her mind. She, too, if she were completely honest, would have preferred Anne as a daughter-in-law, but that was just natural prejudice, and because it was simpler to get on with someone you knew than a stranger. She had thought for many years that Anne and Richard would eventually make a pair, but then Ivo had come on the scene. It was obvious from the first that he was attracted to Anne; and when she appeared to return his affection Penelope put aside her dreams and accepted the inevitable. There was no doubt in her own mind that Anne was missing him. She looked downright peaky.

'It'll do you good to get out with Trish,' Penelope said approvingly. 'Is she coming to supper? You know she's always welcome. A pity Cliff won't be here, though. He's very fond of her. She makes him laugh and isn't over-awed by his reputation.'

Anne shook her head. 'We've arranged to meet outside the Odeon at half-past eight, in time for the main feature.'

'She *is* coming to the birthday-party on Sunday, isn't she? Cliff'll be disappointed if she isn't here.'

'Oh, yes. She's put off going home until Monday. When ... when are Rich and his girlfriend arriving?'

'Early Friday morning. They're travelling down on the overnight sleeper. Do you want to come to King's Cross with me to meet them?'

'What? Oh, no! No, thanks. You won't want me hanging around. Mum and Grandma will be here the following afternoon, by the way.'

'Yes. Barbara just told me. She sent her and Felicity's love. Your grandmother's trying to make head or tail of "The Borgias" on TV and getting in a dreadful muddle.'

That made Anne laugh; and Penelope reflected that it was the first time for a long while that she had heard such a spontaneous expression of mirth from her. Anne was becoming far too serious. She hoped that there was nothing wrong between her and Ivo.

'And this is Georgina.' Richard introduced her proudly. 'Georgy, this is Anne.'

Anne found herself the recipient of a broad grin and an enthusiastic handshake. 'Rich has told me all about you,' Georgina said.

'Only good, I hope,' Anne murmured tritely. She felt that her own smile must look as false as hell, and trusted that the other girl would notice nothing wrong with it.

'Indeed no! He said you were childhood sweethearts, and that he asked you to marry him when you were both about ten.'

Anne forced a laugh. 'So he did. I think I refused him.'

'You did. And dealt my masculine pride a terrible blow.' Richard flung an arm about her shoulders and kissed her cheek. Nothing could have been more friendly or more clinical. 'I don't think I've ever got over it.' The glowing look he sent Georgina belied his protest, and Anne had to blink rapidly to restrain the tears.

She had been up since five-thirty, unable to sleep, prowling restlessly around her bedroom. She had heard Penelope get up, very quietly, so as not to disturb Clifford, and go downstairs to make herself a cup of tea before dressing. Normally, Anne would have joined her in the kitchen, but this morning she was afraid of being press-ganged into accompanying Penelope to the station, so she pretended to be still asleep. It was, after all, the holidays – her last extended vacation before plunging into the chilly waters of the wider commercial world. Mrs Clennan had arrived and, later, Penelope had left the house. Anne, whose bedroom was at the front, had heard her starting the car. (She had abandoned Richard's attic some months ago, preferring, she said, a room which was definitely her own. Penelope, never questioning her reasons, had given her Tim's old bedroom.)

At eight o'clock she had been unable to keep up the pretence any longer, and had showered and got dressed. She found that she was choosing her clothes with care, wanting to make a good impression. To show Richard what he had missed? queried a small cynical voice inside her. Ignoring it, she had selected a long, knife-pleated navy-blue skirt, teaming it with a jade top piped in the navy material. There was also a reversible navy-and-jade jacket, but this she left hanging in the wardrobe. The blouse's softly frilled neckline and cuffs were the latest fashion, made popular by the future Princess of Wales, and suited Anne to perfection. Sheer navy tights and pumps completed the outfit.

Descending to the kitchen for coffee and orange juice, she found Clifford tucking into eggs and bacon, cooked for him by Mrs Clennan. Used to seeing her, at this time of day, in jeans and T-shirt, he raised his eyebrows slightly, but made no comment. Mrs Clennan was not so reticent.

'My, my!' she remarked. 'We *are* all dressed up this morning and no mistake! Anyone would think it's royalty we're expecting.'

With her delicate fair skin, Anne could never disguise embarrassment. The tell-tale colour had stained her cheeks as she took her place at the kitchen table and poured herself a cup of coffee. 'It's the first time I've met Rich's friend. I just thought I should make an effort.'

Mrs Clennan had nodded. 'Oh, well, that's nice, I suppose.'

Clifford had still said nothing. His silence made Anne uncomfortable, and she escaped upstairs to the

228

drawing-room as soon as possible, settling down with a magazine to await Penelope's return and the inevitable introduction to Georgina.

Now it was over, the dreaded moment safely past, and with Clifford's carefully timed entrance into the room Anne was at liberty to resume her seat and study at leisure this girl whom his mother thought Richard would surely marry. A very attractive girl, she admitted grudgingly, in spite of the snub nose, abundance of freckles and that impossibly carrot-coloured hair. No, *because* of them, Anne admonished herself sharply. She was ashamed of being so mean. Georgina was like a breath of fresh air; sweet and unaffected. Nor was she unintelligent as Clifford had hinted; she simply looked at life from a less jaundiced point of view. And Richard plainly doted on her.

That much was painfully obvious to Anne within the first five minutes. His eyes followed Georgina's every move, his voice took on a tender note when he addressed her. He was in love all right, Anne decided bitterly. He had never in his life looked at or spoken to her like that, as though she were some deity on a pedestal.

Clifford was being charming, with that extra-special brand of charm which he reserved for people with whom he was ill-at-ease or to whom he had taken an irrational dislike. She saw him make a face at Penelope behind the couple's back, as though to reassure her that he intended to be on his best behaviour.

At last, Penelope bore Richard and Georgina off to the kitchen for breakfast, with a parting injunction to Clifford to see to the cases. He gave a resigned nod; and Anne reflected, not for the first time, on the dichotomy between his public life, with its degree of sycophantic adulation, and his home life, where he was treated very much as an ordinary human being. It must surely need an extremely stable character to make the frequent transition between one world and the other.

Clifford's voice interrupted her thoughts. 'Why are you looking at me like that?' he demanded.

'Like what?' Anne was not even aware that she had been staring at him.

'With – although modesty almost forbids me to say it – a kind of admiration. It's very embarrassing.'

Anne laughed, got up and went over to where he was sitting, stooping to kiss his cheek. 'I have a touch of indigestion. It always gives me that constipated expression.'

He gave an answering laugh, but then became serious, catching hold of her hands. 'Chin up,' he said. 'Rich is a fool to prefer her to you. And don't bother giving me a lot of nonsense about pining for Ivo. You may be able to fool the others, but not yours truly.'

Anne flushed and pulled her hands away. 'I don't know what you mean,' she told him.

Clifford shrugged. 'OK. If that's how you want to play it. I just thought you might like to know that someone else shares your secret and understands how you're feeling. Don't worry. I shan't tell anyone, not even Pen.' He put up a hand and smoothed her face. ' "What shall Cordelia do? Love and be silent." '

Anne felt tears sting her eyelids. She gave a travesty of a smile and fled to the peace and comfort of her own room. On Monday, thank God, she would be going home to Bristol, putting over a hundred miles between her and Richard. But first there was Clifford's birthday-party to get through.

'You're drinking too much,' she said to Imogen. 'That's your third gin and tonic in under half an hour.'

'So who's counting?' Imogen demanded nastily. 'Except you, my suddenly oh-so-pious little sister! Why don't you mind your own damn business?'

The birthday-party was in full swing. Imogen had arrived on her own thirty minutes ago, Tim having refused point-blank to accompany her because Chris and Irene would be present. The ensuing row had been long and acrimonious, causing the inmates of the neighbouring flat to shrug resignedly and remark that the Haldanes were 'at it again'.

'If Sylvia Gibson really means nothing to you any more, as you keep saying,' Imogen had shouted, 'why can't you forgive Chris and Irene? God! They've been married for well over four years. It's all so long ago!'

But she could not move him. Tim would have nothing to do with either his elder brother or his sister-in-law. In the end, Imogen had slammed out of the flat in a fury.

She had arrived at The Laurels to an effusive welcome from Clifford and Penelope, which unsuccessfully masked their hurt at Tim's absence.

'I'm sorry,' she told them simply. 'I did my best to make him come with me.'

Both parents-in-law assured her it didn't matter. 'If that's how he feels,' Penelope said airily, 'that's how he feels, and there's nothing anyone can do about it.' But she was not slow to assess the implications of Tim's continuing vendetta against Chris. He was still in love with Sylvia Gibson. She swore silently to herself. She had hoped that he and Imogen would have another child to replace the one that had miscarried, but so far there was no sign of her younger daughter-in-law being pregnant. And, as it also appeared that Irene either could not, or would not, have any more children, Penelope had resigned herself – until Richard married, at least – to having no grandchild of her own, only her step-granddaughter, Deborah Grantham.

The trouble was that she did not really care for Deborah. The child had celebrated her ninth birthday

231

the previous month, but Penelope found her precocious for her age. Irene and Chris both spoiled her, catering to her every whim and rarely checking her behaviour. Penelope guessed that they felt guilty about her – a situation which Deborah understood and ruthlessly exploited. Jeremy was allowed regular access to his daughter, who played him off against Irene with a calculated cynicism far beyond her years. Whatever one parent gave her, the other matched in value; and as Chris was now being offered many good parts, both in films and on television, he and Irene were, between them, able to lavish the most expensive presents on her. Penelope watched in tight-lipped silence, knowing that any interference from her would be not only resented, but also useless. Guilt sabotaged people's better judgement. And, to do the child justice, Deborah was neither as selfish nor as grasping as she might have been in the circumstances. But she was accustomed to getting her own way in most things.

Penelope, descending to the dining-room, where, as usual, the buffet was laid out and the bar set up, saw Deborah apparently absorbed in helping herself to food, but quite obviously eavesdropping on Anne and Imogen. It was also obvious to her that Imogen was, if not drunk, then well on the way to becoming so, and that Anne was remonstrating with her. She walked over to them, intervening and putting an arm about their shoulders.

'Enjoying yourselves, my darlings?' she asked. 'That's right. Im, I want you to come upstairs and meet Dorothy Nicolson. You've spoken so often to her on the phone without actually having met her, and she's dying to see you.' She turned to Anne. 'Dorothy's my new editor at Herrald's, and she reckons Imogen is a very efficient secretary. Says she keeps me up to the mark and makes sure all their queries are answered promptly. Good thing, too, because left to myself I'd never reply to correspondence. Hello, Debbie,' she added, as though noticing the child's presence for the first time. She glanced pointedly at the laden plate. 'Don't make yourself sick, will you?'

Deborah smiled sweetly, the round blue eyes limpid in the softly pretty face. The auburn hair, so like her mother's, was swept back into a pony-tail and held in place with a shiny blue ribbon. 'I'm never sick,' she answered smugly.

'There's always a first time for everything,' Penelope responded callously, and led the way out of the room and upstairs, Imogen and Anne dutifully following. 'That child', she hissed at them over her shoulder, 'gets right under my skin.'

The drawing-room, as always on this sort of occasion, was crowded with people. The Haldanes never did things by halves, and when they had a party invited everyone they knew. While her sister was piloted towards a large lady in a severe grey suit, Anne stood in the doorway, surveying the scene. She spotted Richard and Georgina straight away, their arms entwined, talking to her mother and grandmother. Clifford was at the other end of the room, the centre of a group of admirers. She felt very lonely and suddenly wished that Ivo was present.

Someone squeezed her arm. Turning her head, Anne saw Trish Ransome, who had just arrived, her face alight with pleasure.

'This is nice,' she said in her gruff voice, tossing back the lank strands of black fringe, which threatened to get in her eyes. 'I love a crowd of people.'

'Stick around,' Anne laughed. 'It'll probably get even thicker. Come downstairs and get something to eat.'

The dining-room was empty when they got there, Deborah having vanished to gorge herself somewhere on her plateful of goodies. And no-one else seemed inclined for food just at the moment. Anne handed Trish a plate. 'Help yourself,' she invited.

Trish, who existed on a very small grant and was perpetually hungry, needed no second bidding. She grabbed a chicken-and-mushroom vol-au-vent and bit into it. Some of the creamy filling ran down over her chin, staining the front of the ancient Indian cotton dress she was wearing. Anne regarded her affectionately, and was about to say something when she became aware that Richard and Georgina had come in. Richard was looking so happy, her heart sank. She guessed what was coming.

He held out his hands to her. 'Anne! You've always been my best friend, and we both wanted you to be the first to know. Georgy and I are engaged to be married. I hope that one day you and Ivo will be just as happy.'

CHAPTER SEVENTEEN

TRISH SAID: 'So this is where you've got to. Your mother thought you must be out in the garden somewhere.'

Anne glanced round and smiled contritely, 'Sorry. Disappearing in the middle of breakfast isn't a very polite way to treat one's guest.'

'Blow that.' Trish flopped down on the garden seat, sprawling denimed legs in front of her. Although only nine in the morning, the August sun was already hot. The hydrangea bushes wilted, and even the animal noises from the nearby zoo sounded half-hearted. 'Today's the wedding, isn't it? I'd forgotten.'

Anne nodded. Apart from Clifford, Trish was the only person aware of her feelings for Richard, and it was a comfort not to have to dissemble.

Trish asked: 'Did you get an invitation?'

'Oh, yes.' Anne gave a twisted smile. 'Georgina asked me to be bridesmaid, as Rich doesn't have a sister of his own.'

'Ouch! How did you get out of that one?'

'I invited you to stay for a couple of weeks.' Anne glanced ruefully at her. 'Do you mind?'

Trish chuckled. 'What are friends for if not to be used in emergencies? So who's gone up to Scotland, apart from Sir Clifford and Lady Haldane?'

'Chris and Irene. Deborah. Imogen, but not Tim. That's because Chris has gone, of course.'

Trish grimaced at a bed of Ena Harkness roses. 'It must upset Lady Haldane quite a bit.' There was

235

silence, broken by the chattering of some sparrows perched in a row along the garden wall.

Felicity appeared and fed them with a plate of crumbs. 'Here you both are, then,' she said to the girls. 'Anne, aren't you going to finish your breakfast? Your mother wasn't pleased at your going off like that.'

Anne kissed her. 'Don't worry, Grandma. I promise I'll be the perfect hostess and daughter tonight when she gets home from work. Trish and I are just coming in to do the washing-up.'

'I'll do that.' Felicity was adamant. 'Strange as it may seem, I like housework nowadays. It keeps me busy and makes me feel a little less old and useless.' She sat down beside them. 'So! What does the future hold for you two now that your student days are finally behind you?'

Trish groaned. 'Don't, Mrs Bryce! It's quite frightening to discover that the last thing anyone wants is a couple of would-be stage designers.'

Felicity frowned. 'I'm sure with all your connections in the theatre you won't find it hard to get a toehold somewhere.'

Trish shook her head, and Anne laughed. 'It doesn't work like that, Grandma. No-one's going to employ two inexperienced designers. There's a lot of hard graft ahead of us, and that's only if we can find ourselves a job to start with. You know what any branch of the theatrical profession is like. Too many people chasing too few jobs. Luck always plays as important a part as talent.'

'Then your luck', Felicity retorted, 'is that you both know Clifford Haldane, so trade on that connection as much as you can. How do you think half the successful people in this world have got where they are? Naturally, they have to be good at what they do or they won't go very far, but that doesn't stop them making the most of who they know as well.'

Her granddaughter smiled. 'You always were a realist, Gran. Cliff and Penelope have asked Trish and me to spend a week with them in Devon. I take it you think we should accept.'

Felicity struggled to her feet, cursing the arthritic joints which were making her less mobile.

'Of course you should accept! Now, don't be foolish, Anne. Phone them as soon as they get back from Scotland.'

Clifford met Anne and Trish at Plymouth station and drove them across the moors to Fourmile Cottage, where Penelope was waiting to greet them.

'Are we glad to see you!' she said. 'Cliff and I were just beginning to get on one another's nerves. We're so used to this place being filled with people that a holiday on our own is something of a penance.'

Cliff paused in his task of humping the girls' hold-alls out of the car boot. 'Speak for yourself,' he told her. 'Thy presence to me is ever fair.'

'Liar!' his wife responded amiably. 'What's that a quotation from?'

'I don't know. I think I must have made it up.' He kissed her. 'But none the less true for that.'

Penelope laughed and led the way indoors, where tea was laid ready in the oak-beamed dining-room. She indicated the plate of Cornish splits, the bowl of clotted cream and the saffron cake, bought fresh that morning from a baker's in Tavistock. 'When in Rome . . . ' she said. 'And don't let me hear either of you say you're on a diet.'

'No chance of that with Trish,' Anne muttered disgruntledly. 'She never puts on an ounce of extra weight. And thank you both for asking us to stay. It's very kind of you.'

'Rubbish! This is practically your second home. And, as I said, you're doing us a favour. We're both suffering from post-wedding blues, although we didn't, of course, have all the excitement of preparation.'

Anne's heart sank. She knew she would have to hear about Richard's wedding, but could not bring herself to ask the necessary questions. Trish stepped nobly into the breach. 'How did it go in Edinburgh?' she queried. 'Did you and Sir Clifford have a good time?'

'For God's sake, call me Cliff!' He had come in behind them, having taken their luggage up to their rooms, and they all sat down at the table. 'And, yes, we both thoroughly enjoyed ourselves. Once Georgina's mother was finally convinced that Pen isn't at all like the people she writes about, they got on like a house on fire. And Callum is a very nice chap.'

Penelope launched into a detailed description of the wedding while Anne ate her tea, relying on Trish to make all the right noises. She was uncomfortably aware of sympathetic glances from Clifford, but fortunately Penelope did not seem to notice her silence.

'Rich still has another two years to go before he takes his Finals, so he and Georgy will live with her parents until then, and she'll keep on her secretarial job to help support them. We're also making Rich a small allowance until he qualifies. Anne love, it's good to see you eating so well. Have another Cornish split.'

'I'll split if I do.' Anne smiled feebly at the weak little joke and passed her cup for a refill.

'That's enough about the wedding.' Clifford rested his elbows on the table. 'What plans are you two hatching, now that you're out in the big cruel world?'

His over-hearty tone made his wife glance suspiciously in his direction, but Anne plunged in before Penelope could ask any awkward questions.

'We honestly haven't a notion what we're going to do yet. We really ought to be in Town, chasing up every job that's going.' The colour stained her cheeks. 'Actually, it was Grandma's idea that we might be better off down here, talking to you.'

Clifford grinned understandingly. 'Trust Felicity,' he said. 'An eminently sensible woman, never averse to a bit of nepotism. Let me think it over while you're here. I can't promise anything, but you know that. You're both totally inexperienced, and it's a branch of our profession, unlike acting, where strokes of phenomenal luck just don't occur. Never mind. As I said, I'll give it some thought and whatever I can do I will. Now, if we've all finished eating, how about going for a walk to get rid of the effects of too much food?'

They climbed to the top of the ridge where Anne had climbed so often with Richard in the past. The rolling vista of moorland, with its outcropping of granite rock, brought back memories almost too painful to bear. She could hear Richard's voice, identifying this or that bird, whispering urgently to her to look at the hare before it vanished into its form, feeding the wild ponies with lumps of sugar. Resolutely, she shut her mind against the crowding pictures and forced herself to concentrate on what the others were saying.

'I'm trying to get a company together for a production of the *Dream*,' Clifford was telling Trish, 'some time next year. A short season at Her Majesty's.' He seated himself on the close-cropped turf, resting his back against a boulder. 'But how to do it from a different angle, that's the problem.'

The girls and Penelope sat beside him, Trish leaning forward, her hands locked around her knees, Anne reclining full-length, supporting herself on one elbow, and Penelope, grumbling that she was not as young as she used to be, finding a chair-like niche in the rock. Nearby, a patch of harebells quivered in the evening breeze, the delicate pale-blue heads drooping at the end of long wiry stems.

Trish said thoughtfully: 'You mean fresh ideas are thin on the ground where Shakespeare's concerned.'

Cliff nodded gloomily. 'Modern-dress productions started years ago, since when we've had Shakespeare on swings, a Japanese *King Lear*, actors coming on in jeans and T-shirts, then switching to costume halfway through, cocktail-dresses at Elsinore . . . You name it, we've had it. So what do I do that's new?'

A curlew rose skywards with a flapping of wings, moving slowly and majestically westwards in the direction of the sea. Anne rolled on to her back and stared at the panorama of fast-scudding clouds.

'Perhaps', she volunteered shyly, 'what would surprise audiences nowadays would be a completely straightforward production. Proper fairies with wings, historically accurate Athenian costumes, real, old-fashioned, pantomime-type scenery. People don't expect that any more when they go to see Shakespeare. They might just enjoy the novelty of it all.'

Trish said excitedly: 'Yes, why not? You could bill it as a revival of the Sir Henry Irving production. You could even have the live rabbits running round the stage.'

Clifford flung up a hand. 'Heaven forbid! I draw the line at that. I can't have my actors risking a broken leg by tripping over some recalcitrant bunny who doesn't know upstage from downwind. But as far as the rest of the idea goes . . .' He stared musingly at the blue distances for a moment or two before giving a decisive nod of his head. 'Yes, it might just work. A good old-fashioned production could prove to be a novelty for a limited period if – and it's a big if – the production costs can be kept down. It was all right for Irving to have umpteen changes of costume and sets, but we're talking about the days

240

when you could buy a four-course dinner at Romano's, engage a box for three at the Adelphi and still have change out of half a crown. What's more, your modern audience doesn't like to be kept waiting while the scenery's moved. However, when I get back to town, I'll put the idea to Ralph and Aileen and see what they say.' Ralph Hogan had been creating the sets for Clifford's productions for some years now, and together with his wife Aileen, who ran her own theatrical costumier business, represented the cream of British stage design. The girls were overwhelmed at the mere thought of their names and ideas being mentioned in such exalted company, and could hardly believe their luck when Cliff added: 'I might even persuade them to take you on for a trial period. In a very lowly capacity, you understand.'

Later, as they walked back to the cottage, Penelope, one arm linked companionably through her husband's, murmured: 'Was it wise to raise the girls' hopes like that? Ralph and Aileen can take their pick of aspiring young stage designers any day of the week from anywhere in the British Isles.'

Clifford shrugged. 'I can but ask, and that's all I promised. Trish and Anne aren't fools. They don't expect miracles. They know the pitfalls of this business as well as I do. They haven't any false notions that it's going to be easy. And there's always the possibility that Ralph and Aileen will dismiss the idea of an Irving-style revival out of hand as far too costly and impractical.'

Penelope sighed. 'That would be a pity. It would be lovely, just for once, to have a Shakespearian production which doesn't look as though the costumes have been designed by Ronald Searle and the scenery by Emmet.'

Her husband laughed, causing the two girls, who were some way ahead, to turn and smile at him, enquiringly.

He squeezed Penelope's arm. 'Your notions of theatrical design, my darling, were old hat when Noah set sail in the ark.'

Penelope stuck her tongue out at him before lapsing into a giggle.

'They're the ideal couple, aren't they?' Trish asked much later, wandering into Anne's bedroom dressed in her pyjamas and perching on the edge of the window-seat. 'There can't be many marriages as good as theirs.'

Anne, who was seated at the dressing-table, brushing her hair, smiled at her friend in the mirror. 'You're a cynic,' she said. 'But you know that.'

Trish was indignant. 'I'm not. I just think that the odds against picking the right partner are enormous. Frighteningly so. I mean, people change as they get older. So someone who suits you at twenty won't necess-arily suit you when you're forty because the pair of you will have matured at different rates. Sir Clifford and Lady Haldane have been lucky enough to keep in step.'

Anne finished doing her hair and laid down the brush, staring at her reflection in the glass. The delicate heart-shaped face stared back at her, the grey eyes dispirited and ringed with dark circles. She felt sure it could have been the same for herself and Richard. Would it be like that for him and Georgina?

She had no idea she had spoken her thoughts aloud until Trish said bluntly: 'Forget about Richard. He's married now. He's happy.'

And that, Anne supposed, was the nub of the matter; the heart of her deep-seated resentment against Georgina Frere – or Haldane as she must now learn to call her. Richard so obviously loved her; and she, equally obviously, loved him. They were destined to be happy: it was written in their stars. So where did that leave her, Anne Seymour? With her work and the ever-adoring Ivo. But even he wouldn't go on adoring her for ever without a little encouragement now and again. She hadn't written to him for weeks, not bothering to answer his letters, and her conscience pricked her suddenly. She would write to him tonight, before she went to bed, a long newsy letter which would disguise the fact that she had nothing more personal to say. And next time he came to London she would be extra nice to him. Why not? What did she have to lose?

'Now,' Aileen Hogan explained patiently, 'if we use this yellow velvet for Hermia's costume and also for the underskirt of Hippolyta's wedding dress plus Lysander's cloak-lining, then we don't waste so much material and we save money. Right? So, if you promise to be very careful, you can pin together the sleeves of Hermia's bodice – only don't, for God's sake, put a stitch in them until you've shown me. OK? OK.'

The Hogans had accepted the suggestion of a straight production of *A Midsummer Night's Dream* with some reservations as to the cost; but after careful consideration had agreed that it might be feasible to stage a 'Henry Irving revival' as very few people would have any clear idea what the original was like. And, as far as the costumes were concerned, Aileen Hogan admitted that they could always be adapted for other shows. They had also agreed, as a great favour to Cliff, to allow Anne and Trish to gain some much-needed experience in their workshops; and as both girls wished to specialize in costume design they went each day to Aileen Hogan's studio in Soho – the whole top floor of a building which housed a strip club underneath.

For the first few weeks, the jobs they were given to do were so boring that Anne seriously began to wonder if she would not have been better off going to secretarial college and then working in an office.

Gathering up scraps of material from the floor, which she also had to sweep, and taking out basting stitches from garments someone else had sewn, was not her idea of being gainfully employed. It needed Trish to point out how much useful information she was acquiring in the process.

'Aileen's worth listening to,' Trish advised her friend. 'And she doesn't try to keep trade secrets to herself. She's a generous woman.'

Soon Anne found that she was looking forward to the day's work, however menial, and was enjoying herself; so much so that when Ivo unexpectedly turned up at the studio one lunchtime she was able to submit to his bear-like hug with a good grace and even look pleased to see him.

'So this is where you're working, for the great Aileen Hogan,' he said. Aileen, who had glanced up in annoyance at his unceremonious entry, succumbed to his charm. 'I've been round to Cameron Road,' he went on, 'and Cliff told me where you were.' He grinned at Trish. 'You must be the Trish Ransome I've heard so much about.'

'Sorry,' Anne hastily made the introductions. 'I forgot you two haven't met.'

'I feel we should have done.' Ivo held out his hand and winced slightly at the firmness of Trish's grip. 'I've heard so much about you from Anne.'

'Well, I hope you're not disappointed,' Trish answered gruffly as she released his fingers, and for no apparent reason she blushed.

'Young man,' Aileen Hogan said sternly, 'I don't know who you are, but I can't afford to have you wasting my assistants' time. Kindly make yourself scarce.'

Ivo did his injured-innocence look. 'I was hoping to take Anne out to lunch. I'm down from Nottingham for a couple of days. I'm assistant stage manager at the Playhouse. Clifford Haldane is my cousin.'

Aileen regarded him thoughtfully, then said grudgingly: 'Half an hour, no more. Take her to the pub on the corner. Anne, mind you're back promptly at one-thirty.'

Anne protested: 'I've brought sandwiches. I don't have to go.'

'Oh, for heaven's sake! The boy will think I'm a slave-driver.' Aileen waved her away. 'Go and enjoy yourself, but don't make a habit of it.'

Reluctantly, Anne fetched her coat and allowed Ivo to escort her to the pub, which was already packed with the lunchtime crowds.

'I wish you wouldn't do this sort of thing,' she grumbled when they had finally found a seat and Ivo had ordered drinks and food. 'It's so embarrassing. Do you realize how lucky I am to get a place in Aileen's studio? She's only taken on Trish and me as a great favour to Cliff.'

'You're too easily impressed,' was the airy reply. Ivo took a bread stick and snapped it in two. 'But I'm truly sorry if I've made you uncomfortable. I honestly didn't mean to. I apologize.'

Anne refused to be mollified. 'And you could have asked Trish to come, too.'

Ivo grimaced. 'I can see it's one of those days when I'm not able to do anything right. Which is a pity because I've something I want to ask you.' They were sitting side-by-side on a high-backed bench, and he slid an arm about her waist.

Anne sighed and tried to wriggle free but, without making a scene, found it impossible.

'Ivo love, I'm not prepared to throw up this job to shack up with you in Nottingham.'

He looked hurt. 'Who said anything about shacking up?' His arm tightened around her. 'Look, Anne, I know this is a dicey business and that my present

245

prospects are hardly brilliant, but things'll change, you'll see. I know they will. I feel it. I'm destined for a great career. I have this gut instinct about it. So what do you say? Let's take a chance and get married.'

Anne stared at him in disbelief, unable to speak for the moment. Taking advantage of this fact, he kissed her, much to the amusement of an elderly couple seated at a neighbouring table. Anne pushed him away.

'Stop it, Ivo. I don't want to get married. What about my career, or doesn't that count with you? I don't want to throw up this job with Aileen Hogan. I won't get such a good chance again. And for what? For the honour of becoming Mrs Ivo Kingsley? You really have a nerve. What about *my* future, *my* gut instinct?'

'I didn't know you had one.' Ivo spoke sulkily, but looked so defeated that Anne wished she hadn't been quite so vehement.

She impulsively rubbed her cheek against his. 'Ivo, you know I'm fond of you. But I'm ambitious, too. I'm not willing to leave London at present, and I don't want to get married.'

'You might, if you thought about it seriously.' He brightened. 'I'll throw up this job and come back here. Something's bound to turn up for me sooner or later.'

'No.' Anne managed to free herself from his embrace. 'Can't you understand? I don't want to get married yet. Not to you, not to anyone.'

But she knew it wouldn't have been true if Richard had asked her. For him she would have been prepared to sacrifice almost anything.

CHAPTER EIGHTEEN

WHAT WAS BILLED, somewhat inaccurately, as the Sir
Henry Irving revival of *A Midsummer Night's Dream*
achieved a reasonable success during its twelve-week
run, although not always playing to capacity houses.
Criticisms varied from accusations of trying to put
back the clock and being 'too gimmicky' to admissions
of pleasure and acknowledgement that there was still
an audience for 'straight' Shakespearian productions.
Clifford, who played the part of Bottom as well as
directing, came in for his customary share of praise,
as did his young and largely unknown cast; but it
was the Hogans' sets and costumes which garnered
most acclaim. But at the last-night party, held on the
stage of Her Majesty's, Clifford, in his speech, made
sure that Anne and Trish received a mention as the
authors of the original idea.

Tim, who had auditioned for and won the role
of Lysander entirely on merit, gave Anne's arm a
squeeze. 'Bully for Dad,' he whispered. 'It wouldn't
have been fair if Ralph and Aileen had taken all the
credit.'

Clifford's voice boomed on. 'I think we can congratulate ourselves on having done extremely well,
considering the competition. *Guys and Dolls* at the
National and an even greater attraction on TV. I
refer of course to the Falklands War.' This raised a
laugh and a cheer. 'So enjoy yourselves. You deserve
to.'

There was a general murmur of self-approbation
which masked the actor's perennial worry about where

247

the next job was coming from. But, for tonight, everyone was determined to have a good time and forget about tomorrow, drowning their worries in free champagne. Clifford, always the perfect host, moved among his guests, making sure he spoke to the most insignificant member of the cast and backstage team. He was still in costume and full make-up, an imposing sight as he finally descended on Anne and Trish with outflung arms.

'Bless you, my children! I hope you appreciated the little chuck-up I gave you just now.' He smiled over their heads. 'And here's Imogen with Pen. Come on, you two, you're late.' He adopted an injured air. 'You might at least have sat through the last performance.'

'We've each seen it five times already,' his wife complained. 'Any more and Imogen and I could have taken all the parts ourselves and saved you a lot of expense. Anne darling, it was a very good idea of yours and Trish's, and I insist on drinking a toast to you both. Stir yourself, Cliff! Four glasses of champagne.'

Imogen kissed her sister's cheek. 'Yes, congratulations, love. It was a brilliant notion. A great production. I'm sorry it's ended so soon.'

Anne helped herself to a smoked salmon sandwich from a plate on the long trestle-table which the caterers had set up on stage after the end of the performance. Around her, Theseus' marble palace, with its myriad gleaming lights, was revealed for the make-believe world that it really was. A strange way to make a living, she reflected; insubstantial in many ways, ephemeral, like living in Fairyland while all around you other, more sensible people mined coal or dug holes in roads. But she loved it; it was what she had dreamed of ever since her grandmother had taken her to her first pantomime. The smell of the size as she entered a theatre never failed to set her pulse racing. It was like coming home.

'Penny for them,' Trish said; and Anne laughed, shaking her head.

And it was at that moment that she became conscious of Tim's fixed gaze as he stared past Imogen towards the back of the stage, where the actor who had played Theseus – tall, florid, good-looking and just a little elderly for the part – had arrived at last from his dressing-room with Sylvia Gibson in tow. Anne liked Sylvia, but was none the less indignant at what she saw as a blatant disregard for other people's feelings. Sylvia had to know that Tim would be present, as well as taking into account the possibility that Chris and Irene would be there as well. To be fair to her, she was not to know that it was the first time the brothers had been under one roof for many years, nor of the blood, toil, tears and sweat it had cost Penelope to get Chris and Irene invited. There had been many impassioned appeals to Tim's better nature, all of which had fallen on stony ground. It was only when Penelope had threatened to boycott the last-night party herself, which would have upset his father, that Tim finally caved in.

'All right. But don't expect me to be civil to either of them. Just tell them to keep their distance.'

'Very well. I promise.' His mother had regarded him straitly. 'But don't you think it's high time you dropped this vendetta on another woman's behalf? It's insulting to Imogen. I thought you two were getting on better these days.'

Tim had grunted noncommittally, but the truth was that over the past few months he and Imogen seemed to have reached a better understanding. How much this was due to the fact that he had not set eyes on Sylvia for several months, while she had been filming abroad, he had been unprepared to question. Suffice it to say that he had been happier than for a long time past, and that he and Imogen were managing to lead a far more satisfactory life together.

And now, suddenly, after all this time, here was Sylvia just an arm's reach away, and looking as beautiful as ever. The luxuriant hair, knotted in a chignon at the nape of her neck, gleamed like a raven's wing in the artificial light, with not even a hint of grey to betray her forty-one years. Her face, with its high cheekbones, was tanned a delicate golden brown from whatever sunny clime she had been filming in, making her appear more exotically foreign than ever. She wore a flame-red chiffon dress, embroidered with beads, which sparkled with her every movement. Her high-heeled evening sandals gave her an added height, making her immediately visible over the heads of everyone around her.

'Shit!' Anne said under her breath and took her sister's arm. 'Come on! Let's have a look round. I always think there's nothing more spine-tingling than an empty theatre.'

'Hardly empty,' Imogen protested, laughing. 'Not with all this noisy crowd up here. Still, if it'll humour you, lead on. You coming, too, Tim?'

'What?' He turned blank eyes towards his wife, like someone waking from a dream. 'No ... No, I'll stay here, thanks. I ... I just want a word with Clinton Ames.'

Clinton Ames was Sylvia's companion, and Anne's heart sank. She was conscious of an overwhelming desire to take Tim by the shoulders and shake him violently. 'Come on, Im,' she said abruptly.

But Imogen, turning to set down her empty glass, came almost face-to-face with Sylvia. Indeed, her attention had already been alerted to the newcomer's presence by the inevitable cries of 'Darling!', 'Look who's here!' and 'How wonderful you're looking!' She stared for a long moment into the other woman's eyes before reaching instinctively for another glass of champagne, which she downed in very nearly one swallow. Then she asked for a refill from the waiter standing behind the makeshift bar.

'Im!' Anne tried to sound impatient rather than tense, but failed. 'Come on! You said you wanted to look round backstage.'

'No. *You* said that, not me. I'm staying right where I am.' Imogen was swaying slightly. 'Tim, here's your friend, Sylvia.' She enunciated the name carefully, as though it were of vital importance that it was clearly audible to everyone present. 'Sylvia! Hi! Have some bubbly.' And before anyone could divine her intention, or make a move to stop her, Imogen had thrown a full glass of champagne over her rival, drenching the flame-red dress and leaving a spreading stain.

For a moment, Sylvia stood perfectly still before turning savagely on her escort.

'You told me that neither Tim nor his wife was going to be here. You said Tim had told you he definitely wouldn't be at the party.'

Clinton Ames's slightly flabby features creased into a malevolent grin. 'Sorry, darling. I must have misunderstood him. A thousand apologies.'

'Just one would do if it were sincere, you bastard!' Sylvia was shaking now as much as Imogen. 'You lied to me on purpose, didn't you? One of your little diversions to liven things up a bit. God! Why did I believe you? I should know by now that you're a bitchy old woman!'

'Naughty naughty! That's sexist, darling.' Clinton Ames was plainly enjoying the havoc he had created.

By this time, the scene had attracted general attention. Clifford came across, looking perturbed and angry. Penelope broke off the conversation she was having with Irene and drifted over.

'What's wrong?' she asked.

251

But one glance at Imogen's flushed face, Sylvia's stained dress and Clinton Ames's expression of malicious satisfaction was enough to put her in the picture. She placed a protective arm around her daughter-in-law's shoulders.

'Come along, my dear,' she said firmly. 'Anne and I will take you home.'

Sylvia put out a hand to the younger woman. 'Imogen, I'm sorry. Truly. I didn't intend this to happen.'

Imogen shrank back, as though afraid that Sylvia's touch might contaminate her. 'Why can't you just leave us alone?' she demanded breathlessly, and burst into tears.

'Why the hell don't you do something?' Anne asked fiercely of Tim.

'Yes, why don't you, Tim?' It was Chris who had come up behind his brother. He ignored his ex-wife, although it was obvious to Anne that Sylvia had been aware of him for several seconds. The colour had crept into her cheeks, scoring two bright red marks high on the cheekbones beneath her tan. She stared at him defiantly, but he avoided her eyes.

Until that moment, Tim had been schooling himself to do what was right by Imogen, but the expression on Sylvia's face as she looked at his brother snapped his resolve.

'Why don't you all just go to blazes!' he shouted and stormed off the stage.

Chris, glancing round at the faces full of avid curiosity and surmise, felt that he had been here before and that this time it was once too often. He made a silent resolve that, as long as Tim continued to feel as he did, he would never again permit his mother to arrange a meeting between them. It was a thousand pities that Tim was able neither to forgive nor forget, nor to alter his feelings for Sylvia, because Chris missed his brother's companionship. They had been good friends when they were younger, covering for one another, standing together against authority, sharing the same ambition to be better actors even than their father. But now, because of Tim's unremitting enmity, he had lost that relationship, perhaps for ever.

He said quietly to Penelope: 'You and Anne must stay. For Dad's sake. Irene and I will drive Imogen home. Come along, Im love, let's find your coat.' And he signalled to Irene that they were leaving.

'Anne! We're both so pleased you're here, aren't we, Rich? Welcome to Edinburgh.'

Standing on the draughty railway platform, Anne wondered why she had come; why, after all this time, she had finally accepted Richard and Georgina's pressing invitation to pay them a visit. She had been asking herself that question all the way from King's Cross without arriving at any satisfactory answer. It had meant asking for a week off; but as things were quiet at the studio for the moment, Aileen Hogan had raised no objections. Indeed, Anne had been surprised by Aileen's offer to take her on the strength full-time, and detected Clifford's hand once again pulling strings behind the scenes. Trish had received the same offer but, after much agonizing, had declined. She had decided to risk freelancing after receiving a commission from an amateur operatic group to design them new costumes for *The Yeomen of the Guard*. There was very little money in it, but it just might lead to bigger and better things. Moreover, Trish, her head teeming with ideas, did not take kindly to working for someone else, and she and Aileen Hogan did not really get on.

But, then, Trish appeared to be at odds with everyone at present. Much as Anne was loath to admit it, there had been a slight strain on their friendship in recent months. Looking back, the rift seemed to date from mid-summer and Ivo's permanent return to London. While acknowledging that he had learned a great deal about his craft during his eighteen-month stint in Nottingham, he had none the less declared his intention of accepting no further work outside the capital – at least, in the immediate future. Anne had told him not to be stupid, that he was arrogant, that chance would be a fine thing, and finally that if he wanted to work in a very overcrowded profession he would have to take what he could get and be thankful for it. Somewhat to her annoyance, Trish had backed Ivo.

'You do what you feel is best for you,' she told him. 'Instinct is often a very sound guide in these matters.'

The last thing Anne had wanted was Ivo hanging around, unemployed and restless, monopolizing her time.

'I wish you'd mind your own business,' she had said tartly to Trish.

'Why?' Her friend had been equally acerbic. 'You bully that man something rotten and he's absolutely devoted to you.'

Anne had made a pettish rejoinder, and she and Trish came close to quarrelling. Perhaps it was that which had decided Anne on going to Scotland. A break from both Ivo and Trish would do her good; so, once she had obtained Aileen's permission, she telephoned Richard and told him she was coming. He was delighted and said that he and Georgina were looking forward to her visit. He suggested the end of October because his parents-in-law would be away and they could have the house to themselves. Which was how Anne came to be shivering on Waverley station in an autumn temperature several degrees lower than the one she had left behind in London.

She kissed Georgina and gave Richard a quick sisterly peck on the cheek before following them out to

254

where their ancient Ford Sierra was parked. Richard lifted her case into the boot, then climbed in and took the wheel.

'One of the things I've promised Georgy, as soon as we can afford it, is some decent transport. It's one of our priorities, isn't it, darling?'

'It'll have to be,' Georgina answered cheerfully, 'if you're going into practice in the wilds of Dartmoor.'

Anne was jolted into genuine interest. 'You're moving to Devon when you qualify?'

'Yes. Why does that surprise you?'

'I always assumed you'd stay in Scotland.' It was raining slightly, a fine misty drizzle, and the headlights of the oncoming cars blossomed from distant yellow pinpricks into dazzling golden flowers. 'But what about you, Georgina? Don't you want to stay up here?'

'Oh, I'll be happy if Rich is happy.' Georgina half-turned to look over her shoulder, and even from that brief glimpse of her face Anne could see that she meant what she said. Richard was her world, and there was no room in it for anyone else. 'He's a man of the south really,' she teased playfully. 'A soft liver, not like we hardy denizens of the north. By next summer, when he qualifies, he'll have had more than enough of cold winters and springs, and summers that aren't all that much warmer.'

Richard took his eyes briefly from the road ahead to give his wife a grin. 'You make me sound a right wimp. Anne, don't believe anything she tells you. It's simply that I've had a letter from old Merrison – you remember, the vet who lives near Yelverton – to say that next year he'll be looking for a new assistant, because his present one has been offered a partnership in Truro as from next September. It couldn't be better-timed from my point of view, and I've always loved Dartmoor. So now all I have to do is qualify.'

'You'll do that all right,' Georgina assured him. 'Dad says you're a natural, and you work so hard.'

'Thanks to you and all the support you give me. Sorry, Anne. Georgy's father complains we're a mutual admiration society, and he's not far wrong. We must try to curb it. It must be sickening for other people.'

The following days were to prove the truth of this statement. Whenever Richard was at home, Anne felt almost like a voyeur, so thick was the atmosphere with erotic overtones. 'They just can't stop touching one another,' she wrote to Trish. 'I feel that if I weren't here they'd be in bed, making love.'

It was, she realized from the first, an intensely physical relationship. Apart from the fact that her father was a vet, Georgina had very little in common with Richard. Their backgrounds – Scots Presbyterian and freewheeling theatrical – were totally dissimilar. And, whereas Richard was basically a serious person with a mature sense of humour, Georgina was a happy-go-lucky extrovert with an outsize sense of fun. There were moments when Anne found herself wondering how the marriage would wear, only to tell herself that she was suffering from a bad case of wishful thinking. And she liked Georgina. She liked her very much.

Georgina had taken the week off work so that she could be with Anne and show her the sights. Barkis, the dog, might have been jealous had he not long ago switched his allegiance to Richard, who now had all his devotion. The death of Sir Cloudesley Shovel had meant that Richard was able to reciprocate this affection without feeling guilty; and the Freres had resigned themselves to the fact that, when Richard and Georgina eventually left Edinburgh, Barkis would go with them.

In the long run, the week proved to be too busy for Anne to brood much, and for this she was grateful. By the time she had 'done' the castle, Holyrood Palace, Saint Giles, John Knox's house, walked Barkis up and down Calton Hill and shopped in Princes Street from end to end, all she wanted to do at night was to fall into bed and sleep. The colder air and rarer atmosphere also tired her and gave her a decent excuse to retire early. She was finding Richard's transparent happiness almost more than she could bear. She was glad she saw so little of him; but on the Friday evening, her last in Edinburgh, while Georgina was preparing supper, he came through from the study where he had been working and sat beside her on the sofa, stretching his long legs to the fire.

'Anne love, we haven't really had a good chat since you arrived. My fault, and I'm sorry. But you and Georgy seem to have got on well together. She's certainly loved having you here, and I hope that when we have our own home, in Devon, you'll visit us often.' He grinned at her companionably. 'So how's Ivo? When are you two going to get married? Don't pretend he hasn't asked you.'

Anne forced a stiff-lipped smile. 'You know how it is with the acting profession. We both feel we have a long way to go before we have any financial security.'

Richard raised his eyebrows. 'Didn't stop Mum and Dad. Doesn't stop most actors. They learn to live with that insecurity.' He tilted his head to one side, regarding her fondly. The soft shaded glow from the wall-lamps and the flickering shadows cast by the fire made him look vulnerable, the way she remembered him when he was young. 'Funny, isn't it? There was a long period when I was convinced I wanted to marry you or no-one. I couldn't imagine spending my life with anyone else. But first you had a crush on Chris, and then my cousin came along. At one point, I could cheerfully have murdered Ivo. But I could see you were smitten, and your happiness was the most important thing. And shortly after that I met Georgy.' He smiled tenderly at the recollection. 'Strange how life turns out. One moment you think it's blighted for ever, and the next something wonderful happens.'

Anne turned away so that her face was in shadow; so that he was unable to see her bleak expression. She knew she should be glad that he had found such contentment, but the words of congratulation stuck in her throat. Fortunately, before he could notice her silence and find it odd, Georgina opened the door to announce that the meal was ready.

The following day, they both went to the station with her to see her off on the early-morning train. Anne's last sight of them, as their figures receded, was of the pair of them holding hands, shoulders and thighs touching, pressed so close that there was no room to get even a postcard between them. Withdrawing into the carriage and shutting the window, Anne sank into her seat with a sense of something ended, as though a chapter of her life had finally closed. Of course it had really closed a long time ago; it was just that only now had she come to accept it. She thought of London, and suddenly that great sprawling giant began to feel like home. She thought of Trish, and was filled with a warm glow of affection. She thought of her future in the theatre and experienced a sense of mounting excitement. She thought of Ivo . . .

So what was she going to do about Ivo? He loved her. He wanted her. He had remained faithful for years. There were plenty of women who would settle for less. She had neglected him, ignored him and, if Trish were to be believed, bullied him, but it had made no difference to his feelings for her. He deserved his reward. She wasn't in love with him, but what did that matter, so long as he didn't suspect? As soon as she got to Cameron Road she would call him.

'Ivo,' she would say, 'let's get married.' He would be so delighted by her unexpected capitulation, he wouldn't pause to wonder what had made her change her mind. Trish and Clifford might guess the truth and have reservations, but they wouldn't interfere.

Anne closed her eyes, suddenly drained of emotion. She had come to a decision and she would see it through. That was all there was to it. Now she could empty her mind and sleep until the train reached London.

CHAPTER NINETEEN

'IF YOU WANT ME to finish this dress in time for the wedding, for goodness' sake, stand still!' Trish scolded. 'How am I supposed to pin this hem straight if you fidget like a cat on hot bricks?'

'Sorry.' Anne pulled down the corners of her mouth. 'It's just that I feel so restless.' She fingered the swathes of ivory satin which made up the skirt. 'Am I doing the right thing, Trish?'

'Oh, for pity's sake!' Her friend stabbed the material viciously with a pin. 'You've had nearly a year to make up your mind. You can't call the wedding off at this late stage. Think of Ivo. Think what it would do to him. If you had doubts, you shouldn't have got engaged in the first place.' She went on shrewdly: 'It was that holiday in Edinburgh, wasn't it, that made you decide to marry him? When you saw how happy Richard is with Georgina, you realized there was no hope for you, so you thought you'd put poor Ivo out of his misery instead.' She shrugged. 'OK. Why not? But in fairness to him, Anne, you have to try to make the marriage work.'

Anne stared down from the drawing-room windows at the windswept front garden of The Laurels. Although still August, the weather had turned cold and overcast, with a sharp breeze which whipped the big hydrangea to a frenzy. The new gardener, who had replaced John Bone, was attempting to mow the lawn hampered by the padded sleeves of his anorak. The wedding was only three weeks away, and everyone was hoping that things would improve. For Penelope, it was an almost daily topic of conversation. Anne wished she could feel a corresponding interest.

Everyone had been delighted when she and Ivo announced their engagement the previous October; everyone with the exception of Clifford and Trish. Neither of them was easy to persuade that this was what she really wanted, although Cliff was more willing to be convinced than Trish.

'If you're certain you're not in love with Rich any more . . .' he had murmured dubiously.

'You can't go on loving someone who doesn't love you,' Anne lied. 'At least, not in real life.'

Trish had stubbornly refused to believe that Anne no longer felt anything for Richard. 'Pull the other one; it's got bells on,' she kept saying – a reaction that seemed increasingly justified as Anne repeatedly refused to set a date for the wedding. To begin with, she defended the postponement on financial grounds; but when Ivo, falling on his feet as usual, started to earn some money by doing voice-overs for a television dog-food commercial, the argument seemed less cogent.

'I told you something would turn up, didn't I?' he crowed triumphantly, catching her in his arms and kissing her ruthlessly. 'I knew if I hung around long enough, instead of rushing off to the wilds of Northumberland or wherever, the luck would run my way. It always does.'

'It's hardly acting,' she protested feebly. 'Not what you were trained for. What happened to all that vaulting ambition?'

He grinned. 'You are a snob, Annie.' Lately, he had taken to calling her by Tim's pet name, and it irritated her. 'My ambition's no less, but you told me yourself that an actor has to get work where he can find it, so you're hoist with your own petard. With the money I earn from this, we can at least start looking for a furnished flat.'

Anne was trapped. She had told Ivo she would marry him and did not have the courage to back out now. She wasn't even sure that she wanted to. Richard had passed his final exams with flying colours, and a week or two earlier, during the move south to Devon, he and Georgina had spent several days at The Laurels, while he collected some of the things he had left stored in the attic. Once again, Anne had been aware of that almost overwhelming sense of physicality which sparked between them. She was conscious, even more than in Edinburgh, of the way they constantly touched each other, of their long languorous looks when they thought they were unobserved. Anne wasn't sure that she was capable of such sensual passion.

Richard and Georgina's relationship had been in stark contrast to that of Tim and Imogen, whenever the latter two had been at Cameron Road. Since the ill-fated last-night party which had ended the run of *A Midsummer Night's Dream*, matters between them had reached an all-time low. Imogen had started drinking steadily, although Penelope was able to report to Anne that it had not as yet affected her work.

'She's still the most efficient secretary I've ever had,' she said with evident relief. 'She doesn't drink during working hours, but Tim said she heads for the whisky-bottle as soon as she gets home at night.'

'Then, perhaps Tim should ask himself whose fault it is,' Anne replied crisply.

But, she thought guiltily, wasn't she doing exactly as Tim had done? Wasn't she marrying one person while she was in love with another, hoping against hope that she could make it work? She had often wondered why Tim and Imogen had stayed together when they were patently so unhappy, and had come to the conclusion that their very unhappiness made them emotionally dependent on one another. Each, ironically, understood what the other was suffering, and neither had anywhere to run. Imogen couldn't leave Tim because she loved him, and Sylvia didn't want Tim, who loved her. So they stayed together, feeding one another's sense of loss.

Anne shivered uncontrollably, and Trish swore as she pricked her thumb with a pin.

'Can't you stand still for more than two minutes? There'll be blood all over your dress at this rate.'

Anne apologized for a second time and forced some enthusiasm into her voice. 'It's going to look lovely, and I'm truly grateful. It's far better than anything I've seen in the shops at three times the price. Ivo will be thrilled. And they say', she added gaily, 'that a woman's wedding day is the most important of her life.'

Trish glanced up, startled by the change of tone. 'So I believe,' she answered drily. 'But nowadays it's difficult to know which one they're referring to – first, second or even third.'

'I don't know why you couldn't get married from home,' Barbara protested, helping herself to a second glass of champagne. 'I don't know why you always have to let Pen and Cliff do everything for you.' But it was a complaint without substance. In reality, Barbara had been more than content to leave her daughter's wedding arrangements in Penelope's capable hands, and the deep long-standing friendship between them removed all sense of obligation. Even Felicity had been reconciled to her favourite granddaughter being married in London when Anne explained that the majority of her and Ivo's friends were there. She had devoted her energies instead to ensuring that Barbara did not buy something totally unsuitable to wear. The resulting dress and coat, in a rich mustard yellow, with black accessories, had been a pleasant surprise for everyone.

'Mother's looking smart,' Imogen remarked to Anne as they stood, together with Ivo, receiving guests. After much persuasion, she had consented to be her sister's matron of honour, with Trish as chief bridesmaid. The other bridesmaid, much against Anne's personal inclination, was Chris's stepdaughter, Deborah Grantham, now eleven years old.

The problem of finding a colour which suited Imogen's fair prettiness, Trish's dark gypsy appearance and Deborah's auburn hair had been a knotty one. In the end, they had settled on dresses made of the same ivory satin as the bride's, but in a less showy pattern. It had worked very well, and the overall effect had been quite dramatic. Ivo, in hired morning suit, had signalled his approval at the altar. Back at The Laurels for the reception, he had demonstrated it in more practical fashion by kissing his wife and all three attendants with enthusiasm. Now, standing at the head of the receiving line, his exuberance knew no bounds.

'Don't they look marvellous?' he demanded of his guests. 'Trish made all the frocks herself.'

Out of the corner of one eye, Anne could glimpse the faint expression of contempt on Deborah's pert little face, and longed to wipe it off with a well-aimed swipe. She was embarrassed herself at times by Ivo's lack of inhibitions, but that he should be the butt of Deb Grantham's sneers angered her beyond bearing. She had never liked Irene's daughter, but had told herself in the past that Deborah was only a child, and would grow out of her less appealing ways as she got older. This had not happened, and Anne's dislike of her was as strong now as it had ever been. The only reason she had agreed to have her as bridesmaid was in order to please Penelope, to whom she owed so much that to refuse would have been unbearably churlish.

Neither Richard nor Georgina was present at the wedding, for which Anne was profoundly grateful. Richard had felt he could not ask for time off so soon after joining Sidney Merrison's practice, and Georgina was expecting a baby. Richard wrote that she was three months pregnant, but they had waited to tell everyone until they were certain that nothing was wrong and that Georgina would not miscarry. The news had naturally delighted Penelope and Cliff, who had secretly been afraid that they would never be grandparents. It also set the final seal of happiness on Richard's marriage, and in one way made things easier for Anne. She was more reconciled to the decision she had made and therefore more content than she had been for many months past. This morning, when she woke, she had even felt the stirrings of excitement, like any normal bride. She had sung in the bath.

Now, standing by Ivo's side, receiving the congratulations of their friends, she felt convinced she could make a go of the marriage; that she could put Richard out of her mind once and for all. Chris and Irene arrived; Chris, in his early thirties, even handsomer than he had been when younger. It was the face which set so many female hearts a-flutter, both on stage and on screen, but which had no effect whatsoever on Anne. She found this all the more surprising when she recalled how she had hero-worshipped him as a child. Nowadays, the memory of that schoolgirl crush only embarrassed her and made her wonder what she had seen in him compared with his youngest brother.

Irene, of course, had eyes only for Deborah. 'Baby, you look wonderful,' she said, 'and so grown-up. Chris and I are so proud of you, aren't we, darling?'

Thus appealed to, Chris kissed his stepdaughter dutifully on the cheek. 'You look great, Debs, just great.'

It occurred to Anne that perhaps Chris was not very fond of Deborah; that he could see through the sweet-as-syrup exterior to the ruthless determination underneath. She wondered why he and Irene had never had children of their own. Maybe they couldn't, or maybe Irene had decided against having another baby. But, for whatever reason, Deborah remained her only child, the sole recipient of all her maternal affection.

Tim had refused to come to the wedding; and, although Anne was sorry for her sister's sake, she was also relieved. She did not want any unpleasantness to mar this of all days. It was, she told herself firmly, a happy day; a day she would remember for the rest of her life. And for the most part she was happy. Imogen drank a little more than she should have done; Ivo became a fraction too exuberant; Clifford, who had given Anne away and knew too much, gave an over-fulsome speech to compensate for that knowledge. Anne enjoyed herself nevertheless and was still humming the Wedding March when she went upstairs to change. It was then that she discovered herself alone with Deborah Grantham.

'Where are Trish and my sister?' she asked in surprise as Deborah followed her into the bedroom and shut the door. 'I thought you were finding them for me.'

'Imogen's a bit squiffy,' Deborah answered frankly, 'and I couldn't see Trish. But it doesn't matter. I'm perfectly capable of helping you to get ready.' She glanced critically at the pale blue suit laid out on the bed. 'Is this what you're wearing to go away on honeymoon?'

'Yes.' Anne removed her veil. 'Don't you approve?'

'It's all right. A bit plain, but quite nice.'

'What would be your choice?'

Deborah shrugged. 'Something a bit more *with it*. But I suppose you're getting on rather now.'

266

If any other eleven-year-old had said such a thing, it would have made Anne laugh. But there was something studiedly offensive about Deborah's words, and she felt her hackles rise. She replied rather coldly: 'I'm twenty-three next month. Even someone of your limited intelligence could hardly believe that was old.' She instantly regretted the cheap jibe, but there was no retracting it. She saw the child's eyes narrow with dislike before the heavy almond-shaped lids hid them from sight. She felt uneasily that she had made an enemy, but why it should bother her she had no idea. 'That was rude of me,' she added, 'and I'm sorry. Unhook the back of my dress for me, would you, please?'

Deborah obliged and, when Anne had stepped out of the folds of rustling ivory satin, picked up the dress and laid it carefully on the bed.

'Will you and Ivo be coming back here to live after the honeymoon?' she asked.

Anne dragged a brush through her ruffled hair and reached for the skirt of her suit.

'Just for a while, until we can find a flat. Penelope's very kindly letting us use the attic, which used to be Richard's. It's big enough to turn into a bed-sitting-room for the time being. It means we can have a bit of privacy when we're at home. Our friends can come and visit us without imposing on Penelope and Cliff.'

Deborah sat down on the edge of the bed, abandoning all pretence of helping.

'Do those friends include Trish Ransome?' she enquired.

Again Anne felt a surge of irritation at what, in another child, she would merely have regarded as a normal curiosity. 'Yes,' she answered curtly, restraining the impulse to ask why.

Deborah swung her sandalled feet, watching them

appear and disappear beneath the long skirt of her bridesmaid's dress. 'Do you think that's wise?' she demanded pertly.

Anne paused in the act of pulling on her jacket. 'What on earth do you mean by that?' she asked in amazement.

Deborah raised limpid eyes to meet hers. 'Well, I rather thought . . . I mean, it's obvious to me at any rate . . .'

'Go on!' Anne said impatiently. 'What's obvious to you?'

'That Trish is in love with Ivo.'

Anne stared for a moment, then burst out laughing. 'Honestly! I never heard such rubbish! Whatever's led you to that conclusion?'

If she had hoped that her scorn would discomfort her youthful informant, she was unlucky. Deborah gave her a superior smile which would have done credit to someone twice her age, and answered: 'The way she looks at him when she thinks she isn't being watched. And she always gets really nasty if I say anything the least bit rude about him. I merely remarked that he was behaving like a clown this afternoon, and she bit my head off.'

Anne was disconcerted. She herself could remember times when Trish had taken Ivo's part against her; when she had taken her to task for her treatment of him. All the same . . .

'I expect she just thought you were an impertinent little girl, criticizing your elders.' Heavens! She sounded like her mother.

Deborah got to her feet. 'She's in love with him. You can take it from me.'

The bedroom door opened and Trish appeared, looking flustered.

'Anne love, I'm so sorry. I didn't realize you'd come up to change. You should have told me. I was in the garden with Ivo. He was explaining how difficult some of these television commercials are to make. Fascinating. He didn't realize you were changing, either, until your mother told us. Anyway, I've packed him off to his room, and he should be ready almost as soon as you are. Hi, Debs! Thanks for standing in for me.'

Deborah smiled sweetly and moved towards the door. Once out of Trish's range of vision she winked knowingly at Anne. Then she was gone, closing the door softly behind her.

'God! She's an awful child!' Anne exclaimed violently, causing Trish to raise her eyebrows.

'She's not the most likeable of children, certainly, but I wouldn't go so far as to say that she's awful. What brought that on?'

'Oh . . . nothing. Well, just some things she's been saying. She just gets up my nose, that's all.' Anne picked up her handbag and linked one arm through her friend's. 'Come on, let's go down and face all that confetti that Pen's been storing up for the past few weeks.'

'You're very quiet,' Ivo said. 'Have I done something to upset you?'

The big double windows, leading on to the balcony, were wide open, and for the time of year it was unusually warm, confounding all those critics who had said they were mad going to the Lake District for their honeymoon.

'It'll pour with rain the whole time, and you'll freeze to death. That is, if you get out of bed long enough to find out.' Nudge nudge, wink wink. Anne had endured the innuendoes with gritted teeth. Ivo, on the other hand, had seemed to enjoy them.

She turned her head to look at him, lying on the bed beside her. 'No, of course not,' she assured him. 'I'm just tired, that's all. I'm not a good traveller.' They had stayed at a hotel in London overnight and driven up to Windermere today, starting early that morning. She reached out and smoothed his bare shoulder. 'Once we've had dinner, I'll recover, you'll see. Then I'll be my usual sparkling self again.'

'Good.' Ivo got out of bed and shrugged on his dressing-gown, wandering across to the window to look at the view. It was already dusk, but there was still sufficient light to see the last of the sun's rays dancing across the surface of the water. The wooded slopes of the lake's opposite shore were slowly changing from copper to purple to black, turning into places of menace and mystery. Two boats, moored at the hotel landing-stage, bobbed and curtsied with the movement of the current. It was an enchanted setting, and he should have been the happiest man alive, married to the woman he loved, but somehow he wasn't. He felt vaguely dissatisfied and, not normally analytical, he tried to fathom out why.

Their love-making of last night and this afternoon had been perfectly satisfactory, Anne responding to his caresses with an ardour and eagerness which apparently matched his own. Why, then, did he feel that he was being cheated? That a part of her eluded him, lost in a private world where he was unable to follow? That he did not, and probably never would, know exactly what she was thinking and feeling? He told himself that he was imagining things; that, like Anne, he was tired and tense after the last couple of days. A good meal, a bottle of wine and he would regain his usual buoyancy and optimistic outlook on life. They had only a few days here because he was due back in London at the end of the week to do a toothpaste commercial; one in which, this time, he was to be seen as well as heard. So they mustn't waste precious moments. He turned back to the bed, holding out his hand.

'Come on, lazybones! Get dressed for dinner. I'm starving. Then a walk by the lake, I think, and an early night.'

Anne tried to smile at the prospect, mindful of Trish's words that it was her obligation to make this marriage work. She had made her bed and now, literally, she must lie on it. But the thought of her friend made her pause.

'Ivo, what do you think of Trish? You like her, don't you?'

He looked startled, as well he might.'Yes, of course I like her. She's a nice girl. What is all this? Why do you suddenly want to know how I feel about Trish?'

'Oh . . . no reason.' Anne slid out of bed. 'Bags I the bathroom first. And don't forget we have to go and see your mother tomorrow.'

Mrs Kingsley had not come to the wedding, pleading poor health, so Anne and Ivo were committed to a visit to Grange-over-Sands the following day. Anne was not looking forward to it. On the one occasion she had travelled up with Ivo to see his mother, she had felt that Sarah Kingsley did not approve of her, nor of the fact that she and Ivo were, by then, sleeping together – a state of affairs he had not bothered to conceal. Anne had felt she was somehow being blamed for leading Sarah's one lamb astray.

Ivo caught her round the waist as she made a dive for the bathroom, letting his dressing-gown swing open and pressing her naked body close against his own.

'Happy?' he asked. Then, with a resurgence of his old self-confidence, added: 'What does it feel like to be Mrs Ivo Kingsley?'

Anne laughed, relieved. She could cope with this

Ivo, but the serious, unnaturally subdued one made her uneasy.

'Brilliant,' she smiled, gently releasing herself.

He opened the bathroom door for her with a flourish. 'Of course,' he grinned. 'If you're being honest, what else can you say?'

CHAPTER TWENTY

'IT'S A BOY! Ewan Callum Richard Haldane. Seven and a half pounds. Not a whopper; but, then, you wouldn't expect a child of Richard and Georgy's to be a big baby, would you? I hope I'm not interrupting, but I just had to come round and let you know. The telephone seemed far too impersonal for such exciting news.'

Penelope stripped off her heavy camel-hair coat and laid it on a vacant chair. Aileen Hogan's studio was hot, making a pleasant contrast to the cold March wind which was blustering along the London streets. Beneath the coat she wore a pair of tailored slacks and a smart red blouse. There was colour in her cheeks, and happiness had given her blue eyes an added sparkle. Her tangle of brown curls was even more unruly than usual, making her seem far less than her fifty-seven years. Anne wished that time had been as kind to her mother; but Barbara, the same age, was beginning to look lined and careworn.

'I work for a living,' she had replied tartly when her younger daughter, in a moment of tactlessness, had pointed this out to her. 'I don't idle my time away writing tra— Well, novels.' Anne suspected that the word her mother had bitten back was 'trashy', but had not dared to seek confirmation. There were, after all, jealousies and disagreements between the firmest of friends, as she and Trish had discovered.

She kissed Penelope's cheek and offered congratulations, noting out of the corner of her eye that Aileen was not looking best pleased at this disruption to their

273

morning routine, but unable to protest to the wife of a valued, and valuable, client. Instead she said: 'How wonderful. When did you hear? Wait a minute. I think we may have a half-bottle of wine somewhere. We must all wet the baby's head.' She opened a cupboard in one corner of the room, and most of the contents spilled out to meet her. 'Oh, God! Anne, I thought I asked you to tidy these shelves last week.'

'I've straightened them three times in the last six months,' Anne muttered, but gave her most ingratiating smile. 'I'll do them this afternoon, Aileen, without fail.' She received a grimace and a sympathetic grin from the studio's two full-time seamstresses.

Penelope pushed a pile of cartridge paper to one side and perched on the edge of a trestle-table. Aileen Hogan held no terrors for her, and she had every intention of making the most of her news. 'Georgy's labour started late last night, and she had the baby at eight o'clock this morning. Rich phoned us after you'd left, Anne, while the rest of us were still having breakfast. Mrs Frere's on her way from Edinburgh now.'

Anne laid down her pencil and wiped the back of her hand across her forehead. Normally she liked warmth, but the studio heat seemed suddenly unbearable. The portable radio, tuned permanently to Radio 1, was playing Ravel's 'Bolero' for what felt like the ten millionth time since Torvill and Dean had skated to a gold medal with it in the Winter Olympics.

'I'm afraid I can't find the wine, Lady Haldane,' Aileen Hogan said without much regret. 'We must have drunk it, although I can't remember when exactly. It'll have to be instant coffee if you can stand it.'

She was plainly hoping that her unwanted guest would refuse, but Penelope answered cheerfully: 'Anything. I don't care. I'm so happy I'd probably drink hemlock if you offered it.' And, without realizing that she was tempting fate, continued: 'Our own grandchild at last. I can't quite believe it.'

'Have you told Tim and Imogen yet?' Anne enquired, going to fill the kettle from the tap above the old stone sink at one end of the room, then plugging it into the nearby electric point. She wondered how her sister would take the news. Imogen had so wanted to give Penelope and Cliff their first grandchild.

Penelope lost her sparkle and looked as unhappy as she could do in such joyous circumstances. 'I told Im as soon as she arrived this morning, and she phoned Tim. He's rehearsing at the moment. A revival of *Richard of Bordeaux*, playing Thomas of Gloucester. Cliff says he's miscast; he'd have been better as the favourite, Oxford. Well, that's show business for you. I thought you were going to be asked to do the costumes for it, Aileen, but Tim tells me no. Never mind, you can't win them all.' She turned back to Anne. 'They're both delighted, naturally. About the baby, I mean.'

Anne wondered just how delighted her sister and brother-in-law really were, and guessed that Penelope was investing them with some of her own emotions, but she made no comment.

'So', Penelope went on when Anne had made the coffee, and everyone was drinking it from an assortment of none too clean mugs, 'when are we going to hear some good news from you and Ivo? Six months is plenty of time in which to start a family.'

'We don't want one yet,' Anne replied hastily. 'We have our respective careers to think of. Did I tell you that Ivo's been offered the job of hosting a new children's programme that the BBC is planning for the autumn? They wanted someone not too famous, but familiar, and those toothpaste ads he did were very successful. Younger viewers seem to have liked them anyway.'

'Mmm.' Penelope pursed her lips. 'You did tell me, as a matter of fact, and I was talking to Trish about it. She doesn't think you should encourage him. She says it's not what he set out to do. She says he's a good actor, and he is. I remember being very impressed with his Thomas Mendip in a RADA production of *The Lady's Not for Burning* which Cliff dragged me to.'

Anne looked thoughtful. 'Trish seems to take a very great interest in Ivo's career, so perhaps she'd care to know that, like most actors, he's happiest when performing to an audience, and there will be a live children's audience in the studio. And then, of course, there's the money, which we could do with if we're ever to get a place of our own.' She changed the subject. 'So when will you and Cliff be going to Devon?'

'I shall go as soon as I can.' Penelope set down her mug and got to her feet. 'I'm between books at the moment, but Imogen's already typing up my notes for the next one.' She sighed. 'I sometimes feel my novels are like Banquo's descendants, stretching out to the crack of doom. Still, as long as someone wants to read them . . . Cliff's filming out at Elstree at the moment, so his visit will have to wait.' She put on her coat. 'Sorry, Aileen, to have barged in like this. Love to Ralph.' And with a wave of her hand she was gone.

After work, Anne went straight to Earls Court, anxious to see for herself how Imogen was taking the news of the baby. She had offered to work late, to make up for time lost in the morning, and it was gone seven when she finally left the studio. Ivo was at Television Centre for a meeting with the producer of the proposed children's programme and had warned her to expect him when she saw him. Trish, who was designing costumes for an end-of-term school show, had telephoned to know if Anne would care to spend the evening with her in her tiny bed-sitter, but had seemed relieved when her friend said no. Conversation between them had been strained since Anne's marriage, and Anne was reluctantly coming to the conclusion that Deb Grantham had been right when she said that Trish was in love with Ivo.

When she finally reached Earls Court, the escalator bore her upwards, past the graffiti-covered walls, to the flat where Tim and Imogen continued to live because neither could make the effort to move, and which was growing a little shabbier with every passing year. There was an air of neglect about it which showed in the unswept carpets, the stained unpolished furniture and the film of dust which lay over everything. A vase of dead flowers stood in the middle of the dining-room table, a heap of magazines cluttered one armchair, and a wastepaper-basket was full to overflowing with unwanted circulars, discarded envelopes and old newspapers. Anne, following her sister through to the kitchen, noticed two bottles of whisky, one still in its wrapping, fresh from the off-licence, the other half-empty, standing on the sideboard.

'Tim's not here,' Imogen said. 'First run-through or something. They couldn't hire the hall until this evening. I'm making myself a sandwich. Do you want one?'

Anne demurred. 'Aren't you cooking yourself anything?'

'Can't be bothered.' Imogen indicated the sliced loaf, butter, cheese and tomatoes. 'This'll do me. I'm not very hungry, but there's bacon and eggs in the fridge if you want them.' She added: 'Put the kettle on if you fancy some coffee. I'm going to have a whisky. A stiff one.'

'You drink too much.' The words were out before Anne could stop them.

To her surprise, Imogen made no effort to refute the allegation.

'Maybe you're right, but it stops me thinking.'

Anne had no need to ask what about. Imogen had always loved Tim, even long ago when they were children. There had never been anyone else for her, and she had had no other boyfriend. And Tim had always loved Sylvia Gibson . . . And Ivo loved her, who loved Richard, who loved Georgina. Trish loved Ivo. What an absolutely God-awful mess! There seemed to be a peculiar malignancy about the way Fate engineered people's affections. Why couldn't life be nice and easy, with everyone falling for the right partner? It would make for so much more happiness in the world.

Anne settled for a sandwich, made herself a cup of coffee, put it all on a tray and returned to the dining-room where Imogen was already seated at one end of the sofa. Her plate, still full, was on the floor beside her, and both hands were folded around a tumbler of what looked like neat whisky. She downed the contents in several large swallows, then rose and poured herself another from the opened bottle on the sideboard.

'Pen called at the studio with news about the baby,' Anne said, sitting down at the other end of the sofa and biting into her sandwich. 'She was terribly excited.'

Imogen resumed her seat and sipped her drink, trying to make it last a little longer than the previous one.

'She would be. Ewan's her only real grandchild.'

Anne hesitated before asking: 'Im, are you sure you can't have another child? I know the doctor said so after you lost the baby, but doctors have been known to be wrong.'

'Well, that one wasn't,' Imogen retorted. 'Do you think I haven't taken a second opinion? And a third and a fourth? It's always the same story. I can't have any more children.' She began to cry noiselessly, the tears running down her cheeks. 'I've always felt that

278

things would have been different between Tim and me if we could have had children. They would have made a bond, something we shared, just the two of us. He'd have forgotten about Sylvia in the end.'

'It doesn't necessarily work that way,' Anne pointed out gently. 'Lots of men have children and still leave their wives. At least that hasn't happened to you. Tim's still around.'

'Only because Sylvia doesn't want him!' Imogen replied scornfully. 'I'm not a fool, Anne. Sometimes, if he's worried about a part, or not getting one, he talks in his sleep. It's not my name he mentions.'

Anne sipped her coffee, noting that her sister had almost finished the second glass of whisky. 'What are you going to do about it?' she asked.

'Nothing. What can I do?'

'You could leave Tim. Start afresh.'

Imogen shook her head. 'I'll never leave him as long as he wants me. I wouldn't be any good on my own.'

'You might get back your self-respect and stop drinking so much. Secret, solitary drinking is the very worst kind.'

'Spare me the sermon.' Imogen put her empty tumbler on the floor beside her nearly full plate. Her eyes strayed longingly towards the bottle on the sideboard. 'You'd think I was an alcoholic to hear you talk. I can control it. I don't touch a drop during the day. Have you ever heard Penelope complain about my work?'

'No, but—'

'But what?'

'There could come a time when you can't control it. And it's dangerous. You drive a car.'

Imogen was insulted. 'I never drink and drive, you can take my word for it. It would be irresponsible.' She gave her sister a sideways glance. 'It's getting late. Won't Ivo be expecting you?'

Taking the hint, Anne got reluctantly to her feet.

279

There was no point in staying longer. Imogen did not want her company and was dealing with the news of the baby's arrival in the only way she knew how.

'Ivo's out,' Anne said, 'but I'll be going all the same.' She stooped and kissed her sister. A string of platitudes rose to her lips, but she dismissed them. They would do no good in Imogen's present frame of mind.

But as she made her way downstairs to the flats' main entrance, Anne had an uneasy feeling that her sister's mood might be a permanent one.

Trish was in her dressing-gown, boiling a saucepan of milk on the gas-ring, when she heard a knock at the door. She opened it to find Ivo standing on the landing. He looked a little taken aback when he realized she was ready for bed.

'Sorry,' he said. 'I didn't mean to disturb you, only the meeting at the Beeb broke up early and I didn't fancy staying in Cameron Road. Anne's not there. Pen says she's gone to see Imogen. Richard and Georgina's baby was born this morning, so I suppose Anne thought her sister might be taking it badly.'

'It's about time she let Imogen sort out her own problems,' Trish answered with asperity. 'Come in. I can do you some hot milk if you'd like it. I dare say I could even find you some food.'

'I've eaten, thanks. But if you're sure it's OK I will stay for a bit. I hate being on my own upstairs, and I can't keep imposing on Pen and Cliff. You're sure I'm not keeping you from your beauty sleep?'

Trish laughed shortly and held the door open. 'All the sleep in the world wouldn't turn me into a beauty. Do you want some milk? I can lace it with a little brandy for you which I truly do keep for medicinal purposes.'

'Right. Thanks. That would be fine.' Ivo shed his coat and looked around him He had been to Trish's bed-sitter once or twice before, but this was the first time he had really been aware of his surroundings.

It was a biggish room with a raised part at one end, separated from the rest by three shallow steps and a flimsy railing. This was where Trish slept, and the vivid patchwork quilt which covered the bed made a striking contrast to the white-painted walls. It was the general theme of the room: pale background against which bright cushions, chair-covers and curtains glowed like jewels. Trish herself was wrapped in a brilliant emerald-green kimono, her dark hair tumbled about her shoulders. The whole effect was typical of her and very pleasing. Ivo sat down on an old and threadbare settee covered with a large swathe of coral-red velvet.

'I like this,' he approved. 'I love bright colours. I wish Anne was fonder of them.'

Trish lifted the saucepan of milk from the gas-ring and poured the contents into a mug. 'She prefers subtler shades.'

'I know. Smoky soft sort of hues.' He accepted the mug Trish handed him. 'So how's your latest project coming along?'

She shrugged and sat opposite him in a painted wicker chair decorated with bright orange cushions.

'It's work, I suppose. Doesn't make much, and I'm still dependent on the allowance my parents manage to give me. But I'm determined to be famous one day and then I can pay them back.'

Ivo sipped his milk. 'I'm sure you will be. You have the talent. More than most of us have in our little finger.'

She looked astonished. 'Is this Ivo Kingsley – the great Ivo Kingsley – speaking?'

Ivo set his mug down on a glass-topped table with rickety legs and threw up his hands defensively. 'OK, OK! I know what everyone thinks of me, that I'm a bighead. Maybe I am, but I think if you know you're good why not say so? It's the curse of the English to be falsely modest.'

'I guess so.' She grinned at him. 'Let's make a pact. I'll do the costumes for all your plays when you're our most famous Shakespearian actor.'

'Done.' And they shook hands with mock solemnity.

Ivo picked up his mug again. Watching Trish across its rim, he was suddenly aware that she was a very handsome woman. Until this moment, he had always considered her rather too large and gauche to be attractive. Now he realized that he was wrong. She might not be delicately fair like Anne, but her dark gypsyish appearance had a charm of its own. And the Geordie accent, which used to grate on his ears, he now found quite appealing. He smiled at her companionably, beginning to feel warm and at ease.

When he had reached Cameron Road that evening, eager to tell of the successful outcome of his meeting at Television Centre, he had found the attic room empty and in darkness. He knew that he and Anne were both working people, so he had no right to feel as disappointed as he did. He had gone in search of Penelope, who was reading a book in the drawing-room, and they exchanged news. She offered to make him a meal, but he had already eaten in the BBC canteen. Penelope returned to her book, and he felt shut out and resentful.

Every now and then, during the past six months, he had experienced the same sensation as he had done on the second night of his honeymoon, looking out over Lake Windermere; as though there was an invisible barrier between himself and Anne. He supposed, deep down, he had always known that she was not as fond of him as he was of her, but he had assumed that marriage would provide the answer. Once Anne had made a commitment to him, everything would be simple and straightforward. But it hadn't worked out like that. She was affectionate, teasing and, he had to admit, loving, but still elusive. There was still a part of her that was not completely his. She lay in his arms at night and let him make love to her, but her mind was elsewhere. But when he asked her of whom or of what was she thinking she firmly denied that it was of anyone or anything but him.

'It's your imagination,' she would say, kissing him until he was silent; but she never looked him directly in the eyes.

For a while afterwards, he would believe her. He was imagining things. Then, on some occasion like this evening, he would know for sure that he had never possessed her completely and probably never would. The knowledge frightened him, and all he wanted was to get out of the house and run. It was the same tonight, but where would he go? It was too late to ring any of his many friends, and he had no desire to drink alone in a pub. It was then he had remembered Trish.

Her voice brought him out of his reverie. 'I wish you'd stop staring. You're making me uncomfortable.'

He started guiltily. 'I'm sorry. I was just thinking what a nice-looking woman you are and wondering why I'd never noticed the fact before.'

Trish blushed to the roots of her hair, then burst out laughing at his obvious discomfiture.

'Ivo, you'll never win a medal for diplomacy. I hope you watched that tongue of yours at today's meeting. God! How remiss of me! I haven't asked you how it went.'

'I got the job, so I must have been the soul of tact.' His round pleasant face registered concern. 'Anne's always telling me I speak first and think second, and she's right.'

Trish pulled down the corners of her mouth. 'I ought

to congratulate you, I suppose. About the job, I mean. But I can't pretend I'm delighted. I'm afraid a job of this sort will divert you from what you're best at: acting. You could be a really great actor, like Sir Clifford. However, if you're pleased, it's not up to me to cavil. If it's really and truly what you want to do.'

Ivo finished his milk, put down the mug again and leaned forward, his hands linked between his knees. 'Do you mean that?' he asked, staring hard at Trish's earnest face. 'That I could be as good an actor as my cousin?'

'I shouldn't say it if I didn't,' was the gruff reply.

There was silence, except for the hissing of the old-fashioned gas fire. Then Ivo went on: 'And you think I'm doing the wrong thing by taking this job with the Beeb?'

Trish's black eyes met his hazel ones without flinching.

'Yes. Before you know it, you won't be just a TV presenter, you'll be a TV personality and you'll forget how to be anything else. You'll be seduced by the fame and the money. And after a while you won't be able to play anyone but yourself. The public deserve something better from you, because you have the talent.'

There was another silence. Presently Ivo got up and, leaning over, kissed Trish gently on the forehead.

'You're a good friend. I promise to think seriously about what you've said.'

CHAPTER TWENTY-ONE

TIM INVITED ANNE AND TRISH to watch the dress rehearsal of *Richard of Bordeaux*. They sat in the back row of the stalls, whispering criticisms to one another about a production that somehow had a dated feel, as well as some glaring flaws. Cliff had been right: Tim was hopelessly miscast as Thomas of Gloucester.

'Bolingbroke's sleeves are too long in the first act,' Trish muttered. 'Far too foppish for a man of action.'

'What about Tim's hat in Act Two?' Anne muttered back. 'I overheard him telling Penelope the other day that it hurts his head, but the designer insists it's perfect and refuses to change it.'

Trish pursed her lips. 'I'd say the designer's right in this case. He just hasn't got it on properly. Generally speaking, it's the acting and direction that're at fault. No-one seems to have any faith in the play.'

'The colours are a bit garish,' Anne objected, a remark which called forth Trish's scorn.

'They're perfect for the period. I suppose you'd go for gold and white and honey-beige, like the original Gielgud production back in the thirties. Copy-cat stuff.'

Anne felt her irritation mounting. For the last six weeks, she had been dying to have a go at Trish, but had desisted for lack of proof. Now, however, she could contain herself no longer and said angrily: 'I'd be afraid to have such positive views, if I were you, telling other people what's right and what's wrong. Advising them how to feel and think.'

'What's that supposed to mean?' Trish's voice was

necessarily low, but her indignation was apparent.

'It means I think it was you who persuaded Ivo to turn down that job with the BBC.'

There was a guilty silence before Trish asked uneasily: 'Did Ivo tell you so?'

'No. I put two and two together. It was the morning after he spent the evening with you that he suddenly changed his mind and refused it.'

After a moment, Trish murmured defiantly: 'What the hell! All right, I did tell him I thought he was making a mistake. For heaven's sake! You must know it yourself. Ivo has talent.'

The producer, halfway down the central aisle, slewed round in his seat and shushed them. But the moment he called 'Break!' Anne resumed the conversation.

'I'm not saying Ivo was wrong to do what he did. I just wish it had been his own decision.'

'It was.' Trish was defensive. 'All he needed was a push in the right direction. It's like shopping for clothes. Sometimes you know something isn't right for you, but you still want a second opinion.'

'I should hardly compare a career move to buying clothes; and, until you shoved your oar in, Ivo was very happy at the prospect of a job with the Beeb.'

'But it was wrong for him,' Trish insisted. 'A lot of actors could host a children's programme, but very few would make a superb Prince Hal.'

Anne knew that what her friend said was true, and her annoyance increased accordingly. As Ivo's wife, she was the one who should have talked things over with him and given him the benefit of her advice. But she hadn't. She had been content to let him get on with his life while she concentrated on hers. The knowledge upset her and made her unreasonable.

'I wouldn't presume to dictate to him,' she answered.

Trish was hurt. 'I didn't dictate. I merely told him my opinion.'

'You do dictate.' Anne's mouth set obstinately. 'Look at you just now! Implying I don't have any original ideas, just because I thought the costume colours rather garish.'

'I implied nothing of the sort!' Trish gasped and bounced to her feet, letting her seat up-end with a clatter. 'I'm going. I've better things to do than stay here and quarrel with you.'

They did not meet again for several days, and it was almost a week later that Trish called at Aileen Hogan's studio, bearing an olive branch in the shape of an invitation to lunch.

'I've just got paid for that last job I did,' she muttered apologetically. 'I could run to a couple of ploughman's at the pub.'

'Oh, Trish!' Anne hugged her friend. 'I'm sorry. I was bad-tempered because you were in the right and I was in the wrong.' She fetched her jacket and, with Aileen's permission, accompanied Trish to the Dog and Duck. Settled at a table, she resumed: 'We mustn't let differences of opinion about Ivo spoil our friendship.' She hesitated, then added almost shyly: 'I know you're fond of him.'

Trish blushed and stared at her glass of lager. 'Does it show that much?' Anne nodded, and she sighed. 'Oh, well! I'm glad you know – I think! Will it make any difference to us?'

Anne squeezed her friend's hand. 'Our friendship's special. You've always known that I love Richard. If I thought for a moment Ivo wanted you–' She broke off, uncertain how to continue.

Trish finished the sentence for her. 'You'd divorce him tomorrow. Thanks.' She smiled ruefully. 'But he doesn't, so we both have to make the best of our respective situations. But I do promise to keep my mouth shut and my nose out of your and Ivo's affairs in the future. OK?'

'You don't have to, you know. You're Ivo's friend as well as mine. You're probably the best friend he's got.'

In early September, after a few lean months when he came perilously close to regretting his refusal of a lucrative job with the BBC, Ivo was offered a contract for three productions with a provincial repertory company, including a chance to play the lead in *Hamlet*. This performance was lauded by the local newspapers and picked up by the national press, with the result that he was invited to repeat it in London. At first, audiences were inclined to be thin; but by Christmas, word-of-mouth recommendation having spread, he was playing to packed houses, and it was being generally accepted that a new Shakespearian star had entered the theatrical firmament.

'I can't help feeling a little piqued', Cliff complained as he helped Penelope decorate the Christmas tree, 'that it's Ivo, and not Chris or Tim, who's proving himself my successor.'

Penelope looped a tinsel streamer around the lower branches. 'I thought it was Olivier and Gielgud he was being compared with. Has anyone ever told you you're extremely conceited?'

He kissed her cheek. 'Yes, you. At least once a day since I met you. Are these the only fairy lights we have? We'll have to buy more. After all, this is our grandson's first Christmas.'

Richard and Georgina were bringing the baby to London for a few days over the holiday, before going to Edinburgh for New Year. In addition, Barbara and Felicity had accepted with alacrity an invitation to spend a week at The Laurels, so Penelope was able to look forward to what she liked most: a full house and lots of people around her. A family party was being planned for Christmas Day, the only snag being that

Tim would undoubtedly refuse to come if Chris were present.

'I can't help that,' Penelope told Cliff with a sigh. 'If he's so pigheaded, he'll just have to spend Christmas by himself because I'm making sure that Imogen comes. If she's left alone with Tim in that horrid flat, she'll spend the time drinking.'

Somewhat to her surprise, Imogen, when approached, made no protest. 'Tim definitely won't come,' she agreed, fitting a clean sheet of paper into the typewriter, 'but I don't think I care. If he wants to stay home and be miserable, let him.'

Penelope drew up a chair and sat down on the opposite side of the desk, her ancient caftan – much repaired and washed to a nondescript greyish colour – flowing around her. She had been dictating since early morning and felt she deserved a break.

'Don't you love Tim any more?' she asked gently.

Imogen shrugged, her hands poised over the keyboard, intimating that she wished to get on with her work. 'You can't keep loving someone who doesn't love you.' She switched on the recording machine, but Penelope leaned over and switched it off.

'That's a fallacy,' she said. 'There are loads of instances to the contrary. On the other hand, people do fall out of love, particularly if their affection isn't returned. Is that what's happened to you? And don't think I'd blame you if it is.'

Imogen did not answer for a moment, then she abandoned her attempt at work. 'Not really.' Her face was bleak. 'But I'm trying to convince myself that I can lead a separate life from Tim and still be happy. Sometimes, like now, I think I'm winning; then at others I know it's just a mirage. I love Tim. I always have, since I was little. There's never been anyone else as far as I'm concerned. I was never like Anne, with crushes on older men and lots of boyfriends. I love him deep down in my bones. Does that sound silly? But I can't describe it any other way.'

' "A durable fire," ' Penelope murmured. 'Sir Walter Ralegh. "But love is a durable fire in the mind ever burning; never sick, never old, never dead, from itself never turning." '

Imogen nodded. 'Yes. That's it exactly. I'll remember that. What does it come from?'

'Heaven knows! I just remember learning it at school, and it stuck in my mind. It surprises me somewhat because I was never academically inclined. I left that to your mother. All my energies went into hockey and netball in the winter, cricket and rounders in the summer. Not that Barbara wasn't good at sport but, then, she was good at everything.'

'But no dress sense,' Imogen chuckled. 'A constant source of distress to Anne and my grandmother.'

Penelope would have liked to talk more about her daughter-in-law's feelings for Tim, but seeing that she had successfully diverted Imogen's thoughts, if only temporarily, from her troubles she did not care to pursue the subject. Instead she laughed and said: 'Poor Felicity! I wonder what Babs will embarrass her in at Christmas?'

Barbara arrived sporting a brown-and-red check skirt, a pink jumper and a navy cardigan beneath her old and much-worn Burberry. Black shoes and grey tights completed an outfit which made the colour-conscious Penelope wince. But her friend had saved the best for Christmas Day: an electric-blue taffeta dress, embellished with a quantity of glittering jewellery.

'Talk about the fairy on top of the Christmas tree,' Felicity moaned to her younger granddaughter.

But Anne was in no mood to enjoy her grandmother's sense of outrage as she would normally have done. Richard's presence in the house only served to remind her how much she loved him and how much she resented his obvious happiness with Georgina. What made matters worse was his assumption that she was just as happy with Ivo.

The baby, Ewan, now nine months old, was exactly like his father: small, dark, with enormous brown eyes, and giving the same sense of tough wiry strength for all his fragile appearance.

'You should have one, Anne,' Richard said, nursing Ewan on his lap and smiling at her across the baby's head. 'Once you have a child, you realize what you've been missing. Now Ivo's doing so well, you can't be so worried about money.'

'Actors are always worried about money,' she retorted. 'Even people like your father who have no need to be. Why do you think he still grabs at any and every film part he's offered, regardless of what it does for his reputation? And we haven't even got our own home yet.'

It was Christmas evening, and everyone else, having finished dinner, had remained at table to play an uproariously childish game of Tippet. Anne, in the initial stages of a cold, which was manifesting itself in bouts of sneezing, had excused herself and come upstairs to the drawing-room. While she was there, Richard had come in holding Ewan, who had woken up and started crying.

'Ivo would like children,' Richard argued. 'He told me so. He doesn't mind risking it. And as long as you're here with Mum and Dad you're sitting pretty. Unlike most landlords, they'd be over the moon to have a baby around the place. It's you that's being over-cautious.' Fortunately for Anne's peace of mind, he felt that he had now said quite enough on a subject that was not really his business. He abruptly changed it. 'Why isn't Tim here?'

'Need you ask?' Anne blew her nose again. 'He still

won't go anywhere Chris and Irene are invited.'

Richard sighed and kissed the baby's head, nuzzling the soft black down which covered Ewan's scalp. 'It's years now! Why can't he forgive and forget? It's tearing Imogen apart, any fool can see that. She's drinking pretty heavily.'

Anne laughed bitterly. 'You haven't seen the half of it. She's been very moderate today. I don't honestly know what I'm going to do about her.'

'There's nothing you can do. We can none of us live other people's lives for them, however much we'd like to.' Footsteps sounded on the stairs, and a moment later Georgina entered. Richard's eyes lit up at the sight of her. 'It's Mummy,' he said to Ewan, 'come to find us. She can change your nappy while she's here.'

Georgina bent down and lifted her sleepy son into her arms, but her eyes were on Richard. Anne saw the glance which passed between them and, as always in their presence, felt like someone spying through a bedroom keyhole. She got up.

'I must go down and join in; otherwise I shall be accused of spoiling sport.'

'It's very hectic and noisy,' Georgina warned her with a laugh. 'Especially now that Clifford and your Ivo are team captains.'

Anne wanted to scream: 'He's not my Ivo. We don't own one another!' Instead she smiled briefly and moved towards the door.

'Anne!' Richard's voice stopped her. 'Do you think it would be a good idea if we invited Imogen to stay with us for a week or two? I'm sure Mother wouldn't mind. In fact she was telling me she'd been trying to get Im to go away for a while.'

Anne felt a pang of jealousy shoot through her. 'You'd better ask Imogen herself,' she advised. 'I can't answer for her.'

292

Privately, she thought her sister would refuse because she would be afraid to trust Tim on his own. But later, while she was putting on her coat to go home, Imogen told her that she had accepted.

'Rich has asked me to visit him and Georgy in Devon. I said I might go at Easter.'

Anne nodded. 'Very sensible. It will do you good to have a holiday away from Tim. And you've always loved Devon.'

Ivo was going to be a problem, she realized as soon as the attic door had shut behind them. He was immediately all over her, wide awake, adrenalin racing after being on such a high at the party. He had drunk just enough to make him amorous but not sleepy, and insisted on singing 'Do They Know It's Christmas' to her, irritatingly off-key. Anne, on the other hand, was emotionally exhausted, heavy with the onset of her cold and wanting nothing so much as to roll into bed and forget everything until the morning. Her head ached, her nose was blocked and she felt awful.

Ivo suggested a nightcap. 'A drop of whisky. I'll run down and get it.'

'I've drunk enough,' she answered pettishly, 'and so have you. Don't forget you have a Boxing Day matinée tomorrow. I'm going to have a hot bath and go to bed.'

'Good. I'll come and scrub your back.'

'No. Look, Ivo love, I'm tired and I just want to sleep. Tomorrow, perhaps, I'll be better.'

He ignored this and tried to take her in his arms. 'The best remedy for any illness is making love,' he said exuberantly. 'You know that makes sense.'

Angrily she struggled free of his embrace. 'I've told you! I'm tired!'

He stared at her, a slight frown replacing the smile in his eyes. 'It seems to me you're always tired lately.

You don't have to stay at the studio until all hours. I bet Aileen Hogan doesn't.'

Anne was racked by guilt. She knew she had made a lot of excuses these past few weeks for working late and coming home worn out. And Aileen was not a slave-driver. Anne worked late deliberately to avoid making love. She had hoped that the demanding part of Hamlet would sap Ivo's strength for all other activities, but she had reckoned without his seemingly inexhaustible supply of energy. He deserved better treatment from her, and with a sinking heart she capitulated.

'OK. I'll skip the bath and we'll go straight to bed.'

Half an hour later, Ivo sat up in bed, his naked body gleaming with sweat in the shaded glow from the bedside lamp.

'What's the matter?' he asked. 'I can't seem to do anything to please you.'

Anne propped herself up on one elbow. 'I'm sorry, darling. I really am. But I did warn you that I wasn't feeling well. I'm getting more snuffled up by the minute.'

Ivo shook his head. 'It's not only that. There's something else. Something you're not telling me. There's always been something wrong with our relationship, hasn't there?'

'Of course not!' Why couldn't she admit it? Why couldn't she come clean and tell him the truth? He deserved it. But she couldn't stand the thought of hurting him more than she had done already. 'Lie down and we'll try again. It'll be all right this time, I promise.'

But he made no move. 'Oh, I'm sure it will,' he said bitterly. 'You'll fake an orgasm, and poor old Ivo will be happy, then you'll roll over and get your rest.' He leaned towards her, his eyes fierce, one hand gripping her throat. 'But who will you be dreaming of as you drift off to sleep, eh? Answer me that! You've never loved me, have you? What a fool I've been not to realize it before.'

He wasn't hurting her, but Anne's heart was beating uncomfortably fast. His hand felt heavy on her neck, and his fingers were pressing into her flesh. Then fear was replaced by anger and she pushed him away.

'Don't let's play games, Ivo. It's very late and you have to work tomorrow. I'm very fond of you, you know that.'

'And that's supposed to satisfy me, is it?' He threw back the blankets and got out of bed. 'I'm going out for a while.'

'Ivo!' Anne held out her hand. 'Don't be silly! Let's get some sleep and we'll talk in the morning. Everything will look different then, I promise.'

He pulled on jeans and a sweater. His expression was grim. 'Will it?' he queried. 'I doubt it. Oh, don't worry. I'll be back later. I just need some air.'

He let himself out of the attic and went downstairs softly, so as not to wake the rest of the house. Outside, there was still a lot of traffic about, and he could hear home-going revellers shouting at the end of the street. He turned up the collar of his anorak and started walking swiftly, trying not to think of anything much, taking refuge from his unquiet thoughts in exercise. He had no idea how long he had been walking, nor how far, when he realized he was passing the house where Trish had her bed-sitter. He automatically glanced up at her window, although he knew she had gone home to Newcastle for Christmas. So, at first, he thought himself mistaken when he saw a light in her window. He stopped and took several paces out into the road to get a better view. There was a light all right. He stepped forward again and rang her bell.

A minute or so elapsed before she cautiously opened the window and leaned out. 'Who is it?' she demanded.

'It's me.' Ivo lifted his head so that a neighbouring street-lamp illumined his face. 'I thought you'd gone home.'

'Wait,' she said. 'I'll come down and let you in.'

'So what are you doing here?' he asked when he once more found himself in Trish's room, surrounded by the white walls and splashes of brilliant colour.

She shrugged. 'I had a blinding row with my parents yesterday morning and caught the first train back to London.' She tried to smile. 'Silly, I suppose. It's never pleasant spending Christmas Day on one's own. I know I could have phoned Lady Haldane and she would have politely invited me over. But it was a family occasion, especially with Richard and the baby there, and I didn't feel I could intrude. But after a day doing nothing I couldn't sleep. I was sitting up, reading. That's my explanation. Now, what's yours? What are you doing roaming the streets on your own at two in the morning? You look awful. Why don't you sit down?'

For answer, Ivo suddenly put his arms around her, laid his head on her shoulder and burst into tears.

'I'm just so pleased to see you,' he said.

CHAPTER TWENTY-TWO

'IT'S GOOD OF YOU BOTH to have me,' Imogen said, unloading her case from the boot of her Metro and breathing deeply. 'It's lovely to be back at Fourmile Cottage after all these years.'

'Of course.' Georgina nodded. 'I forget you've all been here before. It's very good of Penelope and Clifford to let us use it until we scrape together enough money for a place of our own. And it's so handy for Mr Merrison's house and the surgery. Rich is out on his rounds at the moment, but he's promised to try to get home for tea. Come in. You must be tired after such a long journey.'

'It wasn't too bad. I started at the crack of dawn and beat the holiday rush.' Imogen picked up her case and followed Georgina into the cottage, where she could hear Ewan faintly wailing. He was over a year old now, having celebrated his first birthday a few days earlier, and was seated in his high chair in the kitchen, banging the tray with his spoon. Barkis was crouched adoringly at his feet, and a large tabby cat was looking out of the window. Another cat, a black one, was stretched out on the mat beside the cooker. Georgina introduced them as Iago and Iachimo – 'Iggy and Ikey for short. Richard says they're both Shakespearian villains. I wouldn't know about that, but those two', she added affectionately, 'certainly are. Last night they ate the fish I'd bought for supper. Now, if you'd like to go and unpack, I'll get lunch. I've put you in the bedroom in the extension. That way you get a good view of both the road and the hills at the back.'

Looking out at the familiar scene, framed by the old pink-and-green floral curtains, Imogen was glad that she had come. Everything was so peaceful here; life's hectic pace so much slower. But later, when she and Georgina were finishing lunch, and Ewan was valiantly trying to force a spoonful of mashed potato up his nose, a wave of unease swept over her. What was Tim doing? How was he managing? He had been far too ready to let her come on this holiday without him. True, he was working. The ill-fated *Richard of Bordeaux* had closed after a very short run, but Tim had immediately been offered a part in an American play which had been very successful on Broadway, and which now looked set to repeat that success in London.

'If all goes well,' Tim had said, 'it'll be a nice little earner for some time to come.'

So, as it was Easter and the foreign tourists were already pouring into the capital, there had been no chance of his being able to accompany her. Nevertheless, the alacrity with which he said, 'You go. It'll do you good,' made Imogen suspicious. Would he try to contact Sylvia as soon as he was alone? Imogen found herself wishing that there was something stronger than fruit juice and coffee to drink. Didn't Richard keep any alcohol in the house?

'What's the gossip from London?' Georgina asked, finding conversation with her guest unusually hard going. She recalled Richard saying that Imogen was rather shy and quiet.

'What? Oh, there's no such thing really as London gossip,' Imogen replied. 'It may seem just a huge sprawling city to outsiders – I used to think so myself – but when you live there you know it's just a collection of different villages. I can give you the lowdown on St John's Wood and Earls Court, but nowhere else.'

Georgina flushed, feeling that she had been rebuked. 'I was really asking for news about the family: Anne and Ivo, Rich's parents and . . . and Tim.'

'Oh, they're all right.' I'll faint in a minute, Imogen thought, if I don't get a drink. The silence seemed oppressive. Why had she come? What was she going to do here for a whole week?

'I thought . . .' Georgina hesitated. 'I thought Anne seemed a bit off-hand with Ivo at Christmas. I wondered if they were having problems.'

But she could see by Imogen's blank stare that she had no comprehension of other people's troubles. She had been wrapped up in her own for so long, it never occurred to her that there might be more unhappiness in the world than just hers. She had become self-centred, self-absorbed. Georgina was beginning to regret Richard's impulsive invitation. How was she going to keep Imogen entertained for the next seven days?

'Sylvia? It's Tim. I have to see you. It's OK. Imogen won't know. She's down in Devon. I promise I won't make trouble if you let me come round. I just want to see you, that's all.'

Sylvia groaned. 'For God's sake, Tim, don't you ever give up? I thought we'd finished with all this nonsense a long time ago. I'm forty-four. Menopausal. I can't cope with it. Please, please leave me alone.'

'I only want to talk to you,' Tim pleaded. 'Just reassure myself you're still my friend. I don't know when I'll get another chance. Imogen rarely goes away on her own.'

In spite of herself, Sylvia was touched. 'Just reassure myself you're still my friend.' What woman could resist such a plea? she wondered, and sighed at her own weakness. But she wasn't inviting him round to her flat. She wasn't that stupid.

'Look,' she said, 'I'm meeting my agent at the Savoy for lunch at one. I'll see you in the foyer at quarter to for a quick chat. But that's it, Tim. Five minutes for old times' sake, and after that you leave me alone.'

She replaced the receiver quickly before he had time to demur and at once felt guilty, but she couldn't renege on her promise now. She glanced at her watch and decided she'd better hurry. London traffic was appalling nowadays, especially on Saturdays. She went into the bedroom to dress.

The taxi deposited her at the Savoy's main entrance with five minutes to spare, but when she got inside Tim was already waiting. His face lit up when he saw her, and he kissed her cheek. 'You look wonderful,' he told her.

'I don't feel it,' was the irritable reply. 'Thanks to you, I had to get ready in a hurry. So? What's this about?'

'What I said over the phone. I just want to see you. There's no ulterior motive. I need to be with you for a while.'

'Tim, you're hopeless! What am I going to do with you? It's nearly fourteen years since we were engaged. Thirteen since I jilted you for Chris.'

'Do you still love him?' Tim possessed himself of one of her hands, hanging on to it in spite of her attempts to pull it away.

Sylvia shook her head. 'Not any more. I did for a long time after the divorce, but I'm over it now.' She saw the look in his eyes and added hastily: 'That only means I'm no longer in love with Chris. My heart's my own again, and I intend to keep it that way.' She glanced towards the door to see if her agent had arrived. 'Shit!' she exclaimed. 'There's Clinton Ames. He's spotted us. For God's sake, let go of my hand. You know what a creep he is. The news that we've been seen together will be common knowledge by the start

300

of every matinée performance this afternoon. Which reminds me, don't you have one?'

'Not until three-thirty. Hell! He's coming across.'

'Tim dear boy! And Sylvia darling.' Clinton Ames's urbane tones reached out and caressed them. 'How lovely to see you both.' He pecked Sylvia's cheek and slapped Tim's shoulder. 'Where's that spitfire wife of yours? Not lurking in the shadows, I trust, with another glass of wine to throw at poor old Sylvia?'

'She's staying with my younger brother in Devon,' Tim answered shortly.

'Ah, yes. The estimable Richard. The only one of you three who didn't feel the lure of the greasepaint. Whereabouts in Devon is Rich living now?'

Sylvia tried to catch Tim's eye. She didn't trust Clinton not to make mischief. But Tim was so relieved to escape any innuendoes about himself and his companion that he was only too ready to supply the information. The other man nodded.

'A sensible lad, young Richard. Too bright to take up this damned unpredictable profession. Horse doctors will always be in demand. I don't suppose he knows the meaning of "resting". Incidentally, your cousin's doing bloody well for himself. Ivo Kingsley. Been offered several juicy leads with the National, I understand. How lucky to make one's mark so young, while the rest of us slave away for kicks and ha'pence. Ah, well! I must get along. Toby Wilson's treating me to lunch. Shall we be waving at each other across the restaurant?'

'Only at me,' Sylvia replied tartly. 'With my agent. Tim's just a chance encounter. He was leaving as I was coming in.'

'Of course.' Clinton Ames gave his thin-lipped smile. '*Au revoir*, my dears. We shall meet again, no doubt, at Philippi.' And he sauntered in the direction of the restaurant.

301

'What did he mean by that?' Tim asked uneasily.

'Who knows? He just likes to put on airs to be interesting. And here at last is Pete.' For the first time in years, Sylvia leaned over and brushed Tim's lips with her own. 'Good luck. And take care.'

'Are you feeling all right?' Richard asked, as Imogen resumed her place at the tea-table. 'You're suddenly looking very pale.' A thought struck him. 'That phone call – it wasn't bad news?'

'No.' Imogen spread jam and clotted cream thickly on a scone. 'Just a friend from London, passing on some information he thought I'd be interested to hear, that's all.'

The telephone had rung in the middle of their meal, and Richard had answered, expecting the call to be for him. One of the neighbouring farmer's cows was expected to calve at any time. But he had returned after a few minutes to say: 'Imogen, it's for you. Someone called Clinton Ames, from London.'

Imogen had been astonished. She knew Clinton by name and reputation, and also from that dreadful party when she had drenched Sylvia Gibson with wine. But why he would be phoning her at all, let alone while she was on holiday in Devon, was beyond her comprehension. Clinton, however, was not slow to enlighten her. In his smooth unctuous voice, he regretted being the bearer of bad tidings, but he did think she ought to know that Tim and Sylvia had been holding hands at the Savoy this lunchtime. Of course, they had said it was a chance meeting, and of course they might be telling the truth, but there was never smoke without fire in his experience. Anyway, Imogen could make of it what she liked; he had done his duty, and when it came right down to it that was all that mattered in this life, wouldn't she agree? He did hope she'd forgive him disturbing her holiday, but Tim had mentioned she was staying at Fourmile Cottage, and he just happened to have the number written down because he had once had occasion to phone dear Clifford there. And it was so much better to get these things off one's chest immediately. Then, wishing her a happy Easter, he hung up.

Imogen had stood there, in the narrow passage which ran from the front door to the kitchen, the receiver still clutched in her hand, shaking in every limb. She knew perfectly well that Clinton Ames had a reputation as a malicious and embittered man whose acting career had never lived up to his own expectations, and that he relieved his frustrations by making mischief wherever he could, but she had no doubt he was telling the truth. He had seen Tim and Sylvia at the Savoy this lunchtime; and, like him, she did not believe that the meeting had been fortuitous. It would have been too much of a coincidence the very day she left London. And, because Clinton Ames had carefully failed to enlarge upon events, Imogen assumed that they had lunched together. She took a deep breath to steady her nerves.

Was Sylvia finally relenting towards Tim? Did this mean that the affair was about to start all over again? She walked back to the dining-room on legs that felt like melted butter. She was just conscious of Richard asking her a question, and aware that she mumbled some reply, but after that she sat absorbed in her own thoughts, not hearing a word that the others were saying. Tim and Sylvia; Sylvia and Tim. The words spun round inside her head until repetition robbed them of all meaning. If she didn't think, she couldn't be hurt, but there was no way she could remain in this state of suspended animation. Already pictures were forming in her mind of Sylvia and Tim together, in bed, making love, laughing, talking. Tim would ask her for a divorce;

he and Sylvia would live happily ever after . . .

'Imogen! Are you sure you're all right?' Georgina was leaning towards her, her face creased with worry. 'You are telling us the truth? There isn't anything wrong in London?'

Imogen forced a smile. 'No, of course not. It was just a . . . a friend I hadn't heard from for a while. I was surprised, that's all.' She pushed aside her plate with the scone untouched. 'I'm sorry, that's very wasteful, but I've had enough. I'm sorry,' she repeated.

Georgina laughed. 'Think nothing of it. Rich will eat it. He's one of those lucky people who can stuff themselves without gaining an ounce of extra weight. I put on pounds if I so much as look at anything fattening.' But she was still concerned. 'Would you like to go out this evening? Just you and me. Richard will stay with Ewan, won't you, darling?'

'Yes, willingly. But tell me where you plan on going, just in case I get an urgent call.'

'I thought Imogen would like to go into Plymouth. It'll be a nice drive across the moors, and we can have a quick drink before coming home again. We shan't be late. We can take her car.'

Richard looked startled. After a moment, he said hesitantly: 'Be careful, then, won't you? The police are getting pretty hot on enforcing the drink–drive law around here. We don't want Imogen losing her licence. Can't you go somewhere nearer?'

'Oh, come on, Richard!' Imogen protested. 'You don't think I'd be that silly, do you?'

But, beneath the table, her hands were clasped tightly together in her lap. She needed a drink; she needed one badly. She promised herself a large double brandy or a Scotch and soda, and found herself sweating in eager anticipation. She could taste the fiery liquor on her tongue.

Richard still looked doubtful, but was no match for

the women's determination, and they had made up their minds. 'All right,' he capitulated. 'I suppose, if I do have a call, I can take Ewan with me. The farmer's wife would look after him while I was busy.'

'That's settled, then.' Imogen began to relax now that she had the prospect of a drink to keep her going. And there was nothing to worry about. She fully intended to behave herself. One, maybe two whiskies would be her limit. A measure of calm descended on her troubled spirit. She would think about Tim and Sylvia tomorrow. This evening she would forget about them and enjoy herself.

'Give me the keys,' Georgina said as they left the pub and went in search of the Metro. 'You're in no fit state to drive.'

Any other time Imogen would have complied without hesitation, but tonight she was defiant. The three double whisky and sodas she had consumed had failed to do their work and dull the pictures in her mind's eye of Tim with Sylvia. She was feeling cheated and angry, longing to take her revenge on someone. Georgina was the only person handy.

'I'm perfectly sober,' she answered truculently. 'Nothing wrong with me at all. Look!' And she thrust out a steady hand.

'We have to cross the moors, and it's getting dark,' Georgina cavilled. 'Be sensible, Imogen, please. Let me drive.'

'Not on your life!' Imogen's annoyance was settling into an unrelenting determination. 'I don't let anyone else drive my car.' She noticed Georgina's anxious face. 'Nothing'll happen! People drive over the limit every day of the week and don't get caught. As long as we don't get stopped by the police, we'll be OK. And I'll be very careful until we reach the city limits.'

'And beyond, I hope,' Georgina snapped. She was

beginning to feel extremely uneasy. She made a grab
for Imogen's hand as the other woman took the car
keys from her bag, but Imogen was too quick for her
and bunched them inside her fist.

'I've told you! No-one drives my car but me, so get
in and make the best of it. If you're nervous, look out
of the window or something.'

At the back of her mind, Imogen had the idea that
she was going to regret her behaviour when she woke
in the morning, but for the moment she could not
care less. She fastened her seat belt, let in the clutch
and switched on the ignition.

A little reassured, both by Imogen's swift reaction
when she tried to snatch the keys and by the fact
that she had started the engine without fumbling,
Georgina slid into the front passenger-seat. But a
series of jolts as the Metro pulled away from the kerb
reawakened her misgivings. And by the time they
had made their way through the city and out on to
Dartmoor she was beginning to feel frightened. Near
Mutley Plain they had failed to stop at a pedestrian
crossing while someone was on it, and in Crownhill
the Metro had nearly hit a central bollard. On each
occasion, they had been lucky that no police car had
been passing. Moreover, it was getting dark, the road
a dusky ribbon unwinding before them.

'Stop the car,' Georgina said with what authority
she could muster. 'You must realize by now that
you're in no fit state to drive. We'll change places.'

Imogen ignored her and swerved violently across
the road to avoid a rabbit trapped in the headlights'
glare. She only just managed to return to her own side
before an oncoming car passed them, horn blaring
furiously. A vaguely seen figure in the driver's seat
mouthed abuse. Georgina, terrified, shouted: 'Stop!
Let me get out!'

The fear in her voice at last communicated itself to

306

Imogen, who became flustered and started to panic. The fumes from the whisky were fuddling her brain, and all she could think about was Tim with Sylvia. Her arms felt paralysed, her hands frozen to the steering-wheel.

'I can't,' she gasped. 'I can't remember how to.' Her foot searched for the brake, but found the accelerator. The car plunged headlong into the darkness.

Georgina screamed and made a wild grab for the steering-wheel. The car veered to the left and seemed to rise up in the air, so that for a moment she had the sensation of flying. Then it turned over, landing on its roof with a sickening crash. After that, all was silent.

Anne was undressing for bed. She and Ivo had been to friends for the evening, and it was late. A glance at the bedside clock showed that it was gone two in the morning. But tomorrow was Sunday, and they could lie in until lunchtime. Ivo, who had stopped off in the drawing-room to set the video for a late-night film he wanted to record, followed her into the attic.

He was quiet these days. He had lost much of that ebullience which had been so characteristic of him, and on those occasions when he wanted to make love and she didn't he just shrugged and gave in gracefully, as though it no longer mattered. So, perversely, it began to matter to her. She was no more in love with him than she had ever been, but her affection had ripened and deepened. It was like hurting a very old and very dear friend, and she was prepared to do almost anything to please him. Her sense of guilt where Ivo was concerned depressed her.

He began to shed his clothes, leaving them as he always did for her to pick up in the morning. 'Trish was looking great tonight,' he observed. 'When she wears the right gear, she can be stunning.'

Anne paused in the act of climbing into bed. Trish was striking, it was true, but she would never describe her friend as stunning, no matter what she was wearing. But 'She looked lovely,' she agreed, and waited for Ivo to get in beside her. Then she put up her face to be kissed, sliding her arms around him.

He returned her embrace, but held her lightly. 'You don't have to humour me, you know. We'll only make love if you want to.'

Anne sighed inwardly. She found it difficult to cope with this new, accommodating, slightly blasé Ivo and wished the old one would return. At least then they could have a good row and hurl insults at one another. Making love was somehow easier after that, like two friends patching up a quarrel. But now it was more like having to issue a formal invitation, and she didn't quite know what to say.

Two floors down, the telephone began to ring. She and Ivo drew apart, frowning at one another. Who could possibly be phoning at this hour of the morning? Then it stopped. Penelope or Clifford had answered on the bedroom extension.

'I hope it isn't Melanie to say one of us has left something behind,' Anne murmured. 'It's the sort of daft thing she'd do.'

'Surely not,' Ivo protested. 'Not even Mel could be so thoughtless . . .' He broke off, looking at his wife in dismay. 'Oh, my God. It *is* her. Listen. Someone's coming up the attic stairs.'

The door opened, and the light was switched on. Penelope stood in the doorway, hair awry, eyes staring. She hadn't even bothered to put her dressing-gown over her nightdress. Anne could see at once that something was seriously wrong, and all apologies for Melanie Brent went flying.

'Pen, what is it?' She was out of bed, holding the older woman tightly. 'What's happened?'

Penelope did not answer immediately, and when she did she sounded like someone sleep-walking.

'It's Georgina and Imogen,' she said at last, in a flat unemotional voice. 'There's been an accident. A car crash. They've both been killed.'

PART FOUR
1986–90

CHAPTER TWENTY-THREE

'YOU DON'T MIND ME inviting myself like this, I hope?' Penelope asked as she and Barbara left Temple Meads station in search of a taxi.

Barbara had given up driving herself in the city. 'Don't be ridiculous,' she begged. 'Our friendship goes back too far, and we've been through too much together to stand on ceremony.' They joined the queue at the taxi-stand. 'Things rough at home?'

Penelope sighed. 'They've been better. Richard tries hard, but he doesn't seem to be getting over it. Perhaps I'm expecting too much. It's barely a year yet. I'm not over it myself, and I'm sure you're not. And then there's Ewan. I'm too old to have a young child about the house without his mother. Of course we've engaged a nanny, but I feel guilty at leaving him in her charge all day long, when I'm only downstairs in the basement. So I keep going up to see how he is, and consequently my work suffers. Then I get bad-tempered and frustrated.'

They edged forward a couple of paces in the queue. Barbara asked: 'How's Rich getting on in his new practice? Hackney, isn't it? A far cry from rural Devon. Who's the fellow he's gone in with?'

'Peter Jenkins, one of his old flatmates from his student days in Edinburgh. He was looking for a partner round about the time Georgina died.' Penelope laughed sourly. 'I was going to say that Rich was always a lucky devil, falling on his feet, opportunities there for the taking. And it's true in a way. As for whether he likes it or not, I really couldn't tell you.

He's so quiet now, so withdrawn. The only people he's natural with are Ewan and, strangely enough, Deborah. Mind you, I can see why. She's the only person who doesn't treat him as if he's a piece of rare porcelain, or someone staggering back to health after a near-fatal illness. She's so selfish and spoilt, she hasn't time for anyone else's troubles. Her attitude towards Rich is that, whatever he's suffered, it's as nothing to the trauma of her broken finger-nail when she wanted her hands to look perfect for the next school dance. Totally callous, but probably the best thing for him just at present.'

'How old is she now?' Barbara enquired as they climbed into a taxi. She gave the driver her address.

'Fourteen, going on thirty,' was the dry response as Penelope settled into her corner and stared disparagingly out of the window at her native city. 'God! What are they doing to this place? Hasn't anyone heard the word "preservation"?' She turned her head. 'So far all we've talked about is me. How are you and Felicity coping?'

'Taking it one day at a time. It's better for me than for Mother. I've got my work to keep me going, although for how much longer I'm not quite sure. I'm sixty this year. Well, we both are. And Cliff. But I'll carry on as long as I feel able. But Mother's seventy-eight and has too much time to brood. You don't expect your children to die before you, let alone your grandchildren. Not that I'd know about that. Anne doesn't seem to be producing any. How is she, by the way?'

The taxi negotiated the city centre and began the steep climb up Park Street, the university tower looming at the summit.

'She appears to be coping well,' Penelope said, 'but that's only what one would expect of her. Anne has always met life head-on.'

Barbara grunted. 'She was always the stronger of the two. Even though she was four years younger than Imogen, she seemed the elder. From a very early age she knew what she wanted and where she was going. Although lately I get the impression she might have lost her way. Is everything all right between her and Ivo?'

Penelope was surprised. 'I think so. They seem quite happy together. At least, they've never given me cause to think otherwise. Mind you, I should imagine Ivo gets fed up with Tim hanging around all the time.' It was Barbara's turn to register surprise, and Penelope went on: 'For some reason which neither Cliff nor I can discover, he feels terribly guilty about Imogen's death. He also blames himself for not having treated her better when she was alive. As a result, his work is beginning to suffer. He's losing faith in his ability as an actor. So he clings to Anne – drawing on her strength, I suppose. Now that she and Ivo have their own flat, he's always round there, or ringing her up at all hours. Ivo told me he called her out last week at two in the morning, and off she went to Earls Court in a taxi. Tim was having nightmares. I wish he'd come home to live. Even with Richard and Ewan, there's plenty of room now.'

As they headed for the heart of Clifton, Barbara asked: 'What about Sylvia Gibson?'

'That's the strange part. He doesn't make any attempt to see her or contact her in any way, now that he could do so with a clear conscience. On the other hand, she might make him feel guiltier than he does already. It was his emotional entanglement with her that made Imogen start drinking heavily in the first place.'

There was silence for a moment before Barbara said quietly: 'Pen, I can't tell you how desperately sorry I am that the accident was Imogen's fault. I've been

315

trying to say this ever since the funeral. Can you
and Cliff and Richard forgive me?'

The taxi turned into College Close and came to
rest before the door of number four. Penelope laid
her hand over Barbara's. 'If you ever say anything
as stupid as that to me again, it will be the end of
a long and beautiful friendship. And put your purse
away. I'm paying.'

Ivo ran up the uncarpeted stairs and let himself into
the small flat which he and Anne had found six
months earlier in Tottenham Court Road, not far from
the one where he had lived as a student. He dumped
a bag of groceries in the kitchen and went through to
the living-room, where Trish was ensconced in one of
the armchairs.

'It's all right,' she said when she saw him, 'I'm just
leaving. I know you and Anne are going to the theatre
tonight and want to get ready. The Haymarket, isn't
it?'

'Yes. *The Apple Cart*. Peter O'Toole.' They carefully
avoided one another's eyes.

'How's the TV serial of *The Trumpet-Major* going?
Anne tells me you're playing Bob Loveday.'

'That's right.' Ivo moved a pile of drawings from a
wheelback chair and sat down, as far away from Trish
as possible. 'A more interesting character than the
virtuous John. But I'm not in the scenes they're shoot-
ing today and tomorrow, so I'm having a well-earned
rest. Next week we're off to Dorset on location.'

'Lucky you. Are there any openings in television
for a struggling designer?'

Before Ivo could reply, the telephone rang. 'Don't
answer it,' he advised his wife sharply, but it was
already too late. Anne had picked up the receiver.
She listened intently for a few minutes, then said:
'OK. Tell him I'm coming.' She hung up and turned

316

to the others. 'That was Marilyn Page. She's in this American play with Tim. She wants me to go round to the theatre right away. Tim's suffering from a bad attack of stage fright.'

Ivo asked: 'Why you? There's nothing you can do about it. It's a rotten thing to get, and a bout of it can hit you out of the blue without any warning, but it's something the actor himself has to master.'

Anne sighed. 'I know. But he thinks he needs me, and I can't let him down. I'm the only person he can turn to.'

'That's not true.' Ivo was keeping a tight rein on his temper. 'He has a father and a brother, both of whom know a damn sight more about acting and how to cope with its pitfalls than you do.'

'But he doesn't want them. It's me he's asking for.' Anne tried to sound reasonable. 'Tim would never go to Chris for help anyway, and Cliff will be getting ready to go on stage himself very shortly. You know he's doing six weeks at the National. I'm sorry, Ivo, but you'll have to go on. I'll join you later, in the first interval.'

A mulish expression crossed her husband's face, and Anne's heart sank. He was going to be difficult, and the trouble was that she couldn't blame him. She was herself getting a little tired of Tim's constant demands on her time. He was making no effort to come to terms with Imogen's death, but Anne was the only member of his family who really understood why: she was the only person Tim had confided in. She alone knew of his meeting with Sylvia at the Savoy and subsequent encounter with Clinton Ames.

'Rich says a man telephoned Imogen during tea,' Tim had told her. 'It must have been Clinton. That's why she got drunk. Sylvia warned me he was dangerous.'

Oddly enough, he seemed to bear no grudge against

his vicious fellow-actor but, rather, blamed himself for what had happened. And after almost a year this state of mind was beginning to cause him problems: chronic unpunctuality, an inability to remember his lines and now this debilitating stage fright. Anne longed as fervently as Ivo to be free of this sense of responsibility she felt towards him, but she was his sole source of comfort. Even his mother, sympathetic as she was, did not really understand what he was suffering.

'There's no point in seeing two acts of a play,' Ivo said mulishly. 'If you can't sit through all three, then give your ticket to someone who can. Trish would enjoy it, wouldn't you?'

Trish looked unhappy at being caught in the cross-fire. 'I'm not dressed for the theatre,' she protested. 'Besides, Anne wants to see *The Apple Cart*. She said so.'

'But not enough to see it from the beginning.' Ivo's argument was unanswerable. 'And you've time to get home and change.'

Anne put her arms around her friend and hugged her. 'Yes, you go, love. It's the best solution.'

Trish still hesitated but, sensing that Anne was appealing for her help out of a tricky situation, finally capitulated.

'OK. Thanks. I'd like to.'

'That's settled, then.' Ivo gave his wife a brittle smile. 'You get off, darling, on your errand of mercy. We'll be fine.'

Anne took a step in his direction, but could see by his expression that it was futile to expect his understanding. 'I'm sorry,' was all she could say.

Outside, she managed to find a cruising taxi and gave the name of the theatre where Tim was appearing. The stage-doorkeeper told her that Mr Haldane was in his dressing-room.

Tim was seated in the only armchair, sweating and looking very pale beneath his make-up. Marilyn Page was hovering anxiously beside him, ineffectually patting his hand. Her relief at seeing Anne was palpable. 'I'll leave him to you, then,' she murmured, halfway out of the door before she had finished speaking.

'I can't go on, Annie,' Tim whispered pathetically. 'Every word of dialogue has gone. My mind's like a slate that's been sponged clean.'

'Don't be dramatic, Tim dear.' Anne kneeled beside him. 'Lots of actors suffer from stage fright at some point in their career. It's an occupational hazard. The only thing you can do – and I know because I've heard your father say so – is to force yourself on stage every night until it goes. The chances are that once you get out there the lines will come back to you. But, in case of accidents, pin a few reminders around the set or to your costume, where the audience can't see them. You're a professional actor. You can't spinelessly give in.'

He held her hand tightly, almost cracking the bones. 'I feel awful, Annie. I'm shaking like a leaf. All I can think about is Imogen.'

Anne kissed his cheek. 'The last thing she'd have wanted is for you to wreck your career; particularly now, when it's starting to take off. You've waited a long time for this success, and you deserve it.'

He summoned up the travesty of a smile. 'Ironic, isn't it, that I should begin to be successful as soon as Im's dead?' He let go of her hand and put his arms around her. 'What am I going to do, Annie? What am I going to do?'

'You're going to do exactly as I told you. The rest of the cast will help you. Now, where's the whisky? I'll pour you a drink; just the one, to steady your nerves. After that, it's up to you.'

She rose to her feet. Tim stretched out a hand to

detain her. 'Thanks. I don't know what I'd do without you. I hope I haven't disrupted your evening. You'll stay and watch from the wings, won't you? I shall feel better if I know you're near.'

Anne smiled resignedly. 'All right,' she agreed. 'I won't run away. I promise.'

'Thank goodness you have enough sense to come and stay with us while Ivo's away.' Penelope met Anne at the front door of The Laurels. 'I don't like you being alone in that flat while he's down in Dorset.'

Anne put her roller-bag on the hall floor. 'To tell the truth, I'm ashamed of myself for accepting the invitation. Thousands of women live on their own, let alone stay by themselves for a week or two while their husbands are away.'

'This is London.' Penelope spoke as though that settled the matter and led the way upstairs to the drawing-room. 'Sit down and I'll pour you a sherry. Supper's in about half an hour, when Rich gets in.'

Anne sank into one of the familiar well-upholstered armchairs and let herself relax. 'How was your visit to Bristol?'

'All too short. Your mother and I indulged in an orgy of reminiscence, went to the Old Vic and wallowed in nostalgia, recalled our schooldays at length, and generally behaved like two people who suddenly realize that they are growing old and that their future is now shorter than their past.' She turned round from the side-table where the decanters stood, a glass of sherry in either hand, her face bleak. 'And who, perhaps, are glad of it.'

'Don't say that!' Anne sat forward abruptly in her chair. 'Whatever happens, life is still meant to be lived to the full.'

'I'm not sure your grandmother feels that way.'

Penelope handed her a glass. 'She looks very much older than when I last saw her.'

'I know.' Anne sipped her drink. 'It's sad because she was always such a fighter. What does Mother say about her?'

'She's worried. She's talking about retiring later this year. She feels she should devote more time to Felicity. As it is, your grandmother's on her own a lot and broods.'

'Mother? Retire? I can't believe it. She always seems so young; I forget she was thirty-four when I was born. I'll be twenty-six in October.' Tears filled her eyes. 'Imogen would have been thirty on the same day.' She laughed uncertainly. 'I'm getting maudlin.'

The door opened and Cliff came in, closely followed by Barkis and the two cats, who had found no difficulty in adapting to life at The Laurels. To everyone's amusement, Iggy and Ikey had, from the moment of their arrival, attached themselves to Cliff like two small shadows. Whenever he was at home, they were constantly at his heels.

'It's so nice to have animals about the house again.' Penelope smiled indulgently. 'It reminds me of the old days.'

'It may be nice for you, my love,' her husband retorted with asperity, 'but you don't have the pleasure of the little buggers' company every waking moment. A man does need some privacy. In the lavatory, for example.'

Anne burst out laughing. 'They don't follow you in there surely?'

'Don't they just! I see you are both tippling as usual. How about a whisky and water for the worker?' He sat down, and immediately the cats climbed on to his lap, purring loudly. 'Oh, give me strength!' he begged in the ringing tones which carried easily to the back rows of any theatre. But he made no effort to dislodge the animals; rather, he stroked their heads and murmured dulcetly to them.

Penelope fetched her husband his drink. 'Isn't it time you were off? You'll be late starting your make-up.'

'I can afford another five minutes or so.' Cliff raised his eyebrows at Anne. 'What's this I hear about Tim suffering from stage fright? A little bird told me you've been going to the theatre most nights this week to hold his hand.'

Anne flushed uncomfortably. 'He needed somebody, and . . . I happened to be there. He'll get over it, given time.'

'I'm sure he will.' Clifford nodded. 'Meantime, what does Ivo say? He can't be very pleased about it.'

'Ivo understands.' Anne tried to sound convincing. 'Anyway, he's not around himself half the time. And if he gets lonely he can always go to see Trish. They get on very well together.'

'You mustn't let Tim monopolize you,' Penelope said gently. 'Don't let him come between you and Ivo, and don't let Ivo become too dependent on Trish.'

Anne grimaced. 'There's nothing romantic between them, if that's what you're thinking.'

The young girl who was Ewan's nanny entered, holding the two-year-old by the hand. 'Daddy's coming,' she announced. 'We saw him from upstairs.'

'Daddy,' Ewan repeated, breaking free and trotting over to the window. He stood on tiptoe and peered out. 'Car,' he said, pointing.

Anne and Penelope joined him, staring down into the front garden, now bright with spring flowers. Richard's battered old Ford Sierra was drawn up beside the kerb. After a moment, he got out, locked it and glanced up at the drawing-room window to wave to his son. It was obvious to Anne that this was a nightly ritual because there was no spontaneity on Richard's part, and she suspected that he would have gone through the motions whether Ewan were there or not. Her heart contracted with love and pity, and also with a terrible fear that he was lost to her for ever, walled in behind his pain. When he eventually joined them, she thought he looked even thinner and paler than he had done nine months ago, when he had first returned home to live. He picked up an excited Ewan, hugged and kissed him, stared vaguely at the rest of them, then dropped wearily into a chair. Suddenly, becoming aware of her presence, he smiled.

'Hello, Anne. What are you doing here?'

'I told you at breakfast,' Penelope scolded gently. 'She's staying here while Ivo's in Dorset. Don't you listen to anything I say?'

'Yes, of course. Now I remember.'

It was a lie. He could recollect nothing of the conversation. He had been thinking of Georgina, as he did every morning when he got up. It was then, when he woke, expecting her to be by his side, that he felt her loss most poignantly. It took all his concentration to get himself to Hackney in time for the early surgery, and after that to go out on his rounds. Peter Jenkins, who lived with his wife above the 'shop', was kindness itself, and would gladly have relieved his friend of many of his duties. But Richard insisted on pulling his weight. His work and his son were the only things he had left to cling on to.

The effort involved, however, took its toll, and by evening he was exhausted. All he wanted to do when he returned home was to go to bed, to sleep and forget. He found his mother's over-anxious care oppressive, but would not hurt her by saying so. His father was easier to talk to, but Clifford was unable to disguise his concern completely. He wanted to share his son's grief, but for Richard that was still an intensely private area. And now here was Anne, looking at him with sympathy and pity. He couldn't stand it.

He stood up. 'I'm tired,' he announced abruptly. 'I'm going to bed. I don't want any supper.' He glanced in Anne's direction. 'This house is always too full of people.'

CHAPTER TWENTY-FOUR

'THANKS FOR COMING,' Anne said. 'I've booked a table.' She led the way downstairs to the basement restaurant. The warmth from the adjacent kitchen and closely packed bodies was welcome after the cold outside. As she took her seat, she asked politely: 'Are you all ready for Christmas?'

Sylvia smiled as she settled in the chair opposite. 'Not really. There are so many things which can't be done until the last minute.' She took a menu from a hovering waiter, but after a cursory glance her eyes rested once more on Anne. 'I'm curious to know what this is about. Your invitation was quite a surprise.'

'Shall we order first?' Anne took refuge behind her own menu.

Sylvia's eyebrows went up. 'That serious, eh? OK. I'll have the soup followed by the lemon sole.'

'And I'll have the same.' Anne handed back her menu.

The waiter, an Italian, looked offended by this off-hand approach to food, and muttered something un-complimentary about the English under his breath. Anne and Sylvia both giggled, and the constraint between them dissolved. For the next five minutes, until the soup arrived, they chatted with the easy familiarity of long, if fitful, acquaintance. Sylvia re-counted several amusing disaster-stories of the play she was currently appearing in, and Anne made her laugh with a description of Clifford's sulks when a production of *King Lear* which he had hoped to mount failed to raise the necessary financial backing.

'He was like a spoiled child. Penelope says if he could have found a way of blaming her for it he would have done so.'

Sylvia nodded. 'Typical of Cliff. He gets petulant if he's thwarted, but his moods don't last long. He's very untemperamental for an actor. And he absolutely dotes on Pen. Not that he'd ever admit it, mind you.'

'Oh, no. But she's the same, equally doting, but always putting him down. The opposite of how Richard and Georgina used to be with each other.'

The waiter arrived with the soup. 'How is Richard?' Sylvia enquired as she took her first mouthful.

Anne shrugged. 'Much the same.' She picked up her spoon. 'I know Penelope thinks he ought to make more effort to get over Georgina's death, if only for Ewan's sake. I don't see much of him nowadays. I try to time my visits to The Laurels when he's sure to be out.'

If Sylvia noted the hint of bitterness in Anne's voice, she made no comment. 'So?' she asked. 'Why do you want to see me?'

Anne hesitated, suddenly tongue-tied. She glanced up to meet Sylvia's look of enquiry and plunged in.

'It's about Tim. I want you to take him off my hands.'

Sylvia was nonplussed. 'What exactly do you mean?'

'He's taking up too much of my time. He's in a pretty bad way, blaming himself for Imogen's death. He's been suffering from stage fright, although he's getting over that now, and he has nightmares. Penelope wants him to go home to live, but he won't because he doesn't want to meet Chris. So he rings me up every time he needs help, and I find it very difficult to refuse him. I have to keep going round to the flat or the theatre, and it's playing havoc with my marriage. I'm the only one Tim will let near him – except, of course, you. In fact I've no doubt at all that he'd prefer you. So what

I'm asking is ... well, could you ... would you be willing ...?' Anne paused, floundering.

The older woman was silent for a moment; then she asked: 'Why does Tim feel responsible for your sister's death? Is there something you haven't told me?'

Anne bit her lip, not knowing if she would be justified in breaking Tim's confidence. She salved her conscience, however, with the recollection that he had engaged her secrecy only where his family was concerned. She recounted his suspicions regarding Clinton Ames.

Sylvia's lips thinned until they almost disappeared. 'The bastard,' she muttered at last. 'The sneaky, vicious, slimy toad!' Anne rightly assumed that she was not referring to Tim. 'My God! I shall have a job to keep my hands off him the next time we meet. Of all the lousy vile things to do. Poor old Tim! No wonder he feels rotten. I had no idea.'

'You will contact him, then?' Anne demanded eagerly.

'Now, wait a minute,' Sylvia protested. 'That's going too fast. What you're really asking me to do is to start another relationship with Tim. I don't want that. He'll read something into any overture of friendship that's not intended. I don't want another permanent attachment to anybody. I'm perfectly happy as I am.'

'Then, make that clear from the start,' Anne pleaded. 'But he does need a friend. And I can't go on the way I am now, putting Tim before Ivo. I soon shan't have any marriage left.'

There was another silence while the waiter cleared away the soup-dishes and brought the fish. But when he had at last arranged everything to his satisfaction and departed Sylvia said quietly: 'You're going to think me awfully rude, but I didn't realize your marriage was so important to you. In fact the word backstage is that Ivo's been seeing a lot of Trish Ransome lately. And word also has it that you don't mind.'

Anne laid down her knife and fork. 'Oh dear! I didn't realize . . . And the gossips are right; I didn't mind for a long time. I suppose, if I'm honest, I even encouraged the friendship. It took Ivo off my hands.' She decided to be frank. 'I don't love Ivo. I'm very fond of him; but, as you know, that isn't always enough. When we married, I promised myself I'd make it work, but over the years I've rather lost sight of that commitment. Then, a few months ago, something happened which forced me to accept that life doesn't always work out the way we want it to; that perhaps we ought to make the best of what we have. Not a very romantic concept, but realistic. I want to make it up to Ivo. My neglect, I mean. But I can't do that with Tim perched on my shoulders like the Old Man of the Sea. That's why I'm asking for your help.'

Sylvia ate a mouthful of fish, but it might as well have been sawdust for all she tasted. She felt caught in a trap and saw no way to break free. She asked carefully: 'Have you considered that it might already be too late for you and Ivo?'

'I should have to be a conceited fool not to. However, I feel I owe it to both of us at least to try. But I can't do it without you. I can't just desert Tim and leave him with no-one.' She paused, then added: 'He wouldn't need me if he had you.'

'You're putting me on the spot, you know that, don't you?'

'Yes, and I'm sorry. But I'm desperate.'

'And it might all be for nothing.'

'Again I'm sorry. But I do have to try to make things up with Ivo.'

Sylvia pushed aside her plate, the meal only half-eaten. 'All right,' she agreed at last, 'you win. I'll telephone Tim when I get home.' She sighed. 'And at least he and I will have something in common: a shared sense of guilt over Imogen's death.'

                          *   *   *

'You're never going to believe this!' Penelope's voice
rose with excitement at the other end of the line.'Tim's
agreed to come to our New Year's Eve party, even
though he knows Chris and Irene will be here. And
you'll never guess who he's bringing with him.'

Anne, leaning over the workbench, trying to finish
a costume drawing and conscious of Aileen's eagle eye
upon her, said rather unkindly: 'Sylvia.'

'Oh.' Penelope sounded deflated.'How did you guess?'

'There have been whispers, these past two weeks,
that he's seeing her again. In fact there's even a
rumour that he's moved in with her, but I don't believe that. At least, not yet. I think he might in
time.'

Penelope was aggrieved. 'Why are mothers always
the last to hear things about their children? I blame
Cliff. He never repeats backstage gossip. It's really
most provoking. I suppose Ivo tells you everything.'

Anne dropped her pencil and straightened her back.
'Not everything. What husband does? What wife, for
that matter?'

'Women withhold things from men for their own
good,' Penelope responded tartly.'Husbands just enjoy
being secretive. Look at all those societies they invent.
Masons and Mooses and suchlike. You don't find women
running around with one knicker leg tucked up and
exchanging secret passwords. Anyway, as you guessed,
Tim and Sylvia are coming to the party together. You
and Ivo will be here, I trust? Good. Tell Aileen and
Ralph we're expecting them also. And Trish. Has she
got a young man she can bring with her?'

Anne said as lightly as she could: 'She's coming
with us. She has too much sense to get involved with
any one person.'

'Nonsense!' was the answer. 'She's twenty-six. High
time she was married.'

Anne decided it would be politic to cut the conversation short. 'Look, Pen, we're awfully busy. Have to go. See you Tuesday night.' And she hung up. 'Sorry about that,' she apologized to Aileen.

She resumed work on her sketch, but inspiration had temporarily vanished. Her thoughts were all of Trish and the renewed constraint that had grown up between them ever since Sylvia had re-entered Tim's life, and Anne had more time to spend with Ivo. For Sylvia had been as good as her word. She had telephoned Tim that same afternoon and, from then on, the frantic calls to Anne had virtually ceased. She had received one last week to thank her for all she had done, and to add that he would no longer be a burden to her. If only he had known how relieved she felt, he need not have sounded so guilty.

But the other consequence was that Ivo saw less of Trish. Anne was there for him now when he came home late from the theatre. Trish said nothing, but her silence was eloquent. It was obvious to Anne that her friend was feeling lonely and neglected. Ivo's sentiments were harder to fathom. He seemed pleased enough to have regained Anne's company, but not ecstatic. It was almost as though, nowadays, he could take her or leave her. He had grown used to her frequent absences and had stopped resenting them. Indeed, there were occasions when she wondered if he might not rather have been with Trish. He had developed, too, a habit of making remarks such as 'Trish doesn't do it that way,' or 'That wouldn't do for Trish'. Trish now seemed to be the yardstick by which he measured everybody. Anne couldn't help wondering if he compared their performance in bed.

She had no doubt that Ivo and Trish had slept together. How she knew, she wasn't quite sure: a glance here, a prolonged pressure of the fingers there; a certain air of intimacy between them that would brook no other explanation. Anne wished she could mind more, feel a greater sense of outrage, but found it impossible. The thought of her husband and her best friend making love failed to rouse her to jealousy, however hard she tried to feel wronged.

'Pen's expecting you and Ralph at her New Year's party,' she said to Aileen, who nodded.

'Tell her we'll be there. Wouldn't miss it for the world. But now', she added briskly, 'let's get on, shall we? Just because you've been promoted to designing the odd costume now and again doesn't mean you can slack, you know.'

The New Year's Eve party was in full swing by the time Anne and Ivo got there. Ivo was appearing in a new David Hare play and earning himself rave notices. Tonight he had not reached home until nearly eleven, so numerous had been the curtain-calls taken by the cast. Consequently, it was almost midnight before he, Anne and Trish arrived on Penelope's doorstep.

'We'd very nearly given you up,' she told them. 'Up to the drawing-room quick and grab some glasses. Big Ben's about to strike any minute.'

The drawing-room, as always on these occasions, was crowded; but Anne, searching among the faces, could see no sign of Richard. She tried to tell herself that it did not matter, that she was indifferent to his absence, but in the end she could not forbear from grabbing Chris's arm and asking: 'Isn't Richard here?'

Chris stared around him, his height giving him the advantage of superior vision. 'He was here a while ago.' He turned to his wife. 'Have you seen Richard, darling?'

Irene, stunning in emerald green, said: 'I think he went to his room. Couldn't face the idea of seeing the New Year in, poor lamb.' She squeezed her husband's arm. 'Best smile forward. Tim and Sylvia are approaching.'

The brothers, who had assiduously avoided one another since arriving, at last found themselves face-to-face. It was Chris, inevitably, who made the first move.

'Tim. Sylvia. Happy New Year – in about ten seconds.'

Tim muttered: 'Thanks. Same to you.' Then he took his companion's arm and steered her away. It was not the reconciliation that Penelope, standing behind Anne and Ivo, had hoped for, but it was a beginning. She nodded approval at her eldest son.

'Where's your father?' she asked. 'Has he got the TV on?' She raised her voice above the general hubbub. 'Quiet, everyone, please! Have you all got a drink? Right. Get ready.'

The people standing near Anne suddenly parted ranks as Deborah Grantham pushed her way through, leading Richard by the hand.

'He was hiding away upstairs,' she announced, 'and wasn't going to come down. I soon put a stop to that. Here, let him have your champagne, Chris.' She took her stepfather's glass out of his hand and gave it to Richard. 'You can share Mummy's.'

Richard, Anne noted resentfully, seemed not to mind this autocratic treatment. Rather, it appeared to amuse him. It was the closest to an involuntary smile she had seen on his lips since Georgina died, and it was Deborah who had put it there. She fought hard to stop herself feeling jealous.

Chris's stepdaughter fitted Penelope's description of her as 'fourteen, going on thirty'. She was old for her age even among a generation of girls who seemed to be achieving maturity younger and younger. Her breasts, beneath the Laura Ashley dress, were those of a woman, and the abundant red hair had been permed and allowed to cascade around her shoulders. She looked like a Burne-Jones model, but neither so ethereal nor so languishing. In fact she oozed life and vitality, her imperious blue eyes intimating that she expected immediate compliance with her wishes.

Cliff turned up the volume of the television set, and the chimes of Big Ben came right into the room. As the twelfth stroke of midnight died away, and the crowds in Trafalgar Square exploded into cheers, the guests turned to each other with best wishes for 1987. Anne looked round for Trish and Ivo, but was unable to locate them. Both had disappeared. As she clinked glasses with Chris and Irene, she became acutely aware of Richard at her elbow. A moment later, he slid an arm around her shoulders.

'Happy New Year, Anne,' he said, kissing her cheek.

She held her breath, afraid to move in case she dispelled the magic of that moment. But it was already slipping away from her as Deborah swung round to confront them.

'Happy New Year, Uncle Richard.'

There was something mocking in the way she called him 'uncle', and nothing niece-like in the way she kissed him. She wound her arms about his neck and pressed her parted lips to his. After what seemed to Anne an eternity, he pulled himself free, shaken and laughing.

'And a Happy New Year to you, Debs.' He glanced apologetically at Irene.

But Irene appeared to be fondly amused by her daughter's behaviour. 'You'll have to keep your eye on her, Rich. She's a terrible flirt. Loads of boyfriends. I say to Chris: "God knows what she'll be like by the time she's eighteen." '

Her husband's expression conveyed that he had a

good idea, but knew better than to say anything. And, for some reason, Deborah, normally eager to boast about her conquests, sounded annoyed with her mother.

'Mum! What an exaggeration!' She turned to Richard. 'It's not true, you know. I mean, yes, boys do like me.' She tossed her head, and the red hair floated in a cloud about her shoulders. 'But I prefer older men.' She flashed him a predatory smile.

She's after him, Anne thought; then told herself not to be silly. Deborah was not yet fifteen, still at school. Richard was twenty-six with a two-year-old son. The idea was preposterous. But Anne could not help recalling Penelope's words – 'fourteen, going on thirty'. Deborah was already grown up, with the calculating mind of an adult woman. She knew what she wanted and she intended to go after it with the ruthless determination of someone twice her age. She had marked Richard down as hers, and woe betide anyone who got in her way.

Anne gave herself a mental shake. She was being too fanciful. She returned Richard's greeting and kissed his cheek. 'Happy New Year, Rich. Happier, at any rate, than the last two.'

His eyes met hers, bright with unshed tears, and he nodded. But the renewed warmth and intimacy of a few moments before had vanished. His expression was shuttered, and he had turned in upon himself again. He said abruptly: 'I'm tired. Will you tell Mum I've gone to bed if she asks for me?'

He went, pushing his way through the crowds to the door, ignoring other people's greetings. Deborah glared at Anne.

'That wasn't very clever, was it, reminding him about his wife? He needs to be treated normally, not swamped with sympathy. It's the only way he'll get over it.'

For once, Chris overrode Irene's mild protestations and said with unwonted severity: 'That's no way to speak to Anne. Apologize! Since when has a child of your age been an authority on bereavement? It's high time we were going, too. Get your coat while your mother and I say goodnight to my parents.'

Deborah, her cheeks flaming at this unexpected rebuke, mumbled what might have been an apology and fled. Irene said reproachfully:'I think you were a bit hard on her, darling.'

For answer, Chris took her firmly by the elbow and steered her in Penelope's direction.

Anne suddenly felt an overwhelming desire to be in bed, rather than surrounded by all these noisy and determinedly jolly people. An incipient headache nagged behind her eyes, and she was engulfed by depression. She must find Ivo and ask him to take her home, but no-one seemed to know where he was. One person thought he could be downstairs, eating a belated supper; another that she might have seen him in the study at one point; and yet a third suggested that he had been sitting on the stairs talking to Trish Ransome. Anne thanked them all and resigned herself to a systematic search of the house. She considered it quite likely that Ivo could be with Trish somewhere, as her friend also appeared to be missing.

At twelve-thirty, having looked everywhere else, Anne decided they must be in the basement and hesitated. It was a part of the house she had instinctively avoided since her sister's death: it brought back too many memories of Imogen. A new secretary, Caroline Best, a bright, cheerful, breezy girl with impeccable shorthand and typing skills, not to mention a high standard of efficiency with a word processor, worked nowadays in the little room adjacent to Penelope's. Anne knew it was inevitable that this should be so, but the thought of it hurt none the less. She had therefore wisely refrained from witnessing evidence of this alien occupation until now. Reluctantly, she pushed open the door at the end of the hall and descended the basement stairs, noting as she did so that the light was already on. Before she reached the bottom of the flight, she heard voices.

She judged that they were coming not from Penelope's rooms, but from the large rehearsal studio which was Cliff's domain, where he made recordings of some of his longer speeches and played them back for critical approval. The room was normally sound-proof, but tonight the door stood open. Whoever was in there had evidently not anticipated being disturbed. Anne paused, listening, before walking in. In those few seconds, she had identified her husband and Trish as the speakers, and Trish sounded as though she were crying.

She and Ivo were sitting side by side on a black leather couch which ran the length of one wall. Ivo had his arm round Trish's waist, and her head was resting on his shoulder. As Anne entered, Trish blew her nose in Ivo's handkerchief, then sniffed. These prosaic actions were somehow reassuring and left Anne totally unprepared for the bombshell which followed.

'Trish!' She hurried forward. 'What's the matter? What's wrong? Ivo, why didn't you come and fetch me?'

She would have sat beside them, but her husband prevented her by holding out his hand. At the same time Trish said in a choked voice: 'Don't! Don't touch me! For God's sake, don't be sympathetic, please!'

Anne stopped in her tracks, frowning, noting how thin and pale her friend looked, how dark the circles were under her eyes.

'You're ill,' she began, but Trish started to cry again.

'No, I'm not,' she sobbed, clinging to Ivo's hand. 'I'm pregnant.'

CHAPTER TWENTY-FIVE

'YOU'RE GOING AHEAD with the divorce, then?' Barbara asked, but it was not really a question.

The February day was cold, and a blustery wind whipped across the open spaces of the Downs. Nevertheless, she and Anne had chosen to walk as far as the Clifton Suspension Bridge after lunch, leaving Felicity to rest quietly in preparation for her birthday celebration in the evening. This entailed no more than a few old friends for dinner, but at seventy-nine and in failing health Barbara felt it was as much as her mother could cope with. Anne had come down from London the previous day, thankful that the successful run of the David Hare play provided the perfect excuse for Ivo's absence. It had been agreed between herself and Barbara that there was no need to mention the divorce until absolutely necessary. Felicity had found it hard enough to come to terms with Imogen's death, without adding further to her distress – at least, for the moment.

Anne turned up the collar of her coat and plunged her gloved hands into the pockets. 'I'd really no choice once I knew that Trish was determined to have the baby. Ivo wants the child as well, so I've no option.'

Barbara took the scarf from around her neck and tied it over her head. 'Is he in love with Trish?' she enquired.

Anne considered her answer. At last she said: 'He's not *not* in love with her, if you see what I mean.'

They found a bench in the shelter of some trees whose branches made a natural wind-break. As they sat down, Barbara asked: 'Could you explain that more clearly?'

Anne withdrew one hand from her pocket and rubbed it across her forehead. The gesture was childishly touching, making Barbara feel unexpectedly maternal. She put an arm around her daughter's shoulders and squeezed them. Anne smiled.

'You mustn't feel sorry for me, Mum. The whole mess is entirely of my own making. I wasn't in love with Ivo when I married him, and I'm still not. But I've grown fond of him over the years and I shall miss him. I want him to be happy.'

'And will he be, with Trish?'

'I believe so. She loves him – always has, I think. And as I said just now, he's not *not* in love with her. By which I mean he's not in love with me any more. He was once, but no longer. He's free emotionally. And as soon as he and Trish are married and the baby's born he'll convince himself that she's the one he's wanted all along.'

Barbara sighed. 'You're growing very cynical. I used to think you were more like your grandmother than me, but you'd never hear her express such cold-blooded sentiments.'

'They weren't meant to be cold-blooded.' Anne gave a tiny sob. 'I feel such a mess inside. I don't really know what I want.'

Barbara had removed the scarf from around her head, and a stray gust of wind, penetrating the protecting screen of branches, ruffled her grey hair. She tidied it before asking quietly: 'Don't you?'

Anne demanded sharply: 'What do you mean?'

Barbara thought for a moment, then said: 'It's seemed to me once or twice in the past year that you're very fond of Richard Haldane. Correct me if I'm mistaken.'

For a moment Anne was tempted to refute the

allegation, but the relief of letting her mother into the secret changed her mind. 'No, you're not mistaken. I've always loved Richard. But I won't have Penelope told. I mean that, Mum! You and she have a nasty habit of telling one another everything.'

'All right, if that's the way you want it. But she'd be delighted, you know. Nothing would please her more than the prospect that you and Richard might one day get married. She'd do all she could to help.'

'That's exactly what I'm afraid of.' Anne spoke with suppressed violence. 'Penelope's interference. Given half a chance, she just can't resist arranging people's lives for them. I don't want her throwing Rich and me together with all the finesse of a maternal elephant. Cliff guessed years ago, but he's never told her.'

'Cliff's never been interested in anyone but himself,' Barbara responded drily and a little unfairly. 'He's an egotist. I remember the first time I ever saw him, in a student production at the Bristol Old Vic. I can't recall what the play was now, but it was classical. He was wearing a short tunic, like a cocktail-frock, with a wreath round his head. He could have looked absurd – some of the others did – but not Clifford Haldane. He dominated the stage and revelled in the knowledge.'

Anne grinned. 'I believe you're jealous because he fell for Penelope and not for you, who were always so much better looking.'

'Nonsense!' Barbara got to her feet a shade too abruptly. 'We must get home. Your grandmother will be awake and wondering where we've got to. And don't worry.' She pressed Anne's hand. 'I shall say nothing to Penelope.' They moved out of the shelter of the trees, the wind almost knocking them off their feet, crossed the grass and the road, and plunged into one of the openings between the houses. Barbara continued: 'What's going to happen to you and Trish?'

Anne looked surprised. 'What should happen? We're

friends, like you and Pen. I hope we shall remain so. We're sensible civilized people.'

'It sounds all right in theory.' Her mother was sceptical. 'Just don't mention the arrangement to your grandmother when you eventually have to tell her about the divorce, that's all. She finds it difficult enough adjusting to the second half of the twentieth century as it is, without you upsetting her further.'

'OK. Although I think she's more broad-minded than you give her credit for. And thank God we're home at last. This wind is giving me a headache.'

Once indoors, Barbara headed upstairs to see if Felicity was awake and needing anything. Anne followed in more leisurely fashion, and as she crossed the hall the phone rang. It was Trish.

'I just had to wish Mrs Bryce a happy birthday,' she said awkwardly. 'I hope you don't mind.'

Anne took a deep breath. The hand holding the receiver was shaking slightly. 'That's very kind of you. She's asleep at the moment, but I'll see she gets your message.' How formal and stilted she sounded. 'How . . . how's Ivo?'

'Fine.'

'And you?'

'I'm fine. I went to the clinic this morning for a check-up. Everything's fine. Seem to be repeating myself. Sorry.'

'That's OK.' There was an uncomfortable pause before they both tried to speak at once. When they had sorted themselves out, Anne said: 'Look, I must go now.'

'Yes. Of course. See you when you get back. Ivo says you're moving in with Sir Clifford and Lady Haldane.'

'Again. It's been my second home as long as I can remember.' Anne hastened to extricate herself from what had become an impossible conversation. ' 'Bye,' she said and replaced the receiver just as her mother came running downstairs. 'That was Trish,' she began in explanation, but broke off at the sight of Barbara's face. 'Mum, what's the matter? You're as white as a sheet. Oh, my God! It's Grandma, isn't it?'

Without waiting for confirmation, she dashed upstairs. The front door to Felicity's little flat was open. Anne made her way to the bedroom.

She thought at first that her mother was mistaken. Her grandmother appeared to be sleeping, her eyes closed, lying full length on her bed as she did every afternoon after lunch. It was only when Anne got closer to that peaceful figure that she realized there was no gentle rise and fall of the breast, only a frightening stillness. She called 'Grandma!' once or twice, very softly, but knew, even as she hoped, that there would be no answer, then or ever. She glanced round the room that she knew so well; at the pastel shades of the carpet and curtains, at the neatness and order which had been so much a part of her grandmother, clothes, shoes, jewellery all put away in their appointed places. If she reached out and opened the wardrobe, she would see rows of clothes all carefully chosen to co-ordinate with one another. On a chair next to the bed was the big canvas bag in which Felicity kept her current piece of embroidery. Last night, Anne remembered, she had been stitching a complicated pattern in one corner of a linen tablecloth. Now it would never be finished.

She became aware of her mother standing beside her, busy with her own memories. They turned towards each other and merged into a silent embrace.

Ivo came down for the funeral, returning to London by the afternoon train, in time for the evening performance. Penelope and Cliff were also present, provoking the attention of the local press and providing copy for the reporters. After the funeral, Barbara made lunch with her usual efficiency.

'What will you do now?' Penelope asked her as she helped with the washing-up. 'You only retired early to look after Felicity.'

Barbara smiled wryly. 'I shall find plenty to occupy my time, don't worry. I've never minded my own company. But I shall miss Mother. We didn't always see eye to eye and she was forever criticizing my clothes, but there was a certain rapport between us which I've never had with anyone else but you. However, I shall not be lonely, and I shan't expect frequent visits from Anne, if that's what you're thinking. She has her own life to get on with. I hear she's living with you again, which will no doubt please you. I know how you love filling up that great house of yours. I don't know how you manage to write your books. Incidentally, I found the last considerably more restrained than previous ones. Any particular reason?'

Penelope dried a cup and saucer while she considered the question. 'I'm getting older, I suppose, and the general climate for explicit sex scenes is changing. I've never enjoyed writing them anyway. It's time I did something different. I'm sixty-one and keep hearing "time's wingèd chariot" coming up behind me.' She sighed. 'There's nothing like the death of loved ones for making you realize how short life really is.'

Barbara stripped off her rubber gloves. 'Don't get morbid. Mother would hate that.'

They hugged each other briefly. 'You'll have to come up to Town often,' Penelope urged. 'It's less than two hours by train, and you'll want to see more of Anne now that . . . well, now that her marriage is over.' She added with uncharacteristic venom: 'And to think I always liked that little home-wrecker until now! How could I have been so taken in?'

'If you mean Trish, it's not all her fault, Pen. These affairs can never be laid at the door of just one person. Anne blames herself. She says she was never in love with Ivo and shouldn't have married him in the first place.'

Penelope finished wiping the plates. 'I used to think, years ago, that she and Richard might make a go of it. But it wasn't to be. What a run of tragedy we've had in the past few years. Well, there's one consolation: things can only get better.'

'That's the spirit!' Barbara put away the dried crockery in its cupboard. '*Nil desperandum* and all that rubbish. And, as long as there's cricket to look forward to, nothing's too bad.' She started to laugh. 'Do you remember the match against the school governors – oh, it must have been at the beginning of the war – when Geraldine Curtis . . .'

Within minutes, they were comfortably launched into the cosy safe world of shared reminiscence; girls again, able to smile now at catastrophes which, at the time, had seemed like the end of the world as they knew it. The tragedies and problems of the past two years faded mercifully from their minds. They stood once more on life's threshold.

In the dining-room, Anne said goodbye to Ivo. Clifford had tactfully disappeared.

'It was good of you to come,' she said. 'Gran would have appreciated it.'

They faced each other awkwardly across several feet of floor, almost as though the space between them was marked by invisible electric wires and to take one step forward would mean instant death.

'I was very fond of Felicity,' Ivo assured her. 'She was like the grandmother I never had. Both mine died before I was born. I hope your mother didn't mind me coming.'

'She was pleased. She doesn't blame you for what's

happened. She knows it takes two to make a marriage work or fail. By the way, the flat's vacant now, so you and Trish can move in. That bed-sit of hers must be very cramped for two.'

'Thanks.' There was silence, then Ivo added: 'You've been splendid about the whole thing.'

Anne took a deep breath. 'I haven't always felt splendid, but most of the blame for what's happened is mine. I know that and I can live with it. And I'm still very fond of Trish, in spite of everything.' She smiled bleakly. 'You ought to go. You'll miss your train, and if you wait for the next you'll have an awful rush to make curtain-up. Goodbye, Ivo, and all the best. We'll be seeing one another around.'

'Of course. Frequently. The divorce should go through without any hitch. You must come and visit us when we're settled.' His eyes met hers, and Anne was conscious of a faint pang of regret for something lost; for something which, in different circumstances, might have been worth preserving. He went on: 'I hope things turn out well for you. Perhaps, one day, you'll find someone you can love as much as I once loved you and now love Trish.'

Anne nodded. 'I'm glad you feel like that about her. You'll be very happy together, I can feel it in my bones. And don't worry about me. I'm a survivor. *Au revoir*, Ivo. You really should get going.'

'Yes.' And suddenly the invisible barrier was no longer there. Without either being conscious of making a move, their arms were around one another and they were locked in a gentle embrace. Their lips met in the sort of kiss that could, Anne reflected, be exchanged by brother and sister. There was no bitterness between them, just a moment's poignant anguish for something that was over.

Ivo released her and turned towards the door. With his fingers on the handle, he glanced over his shoulder.

'See you,' he said, and was gone. Anne heard the sound of his voice calling to her mother and Penelope in the kitchen, followed by the slam of the front door and the echo of his feet on the garden path. She stood rooted to the spot, aware of a deep sense of loss, but also of a tremendous upsurge of release; a feeling that she could now get on with her life, freed at last from the debilitating burden of guilt which she had carried for so many years.

It also occurred to her that she was now able to let Richard know how she really felt about him, but she put that thought to the back of her mind. She was not at all sure that he wanted to know just at present, and had a terrifying suspicion that he might never wish to do so. He seemed wrapped in a grief so profound that Anne had more than once been prompted to the disloyal thought that it was a form of self-indulgence. She always dismissed the idea as soon as it had formed, reminding herself how much he had loved Georgina, but it surfaced all the same from time to time. More worrying was the fact that Deborah Grantham was the only person who seemed able to get through to him and ease him out of the blackest moods. Anne's one consolation was that Ewan did not like Deborah, wriggling away whenever she drew near.

With a sigh, Anne began clearing what was left on the dining-room table – place-mats, napkins and finally the cloth itself. Then she wandered into the kitchen where her mother and Penelope were still swapping anecdotes, laughing and giggling like a couple of girls. Anne made herself scarce, frightened away by the ominous words 'Do you remember?' She had no wish just now to be roped in as an audience. She went in search of Clifford, but he was asleep, stretched out on the drawing-room couch, gently snoring. Anne dropped a light kiss on his forehead and went up the two flights of stairs to her grandmother's flat. It felt unbearably empty. Everything was exactly as it had been a week ago, on the day Felicity had died, but the atmosphere of desolation was all-pervading. She tried to persuade herself that her grandmother had just popped out for a while and would soon be back, her footfalls sounding on the stairs. But it was impossible. Felicity was gone, and gone for ever.

'Stop it!' Anne reprimanded herself severely. 'You're getting morbid. All right, so this is a day of endings. Tomorrow, however, will be one of beginnings; the first day of the rest of your life.' The cliché made her smile, and she began to feel better. This time next week she would be back in London, living at The Laurels. She would be under the same roof as Richard and his son, an advantage Deborah Grantham did not have, and if she couldn't make something of it, then that would be her fault. And there was her work. Aileen Hogan provided her with employment when she needed an extra hand in the studio, and commissions were slowly trickling in as one small job led to another. One day, she promised herself, she and Trish would start their own business and become famous. So she had no reason to feel low. She must shake off this sense of loneliness and depression.

She went downstairs again. The phone was ringing in the hall, and she answered it. The shock of hearing Richard's voice, when she had just been thinking about him, almost took her breath away and made her momentarily incoherent.

'Rich? I . . . Rich? Is that you?'

'I just said it is. I wanted to let you and Barbara know how sorry I am not to have come to the funeral. Did everything go OK?'

'Yes. Fine. Mother and I understand. You must be busy.'

'We are. But that wasn't the real reason I didn't come. I'm a coward, Anne. I couldn't face it.'

Her heart sank, but she said sympathetically: 'Of course not. Don't worry. We knew you were thinking of us.' She added with determined cheerfulness: 'We shall be seeing a lot more of each other after this week, once I'm really settled at The Laurels.'

'Yes. I was sorry to hear about you and Ivo.'

'These things happen. Do you want to speak to either of your parents?' When he declined, she went on, reluctant to let him go: 'How's Ewan?'

'Great. He's gone to the zoo this afternoon with his nurse and Debs. Debs is playing truant from school for half a day. I suppose I shouldn't have encouraged her, but she was so keen to go with them I didn't have the heart to dissuade her. She's so fond of Ewan. Irene'll kill me if she finds out. Look, I must go. I'm at the surgery, and it's full. Give my condolences to Barbara, and I'll see you soon.' He hung up.

Anne was left staring into space. Couldn't Richard see what Deborah was up to? Fond of Ewan, my foot! she thought viciously. That girl's never been fond of anyone but herself and never will be. But Deborah wanted Richard; and, as she had never in her life been denied anything she wanted by either parent, it never occurred to her that she might not get him. Anne slammed down the receiver.

'Who was that?' her mother asked as she and Penelope finally emerged from the kitchen. When told, they were both too busy expressing regret that Anne had not called them to the phone to notice her mood of barely suppressed anger.

Clifford, refreshed by his nap, appeared in the drawing-room doorway.

'We should be going, my love,' he said to Penelope. 'It's a longish drive, and I want to be home before

347

dark. My eyesight isn't what it was.' He glanced towards Anne. 'And how is my youngest son? I gathered that was him on the phone just now.'

'Well,' she answered flatly, and turning on her heel went upstairs to her room.

CHAPTER TWENTY-SIX

THE DIVORCE WENT THROUGH smoothly, enabling Trish and Ivo to be married at the end of August. Two weeks later, Trish gave birth to a baby girl who, her proud parents announced, would be called Mabel.

'Why Mabel, for heaven's sake?' Anne wanted to know, sitting beside Trish's hospital bed and helping herself from the box of chocolates she had brought with her. 'It's so old-fashioned.'

'Old-fashioned names are in, or hadn't you noticed? Anyway, Ivo and I like it.' Trish removed her present out of Anne's reach. 'Thanks for the chocolates,' she added drily.

Anne grinned, relieved that the visit was going so well. She had been apprehensive about seeing the baby, wondering how she would feel. But when she bent over the cradle, looking at the tiny, crumpled red face and the mass of dark hair, so like Trish's, she experienced nothing but pleasure for Ivo and her friend. She was finally free of that clinging sense of regret which had haunted her both during and just after the divorce. She was whole again and able to be herself.

Deprived of the chocolates, she turned her attention to the basket of fruit on the locker and nipped off a small bunch of grapes. 'From Penelope and Cliff, I'll bet,' she said, cramming the fruit into her mouth.

'Yes, and the flowers are from Irene and Chris. Everyone's been most kind considering the circumstances.'

'Chris and Irene could hardly be censorious, could they? These are delicious grapes.' The bells were ringing for the end of the visiting period. Anne rose and

349

kissed her friend goodbye. 'When you see Ivo, tell him from me that everything's all right. I think Mabel's wonderful and that he's a very lucky man. But he knows that. Now, let me see if I can find my way out of here. All these corridors look exactly alike. I should have tied a piece of string to the door-handle at the entrance, like Theseus in the Minotaur's lair.'

But, once outside the hospital, Anne's elation left her and she was oppressed by a feeling of anticlimax. She had been gearing herself up all day for the visit, and now that it was successfully over she felt deflated. She thought she might go to the cinema and bought an evening paper to see what was showing. In the end she decided on *Fatal Attraction*.

It seemed years since she had last been to the cinema, either on her own or with someone else, having always preferred the theatre as entertainment. While she hesitated in the brightly lit foyer, looking for a list of current prices, the crowd from the previous performance surged out and engulfed her. A man, bumping into her, made her turn and, descending the stairs behind him, she saw Richard and Deborah Grantham. Ignoring the man's apologies, she took a step backwards so that a pillar hid her from their view. Her heart was beating suffocatingly fast, and any desire to see the film had evaporated. All she wanted now was to get home and be in her room before Richard returned, so that she would not have to face him. The glimpse she had had of Deborah's hand on his arm, and the way his head was bent to catch what she was saying, made her sick with jealousy. She reminded herself, as she had so often done in the past, that Deborah was only a child; but the skin-tight jeans and denim jacket, open to reveal the well-filled polo-necked jumper, argued the contrary. Anne waited long enough to let them get clear of the cinema before she, too, left, heading for the nearest Underground station.

She got home ahead of Richard. Penelope was in the drawing-room, watching an episode of 'Dynasty', but she switched the television set off as Anne came in.

'I get so confused with that programme,' she complained. 'I can never make out who's married to whom. They seem to change partners every other week.' She paused, colouring, aware that she might have made an infelicitous remark. 'Sorry, darling, I didn't mean . . .'

'That's OK.' Anne sat down and stared morosely in front of her. 'Richard's not in, I take it?'

'No. He promised to take Debs to see *Fatal Attraction* and to supper afterwards. I don't know what it is about that child, but she seems able to wind him round her little finger. I've told him what I think: that after work his place is here with Ewan.'

Anne automatically went to Richard's defence, even though she agreed with Penelope. 'He works hard. He's entitled to some relaxation.'

'I suppose so.' Penelope sighed. 'If I'm honest, what really annoys me is that Deborah is the only person who can get through to him. As far as the rest of us are concerned, he barely seems conscious of our existence. I don't want to sound callous, and I appreciate how much he loved Georgina, but surely he should be getting over her death, just a little, by now. It's two and a half years, for God's sake! You and Barbara aren't still parading your grief for Imogen, even though I'm certain you think about her every day. As we all do.' She sighed again. 'At least Tim has straightened himself out, thanks to Sylvia, and he and Chris are on speaking terms after all these years. In fact, when the four of them were here to supper last Sunday, I found the boys having a good laugh over my latest novel, just as they used to do in the old days. And this farce Tim's in is still running, and looks set to do so for another six months at least.

351

Chris has another film and a television serial lined up, and Cliff's never so happy as when he's doing Shakespeare at the National. So everything in the garden would be lovely if it weren't for Richard.' Penelope grimaced. 'What a shockingly selfish point of view, but I know I can say things like that to you without fear of being quoted.'

Anne got up, poured herself a whisky and returned to her seat. 'Do you think he's fond of Deborah?' she asked after a moment's silence.

Penelope eyed her uneasily. 'When you say "fond", you're not implying he might entertain unavuncular feelings for her, are you?'

Anne shrugged. 'Why not? He's not her uncle, after all, and she's a very attractive girl who's quite blatantly throwing herself at him.'

Penelope was alarmed. 'You don't really think so, do you?'

'Isn't it obvious? She's round here all her spare time nowadays, which she never was before. And she does her best to ingratiate herself with Ewan. It's not her fault the child doesn't like her.'

'Shit! I hadn't looked at it in that light. But, now you mention it, she is here a good deal more than she used to be. But I won't believe that Richard regards her as anything other than his niece, the way he's always seen her since Chris and Irene's marriage. To him, she's a child. That's why she's able to get through to him while the rest of us are still shut out.'

Anne finished her drink and stood up. 'I'm for an early night,' she said. 'I'm tired. Hospitals always exhaust me for some reason.'

Penelope was immediately contrite. 'Oh, my dear! I forgot you'd been to see the baby! How ... how did you get on? How are Trish and ... and Ivo?'

'Excited, happy, proud. And the little girl's beautiful. They're calling her Mabel.' Anne waited patiently while Penelope exclaimed, as she herself had done, over the old-fashioned name, then dropped a kiss lightly on her forehead. 'Good night, love. See you at breakfast.'

The following April, Deborah celebrated her sixteenth birthday and left school at the end of the summer term, resisting the efforts of both her parents and Christopher to persuade her otherwise.

'What's the point of staying on?' she demanded of Anne and Penelope. 'I'm not clever, and it's a waste of taxpayers' money to keep me chained to a desk. I've no particular ambitions. I'm just happy to cruise along until I get married, whenever that might be.'

Richard was also present, eating a belated supper, having been called out to a sick cat just as he was leaving the surgery. He smiled at her and slipped a piece of meat to Barkis, an old dog now but with as good an appetite as ever. If Deborah had hoped to provoke some comment from him, however, she was disappointed; and Anne, meanly, could not help feeling pleased. The past nine months had seen a lightening of Richard's mood, and her own relationship with him had improved accordingly. But there were still times when he withdrew inside himself, going about for days as though he were in a trance. But these occasions were growing fewer and further apart, although he was not the gregarious man he had once been. He took Ewan to Scotland every six months or so to see his Frere grandparents, but for several weeks after these visits he was quiet and remote. Nevertheless, Anne felt more optimistic about the future than she had for some time past.

She and Penelope had been in the kitchen, eating their evening meal, when Deborah arrived. Her obvious disappointment at Richard's absence had been short-lived when he put in an appearance half an hour later. Subdued until his arrival, she had immediately launched into the news of her decision to quit school in two weeks' time, describing in detail the arguments she had had with her parents and stepfather.

'What do you think, Rich?' she asked directly, having failed to provoke him with her remark about marriage. 'Isn't it more sense for me to leave school now, rather than hang around for two more years, learning nothing?'

He smiled again, the old sweet smile which Anne remembered so well, and which was like a knife twisting in her heart each time he bestowed it on Deborah.

'I think you should do what you want to do,' he said. 'Life's too short to waste it on doing things you don't like doing.'

Deborah was triumphant. 'I knew you'd understand,' she crowed. 'You're wonderful! And I shall rely on you to back me up if Chris and Mummy canvas your opinion.'

'You have my word,' he promised, and fed another scrap to the attentive Barkis.

Later, he drove her home through the warm July dusk, returning to The Laurels to find his mother retired for the night and Anne, in the nursery, holding a tearful Ewan on her lap. He paused in the doorway.

'Something wrong? Where's the nurse?'

'It's her night off,' Anne replied tartly, 'and she's never in much before midnight. Ewan woke with a tummy-ache, but he's all right now. We're just having a cuddle before he goes back to bed.'

Richard kneeled beside the rocking-chair, ruffling his little son's hair. 'What's the matter, old chap? Been eating too many strawberries?'

Ewan clasped his arms around his father's neck, shaking the bright head so like his mother's. 'No!' he denied indignantly. 'They was rasbies.'

Richard chuckled. 'Same difference, so there's no cause to sound so offended. Here,' he added, straightening up and holding out his arms, 'let me take him. Come on, old fellow, back to bed with you.'

Ewan wriggled. 'Want Anne tuck me in and say goo'night.'

'He's very fond of you,' Richard remarked when Anne had pulled up the bedclothes, kissed the soft little lips and been ruthlessly hugged in return. He switched off the nursery light and they crept downstairs to the drawing-room.

'I'm very fond of him, too,' Anne said, suddenly aware that they were alone together for the first time in ages; for, although they lived under the same roof, there invariably seemed to be someone else present. They sat down, carefully distancing themselves from one another, Anne on the furthest end of the couch from the armchair Richard had chosen. The two cats, who had been asleep on the second armchair, now woke, stretched, jumped down from their perch and headed for Richard's lap, purring loudly.

Anne said: 'You still have the magic touch with animals.'

Richard stroked Iago's head, and was immediately given a friendly nip by Iachimo to remind him of his presence. 'I shouldn't be much of a vet if I didn't.'

There was silence except for the vociferous pleasure of the cats. Anne racked her brain for something to say, anything except the one question she wanted to ask: 'What do you really feel for Deborah Grantham?' But it was Richard himself who broached the subject.

'I don't think Chris is too pleased with me,' he said sleepily, tilting his head back against the cushions. 'Deborah enlisted my support, when I took her home earlier, in the fight she's having about leaving school.'

'And he thinks it's none of your business.'

355

'Nor is it, but I couldn't let her down. I like her. She's a nice kid.'

Anne felt dizzy with relief at this description, but could not stop herself asking: 'Is that how you see her? As a child?'

Richard's eyes widened in surprise. 'She's only sixteen. How would you describe her?'

'I'd call her a woman. She's very mature for her years.'

Richard blinked a little. 'Is she? Yes, now you mention it, I suppose she is.'

'And used to getting her own way. She'll win this argument about leaving school without your help. Oh, her parents and Chris will put up a show of opposition, but they don't really stand a chance against her. Debs has made her decision, and that's it.'

'You make her sound rather formidable. I don't know that I'd recognize her from your description.'

'Then, perhaps you should think about it. She's a very determined young woman.'

Richard frowned. 'Why should I think about it? It has nothing to do with me. I'm only her uncle.'

'Step-uncle. There's a difference. At least, there is for Deborah, you can take my word.'

He laughed suddenly, getting up – to the intense annoyance of the cats – and moving to sit beside her on the couch. He took one of her hands in his.

'I think you're trying to tell me that Deborah's fond of me. Well, I know that already, but only in the way I'm fond of her. I can't think there's any other probability.'

Anne pressed his fingers, avoiding his eyes, afraid that he would see hers brimming over with love. 'I'm saying be careful, that's all. As I said just now, what Debs wants she gets, and she wants you. I'm certain of it.'

'I'm not. But, even if I were, it wouldn't matter. I've no intention of ever getting married again.'

Her head jerked up. 'What nonsense! You're only just twenty-eight. Of course you must marry again, if only for Ewan's sake. A child of that age needs a mother.'

'He and I are all right as we are,' Richard answered quietly, dropping her hand. 'I realize a nurse isn't the same as a mother, but he's also got Mum and Dad. They make a terrific fuss of him.'

'But they're not here all the time. Besides, they're busy people as well as being a great deal older than he is. Ewan needs someone younger, who's close to him.'

'He has Debs. That's why I encourage her to come on jaunts with us, to come round here a lot. She's nearer Ewan in age than any of us.'

Anne sighed to herself. There seemed no point in pursuing the conversation. She was not going to convince Richard of Deborah's self-interest. Not that she suspected for a moment that Deborah loved him: Anne considered her incapable of any such emotion. She fancied him, wanted him and was determined to have him; and when eventually she tired of him she would leave him for somebody else. But as Richard refused to heed Anne's warnings all she could do was to stand by, ready to pick up the pieces.

Richard's face softened, and he again took hold of her hand. 'Don't look so worried. I'm not offended. I know that whatever you say and do is because you have my interests at heart. You've been my best friend ever since we were little. You used to lecture and scold me then. We've lost touch a bit over the past few years, but I've always known you were there if I needed you. And I'm ashamed to admit that that's more than you could say of me. When your marriage to Ivo was going wrong, I was so obsessed with my own troubles that I was no earthly good to anyone, and I'm sorry.'

She gave a watery smile. 'You don't need to be. What happened to you and what happened to me are not comparable in any way. And the break-up of my marriage was mainly my own fault. You mustn't blame Trish or Ivo.'

'If you say so.' The ormolu clock on the mantelpiece struck eleven, but although he had seemed so tired a while ago Richard made no move to go to bed. He appeared content, for the moment, just to sit and continue talking. 'But these things are never completely one-sided in my experience. Is there anyone else in your life at present? Any other man, I mean? Someone you're fond of.'

'No,' Anne lied. 'I'm happy on my own for now. And I love being here. Your parents have always been so good to me, it's the next best place to home.'

'We've always been like one big family,' he said, squeezing her hand. 'We're almost like brother and sister.'

But, even as he said it, some doubt seemed to possess him. He turned and looked at her more directly, tilting her face up towards him with his other hand. In the subdued glow of Penelope's pink-shaded lamps, it was difficult to read his exact expression, but Anne found herself trembling. She remained as still as possible, her clear grey eyes wide with hope. They were enclosed in a magical silence, and nothing must break the spell. His head bent towards her, his lips brushed hers, experimentally at first, before the grip on her hands tightened and the pressure of his lips grew more insistent . . .

The drawing-room door opened, and the main light was switched on, revealing everything in a brighter, harsher glare.

'God! How I need a drink!' Clifford announced in his best rolling tragedian's voice. 'My performance this evening was abysmal!' He started back in feigned

358

horror. 'Dear Heaven! It's those bloody moggies! Keep them away from me, Richard dear boy. You know they find me irresistible. A pity they couldn't have witnessed my display tonight. It would have put them off me for life. They'd have died of boredom, like the audience.'

Richard, who had released Anne's hands and drawn back from her at the first sound of his father's voice, laughed and got up. 'What do you want? Whisky?' He crossed to the drinks-table and lifted the decanter. His tone indicated nothing, neither embarrassment nor relief nor annoyance at Clifford's untimely entrance. But, Anne noted miserably, he refused to look at her again once he had poured the whisky, perching instead on the arm of the couch and addressing his father. 'Come on, Dad! You can't possibly have been that bad.'

The two cats were now ensconced on Cliff's lap, purring rapturously. Iachimo, in a frenzy of hero-worship, clawed at his idol's blue silk tie.

'Oh, for Pete's sweet sake!' Clifford exclaimed in exasperation, removing it from the destructive paws and tossing it negligently over one shoulder. 'And if you don't calm down', he admonished Iago, 'you'll overload your motors. Well, believe me,' he continued, sipping his whisky, 'I was dreadful. But, alas, one gets performances like that every once in a while. I have to admit that I've always considered Prospero a dreary old bore, but one can make something interesting of him if one's on form.' He finished his drink at a gulp. 'And now one's going to bed.' He grinned. 'My leading lady's mode of speech is catching. And by the look of you, Anne my dear, it's time you went, too. You look positively haggard.' He stood up, tipping the cats off his knees. They disappeared to sulk in a corner. 'God bless you, my children. Don't forget to turn off the lights before you come upstairs.'

He bowed himself out, waving an airy hand in valediction. Anne sat where she was, waiting for Richard to say something, to come across to her, perhaps to resume where he had left off. But it was a forlorn hope, and she knew it. The spell was broken. He made no move towards her, merely stooping to caress the cats who were cleaning themselves and refusing to be consoled for the loss of their favourite.

'I'll be off to bed, too,' he said awkwardly. 'I have to be up early in the morning.'

'Richard!' Anne faced him across the room.

He paused in the doorway. 'Yes?' His voice was wary. The tension was palpable in every line of his slight, finely drawn body. His eyes, huge and dark in the thin face, looked pleadingly at her.

'Oh . . . nothing,' she answered sadly. 'Just . . . good night.'

'Good night,' he said with obvious relief, and went out, shutting the door quietly behind him.

CHAPTER TWENTY-SEVEN

WHEN ANNE CAME DOWN to breakfast next morning, Richard had already left the house. Penelope was still in bed.

'She's feeling rather tired,' Clifford explained. 'Mrs Turvey is taking her up something on a tray.'

Mrs Turvey had replaced Mrs Clennan two years previously, the latter having at last decided that it was time to retire. It had been a tearful parting, and her successor came in only twice a week, 'obliging', if she were needed, for special occasions. It meant more work for Penelope who, at sixty-two, found it a bit of a strain. Today, fortunately, was one of Mrs Turvey's days, and Penelope was taking advantage of the fact.

Anne poured coffee and helped herself to toast. Clifford remarked suddenly: 'I'm sorry if I interrupted anything last night.'

'You didn't,' Anne replied as coolly as she was able. 'There was nothing to interrupt.'

'Ah!' Clifford stirred his coffee. 'Perhaps I got the wrong impression.'

'Perhaps you did.' Anne's tone was brusque.

The cats strolled into the dining-room and made a bee-line for Clifford, wrapping themselves ecstatically around his legs. He tried to ignore them.

'You mustn't despair, you know,' he went on after a silence. 'Richard's relationship with Georgina was intensely physical, as I'm sure you'd noticed. He's bound to miss that. It's why he likes being with Deborah. She's a very physical person, too. But I sometimes wonder how much real depth there was in his marriage. My own feeling is that in years to come it might have foundered. For one thing, I think, deep down, he's always been a little in love with you.'

Anne laughed drily. 'I wish I thought so.'

Clifford poured himself a second cup of coffee, before reaching out and squeezing her hand.

'You give up too easily. My advice is give Rich time, as much as he needs. Trust to his own innate good sense. All my three sons have a tendency to do stupid things, as you know only too well, but their instinct for self-preservation is strong, and means that they always extricate themselves from whatever mess they're in in the nick of time, even if it means drawing blood, their own and other people's, in the process. So, I repeat, trust Richard. In the long run, he won't do anything that's to his disadvantage.'

Anne was only half-convinced. 'How much time do you suggest I give him?'

'As long as necessary. Trust me. It will all work out in the end, but you must have patience.'

Deborah's birthday celebrations had always been lavish, given one year by Irene and Chris, the next by her father. For her seventeenth birthday, it was Jeremy Grantham's turn.

Jeremy had never remarried – a perpetual reproach, Chris felt, to himself and Irene. The truth was, however, that Jeremy was really a loner at heart, a fact which his brief marriage and subsequent divorce had proved to him. After the initial humiliation of Irene's desertion, he discovered that he actually preferred being on his own. The sense of freedom had been enormous; and without the immediate responsibility of raising Deborah – all the important decisions were left to Irene – he was able to spoil her without suffering any of the unpleasant consequences of his over-indulgence.

Aware that it would fall to his ex-wife to stage the all-important eighteenth-birthday party the following year, Jeremy was determined that his daughter's seventeenth should be the most spectacular so far. To this end, he hired a suite at the Savoy, engaged a well-known orchestra for the more adult guests to dance to, and arranged a disco, complete with live DJ and strobe lighting, for the younger. There was to be a lavish buffet supper around ten-thirty.

'What's he trying to do? Beggar himself?' Irene demanded irritably of her husband.

'Beggar us, more likely. Just don't try to compete.' But Chris knew, even as he spoke, that he might as well save his breath; that next year, whatever else they had to do without, Deborah's coming of age would have priority over every other consideration.

Anne found herself the recipient of a cream gilt-edged invitation requesting the pleasure of her company at 8 p.m. on Friday, 14 April until two o'clock the following morning. Everyone else at The Laurels received one also.

'We can all go in one car,' Penelope said, 'and save petrol.'

Clifford, who was at present 'resting' and thoroughly irritated at so unusual an occurrence, asked peevishly: 'Why do we have to save petrol? We're not on the bread-line yet, for God's sake, and as long as you go on churning out those bonk-busters of yours we never shall be. Rich can take Anne, and we'll go together. That way, we old fogeys won't have to wait around for the youngsters when we want to go home.'

While Penelope took issue with being described as 'an old fogey', and while Anne and Richard, at the age of twenty-eight disclaimed all pretensions to being classed as 'youngsters', it was nevertheless tacitly agreed that they would travel to the Savoy in two separate cars. Clifford gave Anne a triumphant wink which she ignored. She remained unconvinced that there was anything to be triumphant about.

Nine months had gone by since the morning when he had advised her to be patient; and so far that patience had gone unrewarded. True, Richard now appeared to have got over the worst of his grief and was more like his old happy self, but his attitude towards Anne was still simply one of friendship. There had been no repetition of that moment when it seemed that he might kiss her; indeed, he was careful never to be alone in her company if he could avoid it. Anne would have been surprised to know that Clifford, watching closely from the side-lines, interpreted this as a very good sign. To her, it merely underscored Richard's indifference.

Her spare time, in the two weeks before the party, was largely passed wondering what to wear for the occasion. Her lunch-breaks were spent haunting the dress shops and trying on the most unsuitable clothes. With great difficulty, she prevented herself from buying an impossibly low-cut, black satin mini-dress, which cost the earth but did absolutely nothing for her. Moreover, it was probable that Deborah would be wearing something similar and looking a great deal better in it than Anne ever could. Reluctantly, she recalled the assistant and said that she had changed her mind. In the end, she settled for a plain grey silk dress, which exactly matched the colour of her eyes, and wore it with her gold bracelet and long gilt earrings, her fair hair brushed loosely about her face. This restraint was rewarded by Richard's smile as she descended the stairs.

'You look wonderful,' he said appreciatively. 'That really suits you. It's the sort of thing you always ought to wear.'

'Well,' Anne responded a little breathlessly, 'I'll

see what I can do. Shall we go? I don't think your parents are quite ready yet.'

The rooms at the Savoy were already crowded by the time they arrived, mostly with a vociferous crowd of teenagers who had the effect of making Anne feel suddenly old. She and Richard made their way to where Deborah was standing beside her parents and Chris; and Deborah was indeed looking ravishing in a skimpy black mid-thigh-length dress. Thank heaven, Anne thought, common sense had prevailed.

She gave her birthday present, a silk scarf in the shades of blue and pink which Deborah preferred, and was prettily thanked, but the younger girl's eyes were on Richard and the small gift-wrapped package he held in his hand. When opened, it proved to be an antique ring, set with three garnets.

'Oh, Richard! You pet! You bought it for me, after all! I was sure it was too expensive.' Deborah threw both arms around his neck, kissing him soundly.

He extricated himself from this stifling embrace, smiling a little sheepishly. 'You said it was what you wanted.'

'Oh, it is,' she assured him. She explained for the benefit of the others: 'I saw it in a jeweller's window when Rich and I were out with Ewan one day. I fell in love with it there and then, but I never dreamed I should be given it for my birthday.' She slipped it on and held out her hand. 'Isn't it lovely?'

'Not your engagement finger, darling,' Irene reproved her sharply.

'Oh dear! Silly me!' Deborah looked at Richard, and he hastily lowered his eyes.

He took Anne's hand. 'Come on,' he said. 'Let's dance.'

She slid into his arms and they began slowly circling the floor. He was a good mover, extremely light on his feet, and Anne realized that it was the first time they had ever danced together. She remarked on the fact, forcing herself to smile, trying to forget the scene she had just witnessed.

'Oh, I don't know,' Richard answered. 'I seem to recall shunting you round the drawing-room in the Pimlico house, years and years ago at some children's party. We must have been about seven or eight. You complained I stepped on your toes all the time and said you'd rather be dancing with Chris.' The quick-step finished, and the band struck up again with a fox-trot. Richard grimaced. 'I don't know about you, but I feel as old as Methuselah doing this. Shall we try the disco, or do you think we're a bit long in the tooth?'

'Certainly not.' Anne took his arm. 'I don't intend being old until I'm eighty at least. Maybe not even then.'

'Quite right.' They made their way to the adjoining room, passing Penelope and Clifford, who had just arrived, on the way. Clifford gave Anne a conspiratorial wink, but she ignored it. What she really wanted was to sit out somewhere quiet and ask Richard about his relationship with Deborah, but she hadn't the courage. She had no right to pry into his affairs. The noise was deafening, and the strobe lighting soon gave her a headache. Richard, on the other hand, seemed to thrive on it; and, when Deborah was finally able to join her younger guests, was quick to accompany her on to the crowded floor. Anne tried to convince herself that he was merely being courteous to their hostess, but the sight of them laughing and so obviously enjoying themselves only made her feel more miserable. She could hardly credit that this Richard and the withdrawn stranger of the past years and months were one and the same person. And it was Deborah who had wrought this transformation; no-one else.

Long before suppertime, Anne was fervently wishing

that she had never accepted the invitation to the party. All she wanted was to go home, have a long, hot, comforting bath and fall into bed and the arms of oblivion. It occurred to her that if she were to get a taxi and slip away quietly no-one would miss her. But that would be impolite. She would plead illness, then, and her headache was real enough. She went in search of Jeremy Grantham in order to make her excuses.

He was difficult to track down in the crush of guests thronging the suite of rooms, and she was still looking for him when a hand gripped her arm.

'I've been trying to find you for the past five minutes,' Richard complained. 'I've had an emergency call to go out to a Mrs Farrow. It's really Pete's evening on duty, but one of the kids is sick and his wife doesn't want him to leave her. He's just telephoned, madly apologetic and all that, but says it shouldn't take long. I wondered if you'd like to come with me. I know it's a cheek to ask, but—'

'Of course it isn't!' Anne replied eagerly. 'I'd be pleased to come if you want me. I'll just get my wrap. See you in the foyer in a few minutes.'

Once in the car and speeding towards Hackney, Anne enquired: 'What's the emergency?'

'Oh, Mrs Farrow's bitch is in labour and she isn't too happy with the way things are going. I think she's panicking unnecessarily, but there you are! You know how people are where their pets are concerned. And a good thing, too.' He glanced sideways at her. 'I hope you really don't mind coming with me, but I didn't fancy driving all this way on my own and I had a feeling you weren't enjoying the party.'

Anne made no reply to that. 'What's this Mrs Farrow like?' she asked.

'A nice woman. Elderly. Lives alone, except for her animals, since her husband died last August.

Trudi, the bitch, and her two cats mean everything to her. We shan't be long getting there now. She lives near Lansdowne Walk.'

Anne said nothing more until they reached their destination, where they were greeted on the doorstep by an apologetic Mrs Farrow.

'I'm so sorry, Mr Haldane, to have got you out so late. And you at a party by the looks of you, too. I thought for a moment there that Trudi was in trouble, but she's had all the pups right as rain after all. I shall pay you for your visit naturally.'

'That's OK, Mrs Farrow,' Richard answered cheerfully. 'I might as well take a look at Trudi while I'm here. This is a friend of mine, Mrs Kingsley.'

'Miss Seymour,' Anne amended swiftly, her fingers painfully crushed in Mrs Farrow's welcoming grip. 'I'm divorced. I've reverted to my maiden name.'

The older woman clucked sympathetically. 'That seems to happen to the best of young people nowadays. You're all under too much pressure. Wasn't so in my day, of course. Come along in.'

Mrs Farrow preceded Anne and Richard along a narrow passageway which smelt strongly of floor polish and disinfectant. The second door on the left-hand side opened into a crowded sitting-room where framed photographs and china ornaments cluttered every available surface. An old-fashioned coal fire burned in the grate, and curled up in front of it, in a large wicker basket, lay a King Charles spaniel bitch and three squirming puppies. Two cats, one black, one tortoiseshell, surveyed the scene curiously from the comfort of an armchair.

Richard kneeled down by the basket, talking softly to the bitch and stroking her head. The two cats jumped down and came to rub against him.

'They love Mr Haldane,' Mrs Farrow said fondly. 'I'm delighted to see him with a young lady. I keep

368

telling him he ought to get married again, especially with a kiddie to look after.'

The colour burned in Anne's cheeks, and she was relieved to note that Richard appeared not to be listening to the conversation. 'Er ... no,' she answered. 'I'm just a friend. Richard and I grew up together. We're more like brother and sister.'

She was suddenly conscious of Richard's stillness before he raised his head and regarded her fixedly for a moment. Then his attention returned to the bitch, who had roused herself and was starting to lick her offspring. Carefully, he picked up and examined each pup before replacing it in the basket.

'Two dogs and a bitch, Mrs Farrow. And all healthy. You won't have any difficulty selling them later on if you want to.'

Mrs Farrow was indignant. 'I'm keeping all three. I've no children, and all my family are dead and gone. My late hubby's family live in North Wales. What else have I got to do with my time but look after them?' She glanced sternly at Anne. 'You fond of animals?'

Anne nodded. 'Mind you, I can't stand snakes.'

Mrs Farrow snorted. 'I'm not talking about nasty scaly things. I mean proper animals, with fur.'

Richard's lips twitched as he rose from his knees. Politely refusing Mrs Farrow's offer of a cup of tea, they said they had to be going.

'We must get back to the party. Our hostess will think us very remiss if we don't return as soon as we can.'

When they were once more in the car and Richard had started the engine, he asked: 'Is that how you think of me? As a brother?'

Anne said lightly: 'Well, we did grow up rather like siblings. Why?'

'Oh ... nothing.' There was silence for a while before he spoke again. 'Let me ask you for some sisterly advice, then. Do you think a difference of

369

ten years is too great a gap between a man and a woman? For marriage, I mean.'

Anne's breath caught in her throat, and for a moment she was unable to answer. But finally, with an enormous effort of will, she said: 'Are you talking about yourself and Deborah?'

'Of course, I shouldn't dream of asking her to marry me for at least another year, not until she's at least eighteen.' He sounded defensive.

'Are you in love with her?' Anne was amazed how normal her voice was. Inside, she felt as though she were screaming.

Richard hesitated. 'I'm not in love with her the way I was with Georgy, if that's what you mean. But I'm very fond of her, and I think she's fond of me.'

'She wants you,' Anne responded drily. 'And she's used to getting her own way. I really can't give you advice, Richard. I don't feel qualified. I've hardly made a success of marriage, have I? I would say that love is a lot more important than many people imagine; but, apart from that, you'll have to make up your own mind.' She took a deep breath. 'Could you drive me straight to St John's Wood instead of back to the party? I'm not feeling too good. The noise and the disco lights have given me a terrible headache.'

He was immediately all concern, blaming himself for having dragged her with him to see Mrs Farrow, when he should have realized that she was feeling unwell. When they reached The Laurels, he insisted on going indoors with her and seeing her as far as her bedroom door.

'Mind you take a couple of aspirin,' he told her solicitously. 'And don't worry; I'll explain to Deborah and Jeremy Grantham. I'm sure they'll understand.' He smiled at her and brushed her forehead with his lips. 'Now, get some sleep. I'll just look in on Ewan before I go and make sure he's all right.'

He vanished up the next flight of stairs to where his son shared a room with the nurse. A few moments later, Anne heard him run down again, and the soft click of the front door as it closed behind him. Slowly, she undressed, washed, cleaned her teeth and swallowed the aspirin, before finally getting into bed and burying her face in the pillow. And, at last, the tears came, running down her cheeks until it seemed impossible that she could cry any more. But she was still crying when she fell asleep.

CHAPTER TWENTY-EIGHT

'NOTHING'S CHANGED, then,' Barbara remarked as she and Anne climbed into a taxi at Temple Meads station.

Settling herself in the back seat, while the driver stowed her luggage in the boot, Anne asked carefully: 'What makes you say that?'

Her mother laughed. 'Do you think I'm stupid? When was the last time you decided to spend Christmas and New Year at home? Especially now there's just the two of us.'

Anne smiled ruefully. 'I'm not very considerate, am I? I've condemned you to a quiet holiday when you could have spent it with Penelope and Cliff. I'm sorry. I was so anxious to get away, I just didn't think.'

Barbara squeezed her hand. 'Don't be silly. I wish you'd told me years ago how you feel about Richard. It would have made a lot of other things much clearer. Your attitude towards Ivo, for example.'

Anne nodded. She was glad, now, that she had confided in her mother, that February day during their walk across the Downs. It had been foolish, shutting her out; unfair, too, for who had a better right to know the truth? Anne had feared a lecture on what a mess she had made of her life, and instead, Barbara had proved to be overwhelmingly sympathetic and supportive. As a result, the two of them had drawn much closer together. Her mother had also kept her promise not to tell Penelope, a fact which Anne greatly appreciated, knowing what an effort such restraint must have demanded of her. She found herself expressing her fears about Deborah.

Barbara looked thoughtful, but for the moment made no comment beyond saying: 'Richard's a sensible man. Trust him.' She changed the subject. 'What's happening at The Laurels this Christmas? Will it be a gathering of the clans?'

Their driver braked sharply as another driver crowded him at a bend.

Anne looked out of the taxi window at the passing traffic, which seemed to increase in volume each time she returned to Bristol. The complicated new one-way road systems confused her. It happened in London, of course, but this was the territory of childhood where she expected everything to be always the same. Turning back to her mother, she sighed.

'Oh, everyone will be there. Tim and Sylvia. Irene and Chris. Richard . . . and Deborah. Maybe Jeremy Grantham as well. It's open-house season as far as Penelope's concerned.'

'Tim and Chris are friends again, then? That's something to be glad about, as Pollyanna would have said. There was a time when you wouldn't have found them both under the same roof.'

Anne laughed. 'Sylvia refuses to marry Tim, but they seem to have settled down together, so he's quite happy. And Sylvia seems genuinely fond of him. She's no longer in love with Chris, which makes a difference. There's no hint of bitterness or embarrassment nowadays, so that's one worry removed from Penelope's shoulders.' Anne grimaced affectionately, if a little mockingly. 'So she can concentrate all her anxiety on Rich.'

Barbara's eyebrows shot up. 'Pen knows about him and Deborah? Strange, she hasn't said anything to me.'

'Of course she doesn't know!' Anne's tone was acerbic. 'There's nothing to know as yet. But you know Pen.

She's just not happy unless she's worrying about one of her brood of chicks.'

Barbara said gently: 'You mustn't make fun of her. She's had a lot to contend with, one way and another.'

The taxi turned into College Close and stopped in front of number four. The two women got out, Barbara paid the driver and they carried Anne's case inside. There was a quality of silence about the house which it had never had in the old days, and Anne realized anew how much she missed her grandmother. When Barbara had made a pot of tea, which they carried into the greater comfort of the dining-room, she said: 'This house is too big for you. You must be lonely. Why don't you sell up and move to London? You could buy a little flat, and you'd be close to Penelope and me. Lots of theatres; Lord's and the cricket in the summer. What more could you ask for?'

'My life here, my independence, my freedom,' was her mother's firm retort. 'Pen's my best friend and always will be, but she does tend to interfere. She's so used to moving the characters in her novels around at will, making them do her bidding, that she thinks she can do it in real life, and gets frustrated when people won't do what she wants. I bet she's constantly nagging Richard.'

Anne smiled. 'Yes, she is. But she's concerned for him. She wants him to be happy, that's all.'

'Mmm.' Barbara poured herself a second cup of tea and stirred it vigorously. 'She won't be pleased when she knows his future plans. Do you really think he means to marry Deborah?'

'That's what he said. But maybe by the time she's eighteen he'll have changed his mind.'

Barbara studied her daughter's tired face from beneath lowered lids. Presently, she asked: 'Have you ever told Richard how you feel about him? Does he even suspect that you love him?'

'Of course not! How can I possibly tell him when he so obviously doesn't love me? It would be embarrassing both of us for no good reason.'

Her mother put her elbows on the table and rested her chin on her hands. 'Does he love Deborah? Has he said so?'

'Not to me, but why should he? But I can't imagine he'd want to marry her if he didn't.'

'You married Ivo and you didn't love him. There are all sorts of different reasons why people marry. You say she flings herself at his head. Well, maybe he's flattered – an attractive young girl like that, and him so much older. Then, again, the emotional numbness which followed Georgina's death must be wearing off by now; and, if what you say is true, Richard's a very physical man. He needs a woman. All you ever show him is indifference or a sisterly affection.' Barbara smiled encouragingly. 'Darling, I think it's high time you swallowed your pride and your maidenly scruples, and tried to find out what exactly are Richard's feelings. If he is in love with Deborah, or thinks he is, there's nothing you can do except bow to the inevitable and pray hard that she makes him happy. Then put all your energies into getting on with your own life; a life which doesn't include him. You'll be thirty next year and, to be blunt, you can't waste precious time chasing rainbows.'

'And if he doesn't love her?'

'Tell him how you feel about him and wait for his reaction. If it's negative, at least you'll know the truth. You won't be any worse off than you are now, with all this uncertainty.'

Anne sighed and finished her tea. 'Thanks, Mum. I know it's good advice, but . . . '

Barbara laughed and finished the sentence for her. 'But, like most good advice, it will go unheeded.'

Anne shook her head. 'I wouldn't say that. I promise

at least to think about what you've said. Now, let's wash up the cups, I'll unpack and then we'll make plans for Christmas.'

Richard had arrived home early for once, the unpleasant March day, with a touch of sleet in the air, discouraging too many people from attending the early-evening surgery. Dinner was over, having been brought forward so that Penelope and Clifford could get away in good time for the theatre, Ewan was in bed and Anne was reading to him. The nurse, taking a well-earned rest, was watching television in her room.

Anne did not hear Richard come in, being absorbed, like her charge, in the space adventure story. She was only aware of his presence when he sat down on the opposite side of Ewan's bed.

She jumped. 'Goodness, you frightened me! I had no idea you were home. I'll come down in a minute and make you some supper.'

Ewan frowned. 'No,' he protested indignantly. 'You're reading to me. You're not to take her away, Daddy. I won't let you!'

Richard eyed his son with mock severity. 'You're six years old,' he said. 'You shouldn't need anyone to read to you. Besides, you can't monopolize Anne. Other people want her company as much as you do.' He relented slightly. 'I'll ask Nurse to come and finish the story, if you want.'

Ewan vigorously shook his head. 'She doesn't read so nicely.' He smiled winningly at Anne. 'You don't really want to make Daddy's supper, do you? He can get his own.'

'He's had a long day, working very hard; and, as it happens, I quite enjoy cooking, provided it isn't anything which needs too much concentration.'

Ewan was inclined to be sulky, but she kissed him

and promised to read an extra chapter of the book the following evening if he behaved himself tonight. A few moments later, she was able to close the bedroom door behind her and Richard, leaving Ewan happily snuggled down among the pillows.

'He's getting too self-willed,' Richard remarked as he followed her downstairs. 'He needs a mother.'

Anne made no comment for the moment; but when they were seated together in the kitchen, Richard tucking into a plate of eggs and bacon, she said quietly: 'I suppose he'll soon have one.'

Richard was momentarily at a loss, having by then forgotten his remark, but once he understood her meaning he coloured and was silent for a while. Then he said firmly: 'I'm not going to marry Deborah.'

Anne held her breath. When she could finally trust her voice, she asked: 'What's made you come to that decision?'

He laid down his knife and fork and looked at her. 'It was a foolish idea to begin with, and for a long time now I've known that it would end in unhappiness for both of us. I'm very fond of Debs, but as an uncle. Oh, I'm not blind. I'm perfectly well aware that she has a crush on me, but it won't last. Give her a couple of years, and someone her own age will come along and she'll have no compunction in leaving me. And I probably wouldn't even want to stop her. Oh, we'd be fine in bed together for a few months, but after that we'd bore each other silly.'

Anne cast around for something to say that was neither trite nor too self-revealing. 'I think you're absolutely right,' she murmured finally, 'and I can't pretend I'm sorry. You're not really suited to one another. To be honest, I don't believe Deborah is capable of loving anyone for very long. But I may be doing her an injustice.'

Richard shook his head. 'I don't think so. She's

very spoiled and used to having things all her own way.' There was another silence, protracted this time. At last he went on: 'I'm going up to Scotland in a fortnight's time. It's the Easter holiday, and I'm taking Ewan to visit his grandparents. I wondered . . . I wondered if there was a chance you'd care to come with me?'

Anne's heart was beating so loudly she was sure Richard must be able to hear it. But he gave no sign of noticing any agitation on her part, and she answered as casually as she could: 'I'd love to, if you're sure it will be all right with your in-laws.'

'Callum and Margaret will be delighted. That's settled, then. I'll phone them right away and tell them you're coming.' He stood up and came round the table to where she was sitting. Leaning forward, he kissed her lightly on the cheek.

'So this is Calton Hill,' Anne said, leaning with her back against the Dugald Stewart monument and looking out over the panoramic view of Edinburgh laid out below her. 'It's such an impressive city. It's easy to see what all the fuss is about. Why people love it.'

Richard nodded. 'It is beautiful,' he agreed. 'It's a place which gets into your heart and into your soul without you even realizing that it's happened.' He paused, then went on: 'Right here, where we are now, is where I first met Georgina.'

'Oh,' Anne said, a little deflated.

The last few weeks had passed like a dream from which she had been terrified of awakening. The morning following Richard's invitation, Anne had sat up in bed wondering if the conversation of the night before had been no more than a figment of her imagination. But on going down to breakfast she had found Penelope equally elated.

'Rich tells me he's asked you to go to Edinburgh

with him and Ewan at Easter.' She had, unusually, resisted the temptation to probe further, but her face had been wreathed in smiles.

Clifford, too, had seemed quietly delighted. 'I told you patience was the answer,' he had whispered, as he passed her on the stairs one morning.

Anne was immediately wary of them reading too much into the situation; what Richard's motive for the invitation was, she dared not let herself think, for fear of raising her own hopes too high. As a result, her attitude towards him became so casual that he might have been forgiven for thinking that she regretted her decision. In response to his suggestion this morning that they walk as far as Calton Hill, leaving Ewan with his grandparents, she had merely said: 'OK. If you want to.'

She had always got on well with Callum and Margaret Frere on the few previous occasions when she had met them, and they had made her most welcome on her arrival. Yesterday evening, washing up the supper things in the kitchen while Anne dried, Margaret had asked in her blunt Scots fashion: 'Are you and Richard thinking of getting married?'

Anne hadn't known what to say. At last, she came out with: 'He hasn't said anything to me on the subject.'

Margaret raised her eyebrows. 'You surprise me. There's something about the way he looks at you every now and then that made me think ... Och well! Don't mind me. Callum tells me I'm a terrible old matchmaker.'

Anne hesitated, then asked: 'How would you both feel about him marrying again?'

Margaret Frere looked amazed. 'We'd be delighted, naturally, depending of course on the woman. But I can't imagine Richard picking a wrong one. He was too happy with Georgina to risk a bad second marriage. You'd do fine for him.'

Anne had mulled over the conversation all evening, and had woken this morning still thinking about it. But Richard's attitude towards her continued to be sufficiently ambiguous to make her disinclined to show her own feelings. She said now, drily: 'And I expect you can remember exactly what she was wearing.'

'A dark-green knitted hat and mittens,' Richard answered promptly. 'But what else she had on, I've no idea. She had Barkis with her and he nipped my ankle, ruining a brand-new pair of socks I'd put on only that morning. Oddly enough, just before she spoke to me, I'd been thinking about you. I can recall that fact quite clearly.'

'Oh?' Anne's throat was suddenly constricted. 'What had you been thinking?'

'I'm not sure now, after all this time.' But Anne, looking at him, was certain that he remembered. 'Shall we walk on a bit? It's getting chilly.'

He showed her the Nelson monument, the 102-foot tower resembling an upturned giant telescope. Anne confessed herself impressed. Richard smiled wryly. 'But it isn't what you want to talk about, is it?'

'Not really. Rich, why did you ask me to come to Edinburgh with you? Was there a particular reason, or did you simply want someone to help with Ewan?'

He took her elbow and guided her towards a seat. 'Let's sit down for a moment.' When they were settled, he made a movement as though to hold her hand, then seemed to think better of it. He went on: 'I told you just now that I was thinking about you when I first met Georgina. I lied when I said I couldn't recall what I was thinking. I was coming to terms with the idea that you were in love with Ivo.' She started to speak, but he interrupted her. 'So I persuaded myself that I wasn't in love with you, either. And Georgina turning up so exactly on cue ... Well, you know what they say about nature abhorring a vacuum. She slipped into the place you'd always held, until then, in my affections. We loved each other very much, and she fulfilled a hitherto unsuspected need in me for strong physical passion. We were extremely happy together . . . and then she was killed.'

Anne moved a little closer and slid a hand through his arm. 'Do you still blame Imogen?'

A cold spring breeze was blowing and it ruffled his hair, so dark and so unlike his brothers'. 'I did at first, but these things happen, and you can't embitter your whole life by trying to apportion blame. All right, Imogen was drunk, but why did she drink so heavily? Probably because of Tim. Why did Tim behave as he did? Because of Chris and Irene . . . So nothing is ever as simple and straightforward as it appears to be at first glance. In the end, all you can do is put grief behind you and start again.'

'And Deborah?' Anne asked after a moment's silence.

'She made me laugh. She was the one person who didn't treat me as though I were an invalid; who talked about Georgy without those reverently hushed tones most people seem to reserve for the recently dead. But I never wanted to marry her. She's too young, too selfish, too fond of getting her own way.' He took another deep breath. 'I have to confess that my sole reason for touting the idea was in an effort to provoke some response from you. Which brings me to the real reason I asked you to come to Edinburgh with me.' He slewed round on the seat, and this time he took both her hands firmly in his. 'I love you, Anne. Part of me never stopped loving you, even when I was married to Georgina. I need you. Ewan needs you, and I hope you'll agree to become my wife. I asked you to come to Edinburgh, and to come up here to Calton Hill this morning, because I wanted to make absolutely sure that I've laid Georgy's ghost to rest once and for all; to be certain that I could come, with you, to the place where she and I first met without feeling anything more than a deep sadness, untinged by bitterness or regret.'

'And can you?' Anne asked steadily, searching his eyes for the truth.

He nodded. 'She'll always be very dear to me, a part of me and Ewan. But it's a gentle grief now. You're the one who matters. The only thing is, I'm not convinced you feel the same way about me.'

Anne put her arms around his neck and kissed him. 'Be convinced. I've always loved you. I was never in love with Ivo, and some time I'll try to explain how it was I came to marry him. But not just now.' They drew apart a little, smiling at one another, each with the feeling of at last coming home; of being where they belonged. They kissed again, then Anne stood up, holding out her hand. 'Come on! Let's go and tell Ewan the news. Then we'll telephone your parents and my mother. They'll be so pleased.'

And with their arms entwined they began, slowly, to walk down the hill.

THE END

VOICES OF SUMMER
by Diane Pearson

The Hochhauser Operetta Company was probably the tattiest and most unsuccessful theatrical group in the whole of Austria. Composed of *artistes* who were either 'over the hill' (Freddi was tone deaf and Luisa could hardly waddle across the stage) or raw young recruits straight from music school, they had only two assets – the magnificent old impresario, Franz Busacher who kept them all going, and Karl Gesner, the tenor, who looked like a prince, had a voice like an angel, and was without doubt the nastiest and most spiteful man ever to walk the boards.

When Therese Aschmann, the soprano who had left the stage in tragic disgrace years before, was persuaded to join the company, everyone knew there would be trouble. Therese was insecure and desperately trying to make a comeback. Gesner was consumed with jealousy over her talent. No-one, however, could have imagined it was to be the beginning of the most extraordinary season Hochhauser had ever seen, a season of explosive scenes and magical transformations, both on and offstage. Above all it was to be a season where love blossomed, often in the most unlikely places.

'This delightful novel from the author of *Csardas* makes you wish Pearson wrote more often'
Today

'Superb characterisation and fine writing make this an absorbing and enjoyable novel'
Annabel

0 552 13904 1

A SELECTED LIST OF FINE NOVELS AVAILABLE FROM CORGI BOOKS

THE PRICES SHOWN BELOW WERE CORRECT AT THE TIME OF GOING TO PRESS. HOWEVER TRANSWORLD PUBLISHERS RESERVE THE RIGHT TO SHOW NEW RETAIL PRICES ON COVERS WHICH MAY DIFFER FROM THOSE PREVIOUSLY ADVERTISED IN THE TEXT OR ELSEWHERE.

All Corgi books are available at your bookshops or newsagents, or can be ordered from the following address:

Corgi Books,
Cash Sales Department,
P.O. Box 11, Falmouth, Cornwall TR10 9EN

Please send a cheque or postal order (no currency) and allow 80p for postage and packing for the first book plus 20p for each additional book ordered up to a maximum charge of £2.00 in UK.

B.F.P.O. customers please allow 80p for the first book and 20p for each additional book.

Overseas customers, including Eire, please allow £1.50 for postage and packing for the first book, £1.00 for the second book, and 30p for each subsequent title ordered.

NAME (Block Letters)..

ADDRESS ....

....